Good Girl to Goddess

DANCING WITH DESIRE

LACI MAE WYLD

Contents

CHAPTER ONE
The Break-up

It started with a parade of pastel balloons. Some sickly shade of coral, more hospital gown than festive, hovered at eye level as I tried to navigate the tiny birthday banner George insisted was "just for fun." If there was a less appropriate location or time for a break-up than the Bluebird Cafe on East 76th, I'd yet to discover it.

I SAT at our reserved table by the window, my chair positioned, as always, to allow me to fade into the shadows. The spot was popular with the brunch crowd, but at three in the afternoon, the only other patrons were a pair of elderly women locked in competitive silence over a game of backgammon. For once, I envied their steadfast devotion to routine.

I'D CHOSEN my outfit with deliberate care, a crisp white blouse, buttoned primly to the collar, and a pleated navy skirt that hinted at knees but never delivered. I'd pulled my hair into a sleek bun, no flyaways, not even a rebellious wisp at the nape. Sam had begged to do my makeup, "you deserve some

1

birthday glow, babe!" but I'd declined, settling for mascara and one careful streak of tinted lip balm.

I KNEW BEFORE GEORGE ARRIVED. I knew by the way the hostess, fresh out of high school, kept sneaking glances at me from behind the espresso machine, as if she'd overheard a secret. I knew because George was 16 minutes late, and George was never late, not even in college when his entire sense of time revolved around FIFA tournaments and cheap pizza. I knew the way one knows a wine glass will slip before it ever leaves the table, or that a favorite sweater will shrink the instant it's needed most.

HE ARRIVED AT 3:20, in a navy suit and dove-gray shirt, the tie absent but the top button undone just so. His hair was freshly trimmed, shorter than I liked, a little too severe, and his smile was precisely calibrated, as if he'd been practicing in the Uber.

"HEY, BIRTHDAY GIRL."

I STOOD, reflexively, and he leaned in for a cheek-kiss, his cologne (Tom Ford, always) crowding out the ghost of espresso. The gesture was warm in theory, but he barely grazed my cheek. I sat back down, keeping my hands in my lap so he wouldn't see them trembling.

"I TOOK the liberty of ordering for us," he said, sliding into the banquette. "You don't mind, right?"

2

.   .   .

I SHOOK MY HEAD, lips pressed tight. I'd never once minded, not until that moment.

HE PRODUCED A FLAT, gift-wrapped box from his briefcase and set it in the center of the table. The ribbon was hospital-cornered, the paper creased with militaristic precision.

"YOU CAN OPEN IT NOW, if you want. Or after we eat. Up to you." His phone vibrated, and he silenced it without looking.

"NOW IS FINE," I said. My voice sounded distant, as if someone else was speaking for me. I peeled back the tape, careful not to tear the paper, and lifted the lid. Inside was a leather-bound planner, monogrammed in rose gold. My initials, E.J., stared back at me in a font so elegant it might have been designed to host a wedding invitation.

"IT'S BEAUTIFUL," I said, running a finger over the embossing.

"I THOUGHT you'd appreciate it. Since you're always so organized. Color-coded sticky notes, all that." He meant it as a compliment, but it landed like an accusation.

OUR SERVER ARRIVED with two plates of avocado toast, topped

with microgreens and precision-cut radishes. George thanked her by name; her smile flashed, then dissolved.

"You okay?" he asked, once the plates had settled and we were alone again.

"Of course," I said. "Why wouldn't I be?" Maybe my face was betraying my thoughts. When George first invited me to the cafe last week, I thought he was going to propose. I had even made a point of getting a fresh manicure so that if I were to take pictures of my hands, they would look great. However, since arriving, I knew that this was not it.

He watched me for a long moment, his eyes darting to the cuticle on his thumb, then to the condensation ring forming beneath his water glass.

"I don't think this is working anymore," he said finally, each word measured, like coins doled out to a vending machine.

I didn't react at first, not because I was shocked, but because I'd rehearsed this moment a dozen times in my head, always hoping my imagination was crueler than reality. I focused on the texture of the toast, how the knife tore through the crust, the way the microgreens clung to the yolk before slipping away.

· · ·

"I'm seeing someone else," he added, as if the first blow hadn't landed deep enough.

My hands clutched the teacup so tightly I worried the porcelain would shatter. I set it down, careful, precise.

"Who is she?" I asked, though I didn't really want to know.

He hesitated, then: "Madison. From the office. She's in marketing."

I pictured her immediately—Madison, with the glossy hair and Instagram-perfect smile, the way she wore sleeveless blouses even in winter, as if immune to cold or criticism.

"She's spontaneous," George continued, not meeting my eyes. "She's...fun. I just...I feel alive when I'm with her."

I blinked, and the world smudged at the edges. I told myself it was the mascara, the dry winter air, anything but the ache working its way up my throat.

"You're very..put together, Elara. And I respect that. But I just...I need something less...predictable, I guess."

. . .

"Predictable," I repeated. The word tasted like metal.

"It's not a bad thing," he said quickly, "it's just...maybe it's not what I want right now. You understand, right?'

He looked at me, and I realized he genuinely expected me to agree, to bless his choice like an indulgent older sister.

I nodded. What else was there?

"Thank you," he said, as if I'd done him a great favor. "You're handling this so well. I knew you would."

He reached across the table and squeezed my hand, his fingers warm and dry. I didn't pull away, but I felt my spine tighten, vertebra by vertebra, until my posture was as rigid as the plastic chair.

The rest of the meal was a silent negotiation between dignity and devastation. I forced down three bites of toast. George ate with the determined appetite of someone who'd already processed the loss. He asked about my job, my family, and whether I'd considered grad school. I answered, politely, as if reading from a script.

. . .

WHEN THE CHECK ARRIVED, he paid without comment. As he signed the receipt, he looked up at me, his eyes suddenly soft.

"YOU'RE GOING to be fine, Elara. You always land on your feet."

I WANTED to tell him he was wrong, that I'd spent most of my life treading water, my feet never quite reaching solid ground, that he is not the first who has decided to go for someone more appealing over my careful presence. But I just smiled, smoothing the napkin over my skirt until the fabric felt like armor.

"HAPPY BIRTHDAY," he said, and with that, he stood, gathering his briefcase and slipping out the door into the bright, indifferent afternoon.

I SAT FOR A LONG TIME, staring at the planner. The party balloons bobbed against the window, their string caught on the metal latch. I wondered how long it would take for the helium to fade, for the whole display to deflate into something flat and unremarkable.

WHEN THE SERVER FINALLY APPROACHED, her voice was gentler than before.

"WOULD you like a box for the rest?"

. . .

"No, THANK YOU," I said, folding the planner shut and tucking it into my tote. "I think I've lost my appetite."

SHE NODDED, offering a sympathetic smile. It was more kindness than I could stand. My eyes prickled, and I blinked hard, determined not to give in until I reached the safety of home.

I GATHERED MY COAT, looping the buttons one by one with methodical precision, and stepped into the chill that waited outside. My reflection in the window caught me by surprise: the bun immaculate, the blouse still crisp, not a single tear in sight.

IF I LOOKED LONG ENOUGH, I almost believed I was still whole.

THE WALK from Bluebird to the 96th Street station took longer than usual. I moved through the city as if underwater, my limbs heavy, my thoughts flickering in and out like a strobe. I was almost grateful for the rhythmic roar of the train, loud enough to drown out my own thoughts, or at least shake them loose for a few stops.

BY THE TIME I reached my building, the mascara I'd so carefully applied that morning had surrendered to gravity, leaving smoky smudges beneath my eyes. I paused in the lobby, studying the reflection in the elevator's chrome doors. The bun had started to unravel, thin wisps curling against my neck. The collar of my blouse was smudged with a constellation of gray, one button hanging loose where my hand must have trembled too hard to fasten it back in place.

THE APARTMENT WAS silent when I slipped inside, save for the hum of Sam's ring light from her bedroom-slash-studio. The scent of a vanilla candle clung to the hallway, fighting a losing battle against the ambient city smell. I navigated the minefield of discarded fashion magazines and Amazon boxes in the living room, collapsing onto the couch with a sigh I'd been holding since Midtown.

FROM HER LAIR, Sam's voice carried, bright and assertive. "And that is why you should always overline your lips for a date, babes—it's psychological, not just aesthetic—oh! Hang on, comments section, my roomie's home!"

THE DOOR SWUNG OPEN, and Sam emerged, still lit from behind by the ring light, her platinum hair tossed into a high ponytail, oversized T-shirt hitting her mid-thigh. Her eyes locked on my face, and whatever pre-scripted energy she'd had for her followers evaporated.

"FUCK, ELARA. WHAT HAPPENED?"

SHE DIDN'T WAIT for an answer, just beelined for the kitchen, returning with a stemless wine glass and a half-poured bottle of pinot noir. She pressed the glass into my hand, then disappeared again, returning this time with a battered throw blanket that she draped across my shoulders.

"I'm fine," I said, knowing the lie was transparent. My throat was raw from holding back everything I couldn't say in the cafe.

Sam plopped down beside me, pulling her knees up to her chest. "He did it didn't he?" She didn't say George's name, but I saw it in her eyes, all sharp sympathy and calculated anger.

I nodded, clutching the glass with both hands, letting the rim rest against my lower lip.

"Talk to me," Sam said softly, her voice a far cry from the influencer persona she wore for her followers.

I tried to summon the words, but it was like reaching for pearls scattered on the ocean floor; everything beautiful felt impossibly far away.

"He said I was predictable," I managed, staring into the maroon swirl of wine. "That he needed someone with more... excitement. More fun."

. . .

SAM SNORTED. "Translation: Madison from marketing is a slutty party favor, and he wants to fuck her without the guilt."

I WINCED, but not because she was wrong. "He said I wasn't... enough. That he wanted someone who made him feel alive."

"GOD," Sam said, rolling her eyes with enough force to power a small turbine, "he's such a basic bitch."

HER IRREVERENCE MADE ME LAUGH, a brittle sound that cracked in my chest. Sam seized the opening and scooted closer, one arm wrapping around my shoulders. "Listen to me. George has the emotional range of a one-column spreadsheet. You were always ten times out of his league. He just needed a girl who would gas him up for posting a gym selfie. You? You intimidate the shit out of him."

I WANTED TO BELIEVE HER. I wanted to believe anything but the gnawing suspicion that George was right, that something essential in me was broken, or at least irreparably dull.

I DRAINED the glass and set it on the coffee table, careful not to tip over the leaning tower of unopened PR packages Sam had collected for future content.

"HE DUMPED ME ON MY BIRTHDAY," I said, the truth finally

dropping like a stone. "At the Bluebird. With a party balloon and everything."

SAM WAS QUIET FOR A MOMENT, her thumb tracing lazy circles on my forearm. "You want me to key his car?" she offered, half-joking, half-not.

I SHOOK MY HEAD, a shuddery laugh escaping. "He'd probably just bill it to corporate."

SAM GRINNED, baring her teeth like a wolf. "You should have let me do your makeup this morning. Would've scared him into impotence."

"I THOUGHT you said I was out of his league."

"I DID," she replied, "but a killer highlight never hurt a bitch."

FOR THE FIRST time all day, I felt the tiniest flicker of warmth, not from the wine, not from the blanket, but from the reckless, bone-deep loyalty that only Sam could offer.

I TOLD HER EVERYTHING THEN, every excruciating detail of George's monologue, every line he'd practiced in the mirror, every sideways compliment disguised as a condemnation. Sam listened with the patience of a confessor, never once checking her phone, not even when the little blue notification light blinked insistently from the kitchen.

"HE SAID he wanted someone more...spontaneous," I finished, my voice dropping to a whisper. "Someone more spontaneous. He said I'm...very put together."

SAM ROLLED her eyes so hard I worried she'd dislodge something. "Men are such idiots. You're gorgeous, Elara. It's not your fault he has the libido of a faulty toaster oven."

I SNORTED, wiping a tear from my cheek. The gesture left a charcoal smudge, which Sam noticed instantly.

"COME ON," she said, standing and tugging me up by the wrist. "Let's clean you up. You look like you survived a mascara apocalypse.

I LET her lead me to the bathroom, where she produced a fistful of makeup wipes from the ever-expanding stash beneath the sink. Sam set about dismantling my day: the perfect bun, the stubborn streaks of mascara, the last shreds of my dignity.

WHEN SHE FINISHED, she took a step back and surveyed her handiwork. "There. Fresh start. And you know what? We're going to reinvent you, babe. Not for George, fuck him, but for you."

I wanted to protest, to say I was fine as I was, but the truth was I'd spent so long living inside the lines that I didn't even remember what the edges looked like. Maybe Sam was right. Maybe I needed to be ruined a little before I could ever feel whole. She handed me a clean T-shirt—her favorite, soft and threadbare from too many laundry cycles—and I slipped it on, letting the fabric swallow me up.

Back in the living room, Sam poured another glass of wine and queued up a trashy reality show. She built a fortress of pillows and blankets on the couch, then burrowed in beside me, radiating defiant comfort.

For a while, we just existed in silence, letting the glow of the TV and the muted hum of the city fill in the spaces where words couldn't reach.

Finally, Sam turned to me, her eyes glittering with a new kind of determination.

"Tomorrow, we should do a spa day. Hair, nails, lashes, the whole nine. And when you're ready, we'll go out and show this city what George gave up. You're going to be a fucking goddess, Elara. Main character energy. Are you with me?"

. . .

I CONSIDERED IT, the idea of letting go, of surrendering to something wild and reckless and possibly even fun.

FOR THE FIRST time since the Bluebird, I felt something other than emptiness, a flicker of anticipation, sharp and unfamiliar.

"I'M WITH YOU," I said, and I meant it.

SAM GRINNED, triumphant. She tilted my chin up, examining my face with the critical eye of a seasoned stylist.

"BY THE TIME I'm done with you, George will be begging to have you back," she declared, her voice low and conspiratorial. "And you'll be the one saying no."

I BELIEVED HER, even if just for a moment. And that, for now, was enough.

CHAPTER TWO
The Makeover

The words tumbled out of my mouth before I could swallow them back, raw and unexpected even to my own ears. "I want to become a sexy slut." The wine glass trembled in my hand, half-empty and warm from being cradled too long against my chest. I hadn't planned to say it, hadn't even known I was thinking it until the syllables hung in the air between us, sharp and impossible to retract.

SAM FROZE MID-SIP, her eyes widening over the rim of her glass. For a moment, I thought she might laugh or, worse, offer some gentle redirection back to sensible territory. Instead, a slow grin spread across her face, wicked and delighted, as if I'd finally cracked a puzzle she'd been watching me struggle with for years.

"SAY THAT AGAIN," she demanded, setting her glass down with enough force to splatter droplets of wine onto the coffee table.

· · ·

My throat tightened. "I want—" The second time was harder, the words sticking to my tongue like peanut butter. I cleared my throat. "I want to be the kind of woman George would never expect. Someone sexy and confident and... unpredictable."

Sam was already on her feet, her hand extended toward me like a lifeline. "Elara James, you beautiful disaster, get up right now." She bounced on her toes, electric with purpose. "We're doing this. We're absolutely doing this."

Before I could reconsider, Sam pulled me up from the couch and led me down the hallway toward her bedroom, her grip firm on my wrist. Her excitement was contagious, though panic fluttered in my chest like a trapped bird. I had spent twenty-five years building a careful identity—the good girl, the reliable one, the woman who wore cardigans in summer just in case the air conditioning was too strong. And here I was, ready to dismantle it after one glass of wine and a birthday breakup.

Sam flung open her closet door with theatrical flair. Unlike my own meticulous arrangement of beige, navy, and the occasional burgundy, Sam's wardrobe exploded with color and texture. Sequins caught the light, leather gleamed with promise, and mesh revealed tantalizing glimpses of nothing at all. It was a treasure trove of everything I'd been taught to avoid.

"Welcome to your rebirth," Sam declared, diving into the chaos with practiced ease.

She emerged with a black dress so small I initially mistook it for a tank top. The fabric was stretchy but substantial, with a neckline that plunged well past any boundary I'd ever respected.

"This is perfect for your body type," she insisted, pressing it into my hands. "You've got tits for days, babe. It's practically criminal that you keep them locked up in those button-downs."

My cheeks burned. "I can't wear this. It's—it's barely clothing."

Exactly." Sam was already reaching for another hanger, this one holding a crimson wrap dress with a slit that seemed designed specifically for indecent exposure. "This is your coming out party. Your slutty butterfly moment. You've been a caterpillar long enough.

I fingered the silky material of the red dress, my reservations battling with a strange, unfamiliar thrill. The fabric felt dangerous against my fingertips, a whispered promise of the woman I might become if I dared.

"Try them on," Sam urged, adding a leopard-print miniskirt and a sheer black top to the growing pile in my arms. "Trust the process."

I retreated to her en-suite bathroom, my heart pounding against my ribs. The space was a shrine to beauty products—counters cluttered with creams and serums, makeup arranged by color in acrylic organizers, and a collection of perfume bottles that shimmered like jewels beneath the vanity lights. I set the clothes down and stared at my reflection, still puffy-eyed from crying, still wrapped in the armor of my respectable blouse and sensible skirt.

With trembling fingers, I unbuttoned my blouse, folding it neatly despite the absurdity of maintaining order in the midst of such chaos. The black dress slid over my head, the material stretching to accommodate curves I'd spent years disguising. It hugged my waist, accentuated my hips, and yes—displayed my chest in a way that made my breath catch.

I barely recognized myself.

"Let me see!" Sam called, rapping her knuckles against the door.

I opened it a crack, modesty warring with curiosity. Sam pushed the door wider, her eyes sweeping over me with professional assessment.

"Holy shit," she breathed, circling me like a stylist at a photoshoot. "Look at your waist in this. And your ass—Elara, do you even know what you've been hiding under those pilgrim skirts?"

I tugged at the hem, which barely reached mid-thigh. "It feels... wrong."

"Wrong how? Bad wrong, or exciting wrong?" Sam adjusted the neckline, pulling it slightly lower. "Because there's a difference."

I studied my reflection over her shoulder. The dress revealed more skin than I'd shown since childhood swimming lessons, but something in my posture was already shifting—shoulders pulling back, chin lifting to accommodate this new silhouette.

"Exciting wrong," I admitted, surprising myself.

Sam clapped her hands together. "Next one. Go."

The red wrap dress was even more transformative. The V-neckline emphasized my collarbone, drawing the eye downward to the shadow between my breasts. The wrap tie cinched my waist, and the skirt's movement felt like liquid around my legs. When I walked out, Sam actually whistled.

"George is going to swallow his tongue when he sees you in this," she said, adjusting the slit to reveal another inch of thigh.

"This isn't about George," I said, the lie tasting strange in my mouth.

Sam raised an eyebrow. "Fine. Every other man in Manhattan is going to swallow his tongue. Better?"

I smiled despite myself, turning to view the dress from different angles. My usual hunched posture would ruin the lines; I found myself straightening, elongating my neck, letting the dress work its magic.

The leopard skirt paired with the sheer top was a step too far—I felt like an imposter, a good girl playing dress-up in bad girl clothes. But the final outfit Sam had selected, a midnight blue skimpy dress with a halter neckline and form-fitting edge that stuck to my thighs, struck the perfect balance between daring and elegant.

"This one," I said, running my hands over the silky fabric. "It feels like... me, but not me."

"That's exactly right." Sam stood behind me, her hands on my shoulders, our reflections side by side in the mirror. "It's still you. Just the you that's been waiting in the wings while Little Miss Perfect hogged the spotlight."

I studied myself in the dress, taking in the exposed shoulders, the way the fabric draped over my hips. It was sexy without being vulgar, confident without trying too hard. For the first time since the Bluebird Café, I felt something other than hollowed-out despair—a flutter of anticipation, a spark of defiance.

"I think I could wear this," I said softly, more to myself than to Sam.

She squeezed my shoulders. "You can wear anything, babe. The clothes aren't the magic—they're just permission slips for the woman you already are." She met my eyes in the mirror. "Ready for phase two?"

I nodded, surprised to find I meant it. "What's phase two?"

Sam's smile was pure mischief. "Makeup. We're going to paint you into someone you've never let yourself be."

And despite everything in me that should have been terrified, I felt myself leaning toward that promise, hungry for whatever transformation awaited.

Sam's makeup station dominated the corner of her bedroom like an altar to feminine mystique—a large vanity mirror bordered with professional-grade lighting, surrounded by an organized chaos of bottles, palettes, and brushes that reminded me of an artist's studio. I perched nervously on the cushioned stool as Sam circled behind me, her fingers lifting sections of my hair, assessing my face with the clinical precision of a surgeon planning an incision.

"Time to paint that canvas, honey," she announced, pulling her own stool closer until our knees touched. The intimacy of the gesture struck me—this was how close women got when sharing secrets, when building each other into something new.

I eyed the intimidating array of products spread before me. My own makeup routine consisted of tinted moisturizer, mascara, and the occasional sweep of neutral eyeshadow for special occasions. Sam's collection, by contrast, looked like it could supply a Broadway production.

"I don't even know what half of these things are for," I confessed, picking up a strangely shaped sponge and turning it over in my hands.

Sam plucked it from my fingers with a knowing smile. "That's a beauty blender, babe. And don't worry—I'll walk you through everything. By the time we're done, you'll be armed and dangerous."

She reached for a sleek bottle of foundation several shades warmer than my natural skin tone. I must have looked alarmed, because she laughed.

"Trust me," she said, pumping a dollop onto the back of her hand. "Makeup isn't about looking natural. It's about creating the illusion of what nature should have given you. It's armor and weapon both."

The phrase caught me off guard. "Armor and weapon?"

Sam nodded, dipping a wide, flat brush into the liquid. "Armor because it protects you—gives you a face to show the world when your real one feels too raw or vulnerable." She demonstrated on her own cheek, blending the foundation with practiced strokes. "And weapon, because, used correctly, it makes others see exactly what you want them to see. It's control, Elara. Pure control."

There was something in her explanation that resonated deep within me—the idea that I could shield myself while simultaneously directing others' perceptions. After years of being the reliable, predictable Elara, the thought of wielding that kind of power was intoxicating.

"Let me show you," Sam said, wiping her cheek clean before turning her attention to me. The first touch of the foundation brush was cool against my skin, the bristles softer than I'd expected. Sam worked methodically, explaining each step as she went. "We're evening your tone, building a base. Think of it like priming a wall before painting."

The foundation felt heavier than I was used to, but not unpleasantly so. It smelled faintly of something expensive and chemical, a scent I'd always associated with the cosmetics counters I hurried past in department stores.

"Now for the fun part," Sam declared, reaching for a palette of darker shades. "Contouring. This is where we sculpt that beautiful bone structure of yours."

She demonstrated on herself first, sucking in her cheeks and drawing sharp lines beneath her cheekbones, down the sides of her nose, along her jawline. The effect was dramatic—her features suddenly more defined, almost feline in their precision.

"Your turn," she said, selecting a brush with an angled tip. "Close your eyes and feel the transformation."

I obeyed, surrendering to the gentle pressure of the brush as it traced patterns across my face. The sensation was oddly soothing, like being touched by someone who knew exactly what they were doing, who could see potential I'd never recognized in myself.

"Men are simple creatures," Sam explained, her voice low and instructive as she blended the contour into my skin. "They see what you want them to see. A little shadow here, a little highlight there—suddenly you're not just pretty, you're fascinating." The brush tickled the hollow beneath my cheekbone.

"They'll think they're drawn to your natural beauty, but really, you've just learned how to manipulate light and shadow."

I opened my eyes, startled by the stranger looking back at me. Already my face had changed—my cheekbones higher, my jawline more defined, my features somehow both sharper and softer.

"My God," I whispered, tilting my head to examine the effect from different angles.

Sam grinned, satisfied. "We're just getting started. Wait until we do your eyes."

She reached for a compact of shimmering powder, sweeping it along the high points of my face with a fan brush. The powder caught the light, creating an illusion of dewiness that made my skin look alive in a way it never had before.

"This is how you become the girl everyone stares at," Sam continued, selecting an eyeshadow palette filled with smoky, seductive shades. "Not because you're the loudest or the most obvious, but because you're a mystery they can't solve. Is she wearing makeup? Is that just how she looks? They'll never know for sure."

She dipped a fluffy brush into a deep plum shade, instructing me to close my eyes again. The powder felt cool as it dusted across my lids, building in intensity with each pass.

"When was the last time you really looked at yourself?" Sam asked, her breath warm against my forehead as she concentrated. "Not just checking for food in your teeth or making sure your hair is neat, but really seeing yourself?"

I kept my eyes closed, feeling suddenly vulnerable. "I don't know. Maybe never."

"That's what I thought," she said, her voice gentler now. "Women like you—the good girls, the careful ones—you're taught to blend in, not stand out. To be pretty but not too pretty. Attractive but not distracting." The brush moved to my other eyelid, sweeping in precise arcs. "We're breaking those rules today."

When she finished with the eyeshadow, she instructed me to open my eyes. The woman in the mirror had changed again —her eyes deeper, more mysterious, framed by smoky shadows that made the green of her irises look almost emerald.

"Now for the pièce de résistance," Sam declared, uncapping a liquid eyeliner with a flourish. "The perfect wing. It takes practice, so watch first."

She leaned toward the mirror, demonstrating on herself with a steady hand that drew a flawless black line along her lash line, flicking upward at the corner in a sharp, precise wing. The effect was striking—her eyes immediately more feline, more deliberate.

"Your turn to feel the magic," she said, turning to me with the liner poised. "Look up."

The liner felt wet against my lash line, the applicator tip

firm but yielding. Sam worked with careful precision, her brow furrowed in concentration. "This is the part that separates the amateurs from the professionals," she murmured. "A good wing can make a man forget his own name."

When she finished, she leaned back to assess her work, then nodded with satisfaction. "Perfect. Now for the final touches."

The false eyelashes were the most foreign sensation of all —weightier than I expected, creating a strange awareness of my own blinking. They felt like tiny feathered creatures perched on my eyelids, both uncomfortable and oddly glamorous.

"You'll get used to them," Sam assured me, applying mascara to blend my natural lashes with the falsies. "By the end of the night, you'll feel naked without them."

The last step was lipstick—a deep, blood-red shade that Sam applied with a brush, taking her time to define the edges of my lips before filling them in.

"Press your lips together," she instructed, demonstrating the motion. "Gentle, like you're kissing a baby's forehead."

I complied, feeling the waxy texture of the lipstick, tasting its faint chemical sweetness.

"There," Sam said finally, setting down her tools and spinning my stool to face the mirror fully. "Meet the woman you've been hiding."

The face that stared back at me was a revelation—still mine, but heightened, intensified, as if someone had turned up the contrast on a familiar photograph. My eyes looked larger, more dramatic, the green of my irises popping against the smoky shadow. My cheekbones caught the light like cut glass. My lips were a statement, bold and unapologetic.

"I look..." I struggled to find the right word.

"Dangerous," Sam supplied, her reflection smiling next to mine. "You look like a woman with secrets worth keeping. And that, my friend, is exactly what we're going for."

I couldn't look away from this new version of myself—this woman who seemed capable of things the old Elara would never dare. There was power in this face, a kind of deliberate allure that I'd always associated with women like Sam, never with myself.

"Phase two, complete," Sam declared, squeezing my shoulders. "Ready for hair?"

I nodded, still transfixed by my own reflection. "Yes," I said, and my voice sounded different too—lower, more certain. "I'm ready."

Sam circled behind me, her fingers working deftly to release my hair from its practical ponytail. The elastic band surrendered with a snap, and my waves tumbled down, heavy against my shoulders after being constrained all day. I winced as Sam's fingernails scraped lightly against my scalp, combing through tangles with surprising gentleness. "You're hiding gold here," she murmured, lifting sections to catch the light. "All this time keeping it pulled back like you're afraid of what might happen if you let it breathe."

I watched her in the mirror as she assessed my hair with the same critical eye she'd applied to my face. My brown waves fell just past my shoulders, neither straight nor curly, existing in that frustrating middle ground that had always seemed easier to tame than celebrate.

"You know what your problem is, Elara?" Sam reached for a spray bottle, misting my hair with something that smelled of coconut and expensive salons. "You treat your beauty like it's a liability. Like if you let it out, something terrible might happen."

Her words landed with uncomfortable precision. I'd spent so long downplaying every feature that might draw attention —my curves, my hair, even my voice, which tended to drop an octave when I was comfortable or passionate about something.

"What are you putting in my hair?" I asked, deflecting.

"Texturizing spray. Brings out your natural waves," Sam explained, working the product through my hair with her fingers. The sensation was oddly intimate, like being groomed by a more experienced version of myself. "Your hair has amazing potential. We're just waking it up."

She reached for a round brush and a blow dryer, sectioning

my hair with clips that bit gently into my scalp. As she worked, directing warm air and tension through each segment, my hair began to transform—fuller, more deliberately tousled, framing my face in a way that complemented the dramatic makeup.

"While I work on this," Sam said, meeting my eyes in the mirror, "let's talk about how you're going to move in this new body of yours."

"It's the same body," I pointed out, watching as she wrapped a section of hair around the brush.

Sam smirked. "New packaging, same contents. But packaging matters, babe. How you present yourself is half the battle."

She set down the dryer for a moment and moved to stand beside me. "First rule of confidence: posture." She demonstrated, shoulders rolling back, spine straightening, chin lifting just enough to lengthen her neck. The change was subtle but dramatic—she suddenly occupied more space, commanded more attention.

"Your turn," she instructed. "Stand up."

I rose from the stool, feeling awkward under her scrutiny.

"No, no," she said, adjusting my stance with firm hands. "Shoulders back—not military straight, just... aware. Like your body is something worth paying attention to."

I tried to mimic her posture, feeling stiff and unnatural.

"Better," she said, though her expression suggested otherwise. "But you're overthinking it. Try this—imagine a string pulling up from the crown of your head. Everything else just falls into place."

I visualized the string, feeling my spine lengthen in response. Something shifted—subtle, but immediate.

"There it is," Sam nodded, satisfied. "That's your power stance. Now add a hip." She demonstrated, weight shifted slightly to one leg, hip cocked just enough to create an asymmetrical line. "The hip says, 'I'm comfortable in my sexuality.' Men can't resist it—it's like catnip."

I tried the pose, feeling ridiculous at first, then strangely powerful as I caught my reflection. With the makeup, the hair beginning to take shape, and now this new posture, I barely recognized myself—and that, I realized, was precisely the point.

Sam returned to my hair, working a different product through the ends. "Now for eye contact," she continued. "This is crucial. When you meet someone's gaze, hold it for three seconds—not one, not five. Three is the sweet spot between interest and challenge."

She demonstrated, looking directly into my eyes through the mirror. One, two, three—then she glanced away, the gesture deliberate but not abrupt.

"You have to look away first," she explained, reaching for a curling iron. "Make them chase you. If they hold your gaze longer than you do, you've given away your power."

"That seems... calculated," I said, watching as she wrapped a section of my hair around the heated barrel.

Sam released the curl, letting it bounce against my cheek. "All flirting is calculated, honey. The difference is whether you're the one doing the calculations or having them done to you."

There was a wisdom in her approach that I couldn't deny, a strategic understanding of human interaction that I'd always lacked. I'd spent years believing that authentic connection happened naturally or not at all. The idea that it could be engineered, controlled, directed—it should have felt manipulative, but instead, it felt like discovering the rulebook to a game I'd been playing blindfolded.

"When you're talking to someone you're interested in," Sam continued, curling another section, "touch their arm. Like this." She demonstrated, her fingers grazing my forearm with just enough pressure to register. "Not a grab, not a pat—a touch. It says 'I'm comfortable with physical contact' without being desperate."

I practiced the motion, touching her arm as she'd shown me. My first attempt was too timid, barely making contact.

"Again," she instructed. "More confidence. You're not asking permission—you're making a statement."

My second try was better—deliberate but not aggressive. Sam nodded approval.

"Perfect. That's the difference between a girl who gets noticed and one who gets forgotten."

She finished with my hair, spraying it with a fine mist that smelled of vanilla and chemicals. The result was a cascade of waves that looked both effortless and intentional, framing my face in a way that emphasized my cheekbones and drew attention to my eyes.

"Now let's talk about how to sit," Sam said, guiding me back to the stool. "Crossing your legs isn't just ladylike—it's strategic. It draws the eye upward." She demonstrated, crossing one long leg over the other with a deliberate slowness that made the movement itself an event.

I mimicked her, finding that the motion felt different in the tight dress I still wore—more deliberate, more aware.

"The key is to make every movement count," Sam explained. "When you enter a room, pause in the doorway for just a second—let them see you before you see them. When you sit down, do it like you're lowering yourself onto a throne. When you take a drink—" she handed me an empty glass, "—keep your eyes on them over the rim. It's the ultimate power move."

I practiced sipping from the imaginary glass, feeling self-conscious until I caught sight of my reflection. The woman looking back at me—with smoky eyes, tousled hair, and a posture that spoke of secrets—didn't look self-conscious at all. She looked like someone who knew exactly what game she was playing.

"Don't forget to tilt your head when they're speaking," Sam added, demonstrating the slight angle that suggested attentiveness without submission. "It says you're listening, but you're also evaluating what you hear."

We spent the next twenty minutes practicing these moves in sequence—the entrance, the seated pose, the strategic touch, the calculated glance. With each repetition, my movements became less stilted, more fluid, as if my body was remembering something it had always known but rarely been allowed to express.

"It's like a dance," I observed, surprised by how natural it was beginning to feel.

"Exactly," Sam agreed, her eyes bright with approval. "Seduction is choreography. Anyone can learn the steps."

She led me to the full-length mirror on her closet door, positioning me to see my full transformation. "Final test," she announced. "Show me everything. The walk, the posture, the look—I want the full Elara 2.0."

I took a deep breath and imagined myself entering a bar. I paused, letting an invisible audience take in my appearance. I walked with the deliberate confidence Sam had taught me, hips moving just enough to suggest rhythm without trying too hard. I pretended to spot someone across the room, letting my eyes linger for three precise seconds before glancing away with the ghost of a smile. I crossed the room to an imaginary chair, lowering myself with calculated grace, crossing my legs with a slow deliberation that made even me want to look.

Sam watched, arms crossed, head tilted in assessment. When I finished, striking a final pose with my chin slightly lifted, my gaze direct but not challenging, she broke into applause.

"Holy shit," she breathed. "I think we've created a monster. A gorgeous, devastating monster."

I laughed, the sound surprising me with its depth and ease. "I feel ridiculous," I admitted. "But also... powerful?"

"That's because you are powerful," Sam said, coming to stand beside me in the mirror. "You've always been powerful. You just forgot how to show it."

We stood side by side, two versions of feminine potency— Sam with her practiced confidence, me with my newfound awareness. For a moment, I glimpsed what George might see if he encountered me now, this stranger wearing my face, moving with a deliberation that the old Elara would never have dared.

"One last thing," Sam said, her voice softening. "All of this —the makeup, the hair, the moves—they're tools, not crutches. The real transformation happens in here." She tapped my temple gently. "When you start believing you're worth looking at, worth wanting, worth pursuing... that's when the magic really happens."

I nodded, understanding washing over me like a warm wave. "I think I'm ready for that magic."

Sam grinned, squeezing my hand. "I know you are. Now let's see the whole package put together."

"I'll give you a minute," Sam said, her hand warm on my shoulder. "Some revelations are better experienced in private." She slipped out of the bedroom, the door clicking shut behind her with a soft finality. I stood alone before the full-length mirror, surrounded by the evidence of my transformation—discarded makeup wipes, hair product bottles, rejected outfits draped across Sam's bed like abandoned identities. The woman in the reflection held my gaze, a stranger wearing my bones, my history, my heartbreak.

The dress hugged curves I'd spent years concealing beneath cardigans and A-line skirts. It clung to my waist, accentuating the hourglass shape I'd inherited from my mother but had always treated as something to minimize rather than celebrate. The fabric ended mid-thigh, exposing legs that looked longer, more deliberate than I remembered them being just hours ago.

My heart pounded against my ribcage as I turned slightly, watching how the dress moved with me, how it caught the light, how it revealed just enough skin to suggest rather than announce. I'd never worn anything so deliberately seductive, had never wanted to until George's words—"predictable," "too put together"—had burrowed beneath my skin like splinters.

The makeup transformed my face into something both familiar and foreign. My eyes, normally wide and earnest, now smoldered beneath artfully smoky shadow and false lashes that cast feathery shadows on my cheekbones. My lips were painted a deep crimson that made them look fuller, more defined—the kind of mouth that made promises it might or might not keep.

But it was my hair that completed the metamorphosis. Sam had worked some alchemy with her products and tools, transforming my practical waves into a cascade of deliberate tousles that framed my face like a lion's mane. It looked like I'd just risen from someone's bed, disheveled in the most calculated way possible.

I took a step closer to the mirror, tilting my head the way Sam had taught me, letting my gaze travel over this new self with a stranger's objectivity. This woman didn't look like someone who color-coded her planner or organized her spice rack alphabetically. She looked like someone who made impulsive decisions, who stayed out too late, who knew exactly what she wanted and wasn't afraid to take it.

She looked like the kind of woman George would never expect me to become.

I practiced the smirk Sam had demonstrated—one corner of my mouth lifting slightly, suggesting amusement or interest without giving too much away. I tried the confident stance—shoulders back, weight shifted to one hip, chin tilted at the precise angle that conveyed self-assurance without arrogance.

The movements felt foreign at first, like trying on clothes in a language I didn't speak. But with each repetition, they settled more naturally into my body's vocabulary. I crossed the room and back, watching my reflection move with a deliberate grace that I'd never associated with myself.

I was surprised by how quickly it came, this physical performance of confidence. Perhaps because it wasn't entirely a performance—perhaps because somewhere beneath the practical ponytails and sensible shoes lived a woman who had always known how to command attention but had never been given permission to try.

A mix of emotions churned beneath my sternum—excitement, yes, but also fear, a deep-seated terror that this transformation was a betrayal of some essential truth about myself. I'd spent twenty-five years building an identity around being the responsible one, the predictable one, the girl who never caused trouble or invited drama. What would happen if I stepped outside those carefully constructed boundaries?

I thought of George's face when he ended things, the practiced sympathy in his eyes, the implicit judgment in his explanation. He'd made me feel small, contained, like a disappointment he'd finally found the courage to discard. The memory sent a surge of heat through my chest, hardening my resolve.

Maybe this new Elara was a costume, a carefully crafted illusion—but weren't all identities, in some way? Hadn't the buttoned-up, responsible version of myself been just as deliberately constructed, just as much a response to external expectations?

I took a deep breath and met my reflection's eyes directly. There was something powerful in this stranger's gaze, something I recognized from the deepest, most hidden parts of myself—a hunger, a defiance, a refusal to be contained any longer.

"Who are you?" I whispered to the woman in the mirror, half-expecting her to answer with a voice different from my own.

But the question itself was an answer. I was Elara—not George's Elara, not my parents' Elara, not even the Elara I'd convinced myself I had to be. Just Elara, with all my complexities and contradictions, finally allowing myself to explore the edges of my own potential.

A soft knock interrupted my reverie. "Can I come in?" Sam's voice filtered through the door.

"Yes," I called, not taking my eyes from the mirror.

Sam entered, her own reflection appearing beside mine. She'd changed out of lounge wear—and into a black dress that made her look ready for anything—her makeup still flawless but her posture more relaxed. She studied me for a long moment, her eyes registering approval mixed with something deeper, a kind of pride that made my throat tighten.

"Do you think I can really do this?" I asked, my voice stronger than I expected, the question encompassing everything we hadn't explicitly named—the going out, the flirting, the becoming someone new.

Sam moved to stand behind me, her hands settling on my shoulders, our eyes meeting in the mirror. The contrast between us was striking—her with her platinum hair and practiced confidence, me with my newly discovered power, still raw and uncertain.

"Honey, you already are," she replied, squeezing gently. "The sexy was always there. We just let her out to play."

The simplicity of her answer loosened something in my chest, a knot of doubt I hadn't realized I was carrying. Maybe this wasn't about becoming someone new, but about uncovering someone who had always existed beneath the surface, waiting for the right moment to emerge.

I turned to face her, taking in her expression of genuine affection. "Thank you," I said, the words inadequate for the gift she'd given me—not just the makeup or the clothes or even the lessons in flirtation, but the permission to explore facets of myself I'd kept locked away.

"Don't thank me yet," she replied with a wink. "Wait until we take this show on the road. The men of New York aren't ready for what's about to hit them."

I laughed, a sound more relaxed and genuine than any I'd made since the Bluebird Café. "Neither am I, to be honest."

"That's the beauty of it," Sam said, linking her arm through mine and guiding me back toward the mirror. "They don't know what's coming, and neither do you. But I can promise you one thing—" she paused, meeting my eyes in the reflection, "—it's going to be a hell of a lot more interesting than being predictable."

I studied our reflection, this moment suspended between who I had been and who I might become. The woman looking back at me wasn't a stranger anymore, nor was she entirely familiar. She existed in that exhilarating space between safety and risk, between the known and the possible.

And for the first time since George had uttered those devastating words across a café table, I felt something like anticipation fluttering in my chest—a hunger to discover what might happen when I finally stopped following the rules I'd never questioned, when I allowed myself to be seen, truly seen, without apology or restraint.

"So," Sam said, her eyes bright with mischief, "are you ready to break some hearts?"

I nodded, a slow smile spreading across my crimson lips. "Starting with my own."

CHAPTER THREE
The Club

The line outside Pulse stretched around the corner, a winding line of weekend hopefuls dressed in their Friday best. I stayed back as Sam marched toward the bouncer, her platinum hair catching the glow of the neon sign above the entrance. My fingers tugged at the hem of my borrowed dress, which suddenly felt like it had shrunk two sizes since we left the apartment. The bass seeped through the club's walls, each thump a whispered promise of what awaited inside—bodies, heat, eyes that would see this new version of me before I was entirely sure she existed.

"Stop fidgeting," Sam hissed, turning back to grab my wrist. "You look incredible, and you're going to ruin the effect if you keep tugging at that dress like it's on fire."

"It might as well be," I muttered, feeling the night air brush against bare thighs that hadn't seen sunlight since a beach trip three summers ago. "I'm not sure I'm ready for this."

Sam's expression softened for a fraction of a second before hardening into determination. "That's exactly why we're doing it. Ready is boring. Ready is predictable." She leaned in closer, her breath warm against my ear. "Ready is what George thought he knew about you."

His name stung, like a paper cut in a place I thought had already healed. I straightened my spine, recalling Sam's lessons. String pulling up from the crown of my head. Shoulders back, not military perfect, just aware.

The bouncer—a mountain of a man with arms like tree trunks—gave Sam a once-over, his eyes lingering on her expertly contoured cleavage before sliding a stamp across her hand. When his gaze shifted to me, something unexpected happened. His features softened, eyes widening slightly as they traveled from my red-bottomed heels to my smoky eyes.

"First time at Pulse?" he asked, voice surprisingly gentle for someone whose job description probably included the word "intimidating" multiple times.

I nodded, suddenly unable to find my voice.

"You're gonna have a good night," he said, pressing the stamp onto my hand with a pressure that felt oddly protective. "Stick with your friend."

And then we were through, stepping from the quiet of the street into a world made entirely of sensation. The music hit me first—not just sound but a physical force that vibrated through my ribcage and mixed with my heartbeat. Lights cut through artificial fog, painting the crowd in electric blues and purples before plunging parts back into shadow. Bodies moved as a single organism, connected by rhythm and closeness, by alcohol and desire.

Sam grabbed my hand, pulling me deeper into the crush. "Bar first," she shouted over the music. "Liquid courage."

I followed, hyperaware of eyes tracking our progress. A man in a crisp button-down stepped back to let us pass, his gaze lingering on my exposed shoulders. A woman with a geometric haircut nodded appreciatively, raising her glass in a silent salute. Each look was a revelation—I'd spent years trying to blend into backgrounds, and now, suddenly, I was foreground material.

We were halfway to the bar when I saw him.

George sat in the elevated VIP section, one arm casually draped over the back of a curved leather booth. The lighting accentuated the sharp angles of his jawline and the meticulous styling of his hair. He looked exactly as I remembered, but more—more confident, more relaxed in his surroundings, more entitled to the space he occupied.

And draped across him like living jewelry was Madison.

I recognized her immediately from company photos—tall and slender, with dark hair cut in a sharp bob that high-lighted cheekbones sharp enough to slice bread. Her dress was a bright green, the color of success and envy, hugging her body as if painted on by someone skilled in seduction. One manicured hand rested possessively on George's thigh while the other held a martini glass, its contents perfectly matching her dress. As I watched, she leaned in to whisper something in his ear, her lips brushing his skin with deliberate intimacy.

My stomach twisted, acid rising in my throat. The room tilted dangerously, and suddenly the air felt too thick to breathe.

"I can't do this," I gasped, turning abruptly toward the exit. "I need to go."

I made it three steps before Sam's fingers closed around my upper arm, her grip firm enough to leave marks.

"Absolutely not," she said, her voice low and fierce. Her eyes, when they met mine, were blazing with protective fury. "No way in hell are you running. Not now."

"He's here, Sam." The words felt like broken glass in my mouth. "With her. I can't—I don't want to—"

"This is perfect," Sam interrupted, turning me so my back was to the VIP section. She placed her hands on my shoulders, forcing me to look directly at her. "This is exactly what we needed."

"How is this perfect?" I hissed, fighting the urge to look back over my shoulder. "I look like I'm trying too hard. Like I dressed up just to show him what he's missing, when he's clearly not missing anything."

Sam's fingers tightened on my shoulders. "Listen to me. George dumped you because he thought you were predictable, right? Well, the predictable Elara would run away right now.

She'd go home, put on sweatpants, and cry into a pint of ice cream."

My cheeks burned with humiliation because she was right —that's exactly what I would have done.

"But the new Elara? She stays. She dances. She has the time of her fucking life right in front of him. She shows him that not only is she not devastated, she's thriving."

I swallowed hard, my hands still trembling at my sides. "I don't know if I can."

Sam's expression softened a bit. "You can. I promise you can." She tucked a strand of hair behind my ear, careful not to disturb the artful tousle she had created. "Besides, did you see what she's wearing? That dress is trying so hard it's practically screaming for attention."

A surprised laugh escaped me. "Says the woman who dressed me in this."

"Exactly," Sam grinned, triumphant at having cracked my panic. "And you look ten times hotter. Now, are we running away, or are we getting shots?"

I glanced back at the VIP section, where George was now raising a champagne flute in some unheard toast. Madison laughed, the sound lost in the thrum of music, her head thrown back to expose the elegant line of her throat. They looked like a magazine spread—glossy, perfect, untouchable.

Something hardened in my chest. Not quite anger, not

quite determination, but a strange fusion of both that tasted like metal on my tongue.

"Shots," I said, straightening my spine and lifting my chin the way Sam had taught me. "Definitely shots."

Sam's smile was wolfish as she linked her arm through mine. "That's my girl. Let's show George Mitchell exactly what predictable doesn't look like."

As we moved through the crowd toward the bar, I sensed a strange calm settle over me. The panic faded, replaced by a cool, calculated determination. Maybe it was the makeup, maybe it was the dress, or maybe it was simply the realization that I had nothing left to lose. Whatever the reason, with each step I took, I felt less like a woman running from heartbreak and more like one walking purposefully toward something new.

The bar was packed three people deep, a battleground of raised arms and crumpled bills. Sam cut through the crowd with practiced efficiency, one hand firmly holding my wrist to keep me from falling behind. She caught the bartender's eye with a toss of her platinum hair and a smile that promised generous tips. "Four tequila shots," she called over the noisy crowd, holding up fingers to reinforce her order. "Patron Silver." I opened my mouth to protest—I'd never been a tequila person, preferring wine or the occasional vodka soda—but Sam's expression left no room for argument. "Trust me," she mouthed over her shoulder, "you need this."

The bartender, a woman with a sleeve of intricate tattoos and hair shaved on one side, nodded and reached for a bottle. Her movements were fluid, practiced, a dance of their own as she lined up four shot glasses and filled them with clear liquid that caught the pulsing lights.

"Lime? Salt?" she asked, already reaching for both.

"Yes to both," Sam replied, sliding a credit card across the sticky surface. "And leave it open."

I pressed closer to Sam's back, aware of a man behind me, his breath warm on my neck, his chest occasionally brushing my shoulder blades when someone jostled him. The club's crush of bodies was both claustrophobic and oddly intimate—strangers sharing air, heat, fleeting contact.

The bartender pushed the shots toward us, along with a small plate of lime wedges and a salt shaker. Sam handed me a shot glass, her eyes gleaming with mischief.

"Lick, sip, suck," she instructed, demonstrating by licking the back of her hand between thumb and forefinger, sprinkling salt on the damp spot, then raising her glass in a toast. "To new beginnings."

I mimicked her actions, the salt rough against my tongue, and raised my own glass. "To new beginnings," I echoed, though the words felt hollow in my mouth.

We clinked glasses and threw back the shots in unison. The tequila hit my throat like liquid fire, burning a path to my stomach that made my eyes water and my throat close up. I barely got a lime wedge and bit into it, the sour juice mixing with the tequila's heat in a strange, yet oddly satisfying way.

"Jesus," I gasped, setting the empty glass down harder than I intended. "That's terrible."

Sam was already holding out the second shot. "It gets better after the first one."

She lied. The second shot was just as brutal as the first, but the aftermath was different. A warm sensation spread through my limbs, softening the edges of my anxiety. The bass seemed to sync with my heartbeat, and the crowd pressed around me felt less threatening, more like a shared secret.

"Now we dance," Sam announced, grabbing my hand and pulling me away from the bar before I could protest.

The dance floor was a patchwork of bodies moving in varying degrees of rhythm and coordination. Some dancers were clearly there to be seen, their movements calculated and camera-ready. Others were lost in the music, eyes closed, surrendering to whatever internal current moved them. Sam pulled me into a relatively open space near the center, where the lights shifted from blue to purple to deep red in hypnotic succession.

"Just follow me," she shouted over the music, her body already feeling the beat. She raised her arms above her head, hips swaying in perfect time, her movements both natural and intentionally seductive.

I stood frozen, painfully aware of my own stiffness. I'd never been a dancer—had always been the friend who guarded the table and watched the purses. My body felt disconnected from the music, from the rhythm that seemed to move everyone else so effortlessly.

"I can't," I called, leaning closer to Sam's ear. "I don't know how to do this."

Sam took my hands and placed them on my hips. "Yes, you do. Everyone knows how to dance. You're just overthinking it." She showed me, moving her body in a wave from her shoulders down to her knees. "It's not about the steps. It's about feeling."

I tried to mimic her movement, but my body refused to cooperate, joints locked by years of careful restraint. Around us, dancers pressed closer, the heat of their bodies creating a humid microclimate that smelled of perfume, sweat, and desire. Lights flashed across faces transformed by shadow and color, rendering strangers both intimate and anonymous.

"Here," Sam said, stepping behind me and placing her hands on my hips. "Close your eyes. Listen to the beat, not your thoughts."

I obeyed, letting my eyelids drop. The darkness intensified the other sensations—the bass vibrating through the floor into my feet, the brush of fabric against my skin, the gentle pressure of Sam's hands guiding my hips in a circular motion.

"That's it," she encouraged, her voice close to my ear. "Now move your arms. Run them through your hair—men love that."

I lifted my hands tentatively, feeling awkward until the tequila whispered that perhaps awkward wasn't the worst thing to be. I let my fingers thread through my hair, lifting it from my neck in a gesture that felt both vulnerable and strangely powerful.

"Perfect," Sam approved, stepping back slightly. "Now just let the music take you."

The alcohol flowed through my veins, dulling the voice that usually watched over my every move for signs of embarrassment or inappropriate behavior. The beat thumped, and I felt my body responding more naturally, my hips finding a rhythm that matched the electronic pulse. I looked up to see Sam grinning at me, her hands raised above her head as she danced.

"There she is," she mouthed, nodding in encouragement.

Something shifted then—a subtle transfer of weight from my heels to the balls of my feet, a relaxation in my spine that allowed my body to move more fluidly. The music wasn't something to analyze or understand; it was something to feel, to absorb, to respond to.

I let my hands drift to my sides, then up along my ribs, tracing the path of the red dress that hugged my curves. The movement was pure instinct, a physical expression of the warmth spreading through me. Sam nodded approvingly, then demonstrated another move—a slow rotation of her hips paired with a toss of her hair.

I followed her lead, surprised by how natural it felt once I stopped overthinking every gesture. The dance floor had become more crowded, bodies pressing closer, creating a collective heat that beaded sweat along my hairline and between my shoulder blades. The moisture made my skin glow under the shifting lights, a sheen that caught attention like dewdrops in sunlight.

"Look to your right," Sam said, leaning in close. "Don't be obvious."

I turned my head casually, letting my gaze sweep the edge of the dance floor. A man stood there, tall and broad-shouldered, his white shirt a beacon in the dim lighting. He was watching me, his expression a mixture of appreciation and interest.

"He's been staring for the last five minutes," Sam informed me with a smug smile. "And he's not the only one."

She was right. As I continued to dance, more confident now, I became aware of other eyes tracking my movements. A man near the bar, his arm around a willowy blonde, kept glancing in my direction. Another, dancing with a group of friends, made no effort to hide his interest, his gaze bold and direct.

The attention was unfamiliar territory—both thrilling and disconcerting. I'd spent so long being invisible, or at least unremarkable, that being seen felt like a new sense awakening. Each appreciative glance was a spark against my skin, igniting something I hadn't known lay dormant within me.

"How does it feel?" Sam asked, reading my expression with the accuracy of long friendship.

I considered the question, letting the music move my body through another movement, more fluid and confident than before. "Strange," I admitted. "But not bad strange. Just... new."

Sam's smile was knowing. "That's power, babe. The power of being wanted. Get used to it."

I let her words sink in as we continued to dance, my body loosening further with each song. The tequila had fully integrated into my bloodstream now, blurring the harsh edges of self-consciousness, allowing something more primal to emerge. I found myself making eye contact with one of the men who'd been watching me, holding his gaze for precisely three seconds before looking away—just as Sam had taught me.

His smile in response was immediate, a flash of white teeth in the colored darkness. Something fluttered low in my abdomen, a physical response to visual stimulation that caught me by surprise.

"See?" Sam said, catching the exchange. "You're a natural."

And in that moment, surrounded by strangers moving to the same rhythm, bathed in sweat and artificial fog and the sweet release of inhibition, I almost believed her. The woman George had dismissed as predictable was nowhere to be found. In her place was someone new—someone who moved with intention, who accepted admiration as her due, who understood that desire was a currency she could both spend and earn.

For the first time since we entered the club, I completely forgot about George and Madison in their VIP section. They no longer mattered. What mattered was this—the music, the movement, the intoxicating rush of being seen and desired, the slow revealing of a part of myself I had kept carefully hidden for far too long.

I raised my arms above my head and let my body move freely, no longer following Sam's lead but creating my own rhythm. The red dress clung to my skin, alive with the heat of my transformation.

They materialized through the crowd like apparitions conjured by the pulsating lights—two men moving with the easy confidence of those used to being welcomed wherever they went. The taller one immediately locked eyes with me, his gaze sliding down the length of my borrowed dress and then back up, unhurried and appreciative. His friend, shorter but equally well-built, was already smiling at Sam, who flipped her hair in practiced response. I recognized the dance of attraction unfolding, but for once, I wasn't on the sidelines. The taller man was looking at me—only me—with an intensity that made heat crawl up my neck despite the club's artificial chill.

"Don't look now," Sam murmured, though her eyes never left her admirer, "but those are actual hot guys. Not just club-hot. Hot-hot."

She was right. The taller man approaching us had the kind of looks that didn't require dimmed lighting or alcohol-impaired judgment to appreciate. Broad shoulders tapered to a narrow waist, his white button-down rolled to the elbows to reveal forearms corded with subtle muscle. His dark hair was artfully tousled, as if he'd just run his hands through it, and a small scar bisected his right eyebrow, adding a touch of character to what might otherwise have been intimidatingly perfect features.

"Ladies," he said as they reached us, his voice carrying a hint of gravel that vibrated through the single word. "Mind if we join you?"

Sam answered for us both. "We'd mind if you didn't."

The shorter man laughed, immediately engaging Sam in conversation, while the taller one maintained his focus on me, stepping closer until we occupied the same small patch of dance floor.

"I'm Todd," he said, leaning in so I could hear him over the music. His breath was warm against my ear, carrying notes of mint and expensive bourbon. "And you're the most interesting thing I've seen all night."

The compliment was delivered with such straightforward confidence that it bypassed my usual defenses. Before I could respond, Sam reappeared at my side, pressing another shot glass into my hand.

Liquid courage, round two," she announced, already

holding her own. She clinked her glass against mine, then against the ones the men had somehow procured. "To new friends!"

I tossed back the shot, grateful for the burn that masked my nervous swallow. The tequila hit my system faster this time, mingling with the alcohol already in my bloodstream to create a pleasant, floating sensation.

Sam leaned close, her lips nearly touching my ear. "Go for it," she whispered urgently. "He's hot, and he can't take his eyes off you."

Before I could protest, she was backing away, already being led deeper into the dance floor by Todd's friend. Todd himself stood before me, one hand extended in invitation, his smile confident but not presumptuous.

"Dance with me?" he asked.

I hesitated, torn between years of careful restraint and the new, reckless energy rushing through my veins. The old Elara would have hesitated, made an excuse, and stepped back into the safety of observation. But the woman in this red dress, with tequila warming her blood and unfamiliar power tingling in her fingertips—she had different ideas.

"Yes," I said, taking his offered hand.

His fingers closed around mine, warm and secure, as he guided me to a spot where the crowd provided proximity without crushing. Then his hands were on my hips, light but deliberate, each point of contact sending a small shock of electricity through the thin fabric of my dress.

"I haven't seen you here before," he said, his body already moving to the rhythm, guiding mine to follow. "I would have remembered."

The line should have sounded practiced, even cheesy, but something in his direct gaze made it feel genuine. He was close enough now that I could breathe in his scent—an expensive cologne with notes of cedar and something darker, more primal, underneath.

"First time," I admitted, focusing on the movement of my hips beneath his hands, the way our bodies were learning each other's rhythms. "Is it that obvious?"

His smile grew deeper, showing a dimple in his left cheek. "Not obvious. Just... there's a freshness to you. Like you're seeing everything for the first time." His hands shifted slightly, thumbs grazing the curve where my waist meets my hips. "It's compelling."

The word—compelling—lingered between us, more intimate somehow than a more obvious compliment would have been. I felt myself responding to his touch, my body softening against his as the music shifted to something slower, more deliberate.

"Turn around," he suggested, his voice low near my ear. "Sometimes it's easier to feel the rhythm this way."

I complied, turning so my back pressed against his chest. His hands remained on my hips, guiding me into a slow, sensual sway that matched the heavy beat. The position was both more intimate and somehow safer—I couldn't see his face, but I could feel every shift of his body, every subtle pressure of his hands.

It was then, in the middle of surrendering to this new dance, that I saw George.

He stood at the edge of the VIP section, a forgotten drink in his hand, staring directly at me. Even across the crowded dance floor, the shock in his expression was clear. Madison was still beside him, whispering in his ear, but his focus was entirely on me—on the midnight blue dress, on the man whose hands were possessively tracing my hips, on this version of Elara that had never existed in his presence.

Our eyes locked, and for a moment, I felt the old panic rising—the instinct to explain myself, to apologize for taking up space, for daring to exist beyond the boundaries of his expectations. But then something shifted. In the depths of his gaze, beneath the surprise, I recognized something else: desire. Raw and unexpected, it flickered across his features before he could mask it.

A strange power surged through me, headier than tequila, more potent than any confidence Sam had tried to instill with makeup and clothing. George wanted what he had discarded. He wanted what he could no longer have.

Instead of shrinking under his gaze, I deliberately turned my back to him, pressing closer to Todd until I could feel the solid warmth of his chest against my shoulder blades. His breath caught audibly, hands tightening slightly on my hips.

"You're full of surprises," he murmured, his lips close enough to my ear that I could feel their movement. One of his hands left my hip to brush my hair aside, exposing the sensitive skin of my neck. "I like surprises."

The implied intimacy of the gesture sent a shiver down my spine. Todd felt it, his soft chuckle vibrating against my back as he drew me even closer. His body was firm against mine, all lean muscle and deliberate control. I could feel the heat of him through his shirt, through my dress, a warmth that seemed to seep into my bones.

"Is this okay?" he asked, and the question itself was another surprise—this confident man checking boundaries, ensuring consent.

"Yes," I said, and meant it. My body moved against his with increasing boldness, guided partly by the music, partly by the electricity building between us. His hand slid from my hip to my waist, fingers splayed wide against the fabric of my dress, thumb brushing the underside of my ribcage in a gesture just shy of inappropriate.

I let my head fall back slightly, resting against his shoulder, exposing the column of my throat to the shifting lights. Todd's reaction was immediate—a subtle tension in his frame, a slight catch in his breathing. His cologne enveloped me, mingling with the clean scent of his skin and something more elemental beneath.

"You're dangerous," he said softly, the words vibrating against my skin. "Do you know that?"

I didn't answer because I didn't need to. For the first time in my life, I felt dangerous—felt the power in my body, in my movements, in the way I could influence another person without words. It was intoxicating, this new awareness, this ability to generate heat with nothing but proximity and intent.

The song shifted again, something slower but with a deeper bass that seemed to pulse directly through our connected bodies. Todd turned me in his arms, bringing us face to face, close enough that I could see the flecks of amber in his dark eyes, the slight stubble along his jaw that would feel rough against sensitive skin.

His hands settled at the small of my back, fingertips just grazing the curve above. Mine found their way to his shoulders, feeling the solid strength beneath crisp cotton. We moved together in a dance that was barely disguised as such—bodies aligned, breath mingling, the space between us charged with potential.

I was intensely aware of every sensation: the faint dampness of his shirt beneath my palms, the pressure of his thigh occasionally brushing against mine, the way his gaze dropped to my lips when I unconsciously bit the lower one. The old Elara would have been overwhelmed by this intensity, would have made an excuse and pulled back. But this new version of myself—the one born of heartbreak, tequila, and Sam's unwavering makeover—leaned into the heat, curious about how far it might go.

"What are you thinking?" Todd asked, his voice pitched low enough that I had to lean closer to hear him.

The truth slipped out before I could censor it. "That I've never felt like this before."

His slow, devastating smile left a dimple that looked like a secret punctuation mark. "Like what?"

I searched for the right word, finding it in the electric current running between us. "Powerful."

Todd's eyes darkened, his hands pressing more firmly against my back. "You are powerful," he agreed, pulling me infinitesimally closer. "It's what made me notice you. Not just that you're beautiful—though you are—but that something is happening with you tonight. Something... awakening."

The accuracy of his observation startled me. This man, this stranger, had identified in minutes what had taken me years to realize—that beneath my composed exterior lay something wild and wanting, something that had been silenced but never gone out.

I felt myself drawn to him, not just physically but by this recognition, this seeing of something essential in me. My body moved against his with new intent, testing boundaries, exploring the chemistry that seemed to build with each beat of the music.

Somewhere across the club, George might still be watching. Madison might be noticing his distraction. Sam might be keeping track of my adventure from the corner of her eye. But for the first time since the Bluebird Café, since the moment my carefully constructed life had begun to unravel, I wasn't thinking about any of them.

I was thinking only of this—of Todd's hands warm against my back, of the electricity where our bodies connected, of the woman I was becoming with each passing moment. A woman who wasn't defined by a breakup or a makeover or anyone else's expectations. A woman who was, perhaps, finally meeting herself for the first time.

And as Todd leaned closer, his intention clear in the tilt of his head and the heat of his gaze, I realized that this wasn't just about proving something to George or even to myself. It was about discovering what lay on the other side of caution, what waited beyond the boundaries I'd never dared to cross.

I was ready to find out.

CHAPTER FOUR

The Confrontation

odd's lips met mine in the half-second between heartbeats. The kiss was tentative at first, a question more than a statement, his mouth soft against mine as the club lights painted us in electric blue, then deep crimson. I felt myself sway toward him, my body making a decision my mind hadn't fully processed. My fingers slid up his chest to curl around the back of his neck, drawing him closer as something warm and liquid pooled at the base of my spine.

His hand at my waist tightened, palm pressing into the thin fabric of my dress until I could feel the heat of his skin bleeding through. When he deepened the kiss, there was nothing tentative about it anymore—his tongue traced the seam of my lips, coaxing them open with a confidence that made my knees weaken. I tasted bourbon and mint, felt the slight abrasion of stubble against my chin, breathed in the cedar notes of his cologne mixed with the clean scent of his skin.

When we broke apart, his eyes were darker than before, pupils dilated in the low light. "Dangerous," he repeated, his thumb tracing slow circles at the small of my back. "Definitely dangerous."

The music shifted, the DJ blending into something with a deeper, more insistent beat that seemed to vibrate up through the soles of my feet. Todd drew me closer, one thigh slipping between mine as we began to move again. His body was solid heat against mine, all lean muscle and deliberate control. My hands found his shoulders, feeling the subtle shift and play of strength beneath his shirt as he guided our movements.

We weren't really dancing but rather starting something more relaxed and intimate. His hands moved lower, fingers wide as they covered my hips, thumbs pressing into the soft hollows beside my hipbones. Each touch sent little jolt of pleasure through me, intensified by the alcohol and the novelty of being touched this way—like I was something special and desired instead of just dependable and predictable.

"You move like you've been keeping secrets," Todd murmured, his mouth close to my ear, his breath warm against my skin. "Good secrets."

I smiled, my body rolling against his in a way that would have made yesterday's Elara blush to the roots of her sensibly styled hair. "Maybe I have."

"I'd like to discover them," he said, and the promise in his voice made heat bloom across my chest and throat.

It was then, as I turned my face up to his, that I saw George again. I don't think he'd stopped watching me since first noticing me.

He still stood at the edge of the VIP section, now one hand gripping the brass rail that separated the elite from the merely mortal. Even through the haze of artificial fog and the flash of colored lights, I could make out the rigid set of his jaw, the slight parting of his lips, the way his knuckles whitened against the metal. Our eyes locked across the churning sea of bodies, and I watched disbelief register on his face like a physical blow.

Time seemed to fold in on itself—one moment expanding to contain everything: George's stunned expression, the weight of Todd's hands on my hips, the bass pulsing through my bones like a second heartbeat. For an instant, I felt the old panic rising, the instinctive need to explain myself, to apologize for taking up space in a way George hadn't anticipated.

But then something else surged through me—a power so unfamiliar and intoxicating that it stole my breath. George was staring at me, at this new version of Elara in her borrowed red dress and artfully smudged lipstick, with unmistakable desire. Not the mild appreciation he'd shown during our relationship, but something raw and primal that transformed his features into a mask of want.

I watched as his gaze traveled down the length of my body, lingering on the places where Todd's hands splayed possessively across my hips. When his eyes returned to mine, I didn't look away, didn't offer the shy smile that had been my default response to his attention for two years. Instead, I held his gaze, letting him see exactly what he'd given up.

Beside him, Madison shifted into view, her green dress

catching the light as she leaned closer to him. She followed his line of sight, her perfectly shaped eyebrows drawing together when she spotted me. I couldn't hear what she said, but I saw her red lips move, forming words that seemed to reach George through water—delayed, distorted, barely registering. Her hand came up to rest on his shoulder, fingers curling into the fabric of his jacket, but his attention remained fixed on me, on us.

I turned away first, deliberately pressing my body closer to Todd's, sliding my hands up his chest to link behind his neck. He responded immediately, his grip tightening as he guided me deeper into the rhythm. We moved together with an almost practiced synchronicity, my hips rolling against his in a slow, deliberate tease.

"You've got an audience," Todd said, his voice a low rumble against my ear. He'd noticed George watching, but there was no jealousy in his tone—only amused curiosity.

"Ex-boyfriend," I replied, surprised by how steady my voice sounded. "He dumped me for being too predictable."

Todd's laugh vibrated through his chest into mine. "His mistake," he said, his hands sliding from my hips to the small of my back, drawing me impossibly closer. "Though I can't say I'm sorry he made it."

I glanced back toward the VIP section, catching George's expression as it shifted from shock to something darker and more complex. Desire and disapproval clashed on his face, his brow furrowing even as his eyes stayed fixed on where Todd's body met mine. Madison was speaking again, her face tight with irritation as she tugged at his sleeve. This time, he shook her off without even looking at her, his attention never leaving me.

There was a bitter satisfaction in watching Madison's perfect features contort with the same confused hurt I'd felt at the Bluebird Café. She said something sharper this time—I could tell by the way her shoulders stiffened, by the flash of teeth as the words escaped her—but George barely seemed to notice.

Instead, he set his untouched drink on a nearby table and adjusted his tie with a gesture I recognized well—his way of preparing for confrontation, for asserting control over a situation he deemed unacceptable. The familiar motion gave me a chill, not out of fear but of anticipation. This was no longer a passive observation; George was coming to reclaim what he'd abandoned.

I turned back to Todd, tilting my face up to his. "Kiss me again," I said, not a request but an invitation.

His eyes darkened further, one hand coming up to cup my face, thumb brushing across my lower lip in a gesture so intimate it made my breath catch. "With pleasure," he murmured, before his mouth claimed mine.

This kiss was different—deeper, more intentional, a performance for an audience of one that quickly turned into something real. Todd's tongue swept into my mouth, his hand sliding into my hair to cradle the back of my head. I arched against him, feeling the hard plane of his chest against my breasts, the controlled strength in his arms as they wrapped around me.

From the corner of my eye, I saw George step away from the rail, leaving Madison without a backward glance as he made his way through the crowd toward us. His expression hardened, jaw clenched in a way I recognized from our rare arguments—he was coming to make a statement, to reassert his version of who Elara James was allowed to be.

Just then, the music shifted, the DJ dropping the bass into a sudden, thumping silence that seemed to create a bubble of tension around us. Bodies paused in their movements, the crowd inhaling collectively before the beat returned with renewed intensity. In that suspended moment, I felt George's approach like a storm front, electric and inevitable, as Todd's hands tightened protectively on my waist.

George materialized before us, the crowd parting around him as if he commanded the space by divine right. Up close, he looked both familiar and foreign—the same careful haircut and expensive cologne, but his features were twisted into an expression I seldom saw directed at me: raw, unfiltered displeasure. His eyes, usually cool and assessing, burned with something that could have been anger, possession, or both. He looked at Todd's hands on my waist as if they were a personal affront, a violation of territory he still claimed.

"What the hell are you doing, Elara?" George's voice cut through the music, sharp and precise, the same tone he used when someone presented quarterly reports with incorrect figures. His gaze traveled over me, from my tousled hair to my smudged lipstick, down the length of the dress that hugged curves he'd never seen displayed so openly. His disapproval was clear, but beneath it lurked something else—a heat that contradicted his words.

Todd's hand slid from my waist to the small of my back, the gesture both protective and possessive. I felt the solid warmth of him behind me, his presence like a shield against the icy fury of George's stare. He didn't speak, but his body language made his position clear—he wasn't backing down, wasn't intimidated by George's corporate swagger or expensive watch.

For a moment, I felt myself slipping into old patterns—the urge to placate, to make myself smaller, to apologize for taking up space in ways that made George uncomfortable. It was muscle memory, the product of a thousand minor concessions made in the name of keeping peace. My shoulders started to curl inward, my chin dipping in that unconscious gesture of surrender that had become second nature during our relationship.

But then I felt Todd's thumb trace a small circle against my spine, a silent reminder of the woman I'd been just moments before—confident, desired, powerful. I straightened, pulling myself up to my full height, feeling the unfamiliar weight of Sam's false eyelashes as I looked directly into George's eyes without flinching.

"This isn't you," George said, his voice dropping to a near-whisper that somehow cut through the pounding bass. He gestured at my dress, my makeup, the way I stood pressed against a stranger. "This whole... performance. This isn't the Elara I know."

The words were meant to be a reality check, a wake-up call, but they landed like fuel on the embers of my anger. Who was he to define me? To decide which parts of me were authentic and which were performance? He had rejected me for being too predictable, too controlled, and now he had the nerve to be upset when I proved him wrong.

"You don't get to decide who I am anymore," I replied, surprised by the steadiness of my voice despite the adrenaline coursing through my veins. The tequila in my blood gave my words a reckless edge, but the sentiment behind them was stone-cold sober. "You gave up that right at the Bluebird Café, remember? 'I need something less predictable.' Those were your exact words."

George's jaw tightened, a muscle jumping beneath his skin. He wasn't used to me pushing back, to me having a voice that didn't automatically bend to accommodate his. "That's not—" he started, then cut himself off, eyes darting to Todd and back to me. "Can we talk? Alone?"

"We're kind of in the middle of something," Todd interjected, his voice a low rumble against my back. His hand remained steady at the base of my spine, neither possessive nor controlling, just present—a reminder that I wasn't facing this confrontation alone.

George's eyes narrowed, his composure slipping further. He reached for my arm, his fingers brushing against the bare skin above my elbow. The touch was light but insistent, familiar in a way that sent an unwelcome shiver down my spine. "Five minutes, Elara. That's all I'm asking."

I stepped back, away from his reach, deliberately moving closer to Todd, a move that didn't go unnoticed by George. His expression darkened, and something ugly flickered in his eyes.

"You're making a fool of yourself," he hissed, his voice dropping to ensure only I could hear him. "Is this really what you want? To be grinding on some random guy in a club? To be just another slut?"

The word hit me like a physical blow, sharp and unexpected. Slut. Such a small word, four simple letters, yet loaded with centuries of judgment and control. It was meant to shame me, to make me fold into myself and retreat to safer, more acceptable territory. Six hours ago, it might have worked—might have sent me home with my tail between my legs, desperate to reclaim the "good girl" identity I'd worn for twenty-five years.

But something had shifted inside me, a tectonic plate moving beneath the careful structure of who I thought I was. The woman who'd spent her whole life worried about being proper, about meeting expectations, about never taking up too much space—she wasn't gone, but she was no longer in control. In her place stood someone new, someone who understood that "slut" was just another word for a woman who owned her desire, who refused to be small, who dared to want and be wanted on her own terms.

I looked at George, really looked at him, and saw not the

sophisticated man I'd once placed on a pedestal but a boy in expensive clothing, threatened by the idea that I might exist beyond the narrow confines of his imagination. The realization was both terrifying and liberating—I'd given this man so much power over my self-perception, and now I was taking it back.

Without breaking eye contact with George, I turned in Todd's arms until we were face to face. His eyes widened slightly in surprise, but there was understanding there too, a recognition of what I needed in this moment. I slid my hand up his chest and behind his neck, fingers threading through the soft hair at his nape.

"Kiss me," I whispered, the words meant for Todd alone.

He hesitated for a heartbeat, his gaze searching mine to confirm this was what I truly wanted. Then his mouth came down on mine, gentle at first, then deeper as I pressed myself against him. His arms encircled me completely, one hand splayed across my back, the other cradling my head as our lips parted and our tongues met in a dance more intimate than anything we'd shared on the floor.

This wasn't a kiss for show, though it certainly made a statement. It was a claiming of agency, an embrace of this new Elara who could want without apology, who could take pleasure without permission. Todd seemed to understand this instinctively, his kiss neither performative nor possessive but collaborative—we were creating something together, a moment of genuine connection amid the artificial lights and calculated gestures.

I heard George's sharp intake of breath, felt the weight of

his stare as Todd's hand slid lower on my back, pulling me closer until there was no space left between us. The kiss deepened, becoming something hungry and honest that made my skin flush and my heart race. Todd tasted like possibility, like a future unscripted by anyone's expectations but my own.

When we finally broke apart, I turned back to face George, my lipstick smeared across my mouth and possibly Todd's as well. My chest heaved with each breath, my pulse a wild thing beneath my skin. George stood frozen, his face drained of color beneath the club's shifting lights, his expression a complex mixture of desire, anger, and—most surprisingly—loss.

"I think we're done here," I said, my voice husky but clear. I didn't raise it to be heard over the music; I didn't need to. I knew he was hanging on every word, every gesture, every breath.

The George Mitchell who had walked away from our table at the Bluebird Café had been calm, in control, and confident in his decision. The man standing before me now looked shaken to his core, as if the foundation of his understanding had cracked beneath his feet.

Good, I thought. Let him feel unsteady for once. Let him question his own perceptions instead of mine.

I touched my fingers to my lips, feeling their tender swelling from Todd's kiss. My heart thumped against my ribs like a captive bird, each beat sending a rush of adrenaline and something darker, more primal, through my veins. The woman who had entered this club hours ago—tentative, apologetic, haunted by a birthday breakup—was gone. In her place stood someone new, someone who recognized the power in her own desire, who understood that "predictable" was just another word for "controlled."

The red lipstick Sam had so carefully applied was now smudged beyond salvation, probably transferred to Todd's mouth in crimson evidence of our connection. I could feel the heat of his body still pressed against mine, his hands steady on my hips as if anchoring me in this moment of transformation. His eyes, when they met mine, held neither triumph nor possession, but a warm curiosity tinged with unmistakable want.

Todd's thumb brushed lightly across my lower lip, wiping away a smear of lipstick with a gentleness that contrasted with the hunger of our kiss moments before. The gesture was unexpectedly intimate, more so than the public display we'd just enacted. It felt like something private, a small tenderness not meant for George's eyes or anyone else's.

"You okay?" Todd asked, his voice low enough that only I could hear it over the pulsing beat that had resumed its dominance over the club.

I nodded, surprised to find it was true. I was more than okay—I was awake, alert, present in my body in a way I hadn't been for years, maybe ever. The realization came with a clarity that cut through the haze of tequila and artificial fog: I wanted more of this feeling. More of this night. More of Todd and the way he looked at me like I was a mystery worth solving.

"We should leave," I said, the words coming out huskier than I'd intended, charged with meanings neither of us pretended to misunderstand. This wasn't about escaping George or proving a point anymore—it was about following this current of desire to whatever shore it might lead me.

Todd's smile spread slowly, revealing that left dimple that had caught my attention from the start. "Lead the way," he said, and the promise in those three simple words sent a shiver across my skin that had nothing to do with the club's over-zealous air conditioning.

I glanced at George one last time, finding him still frozen in place, his expression locked in a mask of disbelief. Madison had appeared at his elbow, her green dress a slash of color in the dim lighting, her face tight with barely controlled fury as she tugged at his sleeve. He didn't seem to notice her, his eyes still fixed on me with an intensity that would have made the old Elara shrink and apologize.

The new Elara simply turned away, took Todd's hand in mine, and intertwined our fingers in a gesture that felt both casual and meaningful. His palm was warm against mine, his grip steady but gentle as I started to make my way through the crowd toward the exit.

Bodies pressed against us from all sides, the dance floor now packed with weekend revelers lost in the rhythm and their own private pursuits. The DJ had transitioned to something with a deeper, slower beat that seemed to vibrate through the soles of my feet and up my spine. Todd stayed close behind me, his free hand occasionally settling at the small of my back to guide me through particularly dense patches of dancers.

Each touch, no matter how brief, sent sparks of anticipation through my system. There was a delicious tension building between us, an unspoken agreement that this night was headed somewhere neither of us had expected when it started. The knowledge hummed in my blood alongside the tequila, making me both lightheaded and hyperaware of every sensation—the brush of his fingers against mine, the pressure of his palm at my back, the way his eyes seemed to follow my movements with appreciative heat.

We were halfway to the exit when I spotted Sam near the bar, her platinum hair catching the blue lights as she leaned against the counter, nursing what looked like a vodka soda. She wasn't alone—the friend Todd had arrived with stood close beside her, saying something that made her throw her head back in genuine laughter. But despite her apparent engagement in conversation, her eyes kept darting to the dance floor, scanning the crowd until they locked on me.

The moment she saw us—saw our linked hands, the smudged lipstick, the intention clear in our body language— her expression shifted from concerned vigilance to unabashed delight. She straightened, abandoning her companion mid-sentence to focus entirely on what she clearly viewed as her masterpiece coming to life.

I felt a surge of affection for this fearless friend who had pulled me from the wreckage of my heartbreak and refused to let me hide in the comfortable shadow of predictability. Without Sam's makeover, without her insistence that we come to this club, without her shots of tequila and lessons in confidence, I would be at home right now, curled into myself like a wounded animal, nursing my hurt instead of embracing this new possibility.

I raised my free hand in a wave that was part greeting, part victory signal, unable to suppress the bright smile that spread across my face. It felt strange, this unburdened happiness, this sense of moving toward something rather than away from pain. My smile wasn't the careful, measured expression I usually offered the world; it was wide and genuine, slightly wild around the edges, belonging wholly to this new version of myself.

Sam's response was immediate and enthusiastic—a double thumbs-up followed by an exaggerated wink that made me laugh despite myself. Her grin was fierce with pride, with the satisfaction of a plan perfectly executed. She raised her glass in a toast that managed to be both congratulatory and slightly wicked, then mouthed something that looked suspiciously like "Get it, girl!"

The simple exchange felt like a benediction, a passing of the torch from Sam's brand of bold confidence to whatever version I was creating for myself tonight. I squeezed Todd's hand, feeling his answering pressure as we continued toward the exit, the cool night air beckoning beyond the club's heavy doors.

As we reached the threshold, I couldn't resist one final glance back. George remained where we'd left him, a statue in the midst of movement, his face still frozen in that expression of stunned disbelief. Madison was speaking rapidly now, her perfectly manicured hands gesturing with increasing agitation, but she might as well have been invisible for all the attention he paid her. He was still staring at the spot where Todd and I had stood, as if he could rewind time through sheer force of will.

For a moment, I almost felt sorry for him— for the man who had only known me as he wanted me to be, who never bothered to look beneath the careful surface I had presented. But the feeling quickly passed, replaced by a surge of anticipation as Todd held the door open, his smile promising discoveries that had nothing to do with my past and everything to do with the woman I was becoming.

I stepped into the night, the cool air a shock against my flushed skin. The red dress caught the streetlight as we emerged, a final flash of color before the club door swung shut behind us, sealing George and all his expectations on the other side of a boundary I had no intention of crossing again.

CHAPTER FIVE

The Alley Encounter

The side door of Pulse slammed shut behind us, sealing away the throbbing music into a muffled heartbeat against brick. Todd's hand remained firmly intertwined with mine as we stumbled into a narrow alley, our bodies instinctively seeking each other in the dim glow of a distant streetlight. The cool night air kissed my flushed skin, a stark contrast to the heat radiating between us as his mouth found mine again, hungrier this time, more urgent than the calculated display we'd performed for George's benefit inside the club.

My back pressed against the rough texture of the wall, the brick catching on the thin fabric of my borrowed dress. I inhaled sharply, taking in the complex scent of the city at night —damp concrete from an earlier rain, the faint sweetness of spilled alcohol, and the cedar notes of Todd's cologne blending with the salt of his skin. Somewhere in the distance, a siren wailed, then faded, leaving only our ragged breathing and the persistent thump of bass filtering through the club's walls.

Todd's hands cradled my face, his thumbs tracing my cheekbones with surprising tenderness given the urgency of his kiss. I felt myself melting into him, my body yielding in ways it never had before—not with George, not with anyone. But then something shifted inside me, a tectonic plate of desire moving beneath the careful structure of who I'd always been.

I pushed back, not to create distance but to redirect our momentum. My palms found his chest, solid and warm beneath the crisp cotton of his shirt, and I guided him backward until his shoulders pressed against the opposite wall. His eyes widened in surprise, the dimple appearing as his lips curved into an appreciative smile.

"Well, look at you," he murmured, his voice rougher than before, edged with a desire that sent shivers down my spine.

I didn't answer with words. Instead, I took his mouth with mine, my tongue exploring the heat of him, tasting bourbon, mint, and the faint sweetness of whatever he'd been drinking at the club. My hands moved with new confidence, tracing the contours of his chest, the firm planes of his stomach, the narrow cut of his hips. Each touch was a discovery, an exploration of territory I had never dared to claim before.

Todd groaned against my mouth as my fingers found the button of his pants, fumbling slightly before managing to work it free. The sound vibrated through me, igniting something primal and hungry that had nothing to do with the woman I'd been just yesterday.

"Are you sure?" he asked, his breath warm against my ear as I nipped at his earlobe.

In answer, I drew back just enough to meet his gaze. The

old Elara would have hesitated, would have second-guessed, would have worried about judgments and consequences and what it all meant. But this woman—the one wearing a stranger's dress and smudged lipstick, with tequila still sweet in her blood—she knew exactly what she wanted.

"I'm sure," I said, my voice steadier than I expected as I sank slowly to my knees on the cracked pavement.

The concrete was cold and hard beneath me, gritty with the city's residue. In the faint light, I could make out layers of graffiti spanning the alley walls—jagged letters and faded colors, generations of midnight declarations stacked atop one another like geological strata. Somewhere nearby, a bottle rolled across pavement, its hollow sound echoing between the buildings before fading into silence.

I looked up at Todd, taking in the sight of him from this new vantage point. His chest rose and fell with quickened breath, his eyes dark with wanting as he watched me. Power surged through me—not the practiced seductiveness Sam had taught me, but something rawer, more instinctive. This was what it felt like to be desired, to be the architect of someone else's pleasure.

My fingers worked his zipper down with more confidence than I felt, the metal teeth parting to reveal black boxer briefs stretched taut over his evident arousal. The realization of what I was about to do—what I wanted to do—sent a rush of heat to my core. I'd done this before, but never like this—never in an alley behind a club, never with someone I'd just met, never with such deliberate, unapologetic intention.

I tugged his pants and underwear down just enough, freeing him into the cool night air. He was already fully hard, the sight of him sending another pulse of desire through me. I wrapped my fingers around him, feeling the velvet skin over rigid heat, the subtle throb of his pulse against my palm.

"God, Elara," he breathed, his voice strained with restraint.

I looked up, catching his gaze as I took him into my mouth. His sharp intake of breath was its own reward, a clear sign of the power I wielded in that moment. I moved slowly at first, learning the taste and feel of him, finding a rhythm that made his thighs tense beneath my free hand.

The bass from the club provided a backbeat to our encounter, a primal soundtrack that seemed to sync with my movements as I took him deeper. Todd's fingers threaded through my hair, not forcing, just holding, the gentle pressure guiding rather than controlling. I allowed him this much direction, while still maintaining the pace, still orchestrating his pleasure with deliberate skill I hadn't known I possessed.

"Fuck," he gasped as I hollowed my cheeks, increasing the suction while my hand worked in tandem with my mouth. "You're incredible."

The compliment landed like sparks on my skin, each word a validation of this new self I was discovering. I hummed in response, the vibration making him tighten his grip in my hair, his hips jerking forward involuntarily before he caught himself.

"Sorry," he murmured, but I shook my head slightly, granting permission for what his body clearly craved.

I braced my free hand against his hip, feeling the muscles there flex and strain as he fought to maintain control. The roughness of the brick wall scraped against my knuckles, a sharp counterpoint to the warm, smooth skin beneath my other hand. The contrast was exhilarating—comfort and discomfort, pleasure and pain, the proper Elara of yesterday and this wild creature of tonight existing simultaneously in one body.

Todd's breathing became more ragged, his exhales punctuated with low sounds of pleasure that echoed in the narrow space between buildings. I felt him tense, felt the subtle shift that signaled he was close. Instead of pulling back, I increased my efforts, a surge of triumph rushing through me as his fingers tightened almost painfully in my hair.

"Elara," he warned, his voice strained. "I'm going to—"

I didn't relent, driven by a newfound determination to see this through, to claim this experience fully. His entire body went rigid, a tremor running through him as he reached his peak. I stayed with him through it, accepting everything he had to give, feeling strangely powerful in my surrender.

When it was over, and his breathing began to slow, his grip in my hair softened to something almost tender, I drew back, wiping my mouth with the back of my hand in a gesture that felt both vulgar and freeing. My knees ached from the concrete, my lips felt swollen, and somewhere in the middle of it all, one of Sam's carefully applied false eyelashes had come loose, tickling my cheek.

And yet, I had never felt more alive, more present in my own skin. This—this raw, unapologetic pleasure—was what George had never allowed me to be, what I had never allowed myself to become. The realization was dizzying, intoxicating in a way that had nothing to do with the tequila shots and everything to do with finally, finally stepping outside the carefully drawn lines of my own existence.

Todd reached down, offering his hand to help me to my feet. His expression was a mix of satisfaction and wonder, as if he were witnessing something extraordinary happening right before his eyes. Maybe he was. Maybe I was extraordinary — not because I was breaking the rules of propriety, but because I was daring to.

I rose slowly to my feet, my legs tingling from kneeling on the cold concrete. Todd's eyes followed my movement, dark with lingering pleasure and renewed interest as I pressed my body against his. The alley suddenly felt too confined, too public, and yet not public enough—a liminal space where the standard rules didn't apply, where I could be someone I'd never dared to become. I leaned in, my lips brushing the shell of his ear, and whispered words I'd never imagined saying aloud: "Are you going to take me somewhere else, or are you going to fuck me right here?"

The profanity felt foreign on my tongue, thrilling in its wrongness. Just yesterday, I'd been the woman who said "oh gosh" when stubbing a toe, who apologized to furniture when bumping into it. Now I was propositioning a near-stranger in an alley, the taste of him still lingering in my mouth.

Todd's sharp intake of breath was answer enough, but I didn't wait to hear his words. Something wild had taken hold of me, something that couldn't be contained by polite conversation or careful consideration. I turned around, facing the graffiti-covered brick, and braced my palms against the rough surface. The dress—Sam's dress—rode high on my thighs as I widened my stance, glancing back over my shoulder at Todd with a challenge in my eyes that I felt down to my bones.

"Well?" I asked, the single word carrying more confidence than I'd ever felt in my life.

For a moment, Todd remained frozen, his expression caught between disbelief and raw hunger. Then something shifted in his eyes—a decision made, permission granted. He closed the distance between us in a single step, his hands finding my shoulders and spinning me around to face the wall completely. The brick scraped against my palms as I caught myself, the slight pain a counterpoint to the pleasure coiling tight in my abdomen.

"You're full of surprises," he murmured, his voice rough against the nape of my neck as he pressed his body along the length of mine. His hands slid down my sides, fingers digging into the curve of my hips with an urgency that would likely leave marks—evidence of this night that I'd carry into tomorrow.

I felt him hardening again against me, his recovery impressive given what had just transpired. One of his hands slipped beneath the hem of my dress, finding the edge of my underwear and dragging it down with an impatience that sent a fresh wave of heat through me. The air was cool against my exposed skin, raising goosebumps that had nothing to do with temperature and everything to do with anticipation.

"Is this what you want?" Todd asked, his fingers tracing a path along the inside of my thigh, teasing higher but never quite reaching where I ached for him to touch. "Tell me, Elara."

The sound of my name in his mouth, rough with desire, was startlingly intimate. I'd heard my name spoken thousands of times, but never like this—never as an invocation, a question, a demand all at once.

"Yes," I breathed, pushing back against him, wordlessly asking for what my body craved. "Please."

His fingers found me then, sliding through slick heat with a knowing touch that made my knees buckle slightly. I braced myself more firmly against the wall, feeling the uneven texture of the brick dig into my palms as Todd explored me with a deliberate patience that bordered on torment.

"You're already so wet," he murmured against my ear, the crude observation sending another pulse of desire through me. "Is this what you've been thinking about all night?"

The truth was, I hadn't known I wanted this until the moment it began to happen. I'd stepped into that club as one woman and was emerging as another—one who recognized her own desires and wasn't afraid to pursue them.

Before I could formulate an answer, Todd withdrew his hand and positioned himself behind me. I felt the blunt pressure of him against my entrance, my body instinctively tensing in anticipation. His hands gripped my hips firmly, holding me in place as he pushed forward in a single, powerful thrust that filled me completely.

I gasped, my fingers scraping against brick as I adjusted to the sensation of being so thoroughly claimed. Todd stilled, giving me a moment to accommodate him, his breath hot and ragged against my neck.

"Okay?" he asked, the concern in his voice a surprising tenderness amid the rough urgency of our encounter.

"Don't stop," I managed, the words more plea than command.

He began to move then, setting a rhythm that was neither gentle nor punishing but somewhere gloriously in between. Each thrust pushed me against the wall, the friction of brick against my palms creating a duality of sensation—the rough scrape against my hands contrasting with the smooth slide of him inside me. My dress had rucked up around my waist, the night air cool against my exposed skin where Todd's body wasn't pressed against mine.

The partial nakedness—clothed but exposed in the most vulnerable way—added to the forbidden thrill of it all. We were still technically in public, hidden only by shadows and the late hour. Anyone could walk by, could hear the sounds of skin against skin, could witness this transformation from reliable Elara to someone wild and wanting.

The thought should have horrified me. Instead, it intensified everything, pushing me closer to an edge I rarely reached even in the privacy of my own bedroom. Todd seemed to sense the shift in me, one hand sliding from my hip to reach around, finding the center of my pleasure with perfect accuracy.

"Come for me," he urged, his voice strained with his own approaching release. "Let me feel you."

The command, coupled with the precise pressure of his fingers and the relentless rhythm of his thrusts, catapulted me over the edge I'd been approaching. My climax crashed through me like a wave breaking against rock, powerful and uncompromising. I bit my lip to stifle the sounds that threatened to escape, tasting copper as my teeth broke skin.

Todd followed shortly after, his rhythm faltering as he drove into me one final time, his body going rigid against mine as he reached his peak. For several heartbeats, we remained locked together, our breathing synced in the aftermath of shared pleasure.

Then, slowly, reality began to reassert itself. The distant wail of a siren, the persistent bass from the club, the rough texture of brick against my cheek where I'd pressed my face against the wall. Todd withdrew carefully, his hands steadying me as my legs threatened to buckle beneath the sudden absence.

I turned around, leaning against the wall for support as I quickly adjusted my underwear. My fingers trembled slightly, but not from shame or regret—rather from the lingering aftershocks of pleasure and the strange, powerful realization that I had stepped outside the carefully constructed boundaries of my former self.

Todd was watching me, his expression a mixture of satisfaction and something more complex—perhaps wonder, perhaps uncertainty about what came next. He opened his mouth to speak, but I pressed a finger to his lips, silencing whatever he might have said.

"That was fun," I said simply, surprising myself with how steady my voice sounded.

I reached up to tuck a strand of hair behind my ear, a gesture so normal, so everyday, that it seemed almost comical given what had just transpired between us. Then I straightened my dress, feeling the fabric settle back into place over my thighs, hiding the evidence of our encounter, though my body still hummed with the memory of it.

Todd remained leaning against the wall, his shirt partially untucked, his hair mussed from my fingers. He looked thoroughly, gloriously disheveled—and utterly bewildered by the abrupt shift in my demeanor.

"You're just... leaving?" he asked, his voice carrying a note of disbelief that might have wounded me yesterday but now felt like a badge of honor. I had surprised him. I had defied expectation. I had been anything but predictable.

I smiled, a genuine expression that had nothing to do with apology or accommodation—the first such smile, perhaps, of my adult life.

"I got exactly what I wanted," I replied, the honesty of it thrilling in its simplicity. "Didn't you?"

Without waiting for his answer, I turned and walked toward the mouth of the alley where the street lights cast long shadows across the pavement. My steps were steady despite the slight wobble in my knees, and my posture remained straight and confident despite the tender ache between my thighs. Behind me, I could feel Todd's gaze following my departure, almost tasting his arousal and bewilderment like lingering notes of wine on the back of my tongue.

I didn't look back. The woman who always checked to make sure others were okay, who worried about being polite, who feared taking up too much space—she was gone, or at least transformed into someone new. Someone who walked away from pleasure without apology, who claimed satisfaction as her due rather than her privilege.

As I emerged onto the street, the night air kissed my flushed skin like an old friend welcoming me to a new world of possibility.

CHAPTER SIX

The Vow

I settled onto the barstool at The Crimson Room, a place I'd passed a dozen times but never dared to enter. The whiskey I ordered burned a path down my throat, warming me from the inside in a way the night air couldn't reach. My body still hummed with the memories of what had happened in that alley a few nights before—the brick against my palms, Todd's hands gripping my hips, the thrill of walking away when I was finished with him. I ran a finger around the rim of my glass, watching the amber liquid catch the light. Something had shifted inside me, a fundamental realignment that made the woman who'd cried at the Bluebird Café feel like a distant relative rather than my former self.

The bar cloaked itself in deliberate mystery—dim Edison bulbs casting more shadow than illumination, conversation muted to a low murmur beneath vintage jazz, the occasional clink of ice against glass punctuating laughter. Smoke from someone's illicit cigarette hung in lazy spirals near the ceiling, defying the city's ordinances with the same casual disregard I now felt toward every rule I'd ever followed.

I took another sip of whiskey, letting it linger on my tongue. Just days ago, I would have ordered white wine, something safe and predictable. The thought made me smile against the rim of my glass. Predictable. The word no longer stung—it had become a relic of a life I was shedding like an outgrown skin.

My thighs still bore the ghost of Todd's fingerprints, a delicious ache that reminded me with every shift on the barstool that I had taken what I wanted and walked away before he could. The power in that moment—his bewildered expression, the way he'd tried to reach for me as I straightened my dress—had been more intoxicating than any climax. For the first time in my life, I'd been the one to define the terms of an encounter, to claim pleasure without promising anything in return.

I traced a water ring on the bar's polished surface, my reflection wavering in the mahogany like a woman caught between states of being. The bartender—bearded, tattooed, eyes that had seen enough to know not to ask questions— refilled my glass without being asked. His nod carried a hint of recognition, not of my face but of my purpose. This wasn't a place people came to find connections. It was where they came to forget them.

"Never again," I whispered to my whiskey, the promise settling into my bones with surprising weight. Never again would I build my identity around a man's expectations. Never again would I twist my desires to fit into the narrow box someone else had made for me. Never again would I confuse sex with love, or love with validation.

George had wanted someone less predictable, and in

discarding me, he'd unleashed exactly that—though not in the way he'd intended. I smiled at the irony, imagining his face if he could see me now, perched at a bar most of his friends wouldn't dare enter, my body still carrying evidence of a stranger's touch, my mind already hunting for the next encounter.

The whiskey had softened the edges of my thoughts but sharpened my senses. I sat straighter, shoulders back, chin tilted at the precise angle Sam had taught me—not submission, not challenge, but invitation. My gaze swept the room with new authority, cataloging the men present with a detachment that would have shocked the Elara of yesterday.

Two suits at a corner table—expense accounts and wedding rings. A cluster of grad students celebrating something trivial. A silver fox at the far end of the bar, expensive watch, and an air of practiced disinterest that matched the carefully calculated casualness of his rolled sleeves.

And then—him.

He sat alone at the curve of the bar, close enough to notice but far enough that approaching him would be a deliberate choice. Dark hair falling across his forehead, strong hands cradling a tumbler of something that matched the amber of my own drink. He wore confidence like a second skin, but there was something else in the set of his shoulders—controlled intensity, a banked fire. When he brought the glass to his lips, I found myself watching the movement of his throat as he swallowed.

As if sensing my attention, he glanced up. Our eyes locked

across the bar, and instead of looking away—instead of the shy smile and downcast eyes that had been my default for twenty-five years—I held his gaze. One second. Two. Three. Then I let my lips curve into the barest suggestion of a smile before deliberately looking away, just as Sam had taught me.

I counted to ten in my head, tracing the rim of my glass with one finger. When I looked up again, he was still watching me, his expression a mix of interest and something more primal. The old Elara would have blushed, hidden behind her hair, and made herself smaller under that kind of scrutiny.

The new Elara stood, smoothed her dress over her hips with deliberate slowness, and walked toward him.

He straightened as I approached, his eyes never leaving mine. I slid onto the stool beside him, close enough that the fabric of my dress brushed against his jeans, far enough that he'd have to move to touch me.

"That seat's taken," he said, his voice a low rumble that seemed to resonate directly against my skin.

I raised an eyebrow, letting my gaze slide down to the empty space around him, then back to his face. "By whom?"

His mouth quirked, a flash of white teeth against the shadow of stubble. "By someone with more nerve than most of the men in here."

"And yet," I countered, crossing my legs so my knee grazed his thigh, "I don't see him claiming it."

His laugh was genuine, surprise and appreciation mingling in the sound. He turned to face me fully, one arm resting on the bar, his body creating a private space that excluded everyone else in the room.

"What are you drinking?" he asked, signaling the bartender with a subtle gesture.

"Whiskey," I replied, watching his eyes widen slightly. "Neat."

"A woman of refined taste."

"You have no idea what my tastes are," I said, holding his gaze with newfound boldness.

His pupils dilated, a flush creeping up his neck that had nothing to do with the alcohol in his glass. "I'd like to find out."

The bartender brought over two fresh whiskeys, and as the stranger handed me mine, his fingers brushed deliberately against mine. A current ran up my arm, settling low in my stomach with a warm pulse of anticipation.

"Why are you really here?" he asked, his voice dropping to ensure only I could hear him. "A woman like you could have her pick of places much less... disreputable."

I took a sip of whiskey, letting the liquid sit on my lips before I responded. "Maybe I prefer places where reputation isn't a concern."

He leaned closer, his breath warm against my ear. "And what else do you prefer?"

"Directness," I replied, turning so our faces were inches apart. "I prefer men who know what they want and aren't afraid to take it."

His hand found my wrist, fingers tracing idle patterns that sent shivers up my arm. "And what do you want, mystery woman?"

I leaned forward, my lips nearly brushing his ear. "I want to stop talking about what I want and start experiencing it."

His sharp intake of breath was all the reward I needed. When I pulled back, his eyes darkened to nearly black, his expression caught between disbelief and raw hunger.

"You're not what I expected when I came here tonight," he said, his thumb now tracing the sensitive skin of my inner wrist.

I deliberately bit my lower lip, watching his gaze drop to my mouth with predictable fascination. "Expectation is over-rated," I said, the words carrying a weight he couldn't possibly understand. "I prefer surprise."

His fingers tightened around my wrist, not restraining but claiming, testing boundaries I was increasingly eager to cross. "I have a feeling you're full of those."

I smiled, finishing my whiskey in a single swallow before

setting the glass on the bar with deliberate precision. "You have no idea."

The space between us seemed to shrink with each second, oxygen replaced by something thicker, heavier, charged with intent. His fingers traced slow circles on my wrist, each loop venturing further up my arm, testing boundaries neither of us planned to respect. Without a word, we took our drinks and moved deeper into the bar's shadows, finding a booth tucked behind a brick column where the light deliberately failed. I slid across worn leather, not to make room but to see if he would follow. He did, his thigh pressing against mine with deliberate pressure that sent heat spiraling through my core.

We still hadn't exchanged names. I didn't want his, and he seemed to understand that offering it would break whatever spell we were weaving between us. Names signified connection, representing the possibility of tomorrow. Tonight was about the present, about the electricity sparking when his knee nudged mine, and about the promise in his eyes when they dropped to my lips.

"What's your story?" he asked, his voice pitched low enough that I had to lean closer to hear him.

I shook my head, letting my hair fall forward to brush against his shoulder. "No stories. No histories."

His smile was slow, appreciative. "Just this moment?"

"Just this moment," I confirmed, feeling a rush of power as he accepted my terms without question.

His hand found my thigh beneath the table, fingers splaying wide against the fabric of my dress. Just days ago, I would have stiffened, made excuses, and worried about being judged. Now, I simply shifted, allowing my legs to part slightly —an invitation, not surrender.

"You're not what you seem," he murmured, his thumb tracing the hem of my dress where it had ridden up.

"Neither are you," I countered, though I had no evidence beyond the intuition that men who sat alone in bars like this one were rarely exactly what they appeared.

His fingers inched higher, finding the edge of my underwear with a precision that suggested experience. I kept my expression neutral, though my pulse quickened. The bar's shadows cloaked us, but we weren't invisible—anyone walking past might notice his arm's position, might see the flush spreading across my chest.

"Tell me what you want," he whispered, his lips brushing the shell of my ear.

The question vibrated through me, so similar to what Todd had asked in that alley behind Pulse, yet landing differently against my newly awakened sense of agency. This time, I didn't hesitate.

"I want you," I said, my voice steady despite the heat

pooling between my thighs where his fingers continued their exploration. "But not here."

I captured his wrist, pulling his hand away from my skin with reluctance that we both felt. Then I stood, tugging him with me. His surprise was evident, but he followed without resistance as I led him through the dimly lit bar toward the narrow hallway that housed the restrooms.

The women's door had an "Out of Order" sign hanging crookedly from the handle. I ignored it, pushing open the men's room door instead and pulling him in behind me. The space was barely large enough for two people—a single stall, a wall-mounted sink with a dripping faucet, graffiti layered so thick on the walls that the original color was a mystery lost to time.

A single bulb hung from the ceiling, its flickering light casting strange, moving shadows across his face as he looked at me with obvious hunger. The door had barely clicked shut behind us when I pressed him against it, my mouth finding his with a sudden, fierce rush that caught us both off guard. He tasted of whiskey and mint, his stubble rough against my skin, heightening every sensation.

My hands were already working at his belt, fingers brushing against him through the fabric of his jeans, feeling his immediate response with a surge of satisfaction. His own hands moved to my waist, but I caught them, pinning them against the door on either side of his head.

"My way," I murmured against his mouth, feeling him smile.

"Your way," he agreed, voice strained with want.

The dripping faucet marked time as we lost ourselves in exploration, my hands mapping the contours of his chest beneath his shirt, his breath catching when I found sensitive spots. I trailed kisses down his neck, tasting salt and cologne, feeling the thundering pulse beneath his skin that matched my own.

The door handle suddenly rattled, someone on the other side trying to get in. We froze, his hands instinctively tightening on my hips, my breath catching in my throat. A muffled curse filtered through the wood, followed by retreating footsteps. The interruption should have been a wake-up call; instead, it sent a fresh wave of heat through me—the thrill of nearly getting caught, of doing something forbidden, of claiming space and pleasure that the old Elara would never have dared.

"That was close," he whispered, but I silenced him with another kiss, hungrier this time, my body pressing fully against his.

I led him toward the toilet, my intentions clear in the pressure of my hands against his chest. When the back of his legs hit the closed seat, I pushed him down, climbing onto his lap before he could adjust his position. His hands found my hips immediately, steadying me as I straddled him in the confined space.

"God, you're incredible," he breathed, looking up at me with unabashed admiration.

"Less talking," I instructed, reaching between us to free him from his jeans. He was already fully hard, the evidence of his desire sending a pulse of satisfaction through me.

The cold tile pressed against my knees as I adjusted my position, pushing my underwear aside rather than removing it completely. The faucet's steady drip provided a rhythm as I guided him to my entrance, sinking down slowly enough to make us both gasp.

"Like this," I said, setting a pace that suited my needs, my hands braced on his shoulders for leverage. "Just like this."

He complied, his fingers digging into my hips, leaving marks I would find tomorrow with a mixture of satisfaction and disbelief. The bathroom's fluorescent light flickered above us, casting strange shadows across his features as pleasure transformed them. His eyes never left mine, watching with fascination as I took what I wanted from him.

The sink dripped. The light flickered. Outside, the muted bass of the bar's music vibrated through the walls. But all that existed was the point where our bodies joined, the building pressure low in my abdomen, the heady rush of power as I controlled every aspect of our connection.

"Touch me," I commanded, guiding his hand between us to where I needed him most.

He found the right spot immediately, his touch precise and confident in a way that sent sparks shooting up my spine. The dual sensation—him inside me, his fingers working their magic—pushed me rapidly toward the edge. I bit my lip to contain the sounds threatening to escape, tasting blood and not caring.

"I'm close," he warned, his rhythm faltering slightly as he fought for control.

"So am I," I breathed, increasing my pace. "Don't hold back."

His free hand tangled in my hair, pulling me down for a kiss that muffled his groan as he reached his peak. The feel of him pulsing inside me, combined with the pressure of his fingers, catapulted me into my own release. I buried my face against his neck, teeth scraping his skin as waves of pleasure crashed through me, leaving me trembling in their wake.

For several heartbeats, we remained locked together, our breathing ragged in the small space. The faucet dripped. The light flickered. Reality began its slow return as the intensity of pleasure receded, leaving behind a satisfied languor and the awareness of cold tile against my knees, of his hands still gripping my hips, of sweat cooling on my skin.

I lifted myself off him with careful movements, adjusting my dress with more composure than I felt. He watched me, his expression a mixture of satisfaction and something close to awe, as if he couldn't quite believe what had just happened.

Neither could I, though for entirely different reasons. The woman who had initiated this encounter, who had taken her pleasure without apology or explanation, was still too new for me to fully recognize her as myself. Yet there she was—

reflected in his eyes, in the marks on my skin, in the delicious ache between my thighs.

Someone tried the door again, the handle turning more insistently this time. Our moment of privacy was ending; the real world was pressing in with its expectations and judgments. But for these minutes, in this unlikely space, I had been exactly who I wanted to be—without names, without histories, without tomorrows.

Just desire, satisfied on my terms.

I studied my reflection in the spotted bathroom mirror, barely recognizing the woman who stared back at me. My lips were swollen from kisses, my hair a wild tangle where his fingers had gripped it, a faint red mark blooming at the junction of my neck and shoulder. But it was my eyes that caught and held my attention—they gleamed with something I'd never seen there before, a certainty that bordered on defiance. Behind me, he was tucking in his shirt, adjusting his belt, attempting to recover some semblance of composure. I made no such effort. The evidence of what we'd done—what I'd initiated—wasn't something to hide or apologize for. It was a badge of honor, a declaration of my new reality.

The fluorescent light flickered, casting strange shadows across our faces as we sat in the tiny space that now felt charged with something more intimate than passion—the awkward aftermath that usually follows such encounters. But I felt none of the shame that should have been there, none of the regret or second-guessing that would have consumed the old Elara. Instead, a calm satisfaction settled in my bones, a sense of completeness I had never experienced before.

He caught my gaze in the mirror, his expression a mixture of satiation and curiosity. "You're something else," he said, voice still rough from our activities.

I turned to face him, leaning against the sink with deliberate casualness. "So I've been told."

His eyes traveled over me once more, taking in the disheveled dress, the marks his hands had left on my thighs, the confidence in my posture that hadn't been there when I'd first approached him at the bar. He stepped closer, one hand coming up to tuck a strand of hair behind my ear—a gesture too tender, too familiar for what had just transpired between us.

"I'd like to see you again," he said, surprising me with his directness. "Maybe somewhere with actual lighting and fewer health code violations."

The suggestion hung between us, an invitation to step back into the world of names and numbers, of expectations and explanations. Previously, I might have jumped at the chance— might have mistaken good sex for the promise of something meaningful, might have built elaborate fantasies around a man whose name I didn't even know.

But the woman who had walked away from Todd in that alley, who had sauntered into this bar and chosen this man based on nothing more than physical attraction and the promise in his eyes—she wanted something different. Free-dom. Agency. The power to take pleasure without owing anything in return.

"I don't think so," I said, my voice gentle but firm.

His eyebrows rose slightly, genuinely surprised. "You sure about that? Because what just happened was..." He trailed off, apparently unable to find an adequate adjective.

"Exactly what I wanted," I finished for him. "And exactly what you wanted. Let's not complicate it."

He studied me for a long moment, as if trying to solve a puzzle he hadn't expected to encounter. "At least tell me your name," he tried again. "Or take my number. In case you change your mind."

Instead of answering, I stepped forward, closing the distance between us. I placed one hand on his chest, feeling his heart still beating rapidly beneath my palm. Then I rose on my tiptoes and pressed my lips to his—not the hungry, demanding kiss we'd shared earlier, but something softer, more deliberate. A goodbye.

When I pulled back, his eyes remained closed for a beat longer than necessary, as if trying to memorize the sensation.

"Thanks for the fun," I said with a small smile, then reached past him to unlock the door.

He opened his mouth, closed it again, apparently rendered speechless by this turn of events. The realization sent another pulse of power through me—I had upended his expectations completely, had taken the script men usually followed and torn it to pieces before his eyes.

I walked out without looking back, leaving him standing in that cramped bathroom with its dripping faucet and flickering light. The bar seemed louder now, the music more insistent, the laughter sharper. I moved through the space with unhurried confidence, aware of eyes tracking my progress—men who sensed something had changed, women who recognized the satisfaction in my stride.

No one stopped me. No one questioned my right to occupy this space, to take what I wanted and leave when I was done. The power of it was intoxicating, far more potent than the whiskey I'd abandoned at the bar.

Outside, the night air hit my heated skin like a blessing, cool and clean after the stale warmth of the bathroom. The street glistened from a recent rain, neon signs from surrounding businesses casting red and blue reflections in puddles that stretched across the uneven pavement. I inhaled deeply, filling my lungs with the scent of wet concrete and possibility.

Just days ago, I had sat across from George at the Bluebird Café, watching my carefully constructed world collapse as he explained why I wasn't enough. Since then, I had taken two men to completion without knowing their last names, without promising to call, without needing their validation to feel whole.

The symmetry wasn't lost on me. What George had

perceived as a flaw—my predictability, my careful adherence to rules and expectations—had been protection against exactly this: the wild, unfettered part of myself that took what it wanted without apology. He'd been right to fear it, in his way. The woman I was becoming would never have fit into the neat box he'd tried to keep me in.

I made a silent vow as I walked away from The Crimson Room, my heels clicking against wet pavement with satisfying precision. This would be my new reality—pleasure without attachment, desire without dependency, power without compromise. I would explore every facet of my sexuality, every dark corner of my wants and needs, without the burden of emotional entanglement.

No more tears in café bathrooms. No more reshaping myself to fit someone else's expectations. No more apologies for taking up space, for wanting too much or too little, for being exactly who I was in any given moment.

The city stretched before me, a playground of possibilities I'd never allowed myself to see. Men (and perhaps women—why limit myself now?) waiting to be chosen, to be used for my pleasure and discarded when I was satisfied. The thought should have horrified the good girl who'd spent twenty-five years coloring inside the lines. Instead, it filled me with a buoyant sense of freedom, as if I'd finally shed a weight I hadn't known I was carrying.

I walked with my head high, hips swaying slightly with each step, enjoying the lingering ache between my thighs as a reminder of what I'd taken, what I'd claimed. The night wrapped around me like a lover's embrace, full of secrets and promises I was finally ready to explore.

For the first time in my life, I felt completely, gloriously in control—not just of my body or my choices, but of the narrative itself. I was no longer a supporting character in someone else's story. I was the protagonist of my own dark fairy tale, the wolf rather than the girl in the red cape, hungry and unafraid of the forest's shadows.

And as I rounded the corner, disappearing from the sight of anyone who might be watching from The Crimson Room's windows, I smiled into the darkness—a predator's smile, teeth bared in anticipation of the hunt to come.

CHAPTER SEVEN
The New Normal

I traced the angled brush along my crease with the steady hand of a surgeon, building the perfect smoky eye without a single tremor or hesitation. Six weeks of practice had transformed awkward fumbling into muscle memory, each sweep of shadow creating depth where once there had been only wide-eyed innocence. The woman who had once needed Sam's guidance to apply eyeliner now worked with practiced precision, constructing a face designed for the night's hunt.

"Blend at the edges," I murmured to myself, softening the line between plum and charcoal with my fingertip. The bathroom mirror reflected a stranger back at me – someone with sharp edges and knowing eyes, someone who understood the power of shadows and angles.

Sam appeared in the doorframe, her platinum hair swept into a messy topknot that somehow looked deliberate rather than careless. Her thumbs moved rapidly across her phone screen, but her eyes flicked up to assess my progress.

"You've mastered that smoky eye," she said, nodding with

approval. "Ready to show it off somewhere old tonight? I'm thinking we try Pulse." She leaned her shoulder against the doorjamb, returning her attention to her phone. "We can hit the ridiculous VIP section that overlooks the main floor. Very exclusive. Very scene-y."

"Sounds perfect," I replied, reaching for the mascara wand. Our bathroom counter had transformed over the weeks – once a sparse landscape of basic moisturizer and lip balm, it now overflowed with palettes and potions, scattered makeup brushes and half-used tubes of lipstick in shades I'd never dreamed of wearing before. The air hung heavy with hairspray and the mingled scents of our perfumes – Sam's signature vanilla and my newly adopted jasmine with undertones of amber.

"The bouncer supposedly lets in the hot girls for free," Sam continued, scrolling through what appeared to be the club's Instagram. "Which, obviously, includes us." She angled her phone to show me a dimly lit photo of bodies pressed together beneath blue lights. "Supposed to be impossible to get into the VIP unless you know someone. Or look like us."

I applied a final coat of mascara, my lashes now impossibly long and dark. "And I assume you know someone?"

Sam's smile was sly. "I know of someone, which is almost the same thing. Guy I hooked up with last weekend mentioned he bartends there."

I closed the mascara and turned away from the mirror, crossing to my bedroom where a skin-tight black dress lay spread across my unmade bed. Six weeks ago, I would have hesitated, would have worried about the neckline that plunged almost to my navel, about the hemline that barely covered the curve of my ass. Now I simply stepped into it, relishing the smooth slide of fabric against my skin as I pulled it up and over my hips.

"Zip me," I called to Sam, who appeared behind me, phone still in hand.

"This dress is lethal," she said, tucking her phone under her chin as she pulled the zipper up. "You realize you wouldn't have been caught dead in this a month and a half ago."

"I wouldn't have been caught alive in it either," I replied, adjusting the neckline to ensure it revealed exactly the right amount of cleavage – enough to entice, not enough to appear desperate.

I moved to my closet, pushing hangers aside to find the stilettos I'd bought last weekend. The contrast was stark now – on one side hung my work clothes, a neat row of pencil skirts and button-downs in muted blues and grays, pressed and arranged by color. On the other side, a riot of textures and revealing cuts had taken over – leather pants, satin camis cut low enough to reveal the lace of my bras, dresses that clung like second skins in jewel tones and midnight black.

"Sometimes I still can't believe I live with the same person," Sam said, following my gaze to the bifurcated wardrobe. "Corporate Elara by day, man-eating Elara by night."

I slipped my feet into the heels, instantly gaining four

inches of height. "Who says they're different people? Maybe this is who I was all along."

Sam laughed, but there was a note of uncertainty beneath it, a questioning I chose to ignore. "Wait, stay just like that," she said suddenly, lifting her phone. "The lighting is perfect." She backed up to capture my full outfit, the red recording light blinking as she filmed.

"Turn," she directed, making a circular motion with her finger. "Slower. Give the camera what it wants."

I complied, moving with the languid confidence that had become my nighttime signature. I arched my back slightly, letting my hips lead the turn, my eyes fixed on the camera with an expression I'd practiced in my bathroom mirror – part challenge, part invitation.

"That's it," Sam encouraged. "Now run your hands through your hair, like you just rolled out of someone's bed."

I did as instructed, lifting my dark waves from my neck before letting them cascade back down. The movement felt natural now, where once it would have made me cringe with self-consciousness.

"This," Sam declared to her phone, turning the camera briefly to include herself in the frame, "is what main character energy looks like, bitches!" She shifted the angle back to me. "Tell the people who you are now."

"I'm the girl your mother warned you about," I purred,

delivering the line we'd rehearsed with a smile that promised sin and satisfaction.

Sam ended the recording with a flourish. "Perfect. That's definitely making the story highlight reel." Her fingers flew across the screen, adding filters and text before posting. "Twenty bucks says I get at least three DMs asking who my hot friend is before we even leave the apartment."

I turned to my dresser mirror for a final assessment, checking that everything was in place – the dress that hugged every curve, the heels that forced my posture into a permanent invitation, the hair tousled to suggest recent pleasure, the makeup that transformed my features into something both alluring and slightly dangerous.

For a moment – just a single heartbeat – something flickered in my eyes. A question, perhaps, or a recognition of the stranger who had taken up residence in my skin. A hollowness that all the eyeliner and lipstick in the world couldn't quite fill. I watched it surface and then, with practiced ease, submerged it beneath a smile that never quite reached my eyes but fooled everyone who wasn't looking too closely.

"Ready to wreck some lives?" Sam asked, appearing behind me in the mirror, her own outfit – a silver slip dress that caught the light with every movement – a perfect complement to mine.

"Always," I replied, reaching for my clutch and checking that I had the essentials – credit card, ID, lipstick for touch-ups, condoms because I never left that to chance anymore. "Let's go find some boys to play with."

As I followed Sam toward the door, I caught one final glimpse of myself in the hallway mirror – a predator dressed in human skin, moving with purpose toward hunting grounds already familiar, though tonight's specific territory was new. The hollow feeling whispered again from somewhere deep inside, but I pushed it down, locked it away. Tonight wasn't about feeling. It was about taking, about power, about proving over and over that I was no longer the woman George had discarded for being predictable.

Tonight, like every night for the past six weeks, was about being anything but that.

Pulse lived up to its name – a heartbeat of bass thumped through the floor and into my bones as Sam and I bypassed the line, the bouncer waving us through with an appreciative glance at our outfits. Inside, strobe lights sliced through artificial fog, painting the writhing crowd in electric blue, then deep purple, then back to darkness. Bodies pressed against each other in what could have been dancing or foreplay or both. Six weeks ago, this atmosphere would have overwhelmed me. Now, I breathed it in like oxygen, my eyes already adjusting to the darkness, scanning for tonight's prey.

"This place is insane tonight," Sam shouted near my ear, her voice barely audible over the music. She pointed toward the elevated VIP section where champagne bottles topped with sparklers were being delivered to leather booths. "That's where we're headed next time."

I nodded, but my attention had already shifted to the hunting grounds before me. The dance floor pulsed with potential – men in groups, in pairs, alone at the edges watching. I no longer needed Sam's guidance or liquid courage to approach them. The woman who had once frozen when George appeared at Pulse had been replaced by someone who knew exactly how to get what she wanted.

"Meet back here in two hours?" Sam asked, already eyeing a tall man near the bar.

"If I'm not otherwise occupied," I replied with a smile that made her laugh.

We separated, Sam weaving toward her target while I continued my survey of the room. I moved differently now – each step deliberate, shoulders back, hips leading the way. Men's eyes followed my progress, but I dismissed most with a single glance. Too young. Too eager. Too similar to George.

Then I saw him – dark hair falling across his forehead, strong jaw, leaning against the bar with the casual confidence of someone who knew his own appeal. Our eyes met across the room, and I held his gaze without hesitation, a slow smile spreading across my lips. Six weeks ago, I would have looked away, would have blushed and pretended I hadn't been staring. Tonight, I walked directly toward him, maintaining eye contact until I stood close enough to catch his scent – expensive cologne with undertones of something earthy and masculine.

"Buy me a drink," I said, not a question but a command.

His eyebrows lifted slightly – surprise, then appreciation. "What are you having?"

"Whiskey. Neat."

He signaled the bartender, his eyes never leaving mine. I'd learned that men like him responded to directness, to women who knew what they wanted. The days of waiting to be approached, of giggling nervously at compliments, were behind me.

"I haven't seen you here before," he said, his voice a low rumble that I felt more than heard over the music.

"Maybe you weren't looking properly." I accepted the whiskey, letting my fingers brush against his in a deliberate touch that wasn't accidental at all.

He smiled, revealing perfect teeth that made me wonder briefly about his profession before dismissing the thought as irrelevant. His name, his job, his story – none of it mattered. All that mattered was the way his eyes darkened when I stepped closer, the way his hand found the small of my back with confident pressure.

"Dance with me," I said after downing half the whiskey in a single swallow. Again, not a question.

His hand slid lower, resting just above the curve of my ass as he guided me toward the dance floor. I glanced back once to see Sam giving me an enthusiastic thumbs-up from across the room, her free arm already draped around the neck of her own find for the night. She mouthed something that looked like "Get it!" before turning her attention back to her companion.

The dance floor swallowed us, bodies creating a private universe of heat and movement. I turned to face my conquest, raising my arms above my head in a motion designed to emphasize my curves, to draw his eyes to the plunging neckline of my dress. It worked. His gaze traveled down my body with undisguised hunger, his hands finding my hips and pulling me closer until our bodies aligned from chest to thigh.

We moved together, my back arching slightly to press my breasts against his chest, my thigh slipping between his legs in a deliberate tease. The music shifted to something with a slower, deeper beat that vibrated through the floor and up into my bones. Our bodies responded, grinding against each other with increasing pressure. His hands roamed from my hips to my lower back, fingers splayed wide to claim territory.

"You're fucking gorgeous," he said, lips brushing against my ear in a way that sent a shiver down my spine. "I've been watching you since you walked in. The way you move..." His hand slipped lower, cupping my ass through the thin fabric of my dress. "I want to take you home and peel this dress off with my teeth."

Six weeks ago, such crude directness would have made me blush and stammer. Now, I simply smiled, letting my hand trail down his chest to rest just above his belt buckle, feeling his immediate physical response to my touch.

"Is that all you want to do?" I challenged, my lips close

enough to his that our breath mingled in the small space between us.

He groaned, the sound vibrating through his chest against mine. "I want to taste every inch of you. I want to make you come so hard you forget your own name."

Our bodies moved together, slick with sweat as the club's temperature rose with the crush of bodies and the relentless beat. His shirt clung to his chest, revealing the outline of well-defined muscles. My dress had become a second skin, the fabric clinging to every curve as we moved against each other with increasing urgency. His hands never stopped exploring – my waist, my hips, occasionally brushing the sides of my breasts in touches that could have been accidental but weren't.

I felt the familiar heat building inside me – not from his touch or his words, but from the power I held over him. This man wanted me, would do anything I asked to get me into his bed. The knowledge was intoxicating, far more potent than the whiskey warming my veins. I no longer needed alcohol to feel this confidence, this certainty. I generated it myself now, manufactured it from the desire I saw in men's eyes when they looked at me.

The song changed again, something with a throbbing, insistent beat that matched the pulse between my thighs. I'd had enough of the pretense of dancing. I wanted more, wanted to feel the full extent of my power over this stranger who thought he was seducing me.

I leaned in, my lips brushing his ear. "Follow me."

Without waiting for his response, I turned and moved through the crowd, knowing without looking that he would follow. I led him toward a darkened corner near the back of the club, where shadows provided just enough privacy for what I had in mind. When we reached the spot I'd selected, I turned abruptly, pushing him against the wall with enough force to make his eyes widen in surprise.

"What--" he began, but I cut him off, my mouth claiming his in a kiss that was more demand than request.

He recovered quickly, his hands finding my waist, trying to take control of the kiss. I bit his lower lip in warning, my fingers tangling in his hair to hold him exactly where I wanted him. He groaned into my mouth, surrendering to my lead as my body pressed fully against his, feeling every hard plane and angle.

I wasn't looking for tenderness or connection. I was taking what I wanted, using this man's body for my pleasure the way men had used women's bodies for centuries. The realization sent another pulse of heat through me – this was power, this was control, this was everything George had never allowed me to be.

When I finally broke the kiss, the man was breathing hard, his pupils dilated with desire. "My apartment is ten minutes away," he said, his voice rough with want.

I smiled, letting my hand drift down to cup him through his jeans, feeling his sharp intake of breath at my touch. "I decide where this goes," I told him. "Not you."

The look of surprise on his face was its own reward – he'd thought he was in control, thought he was the hunter. He couldn't have been more wrong.

Pre-dawn light crept through my half-closed blinds, painting pale blue stripes across the tangled sheets and the back of the man who was now pulling on his boxer briefs with his back to me. I couldn't remember if his name was Matt or Mark—something with an M that he'd mumbled in the dark of the club before I'd led him to my apartment. It didn't matter now. The finger-shaped bruises on my hips throbbed dully, physical souvenirs from a night that had already faded in my memory, pleasure reduced to disconnected flashes—his weight pinning me to the mattress, my nails scoring his back, the moment of blankness when I'd finally come with his hand around my throat, exactly as I'd instructed.

He turned, catching me watching him. His smile was tentative, almost shy—at odds with the man who'd fucked me against my bedroom wall hours earlier, who'd whispered filthy promises in my ear as he'd tangled his fingers in my hair. Daylight stripped away the mystique, revealing just another man with bed-head and the faint beginnings of a beard, searching for his socks among the discarded clothing on my floor.

"Last night was..." he began, trailing off as if searching for a word adequate enough.

I said nothing, just watched him dress with the cool detachment I'd perfected over the past months. The silence stretched between us, elastic and uncomfortable. He filled it with movements—tucking in his shirt, running fingers through his hair, checking his pockets for keys and wallet.

"Maybe we could get coffee sometime?" he suggested finally, his voice lifting with a hopefulness that made something inside me curl with disdain. "I'd like to see you again. When we're both, you know, vertical and fully clothed."

It was always the same script, with minor variations. The men who thought our bodies connecting meant something more, who mistook physical intensity for emotional potential. I'd learned to cut them off quickly, cleanly.

"I have an early meeting," I said, not bothering to soften the dismissal with a smile. "And the rest of my week is packed. But thanks for last night. It was fun."

His face fell slightly before he masked it with forced casualness. "Sure, yeah. I get it. Busy is good, right?" He hesitated, then added, "Can I at least get your number?"

"I'll find you if I'm free," I replied, already reaching for my robe, a clear signal that our interaction was ending. I didn't offer my number, didn't suggest another night. The momentary flash of hurt in his eyes registered somewhere distant inside me, then dissolved like steam.

Once he was gone—the front door clicking shut behind him with finality—I headed straight for the shower. I turned the water as hot as I could stand it, letting it sluice over my skin, washing away the scent of him, the dried sweat, the lingering stickiness between my thighs. I scrubbed methodically, watching soap bubbles swirl around the drain, carrying away all evidence of the night before.

By the time I stepped out, pink-skinned and clean, Matt-or-Mark had been erased from my body if not my memory. I wiped condensation from the mirror and studied my reflection —eyes clear despite minimal sleep, mouth unsmiling, hair darkened by water. The bruises on my hips and the faint red mark at my throat were the only remaining evidence of what had transpired. They would fade within days, replaced by new marks from new men whose names I wouldn't bother to remember.

My morning routine proceeded with precise efficiency— hair blown dry and smoothed into a sleek bob, different from the wild waves I wore at night. Makeup applied with a lighter hand, creating a mask of professional competence rather than seductive allure. Moisturizer, foundation, neutral shadow, mascara, muted lip color—each product applied like armor, constructing the daytime version of Elara James that bore little resemblance to the woman who had moaned beneath a stranger hours earlier.

I dressed in a charcoal pencil skirt and ivory blouse, adding a camel blazer that covered any lingering marks on my neck. Pearl earrings completed the transformation—simple, elegant, appropriate. The woman who stared back from my full-length mirror looked incapable of demanding rough sex from a man whose last name she didn't know. She looked like someone who color-coded her planner and brought homemade muffins to office birthday celebrations.

In the kitchen, I brewed coffee in my French press, its familiar ritual grounding me in this version of myself. I checked emails on my tablet, responding to meeting requests and deadline reminders with professional efficiency. By the time I walked out my apartment door, travel mug in hand, I had fully transitioned from night to day, from predator to professional, the compartmentalization so complete it was almost seamless.

Almost.

~

"Wait, he actually cried?" Sam's eyes widened as she lounged across our couch that evening, an empty wine glass dangling from her fingers. She wore oversized sweats, her face bare of makeup—the version of herself reserved for nights in.

"Not full tears," I clarified, curling my feet beneath me in the armchair opposite her. "But definitely got choked up when he came. Called me 'baby' and everything." I recounted the previous night's encounter in explicit detail—how I'd directed Matt-or-Mark's every move, demanding more pressure here, a different angle there, orchestrating the entire encounter like a conductor with a particularly responsive orchestra.

"God, you're such a savage now," Sam laughed, reaching for the wine bottle to refill her glass. But something in her eyes didn't match her laughter—a flicker of concern, quickly masked. "Remember when you used to blush if a guy even mentioned sex on a first date?"

"That was a different lifetime," I replied, my attention already shifting to my phone, where I scrolled through a dating app with practiced detachment. Swipe left, swipe left, pause on a promising jawline, examine the rest of the profile, swipe right. The algorithm had become as familiar as breathing—a ruthless filtering system for potential conquest.

"You've got that look again," Sam observed, her voice softer now. "The hunting expression."

"Just keeping my options open for tomorrow," I said, not looking up from the screen where another face awaited judgment. Too similar to George—swipe left. Too young—swipe left. Strong hands, good shoulders, expression suggesting confidence without arrogance—swipe right. "Tonight I just want to watch something mindless and go to bed early."

"Alone?" Sam asked, attempting to keep her tone light, but the question hung between us with unexpected weight.

"For now," I replied, continuing to scroll. The faces blurred together after a while—interchangeable vehicles for temporary pleasure, for the momentary obliteration of thought and feeling that came with physical release.

As I swiped, a familiar hollowness expanded in my chest— a void that grew larger with each conquest, with each morning dismissal, with each transition between my night and day selves. I ignored it as I always did, focusing instead on the next potential match, the next distraction, the next opportunity to feel something, anything, even if just for the fleeting moments of climax.

A notification appeared—one of my swipes had matched. The man's message appeared instantly: "You're gorgeous. Drinks tomorrow?"

Direct. Efficient. Perfect.

I typed a quick reply setting a time and place, then set my phone down, catching my reflection in its black screen before it went dark. For a moment, the face looking back at me seemed unfamiliar—a stranger wearing my features, eyes empty of everything except calculation. I blinked, and the screen went fully black, reflecting nothing.

"Everything okay?" Sam asked, noticing my sudden stillness.

"Fine," I replied automatically, picking up my wineglass and taking a sip I couldn't taste. "Just planning tomorrow's hunt."

But as I turned back to the mindless reality show playing on our TV, the hollow feeling pulsed once, twice, like a second heartbeat beneath my breastbone—a void growing larger with each man I used and discarded, with each night I spent seeking oblivion in a stranger's arms. I pushed the sensation away, locking it behind the same mental door that contained the Elara from before—the one who had cried in a café bathroom, who had believed in connection, who had wanted more than momentary physical release.

That woman was gone. In her place sat someone stronger, someone who took what she wanted without apology.

Someone who was beginning not to recognize herself at all.

The bathroom stall door rattled against its frame as I braced my hands against the metal partition, my dress hiked up around my waist, a stranger's hands gripping my hips with bruising force. The club's bass vibrated through the walls, providing rhythm to our encounter. "Harder," I instructed over my shoulder, my voice steady despite our position. "And pull my hair." He complied immediately, his fingers tangling in my dark waves, pulling my head back with just enough force to send sparks of pleasure-pain down my spine. I didn't know his name—had deliberately avoided learning it when he'd offered to buy me a drink twenty minutes earlier. Names created connection, and connection wasn't what I was looking for anymore.

When it was over, I straightened my dress with practiced efficiency, checked my lipstick in my compact mirror, and left him leaning against the stall door, still catching his breath. The woman who smoothed her hair in the bathroom mirror bore little resemblance to the one who had sobbed in a café restroom six months earlier. Her eyes were knowing, her smile calculated, her movements precise and controlled.

I was out the club door three minutes later, the night air cool against my flushed skin. Another conquest completed, another momentary distraction achieved, another night of not thinking about the growing emptiness inside.

～

"As you can see from the Q3 projections, we're trending above target in two key demographics." I pointed to the graph displayed on the conference room screen, my voice calm and authoritative. The boardroom table was surrounded by nodding heads, my colleagues impressed by the presentation I'd spent the weekend preparing. None of them would have guessed that beneath the table, my finger swiped through profile pictures on a hook-up app, pausing occasionally on promising prospects.

"Elara, these numbers are excellent," my manager commented, leaning forward with interest. "What do you attribute the increase to?"

I closed the app with a subtle movement, placing my phone face down on my portfolio. "A more aggressive approach," I replied, my lips curving into a professional smile that revealed nothing of the double meaning in my words. "I've found that direct, targeted action yields the best results."

～

"Like this," I instructed, guiding the stranger's hands to my throat as I straddled him on his leather couch. His apartment was minimalist and expensive, all clean lines and chrome accents that would have impressed me once. Now it was just another backdrop, another setting for the same scene I'd been playing out in different locations with different men.

"Are you sure?" he asked, his fingers hesitant against my skin.

"I wouldn't have said it if I wasn't sure," I replied, pressing his fingers more firmly against my throat. "Just enough pressure to restrict, not enough to cut off air completely. I'll tap your arm twice if it's too much."

His eyes widened slightly, but he adjusted his grip as instructed. I closed my eyes, focusing on the physical sensation, the edge of danger that came with controlled breath play. It took more to get me there now—more intensity, more risk, more pain mixed with pleasure. Simple sex no longer provided enough distraction from the hollow space that had been expanding inside me since that first night at Pulse.

When I came, it was with his hand around my throat and my nails digging into his shoulders, the momentary blankness of orgasm providing a few seconds of blessed emptiness before reality rushed back in.

∼

"The Henderson account needs the updated copy by Thursday," my colleague was saying as we walked out of the conference room. I nodded, making a note in my phone while simultaneously checking a notification from another app—a message from last night's distraction asking when he could see me again.

I deleted it without responding, already scanning for new possibilities. Under the conference table, I'd matched with a promising candidate—tall, dark features that weren't quite handsome but suggested intensity, a description that mentioned rock climbing and martial arts, suggesting strength and stamina.

"Are you free for lunch to discuss the campaign?" my colleague asked, not noticing how my attention was divided.

"I have a phone call scheduled," I lied smoothly. "But I can meet at three."

The truth was, I'd already arranged to meet my latest match during lunch. His profile suggested he'd be willing to meet in his car in the underground parking garage of his office building—quick, anonymous, another notch to add to my growing tally.

"Don't stop," I demanded, my voice rough as I dug my heels into the back of a man I'd met forty minutes earlier. The backseat of his car was cramped, the leather sticking to my skin as he complied with my instructions. My head bumped against the door handle, the discomfort adding an edge to the pleasure that coursed through me.

We were in the far corner of a parking structure, the risk of discovery adding another layer of intensity to the encounter. I directed every movement, every angle, every touch—maintaining control even as I allowed him to pin my wrists above my head, even as I encouraged him to bite the sensitive juncture where my neck met my shoulder.

When it was over, I straightened my skirt, applied fresh lipstick using his rearview mirror, and was back at my desk for my three o'clock meeting, carrying the secret ache of fresh bruises beneath my professional attire.

~

I was browsing through a display of bagged salads at the upscale grocery store near my office when I heard his voice. George was standing near the prepared foods section, selecting something from behind the glass counter. He hadn't seen me yet, his attention focused on whatever overpriced dish had caught his eye.

Six months ago, this accidental meeting would have devastated me—would have sent me fleeing to the nearest restroom, tears threatening to ruin my carefully applied makeup. Now, I merely adjusted my course, selecting a salad before walking directly past him, close enough that the sleeve of my blazer brushed against his arm.

His head turned, recognition dawning slowly as he

processed the woman passing by. "Elara?" he called, surprise evident in his voice.

I kept walking, my heels clicking against the polished floor, my posture perfect as I headed toward the checkout. He called my name again, louder this time, but I didn't turn, didn't acknowledge him. The power in that moment—in denying him even the small satisfaction of my attention—sent a pulse of something like pleasure through me, though it faded more quickly than it once would have.

Later, as I ate my salad alone at my desk, I realized I'd felt nothing at seeing him—no pain, no anger, no lingering desire. Just emptiness where emotions should have been.

"Happy slut-iversary!" Sam declared, raising her shot glass in the dim light of Pulse, where it had all begun half a year earlier. The club hadn't changed—same pulsing lights, same crush of bodies, same predatory energy—but I had transformed completely in the months since that first night.

I clinked my glass against hers, the tequila burning a familiar path down my throat. Unlike those first nervous shots, I no longer needed liquid courage to approach men, to take what I wanted. Alcohol was now just a ritual, a punctuation mark between day and night.

"Six months since George did you the biggest favor of your

life," Sam continued, signaling the bartender for another round. She was already pleasantly buzzed, her platinum hair catching blue light as she swayed slightly to the music. "Six months of taking what you want instead of settling for what you're given."

I nodded, scanning the room with practiced efficiency, cataloging potential conquests. The dark-haired man near the DJ booth, watching the crowd with detached interest. The broad-shouldered one in the crisp button-down, laughing with friends but occasionally glancing around, clearly hoping to catch someone's eye. The quiet one sitting alone at the end of the bar, whose intensity suggested promising things for later.

"To never needing a man for anything but his dick!" Sam declared as our fresh shots arrived, raising her glass with a flourish that sloshed tequila onto her wrist.

I smiled and clinked glasses, but the expression didn't reach my eyes. Six months of conquests had left me with an expanding collection of meaningless encounters and a growing void where satisfaction should have been. Each new man, each new position, each new location had provided briefer and briefer moments of escape from the hollowness that had taken up permanent residence inside me.

"You okay?" Sam asked, her head tilting as she studied my face. Even through her tequila haze, she'd noticed something in my expression—a crack in the carefully constructed mask of the new Elara.

"Just deciding who's next," I replied, forcing brightness into my voice as I returned to scanning the room. The dark-haired man had moved closer to the bar, his eyes finding mine across the crowd. I held his gaze for three precise seconds before looking away—the same move I'd perfected over countless nights, the same invitation I'd issued to dozens of men whose faces now blurred together in my memory.

"That one's hot," Sam observed, following my gaze. "Go get him, tiger." She made a playful growling sound, already turning her attention to her own prospects for the night.

I finished my shot and set the glass on the bar with deliberate precision. My body moved on autopilot, sliding from the barstool and smoothing my dress over my hips in the gesture that had become part of my hunting ritual. But as I began walking toward my next conquest, the hollow feeling in my chest expanded, threatening to consume me from the inside out.

Six months. Countless men. Innumerable orgasms. And still, the emptiness grew, a void that no amount of physical pleasure seemed capable of filling. But I pushed forward anyway, my smile practiced, my hips swaying with calculated precision, my eyes fixed on the next temporary distraction from the growing nothingness within.

The man straightened as I approached, his interest obvious in the way his body angled toward mine. I didn't know his name. He didn't know mine. And that was exactly how I needed it to be—another nameless encounter, another brief escape, another futile attempt to feel something, anything, beyond the vast emptiness that had become my constant companion.

CHAPTER EIGHT
Transformation Complete

I slipped into Onyx without hesitation, my black stilettos tapping the polished floor with deliberate precision. The doorman nodded me through effortlessly—my skin-tight dress and practiced smile were all the currency needed at places like this. Inside, the vast space pulsed with expensive sound systems and even more costly perfumes, the crowd a carefully curated selection of beautiful people pretending not to look at each other. I wasn't there to be noticed. I was there to hunt.

The bass pulsed through the soles of my feet, vibrating up my legs and settling low in my abdomen—a physical reminder of why I'd come. Six months into my transformation, I no longer needed Sam's encouragement or tequila's liquid courage. The woman who had once hidden behind modest clothing and careful smiles had been replaced by someone who knew exactly what she wanted and precisely how to get it.

I moved through the crowd with unhurried confidence, aware of the eyes that tracked my progress. My dress—a black sheath that hugged every curve like a possessive lover—had been selected with methodical purpose. The neckline plunged just low enough to suggest access while maintaining the illusion of exclusivity. My hair fell in loose waves past my shoulders, styled to look as though someone had just run their fingers through it. The thought of the fingers that would tangle in it later sent a small smile playing across my lips.

Crystal chandeliers cast prismatic light across the VIP section, where bottle service and privacy came at a premium. I didn't want privacy—not yet. First came the selection, the approach, the familiar dance of desire and intention. I surveyed the room with practiced efficiency, dismissing potential targets with clinical detachment. Too young. Too eager. Too reminiscent of George.

The bar stretched along the far wall, a gleaming expanse of backlit onyx that gave the club its name. Behind it, bartenders in fitted vests performed for their audience, flames dancing above expensive spirits, ice cracking beneath weighted silver picks. But it wasn't the theatrical mixology that caught my attention. It was him.

He sat alone at the corner of the bar, one hand curled around a tumbler of amber liquid, the other resting casually on the polished surface. His suit—charcoal gray and impeccably tailored—spoke of money earned rather than inherited. No wedding ring, though that wasn't always a reliable indicator. His posture suggested confidence without arrogance, a man comfortable in his own skin but not desperate to prove it to anyone else.

Perfect.

I adjusted my trajectory, moving toward him with deliberate steps that made my hips sway in a rhythm calculated to draw his attention. It worked. His eyes found me when I was still several feet away, his interest evident in the slight straightening of his spine, the way his fingers tightened almost imperceptibly around his glass.

I didn't hesitate or glance away. Six months ago, I might have blushed under such direct appraisal, might have questioned whether I was worthy of the frank appreciation in his gaze. Now, I simply returned his look with equal intensity, a silent acknowledgment of mutual interest that required no words.

The space beside him was conveniently empty. I slid onto the barstool, close enough that the fabric of my dress brushed against his suit pants, far enough that he would need to lean in to speak over the music. The bartender approached, but I waved him off with a subtle gesture. I hadn't come for drinks.

"You look like a woman who knows exactly what she wants," the man said, his voice a low rumble that somehow carried perfectly despite the pulsing bass. He didn't offer his name. Good. Neither would I, until absolutely necessary.

"I am," I confirmed, angling my body toward his, one knee grazing his thigh in a touch too deliberate to be accidental. "And I rarely waste time getting it."

His eyebrows lifted slightly—surprise, then appreciation.

He was used to the game, to women who feigned disinterest or played at being difficult to obtain. My directness was novel, an unexpected deviation from the script.

"That's refreshing," he said, taking a sip of his drink, his eyes never leaving mine. "In my experience, most people spend their lives circling what they want without ever reaching for it."

"Most people lack conviction," I replied, letting my hand rest lightly on his forearm, feeling the expensive fabric of his suit, the warmth of his skin beneath. "Or courage."

He set his glass down, turning more fully toward me, his knee now pressing deliberately against mine. "And which do you value more? Conviction or courage?"

"Neither," I said, leaning closer, my lips near his ear, my breath warming his skin. "I value results."

I felt rather than heard his sharp intake of breath, watched with satisfaction as his pupils dilated, the brown of his irises nearly disappearing into black. His cologne—something woodsy with notes of cedar and bergamot—mingled with the underlying scent of his skin, creating a combination that was unexpectedly appealing.

"What results are you looking for tonight?" he asked, his voice dropping lower, acquiring a rough edge that sent a familiar warmth spiraling through my core.

Instead of answering, I placed my hand on his thigh, just high enough to make my intentions clear without crossing into vulgarity. The muscle tensed beneath my touch, a physical confirmation of his interest that was far more reliable than words.

"You haven't asked my name," I observed, my fingers tracing small circles that inched gradually higher.

"Does it matter?" He countered, his own hand coming to rest at the small of my back, thumb brushing against the bare skin exposed by my dress's low cut.

I smiled—not the practiced, alluring smile I'd perfected for these encounters, but something genuine that surprised even me. "I like the way you think," I said. "But it's Elara."

"Henry," he offered in return, though I hadn't asked and wouldn't remember beyond tonight. Names were a formality, a brief acknowledgment of humanity before we reduced each other to bodies and sensation.

His thumb continued its exploration of my skin, each small movement sending sparks of anticipation up my spine. The club's lighting shifted, bathing us in deep blue that turned his white shirt violet and cast shadows across the planes of his face. In this light, he could have been anyone—a canvas for my desires rather than a specific person with specific features.

I leaned in again, close enough that my breasts brushed against his arm, my lips almost touching the shell of his ear. Then I told him, in explicit, unambiguous detail, exactly what I wanted to do to him and what I wanted him to do to me. The words—crude, direct, unapologetic—fell from my lips with practiced ease, each syllable calibrated for maximum impact.

When I pulled back, his eyes had widened, his breathing noticeably quicker. I'd surprised him—this polished businessman in his expensive suit who thought he knew the rules of attraction, who believed he understood how these games were played.

"Right now?" he asked, his voice strained with evident desire.

I stood, smoothing my dress over my hips with deliberate slowness. "Right now," I confirmed, extending my hand.

He took it without hesitation, allowing me to lead him away from the bar, through the press of bodies on the dance floor, toward the more secluded areas at the back of the club. His fingers were warm against mine, his grip firm but not controlling. Another good sign.

As we walked, I felt the familiar thrill of anticipation, the rush of power that came with taking exactly what I wanted. Whatever emptiness had been growing inside me these past months would be temporarily filled with sensation, with the mindless pleasure of bodies connecting without the complication of emotion.

For tonight, for these few hours, it would be enough. It had to be.

We barely made it through the bathroom door before my hands were at his belt, my fingers working the leather with practiced efficiency. Henry kicked the door shut behind us, the heavy wood closing with a solid thunk that sealed us into our temporary sanctuary. The bathroom was all sleek marble and subtle lighting, designed for the beautiful people who frequented Onyx—a far cry from the grimy stalls of lesser establishments I'd utilized in the past. I pushed him against the edge of the sink, my mouth finding his in a kiss that was more demand than request.

His hands fumbled for purchase against the smooth marble, then found my waist, fingers digging into the fabric of my dress with an urgency that satisfied something primal within me. I bit his lower lip, just hard enough to make him gasp, his surprise transforming into a low groan as I pressed my body fully against his. Through the thin material of my dress and his tailored pants, I could feel his immediate physical response—his desire a tangible thing between us.

"Jesus," he breathed against my mouth, his voice hoarse with want. "You're—"

"Don't talk," I instructed, pulling back just enough to meet his eyes. "Unless I ask you a question."

Confusion flickered across his face for a heartbeat before understanding replaced it—then appreciation, then hunger. He nodded once, accepting my terms without argument. Another point in his favor. I rewarded him by returning to his belt, unfastening it completely this time and moving on to his zipper with deliberate slowness.

Music from the club filtered through the walls in muted waves, the bass still palpable even here. The marble was cool beneath my palms as I leaned forward to press my lips against his neck, tasting salt and expensive aftershave. His pulse raced beneath my tongue, a rapid flutter that betrayed his excitement despite his outward composure.

I slid my hand inside his pants, past the silk of his boxers, finding him already fully hard. His sharp intake of breath was its own reward—the visceral proof of my effect on him, of the power I held in this moment. I stroked him slowly, my grip firm but not rough, watching his face as pleasure transformed his features.

"Take off your jacket," I said, my voice steady despite the heat building between my thighs. "And unbutton your shirt."

He complied immediately, shrugging out of his expensive jacket and draping it carefully over the adjacent sink before his fingers moved to his shirt buttons. I continued to touch him as he worked, my rhythm deliberate and unhurried. There was no rush. This place, this moment, this man—all existed in a bubble outside of normal time, a temporary universe where only sensation mattered.

When his shirt hung open, revealing a chest more defined than I'd expected beneath his business attire, I stepped back slightly, evaluating. Not the sculpted perfection of the gym-obsessed, but the solid strength of a man who took care of himself without vanity. Interesting. I traced a finger down his sternum, feeling the shiver that ran through him at my touch.

"Turn around," I instructed.

His eyebrows rose slightly, but he obeyed, turning to face

the mirror above the sink. Our eyes met in the reflection—his dark with desire, mine watchful and calculating. I moved behind him, pressing my body against his back, my hands sliding around to continue their exploration. One hand returned to his erection while the other traveled up his chest, nails scraping lightly across his skin.

"Watch," I murmured against his ear, my eyes holding his in the mirror. "I want you to see exactly what I'm doing to you."

His breathing quickened as my hand moved with increasing purpose, his hips instinctively pushing forward into my touch. I used my free hand to unzip my dress just enough to expose one shoulder, then guided his hand behind him to touch me. His fingers found the bare skin of my thigh, sliding upward with eager anticipation.

"Not yet," I said, moving his hand away. "Not until I say so."

The flash of frustration in his eyes was quickly replaced by renewed arousal—he understood the game now, understood that his pleasure was entirely at my discretion. I continued to stroke him, varying pressure and speed with deliberate unpredictability, keeping him balanced on the edge of satisfaction without allowing him to tip over.

When I finally released him, stepping back to pull my dress up around my waist, his entire body seemed to vibrate with anticipation. I reached into my small clutch purse, extracted a condom and handed it to him with an expectant look. He tore the package open with fingers that trembled slightly, his eyes never leaving mine in the mirror as he rolled it on.

"Now you can touch me," I said, turning to face him, backing him against the sink once more. "Show me what those expensive hands can do."

His touch was surprisingly deft, fingers finding their way beneath the lace of my underwear with practiced ease. I allowed myself a small sound of approval as he found the right spot, the right pressure, the right rhythm. Not all of them did. This one paid attention, responded to the subtle cues of my body, and adjusted without needing explicit direction.

I reached between us, guiding him to my entrance, watching his face as I sank down onto him in one fluid movement. His eyes widened, lips parting on a silent exhale as I took him fully inside me. For a moment, neither of us moved— suspended in the perfect tension of that initial connection, the exquisite fullness.

Then I began to move, setting a pace that suited my needs rather than his, my hands braced on his shoulders for leverage. He tried to take control, hands gripping my hips to guide my movements, but I caught his wrists and pinned them against the mirror behind him.

"My way," I reminded him, my voice husky but firm. "Or not at all."

He surrendered completely then, letting me use his body for my pleasure, accepting the role I'd assigned him in this encounter. The marble edge of the sink must have been digging into his back, the position somewhat awkward for his height, but he made no complaint as I rode him with single-minded purpose.

I watched his face, cataloging the small changes that signaled his approaching climax—the flush spreading across his chest, the tension in his jaw, the way his eyes began to lose focus. When I felt my own release building, I released his wrists, guiding one of his hands between us.

"Here," I directed, showing him exactly where and how to touch me. "Like this."

The dual sensation—him inside me, his fingers working in precise circles—pushed me rapidly toward the edge. I bit my lip to contain the sounds threatening to escape, aware that despite the club's noise, we weren't completely isolated. When the wave broke, pleasure pulsed outward from my core in rhythmic contractions that made my thighs tremble and my breath catch. I allowed him his release then, feeling him shudder beneath me, his free hand gripping my hip with bruising force.

For several heartbeats, we remained connected, our breathing gradually slowing, reality seeping back into our private bubble. Then I lifted myself off him with careful movements, smoothing my dress back down over my thighs with practiced nonchalance. The woman who examined her reflection in the mirror looked remarkably composed—hair slightly tousled in a way that could be deliberate, lipstick faded but not completely gone, eyes bright with the lingering effects of endorphins.

I extracted a compact and lipstick from my clutch, reapplying the deep red with precise strokes while Henry disposed of the condom and rearranged his clothing. In the mirror, I watched him attempt to smooth his rumpled shirt, tuck it back into pants that now bore wrinkles where my hands had gripped the fabric.

"That was..." he began, his voice still rough with the aftermath of pleasure. "You're incredible."

I smiled at his reflection, snapping my compact shut and returning it to my purse. "Thanks for the fun," I said, turning to face him directly. "You were exactly what I needed tonight."

Confusion flickered across his features—he was used to exchanging numbers after such encounters, to the promise of future meetings, to the pretense that what had just transpired might lead to something more.

"Can I get your number?" he asked, already reaching for his phone. "I'd love to see you again."

"That's not how this works," I replied, my tone gentle but firm. "This was perfect as it is. Let's not complicate it."

Before he could respond, I pressed a brief kiss to his cheek —a parting gesture that contained no promise, no sentimentality—and walked out, closing the door on his bewildered expression without a backward glance.

The club enveloped me again, the music washing over my skin like water, the crowd parting unconsciously to let me through. My body hummed with satisfied pleasure, the ache between my thighs a pleasant reminder of what had just transpired. I moved toward the bar, scanning the room with renewed interest. The night was still young, and the temporary relief I'd found in Henry's arms was already fading, the familiar emptiness creeping back into the edges of my awareness.

Perhaps one more encounter before the night ended. Perhaps someone who might provide a different kind of distraction, a different flavor of oblivion. I signaled the bartender, ordered a whiskey neat, and turned to survey my options with the cool assessment of a connoisseur rather than the desperate hunger of an addict.

I was fine. I was in control. I was getting exactly what I wanted.

Wasn't I?

I pushed through the glass doors of Lambert & Associates at precisely 8:45 AM, my heels striking the marble floor with the same deliberate confidence that had carried me across Onyx's dance floor nine hours earlier. The weekend's escapades—Henry in the bathroom, followed by a brief but satisfying encounter with a visiting DJ in his hotel room—had left faint marks on my inner thighs, hidden now beneath a perfectly tailored charcoal pencil skirt. My ivory silk blouse revealed nothing of the woman who had whispered filthy demands into strangers' ears, its high neckline and precise cut projecting polished professionalism instead of predatory sexuality. Different costume, same power.

"Morning, Ms. James," the security guard called, his smile warm and respectful. Six months ago, I would have returned his greeting with a self-conscious nod, uncomfortable with being noticed. Now, I met his eyes directly, my smile measured but genuine.

"Good morning, Carl. Beautiful day, isn't it?"

My office waited on the twenty-third floor, a glass-walled corner that I'd earned through relentless performance rather than time served. The transformation that had begun in my personal life had spilled over into my professional one—the newfound confidence, the unapologetic assertion of my wants and needs, had translated perfectly into boardroom dynamics. I no longer apologized before speaking, no longer couched my opinions in hesitant qualifiers. I stated facts, presented solutions, and expected to be heard.

The results spoke for themselves. Two major client acquisitions in the past quarter. A fifteen percent increase in my department's revenue. A promotion that had raised eyebrows among colleagues who still remembered the agreeable, accommodating Elara from before.

"The Killian Group presentation is set for ten," my assistant said, appearing at my office door with a steaming cup of coffee —black, no sugar, exactly as I preferred it. "Conference room A. Mr. Davidson asked if you could stop by his office beforehand to align on strategy."

Davidson—mid-forties, divorced twice, perpetually threatened by women who refused to defer to him. Six months ago, I would have rearranged my morning to accommodate his "strategy alignment," which inevitably involved him trying to take credit for my ideas. Now, I simply took a measured sip of coffee before responding.

"Tell him I'm finalizing the presentation and will see him in the conference room at 9:50. He can align with me there."

My assistant's smile contained a hint of admiration. "Yes, Ms. James."

I spent the next hour reviewing the proposal I'd developed for The Killian Group—a luxury hospitality chain looking to revamp their entire digital presence. The work was solid, innovative without being risky, exactly calibrated to push their brand forward while maintaining the heritage they valued. I knew it was good. More importantly, I knew I could sell it with the same confidence I now brought to every aspect of my life.

At 9:50 precisely, I gathered my materials and made my way to Conference Room A. The space was designed to impress —floor-to-ceiling windows overlooking the city skyline, a massive table of polished walnut, chairs of buttery leather that cost more than most people's monthly rent. Davidson was already there, of course, speaking with forced joviality to Arthur Killian and his executive team.

"Ah, here she is," Davidson said, his smile not quite reaching his eyes as I entered. "The genius behind the proposal you're about to see."

I nodded acknowledgment of the introduction while assessing the room. Arthur Killian—silver-haired, immaculately dressed, old-money confidence in every line of his posture. His CFO, Janet Mercer—sharp eyes behind sharper glasses, the only other woman in the room. Three more executives whose titles I knew but whose names would remain irrelevant unless they had decision-making power.

"Thank you all for coming," I said, my voice carrying easily across the space as I moved to the head of the table. Not asking permission, not looking to Davidson for approval. Simply taking my place. "I'm excited to share what we've developed for The Killian Group's digital transformation."

I didn't use the projector or slides as a shield. Instead, I provided elegantly bound presentation books, then remained standing, commanding their attention with my presence rather than visual aids. As I outlined our strategy—the comprehensive website redesign, the integrated booking system, the social media approach tailored to their elite clientele—I watched their reactions with the same careful attention I gave to men's responses in more intimate settings. Who was engaged, who needed additional convincing, who was already sold.

"The numbers look ambitious," Janet Mercer interjected, tapping a manicured nail against the projected ROI page. "How confident are you in these conversions?"

Before I could respond, Davidson leaned forward. "Well, naturally there's always some degree of—"

"Actually," I cut in, my voice pleasant but firm, one eyebrow raised just enough to silently communicate that his interruption was both noticed and unwelcome, "these projections are conservative based on our previous work in the luxury sector. If you'll turn to Appendix C, you'll find three case studies with independently verified results that exceeded these targets."

Davidson's mouth closed with an audible click. Janet Mercer's lips curved in a small, appreciative smile as she turned to the referenced page.

"For example," I continued, as if the interruption had never occurred, "our work with Meridian Hotels produced a twenty-seven percent increase in direct bookings within the first quarter, reducing their dependence on third-party platforms and their associated fees. The Killian Group's stronger brand position and more targeted demographic actually suggests potential for even greater returns."

I maintained eye contact with each person around the table as I spoke, my posture relaxed but authoritative. The same subtle dominance I'd perfected in clubs and bedrooms translated seamlessly to this environment—the careful calibration of physical presence, the deliberate modulation of my voice, the absolute certainty I projected. These were different men, different desires, but the underlying dynamics were identical.

"What about security concerns?" one of the executives asked. "Our clients expect absolute discretion and protection of their data."

"A valid concern," I acknowledged, appreciating the directness of the question. "We've developed a multi-layered security protocol specifically for clients in your position." I outlined the technical specifications with precise language, neither oversimplifying nor hiding behind jargon. When another question arose about implementation timelines, I addressed it with equal clarity.

Throughout the presentation, Davidson made three more attempts to interject himself into the conversation. Each time, I navigated around his interruptions with such smooth efficiency that it became increasingly obvious to everyone in the room—he was superfluous to this discussion. By the time I concluded, Arthur Killian was leaning forward with genuine interest, Janet Mercer was making detailed notes, and the other executives were nodding with approval.

"Well," Killian said, closing his presentation book with a decisive motion, "I think we've seen enough. Ms. James, you've addressed every concern we brought to the table and several we hadn't considered yet. I'm impressed with the thoroughness of your approach and your obvious understanding of our brand values."

I allowed myself a small smile. "Thank you, Mr. Killian. We're excited about the potential partnership."

"As are we," he replied, extending his hand across the table. "Janet will work with your team on finalizing the contract details, but consider this a verbal commitment. We want Lambert & Associates handling our digital transformation, with you specifically leading the project."

Davidson's face performed a fascinating dance between the required pleased expression and his actual dismay at being sidelined. "Excellent news," he managed. "Our team is—"

"Your team is clearly in good hands with Ms. James," Killian interrupted, his attention still focused entirely on me. "We'll be in touch later this week to move forward."

After handshakes and pleasantries, the Killian team departed, leaving Davidson and me alone in the conference room. The silence stretched between us, taut with his unspoken resentment and my complete indifference to it.

"Well done," he finally said, the words extracted as if under duress. "Though next time, perhaps we should coordinate more closely on who addresses which aspects of the presentation."

I gathered my materials with unhurried movements. "I'm happy to coordinate whenever necessary, Richard. But today's approach clearly worked." I met his eyes directly, my expression pleasant but unyielding. "Results speak for themselves, don't they?"

Before he could formulate a response, I walked out, my heels striking the polished floor with measured confidence. In the hallway, I encountered Marshall Lambert himself—the firm's founder and CEO, a man who rarely ventured from the executive floor to mingle with the working professionals.

"I just passed Arthur Killian in the elevator," he said, falling into step beside me. "He couldn't stop singing your praises. Said you understood his vision better than his own marketing team."

"The Killian Group is an excellent fit for our services," I

replied, neither boasting about my success nor diminishing it with false modesty. "I'm looking forward to implementing the strategy we presented."

Lambert studied me with frank assessment. "You know, Elara, I've noticed a remarkable change in you these past few months. You've really come into your own—more confident, more decisive." He paused outside my office door. "Whatever sparked this transformation, I hope you keep it up. It suits you."

I smiled, thinking of dark club corners and anonymous hotel rooms, of whispered demands and temporary oblivion. "Thank you, sir. I have no intention of going back to who I was before."

As Lambert walked away, I entered my office and closed the door, allowing myself a moment of private satisfaction. The woman who had once sought validation through accommodation and agreement had vanished completely. In her place stood someone who took what she wanted—in the boardroom as in the bedroom—without apology or hesitation.

The hollow feeling that sometimes plagued me in quiet moments remained at bay, drowned out by the clean, sharp pleasure of professional conquest. This victory, like the physical ones I collected after dark, was evidence that I was moving forward, that George's dismissal had freed rather than diminished me.

I was becoming exactly who I was meant to be.

Wasn't I?

Le Jardin occupied the top floor of a renovated historical building downtown, its glass walls offering panoramic views of the city skyline now glittering with early evening lights. White linen tablecloths, crystal stemware that caught and fractured the soft lighting, fresh orchids floating in shallow bowls—all of it designed to convey a simple message: exclusivity. I arrived five minutes early, requesting a corner table that would allow me to sit with my back to the wall, a habit I'd developed in the months since my transformation. I no longer liked being approached from behind, preferred to see everything coming. The maître d' led me to the perfect spot, pulling out my chair with practiced deference that I accepted as my due rather than an unexpected courtesy.

I ordered a glass of cabernet while waiting, using the time to transition mentally from the executive who had closed a seven-figure deal that afternoon to the daughter my mother expected to see. The roles I played had multiplied in recent months—corporate strategist, nighttime predator, and now, dutiful daughter returning to a script I'd long outgrown. I took a measured sip of wine, feeling it coat my tongue with notes of blackberry and oak, and watched the elevator doors.

My mother appeared precisely at seven, punctual as always. Even from a distance, I could see the careful details of her presentation—pearl earrings that had been my father's last anniversary gift before his death, a conservative navy dress that nonetheless flattered her still-slender figure, sensible heels that spoke of comfort prioritized over fashion. Her hair, once the same rich brown as mine, was now more silver than not, styled in the same shoulder-length cut she'd worn for as long as I could remember.

She spotted me and smiled, that particular expression mothers reserve for their children regardless of age—part pride, part perpetual worry. I stood to greet her, accepting her embrace and the faint scent of Chanel No. 5 that had been her signature since my childhood.

"Elara, darling," she said, holding me at arm's length for inspection. "You look different." Her eyes traveled over my face, my hair, my carefully selected outfit—a cream silk blouse and tailored trousers that projected sophisticated professionalism rather than the overt sexuality of my nighttime wardrobe. "More... confident."

"New haircut," I deflected, though my hair was essentially the same as the last time we'd met, just styled with more deliberate attention. "How was your garden club meeting last week? Did Mrs. Holloway finally admit her prize roses aren't actually heritage varieties?"

My mother laughed, allowing the subject change as we settled into our seats. "She'll take that secret to her grave, I'm afraid. But you should have seen her face when Diane brought in documentation proving those roses weren't developed until the 1950s."

The waiter appeared, offering menus and reciting specials with rehearsed eloquence. I ordered another glass of the cabernet; my mother requested her usual gin and tonic. As we studied the menu options, I felt her gaze return to me periodically, assessing, wondering. The woman sitting across from her was both familiar and foreign—her daughter's features arranged in expressions she didn't quite recognize.

"I heard from Sarah Matthews last week," she said after we'd placed our orders. "Her son just made partner at his law firm. Apparently, they're looking for someone with your background in their marketing department."

I recognized the maneuver—a classic maternal segue designed to gather information about my professional situation while appearing to simply share news. "That's nice," I replied noncommittally. "But I'm quite happy at Lambert. We just secured the Killian Group account today, actually."

"Oh! That's wonderful, darling." Her pleasure was genuine, her pride unfeigned. "Your father would have been so proud to see what you've accomplished."

The mention of my father sent an unexpected pang through the carefully constructed armor I'd built around my emotions. He had died three years ago, before George, before my transformation. Sometimes I wondered what he would think of the woman I'd become—not just professionally, but in all aspects of my life.

"He always said I'd go far if I stopped apologizing for taking up space," I said, the words emerging before I could filter them.

My mother's expression softened. "He was right about that. You always were too concerned with making everyone else comfortable." She took a sip of her gin and tonic, her eyes never leaving my face. "It's good to see you owning your worth more."

Our appetizers arrived—delicate seared scallops for her, steak tartare for me. Six months ago, I would have ordered something less assertive, something that wouldn't draw attention or comment. Now, I savored the raw meat seasoned with capers and shallots, unapologetic in my preferences.

"So," she said eventually, setting down her fork with deliberate precision. "It's been six months since... since things ended with George. Are you seeing anyone new?"

And there it was—the question I'd been anticipating since I'd agreed to this dinner. Despite our closeness, I'd shared minimal details about the breakup, offering only the basic fact that it had happened. I certainly hadn't disclosed how it had catalyzed my complete reinvention, how it had opened a door to desires and behaviors my mother couldn't begin to imagine.

"I'm focusing on myself right now," I replied, the practiced evasion rolling off my tongue with ease. "After George, I needed to figure out who I am on my own terms."

"Of course, darling. That's very wise." She nodded, but her eyes held questions she was too polite to voice directly. "It's just that you seem so different lately. Not in a bad way, but... changed. I wondered if perhaps someone new was influencing that change."

I smiled, reaching for my wine. "The only person influencing me these days is me."

That much, at least, was true. The men who cycled through my bed, through bathroom stalls and hotel rooms, held no power over me. They were instruments, not influences—temporary distractions from the hollow space that had taken up residence inside me since that day at the Bluebird Café.

Our main courses arrived, providing a welcome interruption. The waiter described each dish with theatrical flourish—her roasted salmon with fennel puree, my duck breast with cherry reduction. The plating was artistic, the portions modest, the prices exorbitant. The type of meal designed to impress rather than satisfy, form prioritized over function.

"Janet Wilson's daughter just got engaged," my mother continued after several minutes of appreciative eating. "To that boy she met on one of those dating apps, if you can believe it. Apparently, they're quite successful these days."

Another probe, delicately phrased. "I'm glad it worked out for her," I said, carefully cutting a piece of duck. "Dating apps can be hit or miss."

"Have you tried any?" The question was casual, but her eyes were watchful, concerned. "After being with George for so long, it might be a good way to ease back into things."

My phone vibrated in my clutch purse, a discreet buzz against the table's edge. I ignored it, though curiosity flickered through me. Most likely Sam, but possibly the investment banker I'd met at a charity gala the previous week—tall, arrogant, with hands I'd imagined wrapped around my throat since our brief conversation.

"I'm not really interested in 'easing back into things,'" I replied, meeting my mother's gaze directly. "When I decide to date again, it won't be because I need a relationship to feel complete."

She nodded slowly, absorbing both what I'd said and what I hadn't. "I just want you to be happy, Elara. That's all I've ever wanted."

"I know, Mom." I reached across the table to squeeze her hand briefly. "And I am happy. I'm successful at work, I have my own place, good friends. I'm exactly where I want to be right now."

My phone buzzed again, more insistently this time. I glanced at my mother apologetically before reaching for my clutch. "Sorry, it might be work. The Killian implementation is time-sensitive."

I extracted my phone, angling it away from her line of sight out of habit. The text wasn't from Sam or work. It was from the investment banker—Andrew or Anthony, something with an A —with a suggestion for meeting later that was both creative and explicit. Heat flared briefly in my core as I read his detailed proposition, imagining how the night might unfold if I accepted.

"Not work?" my mother asked, noticing the small smile that had crept onto my lips.

"Just a friend," I replied, tucking the phone away. "Nothing urgent."

"Someone special?" she persisted, hope coloring her voice despite her attempt at casualness.

I took a deliberate sip of wine, considering my response. "Just someone to pass the time with," I said finally, my tone light but final.

The shadow that passed over her face suggested she'd heard more in those words than I'd intended to reveal—some hint of the emptiness I worked so diligently to fill with physical sensation and professional achievement. For a moment, I feared she might press further, might pierce the carefully constructed facade I maintained.

Instead, she nodded and returned to her salmon, respecting the boundary I'd established even if she didn't understand it. That was the thing about my mother—unlike the men I encountered, whose desires made them predictable and therefore controllable, she wanted nothing from me except my happiness. It made her both safer and more dangerous than anyone else in my life.

"Tell me more about this Killian account," she said, offering me the gift of another subject change. "It sounds impressive."

I accepted the redirection with relief, launching into a sanitized version of the morning's presentation. As I spoke, I felt my phone vibrate once more with what was likely another suggestive message from the banker. Two separate worlds, contained in the same moment—the daughter sharing professional accomplishments over an elegant dinner, and the woman who would later follow detailed instructions to a hotel room across town, seeking temporary oblivion in a stranger's arms.

Both were real. Both were me. And the space between them grew wider with each passing day.

CHAPTER NINE
Enter Ryker

I pushed through the heavy oak door of the Obsidian with the precision of a surgeon entering an operating theater. Unlike the pulsing clubs and dimly lit dives that had become my usual hunting grounds, this place offered a different caliber of prey—men with corner offices and net worths that matched their egos. The amber glow from crystal fixtures washed over polished mahogany, casting shadows that deepened the intimacy of velvet-lined booths and softened the sharp edges of tumbler glasses. Perfect lighting to hide intentions, to blur the line between confidence and vulnerability. Not that I needed such advantages anymore.

SIX MONTHS of reinvention had stripped me of hesitation. The doorman had nodded me through without question, black dress a second skin that spoke its own language of invitation and warning. Inside, the space hummed with muted conversation and the gentle clink of expensive glassware, a soundtrack of privilege and restraint so different from the throbbing bass and desperate energy of places like Pulse or The Crimson Room.

. . .

I PAUSED AT THE THRESHOLD, letting the atmosphere settle around me like a familiar coat. There was a time when I'd needed a shot of tequila to steady my nerves, with Sam's encouragement whispering in my ear like a battle cry. Now, I surveyed the room with the detached interest of a collector eyeing potential acquisitions. The banker from the other night had been adequate, eager but ultimately forgettable, like all the others. Tonight, I wanted something with more depth, more challenge—something to fill the hollow space that grew larger with each conquest.

MY GAZE DRIFTED past the obvious candidates, the circle of young executives by the fireplace, too eager in their laughter; the silver-haired man at the center table who kept checking his watch, clearly waiting for someone who wasn't me. Then I saw him, seated alone at the far end of the bar.

HE DIDN'T LOOK up when I entered. Didn't scan the room with hungry eyes like most men did when the door opened. Instead, he maintained a studied focus on the amber liquid in his glass, one finger tracing its rim with unhurried precision. His posture spoke of authority—shoulders squared beneath a charcoal suit that had been tailored to the exact specifications of his frame, spine straight but not rigid. He exuded the quiet confidence of someone who had nothing to prove, to himself or anyone else.

ONLY WHEN I had nearly completed my assessment did he lift his gaze, meeting mine across the room with an intensity that sent an unexpected ripple down my spine. No eager smile, no obvious once-over of my body, just a steady look that acknowledged my presence without betraying any particular interest or disinterest. A perfect neutral that somehow managed to feel more like a challenge than any overt invitation.

I SHIFTED my trajectory without hesitation, moving toward him with deliberate steps that created just enough sway in my hips to draw attention without appearing calculated. The space between us became a runway, each step closing the distance between curiosity and whatever waited at the other end of that unwavering gaze.

HE OBSERVED MY APPROACH SILENTLY, without the usual adjustments men made when they realized I had chosen them —no sudden straightening of posture, no hand running through hair, no fake act of returning to conversation only to glance up with manufactured surprise. He simply waited, one hand curled around his glass, the other resting on the polished bar with casual ownership of the space.

I SLID onto the stool beside him, close enough to create a private sphere between us, far enough to maintain the illusion of choice.

"THAT SEAT MIGHT HAVE BEEN TAKEN," he said, his voice a low rumble that matched the rich wood and leather surrounding us.

. . .

"I DON'T SEE anyone sitting in it," I replied, deliberately echoing the response I'd given to countless men before, testing whether he would follow the familiar script.

HE DIDN'T SMILE or offer the expected comeback. Instead, he held my gaze a beat longer than comfortable, then gave a slight nod as if confirming something to himself. "It was reserved for someone interesting," he said finally. "You'll do."

THE RESPONSE CAUGHT ME OFF-GUARD, not because it was particularly clever, but because it carried no trace of the desperate eagerness to impress that I'd grown accustomed to. He spoke as if making an observation rather than delivering a line, his tone neither flirtatious nor dismissive.

"CONFIDENT OF YOU TO assume I'm staying," I countered, though we both knew I had no intention of leaving.

"CONFIDENT OF YOU TO sit down without asking," he returned, lifting his glass for a measured sip. "I respect the certainty, if not the presumption."

I STUDIED him more closely now that proximity allowed, noticing the strong line of his jaw softened by a shadow of evening stubble; the slight gray at his temples suggesting experience rather than age; the green eyes watching me with an unsettling mix of interest and evaluation. He wasn't just handsome in the way of the men I usually pick, whose good looks often hide a lack of substance. This man's charm lay in something less obvious, a presence that filled the space around him effortlessly.

"I'm Elara," I offered, breaking my own rule about names. Something about him made me want to establish myself as a specific entity rather than an anonymous conquest.

"Ryker," he replied, without extending his hand or adding a last name. Just the single word, offered without elaboration or expectation.

The bartender approached, his expression politely inquiring. Before I could speak, Ryker lifted a finger in a subtle gesture that somehow managed to be authoritative without being ostentatious.

"She'll order for herself," he said to the bartender, then turned to me with a slight lift of his eyebrow that invited rather than demanded.

"Whiskey, neat," I said, choosing my standard drink. "Macallan 18, if you have it."

The bartender nodded and moved away, leaving us in a silence that felt heavier than it should have. I was used to controlling these initial exchanges, to establishing dominance through well-practiced charm and carefully calculated boldness. But Ryker's calm confidence neither surrendered to my tactics nor attempted to overpower them. He simply existed alongside them, acknowledging their presence without yielding to their influence.

"You don't come here often," he said after a moment, not a question but a statement of fact.

"And you'd know that how?" I challenged, curious despite myself. "Do you keep a catalog of every woman who walks through the door?"

"Only the ones who enter like they're stepping onto a battlefield," he replied, his eyes never leaving mine. "You move like someone who expects resistance."

The observation was too precise to dismiss with my usual arsenal of evasions and redirections. I found myself replying with unexpected honesty. "Most worthwhile things require overcoming resistance."

A small smile played at the corner of his mouth, not the eager grin of a man who thinks he's scored a point, but the quiet acknowledgment of someone who recognizes a kindred perspective. "True," he agreed. "Though sometimes the most valuable experiences come when we stop fighting long enough to feel what's actually there."

. . .

THE BARTENDER RETURNED with my whiskey, setting it down on a small napkin with quiet efficiency. I lifted the glass, inhaling the rich aroma before taking a sip that burned pleasantly against my tongue. When I placed it back, I saw Ryker still watching me with that same unnerving intensity, as if he could see past the carefully built facade I'd perfected over the last six months.

FOR THE FIRST time in longer than I could remember, I felt a flicker of uncertainty beneath my practiced confidence. This man didn't fit the patterns I'd learned to exploit, didn't respond to the signals that usually guaranteed compliance. He presented a challenge I hadn't anticipated when I'd walked through Obsidian's heavy door, not just a conquest to be claimed, but a puzzle whose solution remained tantalizingly out of reach.

AND DESPITE EVERYTHING I thought I'd learned about myself, I wanted nothing more than to solve it.

I TOOK another sip of the Macallan, letting the liquid warm my throat while I recalibrated my approach. The usual script clearly wouldn't work with Ryker. He watched me over the rim of his own glass, bourbon, I noticed, aged and appreciated without the need for ice to dull its edges. Like him, it seemed to require no dilution to be palatable. The realization annoyed and intrigued me in equal measure.

. . .

"Most people dilute good whiskey," I observed, nodding toward his glass. "Too afraid to experience the full intensity."

"Most people mistake intensity for quality," he countered, setting his drink down with deliberate precision. "They chase the burn rather than the complexity beneath it."

I leaned forward slightly, allowing the neckline of my dress to shift just enough to draw attention without seeming deliberate. A move that had diverted many conversations in the past six months. "And what complexities do you prefer, Ryker?"

His eyes remained fixed on mine, not even a flicker of acknowledgment toward my exposed skin. "The kind that reveal themselves gradually," he said, "Layer by layer, each more interesting than the last."

I traced the rim of my glass with one fingertip, the gesture both casual and calculated. "Most men I meet aren't interested in peeling back layers. They prefer...immediate gratification."

"I'm not most men." His statement carried no bravado, just a simple certainty that felt like both challenge and promise. "And you're not most women, though you seem determined to play the part tonight."

. . .

THE OBSERVATION STRUCK CLOSER to home than I cared to admit. I shifted tactics, crossing my legs so my knee brushed against his under the bar. "And what part do you think I'm playing?"

"THE SEDUCTRESS," he said without hesitation. "The woman who uses desire as currency while pretending she's the one collecting payment."

MY LAUGH EMERGED MORE GENUINELY than intended, surprise overriding calculation. "You think you've figured me out after ten minutes of conversation?"

"I THINK you're working very hard to ensure I don't." His smile was slight but reached his eyes, softening what might have been an accusation into something closer to admiration. "Which makes me wonder what you're protecting with all this performance."

I TOOK another sip of whiskey, using the moment to compose a response that wouldn't reveal too much. The usual men were so much simpler, so eager to talk about themselves, to impress, to follow the breadcrumbs of innuendo I scattered before them. Ryker reversed the dynamic with unsettling ease, turning my practiced moves into openings for his own exploration.

"MAYBE I JUST ENJOY THE GAME," I offered, leaning in closer. "The back and forth, the tension, the..." I let my voice drop to a suggestive murmur, "anticipation of what my mouth might do next."

It was a line that had never failed to fluster even the most composed men, delivered with precisely calibrated intimacy. But Ryker simply took another unhurried sip of his bourbon, his eyes never leaving mine.

"I'm more interested in what you do with your mind," he replied, his voice carrying no judgment, just genuine interest. "Your mouth, I'm sure, is skilled at many things, including deflection."

The unexpected response caught me off guard. For six months, I'd existed in a world where physical attraction trumped all else, where my body was both weapon and shield. This man had somehow slipped past those defenses with a single sentence, acknowledging my sexuality while refusing to be diverted by it.

I reached for my glass at the same moment he moved to lift his own. Our fingers brushed, a brief, incidental contact that should have meant nothing. Instead, electricity shot up my arm, a jolt of connection that felt more intimate than many of the nameless encounters that had filled my nights. His hand paused for a fraction of a second, the slight hesitation telling me that he'd felt it too.

. . .

Around us, the ambient sounds of the bar—such as the murmur of conversations, the gentle clink of glasses, and the soft background music—seemed to fade into the background, creating a bubble of heightened awareness between us. The air itself felt charged, heavy with something more complex than just desire.

"What do you do, Elara?" he asked, steering the conversation toward safer territory. "When you're not disarming men in bars."

I offered the sanitized version of my professional life, the details I shared freely because they revealed nothing of consequence. "I lead digital transformation projects for major hospitality brands. I help them connect with customers they haven't figured out how to reach."

"You translate between worlds," he observed. "Human desire into data points, data points back into experiences that fulfill those desires."

The insight was unexpectedly perceptive. "That's...actually a good way to put it," I admitted. "Most people just hear 'digital' and assume I build websites all day."

"Most people lack imagination." His eyes held a warmth that hadn't been there before, a genuine interest that felt more disarming than any practiced seduction. "They see the surface and miss the mechanism beneath."

"And what mechanism do you think drives me?" I challenged, curious despite my better judgment.

"That would be presumptuous after twenty minutes of conversation," he replied. "But I'd guess something more complex than the need for validation most people settle for."

The conversation shifted to broader topics: the nature of connection in a digital age, whether authenticity was possible in spaces designed for performance, and the value of experiences versus possessions. It was not the superficial exchanges I'd grown used to, where words served merely as placeholders until bodies could communicate more directly, but real ideas that demanded engagement.

More surprising than the topics was my own participation. I found myself offering opinions that weren't calculated to advance a seduction, perspectives that revealed glimpses of the woman who existed beyond the carefully crafted facade I'd perfected. The woman who had once loved debates in college seminar rooms, who had read philosophy for pleasure rather than professional advantage.

Ryker listened with genuine attention, challenging without dismissing, disagreeing without needing to dominate. His confidence never wavered, but neither did it overwhelm. He inhabited his certainty with a comfort that made it seem less like armor and more like skin, a natural extension of self rather than a constructed defense.

I FOUND myself working harder for his attention than I had for anyone in recent memory, offering increasingly thoughtful responses, seeking reactions that went beyond the physical appreciation I'd come to expect. When I made a point about the performative nature of social media that he particularly appreciated, the small nod of acknowledgment felt more rewarding than dozens of hungry stares.

"You've THOUGHT ABOUT THIS," he said, sounding pleasantly surprised. "Most people just accept the frameworks they are given without questioning the architectural assumptions."

"MAYBE I'M NOT most people either," I replied, unconsciously echoing his earlier statement.

HIS SMILE DEEPENED, creating a small dimple at the corner of his mouth that I hadn't noticed before. "I never thought you were," he said. "That's why I've ignored everyone else who's walked through that door tonight."

THE ADMISSION SHOULDN'T HAVE AFFECTED me; I'd received far more explicit compliments from men with equally impressive credentials. But something about the simple honesty of it, delivered without expectation or performance, sent a warmth through me that had nothing to do with the whiskey in my glass.

I took another sip to hide my reaction, unnerved by how quickly this man had managed to slip past defenses that had kept everyone else at a calculated distance for months. His calm confidence both challenged and attracted me, making me question strategies that had served me well since that day at the Bluebird Cafe.

For the first time in six months, I was less interested in what would happen when we finally left the bar together and more curious about what might develop in the space between now and then. The realization was both exhilarating and terrifying, a crack in the foundations of the new Elara I'd so carefully built.

"Perhaps we should move somewhere more comfortable," Ryker suggested after our second round of drinks, nodding toward a secluded booth in the corner. The simple proposal carried none of the leering undertones I'd grown accustomed to, no suggestive smirk, no loaded pause to transform innocent words into invitation. Yet the prospect of moving to that intimate space with him set a ripple of anticipation through me that felt both familiar and strangely different.

"Lead the way," I replied, sliding from the barstool with deliberate grace.

. . .

He placed a hand at the small of my back as we navigated between tables, not possessive or controlling, just a light pressure that somehow managed to feel both protective and respectful. The touch was barely there, yet I felt it with an intensity that surprised me, heat radiating outward from that single point of contact.

The booth he selected was tucked into an alcove, partially screened from the main room by a mahogany divider. Velvet cushions in deep burgundy absorbed sound, creating a pocket of privacy within the larger space. The amber light from a single wall sconce cast soft shadows that made the world beyond our table seem distant and irrelevant.

I slid into the booth, expecting him to sit opposite me, the traditional arrangement for conversation. Instead, he settled beside me, close enough that I could detect the subtle notes of his cologne—sandalwood and something darker, more primal —but not so near as to eliminate the delicious tension of anticipated contact.

"Better," he said, his voice dropping to a lower register that seemed to vibrate through me rather than merely reach my ears. "I find distance overrated when getting to know someone worth knowing."

. . .

THE STATEMENT WAS simple yet layered with meaning, like everything about this man. In another's mouth, it might have been a line, a calculated step toward seduction. From him, it felt like truth, straightforward yet complex, an observation rather than a performance.

"AND WHAT MAKES you think I'm worth knowing?" I challenged, turning slightly to face him, allowing my dress to ride up just enough to expose another inch of thigh.

HIS EYES FOLLOWED THE MOVEMENT, acknowledging my body without becoming fixated on it. When his gaze returned to mine, it carried appreciation laced with something more substantial than mere desire. "The way you listen," he said. "Not just to respond, but to understand. It's rare."

ONCE AGAIN, his observation caught me off guard. For months, I'd been evaluated based on the curve of my hips, the fullness of my lips, the promise in my eyes—all external metrics of value that required no real understanding of the woman beneath the carefully crafted exterior. This man had somehow seen something I hadn't intentionally revealed, a quality I hadn't considered weaponizing in my arsenal of seduction.

AS OUR CONVERSATION WENT ON, the sexual tension between us grew with every word and gesture. When I laughed at something he said, his eyes traced the curve of my neck with a desire that made heat rise low in my stomach. When he talked about the nature of connection, his hands moved with a steady precision that made me imagine them gliding across my skin with the same careful attention.

Yet unlike my previous encounters, where intellectual exchange served merely as a prelude to physical release, our conversation seemed to exist as its own form of intimacy. Ideas merged and separated, perspectives challenged and aligned, creating a dance of minds that felt as exhilarating as any bodily connection.

The realization was unsettling. I had perfected the art of compartmentalization, body separate from mind, pleasure distinct from emotion, night-self segregated from day-self. This man threatened those carefully maintained boundaries, suggesting the possibility of integration I'd deliberately avoided since that day at the Bluebird Cafe.

Ryker leaned in closer to speak over the music that had grown louder as the night progressed, his breath warm against my ear. "You present quite the puzzle, Elara," he murmured, his voice low and intimate. "Every answer reveals three new questions."

The proximity sent an unfamiliar flutter through my stomach, not just the expected heat of attraction, but something more vulnerable, more dangerous. A response that went beyond physical desire to something I'd thought I'd excised from my emotional repertoire.

.   .   .

"MAYBE SOME PUZZLES aren't meant to be solved," I replied, my voice less steady than I would have liked.

"OR MAYBE THEY'RE worth the time required to understand all their dimensions." His knee brushed against mine under the table, the contact sending a jolt of awareness through me. Neither of us pulled away, the pressure of his leg against mine becoming a constant, grounding presence as our conversation continued.

THE MUSIC SHIFTED to something with deeper bass, requiring us to move closer still to hear each other. The forced intimacy should have been just another tactical advantage in my usual approach. Instead, it felt like exposure, as if the reduced physical space eliminated the corresponding emotional distance I hadn't realized I was maintaining.

"WHAT BROUGHT YOU HERE TONIGHT, ELARA?" he asked, his question cutting through the layers of deflection I'd been carefully deploying. "A woman like you has options. Why Obsidian? Why alone?"

I REACHED for my standard response, something lightly dismissive, vaguely suggestive, carefully revealing nothing of consequence. But what emerged surprised me. "I was looking for something different," I admitted. "The usual places, the usual men, they've started to blur together."

. . .

His eyes held mine, neither judging nor assuming, simply receiving what I offered. "And what made them usual?" he asked.

"Their predictability," I said, the honesty slipping past defenses I hadn't realized had weakened. "They want the same things, follow the same patterns. They think they're pursuing, but they're really just...performing expected roles."

Ryker nodded slowly, as if confirming a theory. "While you've been playing a role of your own," he observed. Not an accusation, just a statement of perceived truth.

"We all play roles," I countered, pulling back slightly from the unexpected vulnerability. "Some are just more effective than others."

"Effective at what?" he pressed, his voice gentle but persistent. "Getting what you want, or avoiding what you fear?"

The question landed like a bomb, tearing through my usual composure. I deflected with practiced charm, "Tonight, I'm more interested in what I want than what I might fear."

His smile held no triumph at having touched a nerve, only a quiet acknowledgment of the boundary I'd reasserted. "Fair enough," he conceded. "Though I suspect what you want might be more complicated than you're willing to admit."

I LEANED BACK SLIGHTLY, reclaiming some distance. "You seem very interested in my motivations for someone I just met."

"I'M INTERESTED IN YOU," he corrected. "The motivations are just part of the complete picture."

"AND WHAT PICTURE IS THAT?" I challenged.

"A WOMAN of exceptional intelligence and beauty who uses both as armor rather than connection," he said, his directness startling in its precision. "Someone who sees physical intimacy as the safest form of closeness precisely because it requires no real vulnerability."

I SHOULD HAVE BEEN OFFENDED by his presumption, should have shut down this line of conversation with a cutting remark or simply walked away. Instead, I found myself momentarily speechless, seen in a way that was both terrifying and exhilarating.

"WHY ARE YOU REALLY HERE TONIGHT?" I asked, turning his question back on him. "Most men don't come to bars like this looking for psychological insights."

. . .

"Maybe I'm not most men," he replied, echoing our earlier exchange. "Or maybe I recognized something familiar in the way you surveyed the room when you entered, someone seeking substance beneath the surface."

The background noise of the bar seemed to fade further as his words settled between us. The booth suddenly felt both too intimate and not intimate enough, a liminal space where the rules I'd established for myself these past months no longer seemed to apply.

Ryker's expression softened as he watched the conflicting emotions I failed to completely conceal. He leaned forward, closing the small distance between us until his lips nearly brushed my ear. My breath caught, anticipating the typical proposition I'd heard countless times before in various forms.

"I'd like to see you again, Elara," he whispered instead. "Not just for what we both clearly want."

He pulled back just enough to meet my eyes, his proposition hanging between us like a challenge and an offering, the possibility of something beyond the temporary physical connections that had defined my existence for just over six months now.

I felt caught between contradictory impulses, the practiced seductress who would take what she wanted tonight and disappear by morning, and something deeper, more authentic, that responded to the genuine interest in his eyes. The hollow space inside me that no amount of conquest had managed to fill seemed to pulse with renewed awareness, with the dangerous possibility of hope.

"WHAT MAKES you think I want anything else?" I asked, my voice barely audible over the music. His smile held no triumph, only understanding. "Because you're still sitting here, having a conversation that has nothing to do with getting me into your bed." He reached out, his fingers brushing a strand of hair from my face with a gentleness that felt more intimate than any passionate embrace. "Though I certainly wouldn't object to that outcome."

A WEEK AGO, fuck even an hour ago, I would have had a ready response, something calculated to maintain control while moving us efficiently toward physical release. Now, I found myself genuinely uncertain, caught between familiar patterns and uncharted territory.

"I DON'T DO RELATIONSHIPS," I said finally, the word feeling foreign on my tongue after months of deliberate disconnection.

"I'M NOT ASKING FOR ONE," he replied. "I'm suggesting we explore whatever this is without unnecessary limitations." His eyes held mine, direct and unflinching. "Unless, of course, you're afraid of what you might discover.."

· · ·

THE GENTLE CHALLENGE in his words stirred something I'd
thought long buried, not just desire, not just curiosity, but the
faint, frightening whisper of authentic connection. For six
months, I had defined myself by what I took, by the power I
wielded over men's bodies and desires. This man offered something far more dangerous: the possibility that I might want to
give something of myself in return.

As I LOOKED at him in the amber light of our secluded booth, I
realized I stood at a crossroads I hadn't anticipated when I'd
pushed through Obsidian's heavy door. The path forward
remained unclear, shrouded in possibilities both thrilling and
terrifying. But for the first time in longer than I could remember, I found myself genuinely curious about what might lie
beyond the horizon of a single night.

CHAPTER TEN
The Night of Passion

The elevator ascended with silent efficiency, carrying us to the top floor of Ryker's building. I stood with my back against the polished wood panel, watching him through lowered lashes as he leaned against the opposite wall. Neither of us spoke. The tension that had built between us at Obsidian stretched taut in the confined space, vibrating with possibilities yet to unfold. My pulse quickened as the numbers climbed higher on the digital display, both countdown and promise of what waited beyond those sliding doors.

WHEN WE REACHED the penthouse level, Ryker moved with the same unhurried confidence that had drawn me to him at the bar. His hand found the small of my back as he guided me forward, the pressure firm enough to direct but gentle enough to suggest respect rather than possession. Unlike the eager fumbling of my usual conquests, his movements carried the precise intentionality of someone accustomed to getting exactly what he wanted.

. . .

THE APARTMENT DOOR opened to reveal a space that matched the man, elegant without ostentation, powerful without needing to announce itself. Ambient lighting casts a warm glow over sleek furniture in shades of charcoal and navy, the clean lines softened by occasional touches of texture, a cashmere throw draped over a leather couch, a handwoven rug beneath a glass coffee table. Floor-to-ceiling windows dominated the far wall, framing the city like a living painting, lights twinkling against the night sky.

RYKER TOOK MY COAT, his fingers brushing against my shoulders with deliberate slowness that sent a shiver down my spine. I hear the decisive click of the lock as he secured the door behind us, the sound somehow both promising and vaguely threatening, a boundary between the world outside and whatever was about to unfold between us.

"BEAUTIFUL VIEW," I said, moving toward the windows with practiced nonchalance, reclaiming some sense of agency through movement. My reflection floated ghost-like against the backdrop of city lights, my expression revealing more vulnerability than I'd intended.

I FELT RATHER than heard him approach, his presence registering as a shift in the air around me, a warmth at my back that preceded actual contact. When his hands settled on my hips, I instinctively moved to turn, to take control as I always did, to push him against the window and claim his mouth with mine, establishing dominance from the onset.

· · ·

His grip tightened just enough to hold me in place, his reflection in the glass watching mine with calm intensity. "Tonight," he said, his voice a low rumble against my ear, "you follow my lead."

Four simple words that should have triggered immediate resistance. For six months, I had orchestrated every encounter, dictated every touch, and maintained absolute control over how and when pleasure happened. Submission wasn't in my vocabulary, wasn't compatible with the woman I'd become after George.

Yet I felt my breath catch, my pupils dilate, my body responding to his quiet command with a rush of heat that caught me entirely off guard. The unexpected thrill of relinquishing control vibrated through me, intensifying rather than diminishing my desire.

"And if I don't want to?" I challenged, my voice betraying me with a slight tremor.

His smile in the reflection was knowing, his eyes never leaving mine as his hands slid from my hips to my waist, drawing me back against him with gentle insistence. "You do," he said simply. "That's why you're still here."

The truth of it stunned me into silence. I could have walked away at Obsidian. Could have selected any of a dozen more predictable men who would have followed my lead without question. Could have maintained the patterns that had defined my existence these past months. Instead, I had chosen to follow this man to his domain, curious about what surrender might feel like in hands steady enough to catch me.

He turned me slowly to face him, one hand coming up to cup my cheek with unexpected tenderness. My usual conquests rushed toward physical connection, fumbling with clothes and limbs in their eagerness to reach climax. Ryker touched me as if we had all the time in the world, as if the journey itself held as much value as its destination.

"I want to see you," he said, his thumb tracing the curve of my lower lip. "Not the performance, not the practiced seduction. You."

I started to reach for him, to pull his mouth down to mine with the urgency that had defined all my recent encounters, but he caught my wrists in one hand, holding them with firm gentleness between us.

"Patience," he murmured, his free hand tilting my chin upward. "Some things deserve to be savored."

When his lips finally met mine, the kiss was nothing like I'd anticipated. Not the aggressive claiming I was accustomed to, not the desperate hunger I'd come to expect. He kissed me with deliberate slowness, his hands framing my face as if it were something precious, setting a pace that built anticipation rather than rushing toward release. I felt myself melting into it, my usual strategies for maintaining emotional distance dissolving under the careful attention of his mouth against mine.

HE TASTED of bourbon and possibility, his tongue exploring mine with the same thoughtful intensity he'd brought to our conversation at Obsidian. I heard myself make a small sound of surrender, felt my body yielding to his guidance, my hands coming to rest against his chest, not to push away but to steady myself as the room seemed to tilt beneath my feet.

WHEN HE FINALLY PULLED BACK, his eyes were darker than before, his breathing slightly uneven, evidence that his control, while impressive, wasn't absolute. The realization sent another pulse of heat through me, the knowledge that I affected him despite his composure adding a new dimension to the desire building between us.

"YOU'RE USED TO RUSHING," he observed, his fingers tracing a path from my jaw to my collarbone with maddening precision. "Taking what you want and moving on before it becomes complicated."

I SWALLOWED, unnerved by how easily he saw through me. "Complications are overrated."

. . .

"So is simplicity." His hand continued its deliberate journey, tracing the neckline of my dress without dipping beneath it, building anticipation through restraint. "Some experiences are worth the complexity they bring."

As he led me deeper into his apartment, his hand once again at the small of my back, I found myself in unfamiliar territory, not just physically, but emotionally. For months, I had been the hunter, the one who selected and discarded, who controlled every aspect of my encounters. Tonight, I was allowing myself to be led, to follow rather than direct, to experience rather than orchestrate.

The strangest part wasn't that Ryker had taken control. It was how much I wanted him to. How ready I was to set down the exhausting vigilance of always calculating the next move, always maintaining emotional barriers while bodies connected. For tonight at least, I wanted to surrender to whatever this man had to offer, to discover what might emerge when I stopped fighting so hard to protect the hollow spaces inside me.

Ryker's bedroom mirrored the rest of his apartment, minimalist luxury with purpose behind every element. A king-sized bed dominated the space, its dark frame low to the ground, the sheets a shade of midnight blue that absorbed the subtle light from recessed fixtures overhead. No clutter, no unnecessary ornamentation, just the essential elements arranged with deliberate intention. Like the man himself, the room revealed nothing it didn't intend to show. My pulse quickened as he closed the door behind us, the soft click marking another boundary crossed.

HE MOVED to stand before me, close enough that I could feel the heat radiating from his body, yet not touching me. Usually, clothes were obstacles hastily removed and discarded, the goal being skin against skin as quickly as possible. Ryker approached undressing me as if it were an art form deserving of attention, his eyes never leaving mine as his fingers found the zipper at the back of my dress.

"TURN AROUND," he said, his voice low but firm.

I COMPLIED, feeling strangely vulnerable with my back to him. The slow descent of the zipper sent shivers across my skin, each newly exposed inch meeting the cool air of the room with a whisper of anticipation. His knuckles brushed deliberately against my spine as he drew the zipper down, the subtle contact more erotic than the overt groping I'd grown accustomed to.

WHEN THE DRESS PARTED COMPLETELY, his hands slid beneath the fabric at my shoulders, guiding it forward and down with measured precision. I felt it pool at my feet, leaving me in the black lace underwear I'd selected with calculated purpose earlier that evening. His breath caught audibly, the small sound of appreciation more satisfying than the crude compliments my usual conquests offered.

HE TURNED me to face him, his eyes travelling the length of my body with unhurried appreciation, taking in every curve and plane as if committing them to memory. His fingers trailed against my skin slowly as he removed my bra, running his hands down my sides until reaching the waist band of my underwear, he lowered his own body as he lowered my underwear, for a moment I thought he was going to nuzzle into my pussy, but instead he just let out a deep breath, the sensation of his hot breath was almost my undoing.

IMPATIENCE FLARED WITHIN ME, the habit of taking control overwhelming my earlier surrender. I reached for him, fingers moving to the buttons of his shirt with practiced efficiency, determined to level the playing field of exposure. Before I could undo the first button, his hands captured my wrists in a grip both gentle and unyielding, raising them and bending them so our hands rested at the back of my neck as he backed me toward the bed.

"PATIENCE," he whispered against my ear, the word both command and promise.

MY BACK MET the cool sheets as he guided me down, still holding my wrists with one hand while the other traced the outline of my collarbone. The unfamiliar position, restrained, at his mercy, should have triggered resistance. Instead, it sent a fresh wave of heat pooling between my thighs, my body arching toward his touch despite my mind's confusion at my response.

He released my wrists only after a look that clearly communicated I was to leave them where they were. I complied, watching as he methodically removed his own clothing, each movement precise and controlled. He never broke eye contact with my eyes, even though my own flicked between his and greedily taking in the view that revealed itself, a body honed by discipline rather than vanity. The planes of his chest, the definition of his abdomen, the strength evident in his thighs, all spoke of power held in careful check.

When he returned to me, now as naked as I was, he didn't immediately press his body against mine as I expected. Instead, he knelt beside the bed, his hands skimming up my legs from ankle to thigh with deliberate slowness. His palms were slightly calloused, creating a delicious friction against my skin that made me shiver with anticipation.

"You're beautiful," he said, and unlike the empty flattery I'd heard countless times before, his words carried the weight of genuine appreciation. His hands continued their journey, fingers tracing patterns across my stomach, circling my breasts without touching where I most wanted him to. When his mouth finally joined his hands, pressing warm kisses along the inside of my thigh, I gasped at the intensity of sensation.

· · ·

He took his time, using lips and tongue and teeth to explore every inch of my skin, deliberately avoiding the centre of my desire despite my increasingly explicit encouragements. My fingers gripped the sheets above my head, the self-imposed restraint adding another layer to the building tension.

"Please," I heard myself say, the word unfamiliar in this context. I never begged, never showed need. I took what I wanted without apology.

He looked up, his eyes meeting mine with a heat that made my breath catch. "Tell me what you want, Elara. Not what you think I want to hear, not what you usually say in these moments. What you truly want."

The question stripped away pretense, demanded honesty I'd avoided in all my recent encounters. "Touch me," I whispered, the simple truth more vulnerable than all the explicit directions I'd given other men.

He smiled, recognizing the surrender in my response, and lowered his mouth to the apex of my thighs. The first touch of his tongue against me was exquisitely precise, finding exactly the right spot with unerring accuracy. I cried out, hips lifting involuntarily toward the source of pleasure. His hands gripped my thighs, holding me open to his attention, his rhythm alternating between gentle exploration and focused intensity that brought me repeatedly to the edge without allowing release.

· · ·

JUST WHEN I thought I couldn't bear the tension any longer, he would ease back, his mouth moving to my inner thigh, my hip bone, my stomach—building the pleasure again from a different angle, a different approach. I writhed beneath him, frustration and ecstasy becoming indistinguishable as he played my body with the skill of someone who understood delayed gratification was its own form of pleasure.

"RYKER," I gasped, my voice breaking on his name. "I need—"

"I KNOW WHAT YOU NEED," he murmured against my skin, the vibration of his voice adding another layer of sensation. "And I'll give it to you. When you're ready to feel it completely."

HE ROSE ABOVE ME THEN, his body covering mine with welcome weight, the hard evidence of his desire pressing against my thigh. His eyes held mine as he positioned himself at my entrance, one hand bracing his weight while the other traced the outline of my face with surprising tenderness.

WHEN HE FINALLY ENTERED ME, it was with torturous slowness, a deliberate inch-by-inch claiming that forced me to feel every moment of connection.

UNLIKE RECENT ENCOUNTERS, where physical sensation served as a distraction from emotional presence, this joining demanded I remain fully aware, fully present. There was nowhere to hide, no way to maintain the detachment I'd perfected.

"STAY WITH ME," he commanded softly, recognizing my instinctive retreat. "Feel this."

HIS PACE WAS MEASURED at first, each stroke deep and deliberate, his eyes never leaving mine, an intimacy more invasive than the physical joining of our bodies. I felt exposed in ways that went beyond nakedness, seen in ways that transcended the merely physical. The hollow space within me that no amount of casual sex had filled seemed to pulse with awareness, with dangerous possibility.

AS THE TENSION built between us, his control began to fray at the edges, his movements becoming more urgent, more primal. The headboard struck the wall with rhythmic insistence, the sound punctuating our increasingly ragged breathing, the slip of skin against sweat-dampened skin. His hand slid between our bodies, finding exactly where to touch to send me spiralling toward release.

"LET GO," he growled, his voice rough with effort and need. "Let me see you."

THE ORGASM CRASHED through me with unexpected force, wave after wave of pleasure so intense it bordered on pain. I heard myself cry out his name, felt my nails digging into his shoulders as my body clenched around him, drawing him deeper. He followed me over the edge moments later, his release triggering aftershocks of pleasure that left me trembling beneath him.

As we lay tangled together, hearts racing in uneven time, I realized what made this encounter so different. For the first time in six months, I hadn't used sex as a way to disappear, to numb myself, to assert control over my emotional landscape. Instead, I had remained fully present, fully aware, and somehow, impossibly, it had been more satisfying than any of the emotionless couplings that had filled my nights since George.

The realization was both exhilarating and terrifying. Ryker had somehow breached defenses I'd thought impenetrable, forcing me to feel rather than experience physical sensation. As his breathing steadied against my neck, his weight a comforting pressure above me, I wondered what other walls might crumble if I allowed this man further access to the carefully guarded chambers of my heart.

My body hummed with the aftershocks of multiple orgasms, muscles trembling with pleasant exhaustion, skin hypersensitive to every point of contact between us. The sheets beneath me were damp with sweat, twisted into abstract sculptures by our movements. Beside me, Ryker's chest rose and fell with gradually slowing breaths, his skin gleaming in the low light. I blinked up at the ceiling, feeling strangely disoriented, not by the physical intensity of what we'd shared, but by the emotional presence I'd maintained throughout. Six months of perfecting the art of being physically present while emotionally absent, all undone by this man who had somehow demanded both without saying a word.

In my carefully constructed post-George world, this moment had a script: catch my breath, offer a casual compliment, gather my clothes, and disappear before emotional intimacy could take root. Physical distance after physical connection, the formula that had protected me from vulnerability since that day at the Bluebird.

Before I could initiate this practiced exit, Ryker shifted beside me. His arm slid beneath my shoulders, drawing me against him with gentle insistence until my head rested in the hollow between his shoulder and chest. His other arm draped across my waist, not restraining but claiming, his hand splayed against my hip with proprietary ease. The position was unfamiliar, intimate in a way that transcended the act we'd just shared, suggesting a comfort with closeness I'd deliberately avoided in all my recent encounters.

"You're thinking too loudly," he murmured, his voice a rumble I felt against my cheek.

I tensed slightly, unaccustomed to being read so easily. "Just cataloging the experience," I replied, aiming for casual detachment but landing somewhere closer to defensive.

· · ·

HIS FINGERS BEGAN TRACING idle patterns against my hip, the touch neither sexual nor demanding, just a gentle connection, an anchor to the present moment." And how does it rate compared to your usual conquests?"

THE QUESTION CAUGHT me off guard, both for its directness and the implicit acknowledgement of my recent patterns. I considered deflecting with humor or evasion, but something about the darkness, the shared warmth of our bodies, encouraged honesty.

"DIFFERENT," I admitted quietly. "More..."

"PRESENT?" he suggested when I trailed off, unable to find the right word.

I NODDED, feeling the movement of my head against his skin. "Yes."

THE SHEETS HAD COOLED where they touched my exposed shoulder, but everywhere our bodies connected radiated warmth, his chest against my side, his arm beneath my neck, his thigh touching mine. Our limbs fitted together with an ease that seemed improbable for two people who had been strangers mere hours ago. I found myself melting into the contours of his body, muscles relaxing despite my mind's cautionary signals.

. . .

"What now?" he asked, the question hanging in the air between us, simple words carrying complex implications.

The script called for me to pull away, to reestablish physical space that would protect my emotional boundaries. Instead, I found myself turning slightly toward him, my hand coming to rest against his chest where I could feel the steady rhythm of his heart beneath my palm. Every part of me wanted to wrap myself around this man and stay, and that thought scared the fuck out of me. I knew I needed to be careful here.

"Now I should go," I said, the words automatic though lacking conviction.

His arm tightened slightly around my waist, not forceful but present. "Should? According to whose rules?"

The question penetrated deeper than it had any right to, striking at the core of the structures I'd built to protect myself. Whose rules indeed? Rules created in the aftermath of heartbreak, designed to prevent its recurrence. Rules that had governed my interactions with men for six months, keeping me safe but increasingly hollow.

"Mine," I replied, though even to my own ears, it sounded more like a question than a statement.

· · ·

I MADE a half-hearted attempt to rise, muscles protesting after the intensity of our activities. "I don't stay over," I explained, the words mumbled against his skin. "It's one of my...rules." Ryker's response was physically simple; his arm remained draped across my waist, neither tightening to prevent my departure nor withdrawing to facilitate it. "Stay," he said, the single word containing neither plea nor command, just quiet certainty.

I COULD HAVE LEFT. Could have pushed away his arm, gathered my scattered clothing, called a rideshare to take me back to my carefully maintained space with its clear boundaries. The Elara who had walked into countless bars and clubs these past months, selecting men like appetizers from a menu, would have done exactly that, preserving the emotional distance that had become both shield and prison.

BUT I FOUND myself in conflict, I felt my body settling back against his, surrender facilitated by physical exhaustion and something deeper, more dangerous, a longing for connection I'd denied for so long I'd almost forgotten its existence.

"JUST FOR TONIGHT," I murmured, establishing a boundary even as I crossed one.

HIS HAND MOVED to stroke my hair, fingers combing gently through the tangles our activities had created. "Tonight is all we have guaranteed anyway," he said, the philosophical observation somehow more comforting than false promises of tomorrow.

THE STEADY RHYTHM of his breathing, the solid warmth of his body against mine, the lingering scent of our shared pleasure, all combined to create a cocoon of unexpected intimacy. I tried to maintain some mental distance, to remember that this was temporary, that vulnerability led to pain, that I had reconstructed myself specifically to avoid the hollow ache George had left in his wake.

BUT MY BODY BETRAYED ME, molding itself more completely against Ryker's as if recognizing something my mind refused to acknowledge. My eyelids grew heavy, the day's events and night's exertions claiming their toll in encroaching drowsiness.

I FOUGHT IT BRIEFLY, aware that sleep represented another boundary crossed, another defense breached. In sleep, we are at our most vulnerable, unguarded, unprotected, unable to maintain the facades we construct in waking hours. To sleep beside someone is an act of trust my post-George self had deliberately avoided.

"REST," Ryker murmured, seeming to sense my internal struggle. His hand continued its gentle movement through my hair, each stroke lulling me further toward surrender.

. . .

THE HOLLOW SPACE INSIDE ME, the void I'd tried to fill with nameless encounters and momentary pleasure, seemed less cavernous in that moment, less echoing with emptiness. As consciousness began to slip away, I wondered dimly what made this man different from all the others. Why his touch penetrated defenses that had repelled even the most determined suitors. Why I was breaking my cardinal rule by allowing myself to drift toward sleep in his arms.

PERHAPS IT WAS SIMPLY EXHAUSTION. Perhaps it was the skill with which he'd played my body, drawing responses I hadn't experienced in longer than I could remember. Perhaps it was the way he'd seen past my carefully constructed facade from the moment our eyes met across Obsidian's dimly lit interior.

OR PERHAPS, my fading consciousness suggested, it was because he'd demanded I remain present, not just physically but emotionally, throughout our encounter. Had refused to allow me the distance I usually maintained, the detachment that had protected me from feeling anything beyond physical sensation for six long months.

AS SLEEP CLAIMED ME, my head tucked beneath his chin, his arm a warm weight across my waist, I had one final coherent thought: this was different. He was different. And most terrifyingly of all, I was different with him, less guarded, more authentic, closer to the woman who had existed before George's rejection had catalyzed my transformation.

. . .

WHETHER THAT WAS progress or regression remained to be seen. But as I surrendered to sleep in a stranger's arms for the first time since remaking myself into the hunter rather than the hunted, I couldn't deny the unfamiliar sense of peace that settled over me, a quiet in the hollow spaces that had known only echoes for far too long.

CHAPTER ELEVEN

The Morning After

I woke to sunlight painting warm stripes across my bare skin, momentarily disoriented by the unfamiliar texture of high-thread-count sheets against my body. This wasn't my bed. This wasn't my apartment. The events of the previous night flooded back with startling clarity, Ryker's hands on my skin, his mouth exploring places I'd allowed countless others to touch but never quite like this. I'd broken my cardinal rule: I'd stayed the night. Worse still, I'd slept deeply, vulnerably, in a stranger's arms. But as I reached across to. The other side of the massive bed, my fingers found only cooling sheets and the lingering impression of his body. He was gone.

A RIDICULOUS PANG of disappointment fluttered in my chest, which I immediately tried to smother. What had I expected? This was exactly how it should be, no awkward morning-after conversation, no pretense of intimacy beyond what we'd shared physically. This was my preferred scenario, played out perfectly, the clean exit I usually orchestrated myself.

· · ·

So why did the empty space beside me feel like an accusation?

I traced the shallow depression where his head had rested hours before, the pillow still bearing the ghost of his cologne. Fragments of the night replayed behind my eyes: his careful attention to every inch of my skin, the way he'd held my wrists above my head, the command in his voice when he'd insisted I stay present, stay with him. Most disturbing of all, how I'd complied, remaining emotionally tethered to the experience in a way I hadn't allowed myself in six months of calculated encounters.

"Just sex," I whispered to the empty room, the words hanging unconvincingly in the morning air. "Just another hookup."

But it wasn't, and the hollowness expanding in my chest knew it. I'd let Ryker past defenses constructed specifically to prevent this feeling, this vulnerable, exposed sensation that made me want to gather my clothes and run before it grew any stronger.

My dress lay crumpled near the foot of the bed, one heel toppled on its side nearby, the other nowhere in sight. In daylight, Ryker's bedroom revealed more details than I'd registered in our entry the night before. The massive windows continued here, though partially veiled by automated blinds that diffused the morning light to a gentle glow. Everything spoke of restrained luxury, furniture in dark woods and smoky blues, art that suggested taste rather than wealth, though clearly both were present.

I SAT UP, letting the sheet fall to my waist as I surveyed the room for the rest of my belongings. My underwear dangled precariously from the edge of a sleek dresser where Ryker had tossed it after removing it. The memory sent a fresh wave of heat through my core, my body responding to the recollection before my mind could intercept it.

THIS WOULDN'T DO. I needed to regain control, to reestablish the emotional distance that had protected me since George. Standing, I moved to retrieve my dress, wincing slightly at the pleasant soreness between my thighs, a physical reminder of the thoroughness of Ryker's attention. I stepped into the dress, contorting to reach the zipper that had descended so slowly under his fingers the night before.

"FOCUS, ELARA," I muttered, scanning the floor for my missing shoe. "Find your stuff and get out."

THIS WAS THE PROTOCOL: wake, dress, leave. No lingering, no morning-after vulnerability, no chance for rejection to strike when defenses were at their weakest. I'd perfected this escape routine over six months of nameless encounters, had it down to a science that protected me from exactly the kind of emotional exposure I was feeling now.

. . .

I spotted my clutch on a chair in the corner, my phone likely inside with several missed messages from Sam wondering about my night. I'd tell her it was fine, satisfying, nothing special, the same report I'd delivered dozens of times before. The lie felt leaden even in anticipation.

The sound of approaching footsteps froze me mid-zip. My heart accelerated from a steady rhythm to a frantic tattoo in an instant. This wasn't part of the script. Ryker was supposed to be gone, to work, to the gym, anywhere that facilitated my clean escape. I wasn't prepared for a morning encounter, for conversation, for those eyes that seemed to see through my carefully constructed persona.

I straightened my spine, summoning the confident mask that had carried me through countless morning-afters. I could handle this. A smile that suggested pleasure without attachment, a casual goodbye, a vague promise to call that we both knew was empty. Simple.

But when Ryker appeared in the doorway, the practiced lines evaporated from my mind like morning mist under a strong sun.

He wore only low-hanging sweatpants, the defined planes of his chest and abdomen on full display in the gentle morning light. His hair was slightly damp at the temples, suggesting a recent shower, and in each hand he held a steaming mug of coffee. The casual domesticity of the image struck me with unexpected force; this wasn't the hasty exit of someone avoiding morning intimacy, but the deliberate return of someone who had anticipated my waking.

"Morning," he said, his voice carrying that same quiet confidence that had drawn me to him at Obsidian. "I thought you might want coffee before you disappeared."

The gentle teasing in his tone indicated he knew exactly what I'd been planning, the quick escape, the avoidance of morning vulnerability. Somehow, he'd anticipated this and chosen to disrupt it with this simple gesture of consideration.

I stood frozen between the bed and the window, dress half-zipped, hair tumbling in what I was sure was a chaotic mess around my shoulders. For six months, I had been the one in control, the one who dictated the terms of every encounter. Now, with two mugs of coffee and his knowing eyes, Ryker had completely upended the power dynamic.

"You made coffee," I said stupidly, my usual eloquence deserting me in the face of this unexpected kindness.

His lips curved into a slight smile. "I did." He stepped further into the room, extending one mug toward me. "I hope I got it right. What helped is that you struck me as someone who appreciates the real thing, not those sugary approximations they sell at coffee chains."

. . .

THE THOUGHTFULNESS of the gesture rendered me momentarily speechless. I had never either stayed or let them stay long enough for coffee, let alone preferences, comfort and desires beyond the immediate physical release we provided each other. Yet here was this man I'd known less than twenty-four hours, offering coffee as if my morning needs mattered to him.

THE HOLLOW SPACE INSIDE ME, the void I'd been trying to fill with nameless encounters, pulsed with dangerous awareness. I'd spent six months perfecting the art of emotional distance, of taking physical pleasure without risking my heart. One night with Ryker, and those carefully constructed walls were already showing cracks.

As I REACHED for the mug, I realized with alarming clarity that the danger I faced this morning wasn't rejection. It was the possibility that with this man, for the first time since George, I might want something more than a single night of forgetting.

"BLACK, NO SUGAR?" Ryker asked as he extended the mug toward me. I reached for it, our fingers brushing in the exchange, the brief contact sending an absurd flutter through my stomach. The coffee sloshed dangerously close to the rim, nearly spilling onto the expensive sheets. I steadied my hand with deliberate focus, disturbed by how such a minor touch could affect me after the intimacies we'd shared hours before.

. . .

"You remembered?" I asked, the surprise evident in my voice. I vaguely recall mentioning my coffee preference during our conversation at the Obsidian.

His lips curved into a slight smile. "I pay attention to details that matter." He moved around to the other side of the bed, settling against the headboard with casual ease, as if sharing morning coffee with a near-stranger was the most natural thing in the world.

I remained standing for a moment longer, caught in the strange liminality of the situation. This wasn't the script I knew by heart: hastily dressing, vague excuses, quick exit before emotions could complicate situations. I had no roadmap for sitting on this man's bed and sharing a coffee after a night that was meant to only be a purely physical encounter.

Finally, I perched on the edge of the mattress, my back against one of the posts at the foot of the bed, as far from Ryker as I could manage while still being on the same piece of furniture. The physical distance was deliberate, a small attempt to reestablish the emotional boundaries that had become danger-ously permeable in his presence.

An awkward silence settled between us, broken only by the gentle sound of sipping. I stared into the dark surface of my coffee, searching for the confident, detached woman who had walked into the Obsidian last night. She seemed to have vanished somewhere between Ryker's precise attention to my pleasure and this unexpected morning kindness.

"This is weird," I blurted out, immediately regretting the unfiltered honesty.

Ryker's eyebrow lifted slightly. "The coffee? Would you prefer juice? I can get something else if—"

"No, the coffee's perfect," I interrupted. "I meant...this." I gestured vaguely between us with my free hand. "The morning after. I don't usually..."

"Stay?" he finishes for me, his tone free of judgment.

"Or linger," I added. "Or drink coffee. Or talk, really."

He took another unhurried sip from his mug, watching me over the rim with those eyes that seemed to see more than I wanted to reveal. "Is that a rule you made, or just a habit that formed?"

The question was gentle but penetrating, cutting straight to the heart of patterns I'd established without fully examining their origins. The answer was both a deliberate rule that had calcified into a habit.

. . .

"Does it matter?" I countered, defensive edges rising in my voice.

"Only if you want it to." He shrugged, the movement drawing my attention to the defined muscles of his shoulders, the slight indent at his collarbone where I'd left a mark with my teeth last night. "I'm not trying to dismantle your boundaries, Elara. Just offering coffee and company."

The simplicity of it disarmed me. I was used to men either wanting more than I was willing to give or nothing beyond the physical release we'd shared. This middle ground, this quiet acknowledgment of connection without demand for continuation, was unfamiliar territory.

I took a long sip of coffee, using the moment to gather my thoughts. It was perfect, strong, rich with hints of chocolate beneath the bitterness. Like the man who'd made it, complex rather than simply intense.

"I have a meeting at eleven," I said finally, offering information I rarely shared with an overnight companion unless using it as an excuse to leave. "Quarterly review with a client."

Ryker nodded, accepting this mundane detail as if it were a gift rather than the distraction I'd intended. "Enough time to finish your coffee, at least," he observed. "Any interesting projects lately?"

THE QUESTION WAS SO NORMAL, so divorced from the sexual tension that usually dominated my interactions, that I found myself answering honestly. I told him about the Killian account, about the digital transformation strategy I'd developed, about Davidson's attempts to claim credit for my work. He listened with genuine interest, asking questions that demonstrated actual engagement rather than polite pretense.

IN TURN, he shared details about his own work, he ran a venture capital firm specializing in sustainable technology, a fact I might have found intimidating if we'd exchanged this information at the Obsidian. Now, it seemed like just another piece of the puzzle that was Ryker Davis, a man who defied easy categorization.

THE CONVERSATION FLOWED with surprising ease, punctuated by comfortable silences that lacked the awkwardness I'd anticipated. I found myself relaxing incrementally, my posture softening, my grip on the coffee mug less white-knuckled. When I shifted to a more comfortable position, my leg extended along the rumpled sheets, bringing me slightly closer to where he sat against the headboard.

THIS QUIET DOMESTICITY, sharing coffee and conversation in the gentle morning light, felt more intimate than the passionate encounters that had filled my nights for months. Sex was a physical connection I'd perfected the art of keeping separate from emotional entanglement. But this, this simple act of being present with someone, fully clothed yet somehow more exposed, was dangerous territory; it terrified me and set off all the alarms in my head, yet I couldn't bring myself to leave yet.

I HAD PRIDED myself on maintaining control through careful distance, through the deliberate withholding of personal details, through sex that satisfied physically while protecting emotionally; it made me the one with the power. Ryker dismantled these defenses not by demanding more but by offering a space where walls seemed unnecessary rather than vital. I felt my power slipping. I wasn't sure I minded.

"WHAT ABOUT YOU?" he asked, interrupting my thoughts. "Any plans after your meeting?"

THE QUESTION WAS CASUAL, carrying no obvious expectation or hidden agenda. Yet I found myself analyzing it from every angle, searching for the trap, the demand, the complication I'd spent six months avoiding.

"JUST WORK," I replied cautiously. "Maybe drinks with Sam later." The mention of my friend felt like offering another piece of myself, another potential point of connection I usually guarded more carefully.

· · ·

Ryker nodded, setting his empty mug on the bedside table. "Sounds like a good day," he said simply.

I finished the last of my coffee, preparing myself for the inevitable question—when would we see each other again? What came next? Would I give him my number? The familiar pressure to define or dismiss whatever had happened between us, to categorize it neatly as either a one-time encounter or the beginning of something more complicated.

But the question didn't come. Instead, Ryker glanced at the sleek watch on his wrist and said, "I should probably get ready for work soon."

The lack of pressure, of expectation, of demand was so unexpected that I found myself momentarily speechless. In the absence of his pushing, I felt no need to pull away—a realization that was both liberating and terrifying.

"Thank you," I said, the words emerging before I could analyze them. "For the coffee."

His smile reached his eyes, creating small lines at the corners that hadn't been visible in last night's dim lighting. "You're welcome, Elara."

The way he said my name—not as a prelude to a request or just as a casual placeholder, but as if the syllables themselves carried meaning—sent another ripple of awareness through me. I'd given my name to countless men over the past six months, had heard it gasped and groaned and whispered in the dark. None had said it quite like this—like it was worth saying correctly, worth savoring.

As I watched him rise from the bed, coffee mug in hand, I realized with unsettling clarity that while last night had been about bodies connecting, this morning had somehow become about people connecting—a distinction I'd deliberately blurred since George, a line I'd carefully avoided crossing.

And I wasn't entirely sure I wanted to stop it from happening.

Ryker took my empty mug, his fingers brushing against mine in a touch that lingered just long enough to seem deliberate. "I need to get ready," he said, moving toward the doorway. "Make yourself comfortable." I watched him disappear into what I assumed was an en-suite bathroom, the quiet click of the door leaving me alone with thoughts I wasn't prepared to examine. Minutes later, he emerged transformed—no longer the man whose skin had pressed against mine throughout the night, but someone else entirely.

He moved with practiced efficiency, selecting a suit from a walk-in closet that revealed rows of meticulously organized clothing. The charcoal gray fabric whispered against crisp white cotton as he buttoned his shirt, each movement precise and unhurried. I watched, transfixed, as Ryker the passionate lover became Ryker the polished professional—cufflinks secured with a subtle click, tie knotted with mathematical precision, jacket settling perfectly across broad shoulders that hours earlier had been bare beneath my grasping hands.

. . .

THE DICHOTOMY WAS JARRING—THIS immaculate businessman had been inside me, had whispered filthy encouragements against my ear, had held me through the vulnerability of sleep. The memory of pleasure collided with the reality before me, creating a dissonance I didn't know how to reconcile. With my usual conquests, I never saw this transition, never witnessed the return to their daytime selves. The compartmentalization was cleaner that way, the boundaries between night and day firmly established.

"Do you need anything before I go?" he asked, adjusting his cuffs as he turned toward me. "Coffee refill? Towel for the shower?"

I stumbled over my response, unaccustomed to such consideration from a man I'd slept with exactly once. "I—no, I'm fine. I should probably get going anyway." The words emerged automatically, the script I'd perfected for hasty exits, though they lacked my usual conviction.

"You don't have to rush," he said, moving to a dresser where he collected his wallet, keys, and phone with the same deliberate efficiency that characterized all his movements. "The shower's through there if you want to use it. Towels in the cabinet beside the sink." He paused, seeming to consider something, then opened a small drawer and extracted a key. "And this is so you can lock up. Just drop it in the mailbox in the lobby."

He placed the key on the nightstand between us, the small metal object carrying implications that made my chest tighten with unfamiliar anxiety. Trust. Consideration. Potential for return. My usual morning-afters involved neither trust nor consideration, and certainly no implication of possible return. I stared at the key as if it might bite, unsure how to respond to this unexpected gesture.

"That's not necessary," I managed, my voice sounding strangely formal even to my own ears. "I won't be long."

Ryker shrugged, leaving the key where it lay. "Just in case," he said. "No pressure either way."

That was the thing about him that I found most unsettling—the complete absence of pressure, of expectation, of the subtle manipulations I'd grown expert at identifying and deflecting. He offered without demanding, suggested without insisting, creating space rather than attempting to fill it.

He checked his watch—a subtle, expensive timepiece that complemented the overall impression of quiet wealth his apartment exuded. "I have a meeting across town," he said, gathering a leather portfolio from a side table. "Help yourself to anything in the kitchen if you're hungry."

I nodded mutely, still perched on the edge of his bed, still wearing last night's dress with its half-fastened zipper, still struggling to process this departure from the morning-after script I knew by heart.

He crossed to where I sat, and I tensed instinctively, anticipating the kind of goodbye I was accustomed to—a perfunctory kiss, perhaps a casual suggestion to "do this again sometime" that we both knew was empty. Instead, Ryker bent and pressed his lips gently against my forehead, the gesture so unexpectedly tender that I froze completely, breath caught in my lungs.

"It was a pleasure meeting you, Elara," he said softly, his breath warm against my skin. Then he straightened, offered a small smile that reached his eyes, and turned toward the door.

I remained motionless, listening to his footsteps recede, the distant sound of the front door opening and closing with a quiet finality. Only when I was certain he was gone did I release the breath I'd been holding, my hand rising unconsciously to touch the spot on my forehead where his lips had pressed—a kiss more intimate than anything I'd experienced in six months of meaningless couplings.

For long minutes, I sat on the edge of his bed, clutching the sheet to my chest though I was still partially dressed, trying to understand the tumult of emotions churning beneath my ribs. This wasn't how these encounters were supposed to go. I was supposed to feel satisfied but detached, physically sated but emotionally untouched. Instead, I felt raw, exposed, as if Ryker had somehow bypassed all my carefully constructed defenses to touch something I'd thought safely buried.

Eventually, the unfamiliar vulnerability drove me to movement. I stood, straightening my dress with hands less steady than I would have liked, and began a slow circuit of the bedroom, studying the space for clues about the man who had so thoroughly disrupted my carefully maintained patterns.

The bookshelves held an eclectic mix—business texts and financial journals alongside philosophy, classic literature, and what appeared to be first-edition poetry collections. I ran my fingers along their spines, noting titles I recognized from college courses I'd once loved before practicality narrowed my focus to career advancement. A small photograph in a simple frame caught my eye—Ryker, perhaps a decade younger, with an older man who shared his jawline and direct gaze. Family. Connection. Context.

My usual conquests remained carefully two-dimensional in my mind—bodies without histories, desires without depths. I deliberately avoided learning the details that would render them fully human, that might complicate the physical satisfaction I sought from them. Yet here I was, absorbing evidence of Ryker's life beyond our night together, curious in a way that threatened the emotional distance I'd cultivated so carefully.

In the bathroom, I found more fragments of the man—a straight razor beside the sink, suggesting patience and precision; expensive but understated toiletries arranged with methodical care; a book of Japanese poetry on the edge of the bathtub, its pages slightly warped from steam. I touched these objects with a strange reverence, as if they might reveal through osmosis why this particular man had affected me so differently from all the others.

The shower tempted me with its multiple heads and sleek glass enclosure, but using it felt like another boundary crossed, another concession to the intimacy I'd spent months avoiding. Instead, I splashed cold water on my face, attempting to shock my system back to its usual detached equilibrium.

The mirror reflected a woman I barely recognized—hair tousled beyond the artful mess I cultivated for nights out, eyes bright with confusion rather than calculation, lips slightly swollen from kisses that had somehow felt like more than physical contact. I looked... affected. Touched not just externally but internally. The realization was terrifying.

I completed my circuit of the apartment, noting the careful curation of the space—art selected for appreciation rather than investment, furniture chosen for comfort as well as aesthetics, a kitchen that showed signs of actual use rather than mere display. Everything spoke of a man who made deliberate choices, who valued substance over appearance while maintaining standards in both.

The key still lay on the nightstand where he'd left it, catching the morning light that streamed through the partially open blinds. I picked it up, its weight substantial in my palm, its implications even heavier. For six months, I had perfected the art of taking without giving, of experiencing without engaging, of remaining untouched at my core while allowing my body to be thoroughly known.

One night with Ryker had cracked foundations I'd thought impenetrable, had shown me glimpses of a connection I'd convinced myself I no longer wanted or needed. The hollow space inside me—the void I'd tried to fill with nameless encounters and momentary pleasure—pulsed with newfound awareness, with dangerous possibility.

I closed my fingers around the key, its edges pressing into my palm with a sharpness that anchored me to the present moment. The woman I'd become after George would have left it behind without a second thought, would have already deleted Ryker from her mental roster, filed him under "complete" rather than "continuing."

But as I gathered my belongings, locating my missing shoe beneath the edge of the bed and my earrings on the bathroom counter, I knew with unsettling certainty that I wouldn't be able to dismiss this night, this man, this experience as easily as all the others.

Something had shifted, a tectonic movement beneath the careful structures of my post-George existence. Whether that shift would lead to collapse or reconstruction remained to be seen. But as I slipped the key into my clutch instead of leaving it behind, I acknowledged what I'd been avoiding since waking in his arms: with Ryker, for the first time in six months, I wanted more than just forgetting. I wanted to remember.

CHAPTER TWELVE
The Aftermath

I stood in front of my full-length mirror, eyes tracing the familiar curves of my body wrapped in black fabric that hugged like a second skin. The dress was a weapon I'd wielded countless times—tight enough to draw attention, short enough to promise access without giving it away too easily. But tonight, as I smoothed my hands over the material, something felt off. My movements lacked their usual precision, as if my body was performing a routine it no longer fully believed in.

My fingers brushed against the zipper, remembering how different hands had lowered it less than twenty-four hours ago —hands with a gentle strength that had made me tremble despite myself. I shook the thought away, reaching for the stilettos that added four inches to my height and a dangerous curve to my posture. The heels that had once made me feel invincible now seemed like props in a play I'd performed too many times.

"Focus, Elara," I muttered, sliding my feet into the shoes with practiced movements.

The apartment felt too quiet, too empty—a sensation I'd never noticed before. I'd always appreciated the solitude of my space, the clear boundary between my nighttime adventures and my carefully maintained sanctuary. Now that emptiness seemed to pulse with phantom echoes, with the ghost of a voice that had somehow managed to slip past my defenses.

My GAZE FELL on the coffee mug sitting on my kitchen counter, white ceramic with a chip on the rim, nothing special, not even a close resemblance to the one I watched Ryker's lips caress as he drank his coffee this morning, but it still took me back there.

I FORCED myself to look away, moving to my bathroom where makeup awaited, the armor I applied each night with precision. Foundation to even skin tone, concealer to hide any hint of vulnerability, bronzer to warm my complexion, highlighter to draw attention to cheekbones and collarbones, the angles of a body designed for temporary pleasure, all in all, it was a mask. What I once perceived as putting on my crown, having all the power, and taking what I wanted, has now transformed into a perception of this layer being nothing but a mask to hide a scared little girl underneath.

My HAND TREMBLED as I reached for my eyeliner, the sharp black pencil hovering inches from my face when an unbidden image flashed behind my eyes—Ryker's gaze in the morning light, studying me with an intensity that had nothing to do with my carefully crafted exterior. He looked at me as if trying to see past the makeup, past the practiced smiles and calculated gestures, to something I'd buried so deeply I sometimes forget it's there.

"Stop it," I told my reflection sharply. "He was just another guy."

But even as the words left my mouth, I knew they were a lie. Another guy wouldn't have brought me coffee exactly as I liked it. Another guy wouldn't have listened with genuine interest as I spoke about work. Another guy wouldn't have kissed my forehead with such unexpected tenderness before leaving.

I finished my makeup with mechanical efficiency, erasing all traces of the woman who had spent last night vulnerable in a stranger's arms. The woman in the mirror looked exactly as she should—eyes smoky and inviting, lips painted deep red, every feature enhanced to maximize impact while revealing nothing of substance.

On my way to the closet for a leather jacket, I passed my unmade bed. I never left it unmade—another rule broken in the strange aftermath of last night. The sheets were still rumpled, tangled from where I'd tossed and turned after returning from Ryker's apartment, unable to find the peaceful sleep that had come so easily in his arms.

I paused, drawn by an invisible thread toward the pillow where I'd buried my face upon returning home. I leaned down, inhaling deeply. His scent lingered there—sandalwood and something darker, earthier—transferred from my skin and hair after our night together. It mingled with my own perfume, creating a combination that sent an involuntary shiver down my spine.

My phone chimed on the nightstand, and I lunged for it with embarrassing eagerness, my heart accelerating before I could remind myself that I didn't care if he called, didn't want him to call, had no reason to expect he would call.

Just Sam, confirming our meeting spot. Not him. Of course not him.

A peculiar heaviness settled in my chest as I typed a quick response, confirming I'd meet her at The Velvet Room in an hour. Six months of training myself not to feel disappointment couldn't quite suppress the hollow ache that expanded beneath my ribs.

I checked the time—still forty minutes before I needed to leave. My usual pre-club ritual involved a glass of wine, maybe a carefully curated playlist to set the mood for the night ahead. Instead, I found myself opening my contacts, scrolling to where I'd saved his number before leaving his apartment that morning.

My thumb hovered over his name. What would I even say? "Thanks for the coffee." "Last night was fun."? Nothing seemed adequate to capture what had happened between us, and anything more substantial would reveal a vulnerability I couldn't afford.

I tossed the phone onto the bed with unnecessary force, turning away as if the physical distance might sever the mental connection that had lingered all day. Tonight would be like any other night these past six months. I would go out. I would find someone suitable. I would take what I wanted and leave before morning threatened any emotional complications. I needed to try to get Ryker out of my head.

I sprayed perfume at my wrists and neck, the familiar scent of jasmine and vanilla settling around me like armor. But as I inhaled, I caught that lingering note of sandalwood again, as if my skin had absorbed his essence and refused to relinquish it despite my shower, despite my determination to erase all traces of the connection we'd shared.

Grabbing my clutch, I did a final check in the mirror. The woman who stared back was everything I'd crafted her to be—confident, alluring, untouchable. Yet something in her eyes betrayed her, a shadow of uncertainty that hadn't been there before last night.

I closed the door behind me with unnecessary force, as if the sound might drown out the whisper of doubt that had taken up residence in my mind. Tonight would be like any other night. It had to be.

The Velvet Room throbbed with familiar energy—bass notes vibrating through the soles of my stilettos, colored lights cutting through artificial fog, bodies pressed together in what passed for intimacy in places like this. I'd walked through these doors dozens of times in the past six months, each entrance a prelude to temporary satisfaction, to moments of forgetting. Tonight, the rhythm felt off, as if someone had slightly shifted the tempo of a song I'd memorized, making each step uncertain where once I'd moved with predatory grace.

Sam waved from a high-top table near the bar, already surrounded by admirers drawn to her platinum hair and effortless charisma. I navigated through the press of bodies, accepting the shot she pushed toward me with practiced enthusiasm that felt hollow even to my own ears.

"About time!" she shouted over the music. "I was starting to think you'd bailed on me!"

I forced a smile, tossing back the tequila with a practiced flick of my wrist. The burn traveled down my throat, but the warmth it spread through my limbs felt different—not the liquid courage I'd once needed, not the pleasant buzz that had become ritual, just heat without purpose.

"Wouldn't miss it," I replied, my eyes already scanning the crowd with methodical assessment. This was familiar territory —cataloging potential conquests, eliminating the too-young and too-eager, identifying those with the right combination of desire and detachment. The calculation had become second nature, a skill honed to perfection since that day at the Blue-bird Café.

My gaze settled on a man near the edge of the dance floor —trim suit that spoke of money, carefully styled hair, a certain hesitancy in his posture that suggested he was out of his usual environment. A banker, most likely, or something similarly buttoned-up, seeking temporary escape from spreadsheets and client meetings. Normally, his type appealed—the contrast between public restraint and private abandon creating an intriguing tension to exploit.

He caught me looking and straightened, confidence visibly expanding under my attention. When he approached, it was with the careful precision of someone accustomed to high-stakes negotiations.

"Can I buy you a drink?" he asked, cologne enveloping me in a cloud of something too sharp, too synthetic. It pierced rather than invited, lacking the subtle warmth of sandalwood and cedar that had clung to Ryker's skin.

"Whiskey, neat," I replied, the same order I'd given in countless bars to countless men whose faces had begun to blur together long before last night.

The banker—Andrew? Aaron? Something with an A—signaled the bartender with a crisp efficiency that would have impressed me a week ago. Now, I found myself comparing the gesture to the quiet authority with which Ryker had summoned the bartender at Obsidian, the subtle difference between someone performing confidence and someone simply embodying it.

"I'm Alex," he said, handing me a tumbler that caught and splintered the pulsing lights. Not Andrew, not Aaron. It didn't matter.

"Elara," I responded, raising the glass in a small toast before taking a sip. The whiskey was good—aged, expensive—but it tasted flat against my tongue, lacking the complex richness of what Ryker had served in his apartment.

Alex moved closer, his hand coming to rest at the small of my back with a tentative pressure that asked permission rather than claimed space. A week ago, I would have leaned into the touch, encouraging more boldness with a deliberate shift of my hips. Tonight, I had to suppress an urge to step away, to break the contact that felt wrong in ways I couldn't articulate.

"You come here often?" he asked, the cliché falling between us like a stone in still water.

I nearly laughed at the predictability of it, at how many times I'd heard some variation of this opening in the past six months. The script was so familiar I could have recited his next three questions without effort—what did I do for work, did I live nearby, was I here with friends or alone?

"Often enough," I replied, taking another sip to avoid elaborating.

My eyes drifted to the DJ booth, where a tall man with dark hair and arms covered in intricate tattoos caught my gaze. He nodded slightly, a gesture of recognition and interest that established the possibility of later connection. Another night, I might have excused myself from Alex to pursue this more intriguing option, or perhaps played them against each other, enjoying the competitive energy my attention created.

Instead, I found myself remembering Ryker's voice in the dimness of Obsidian—"I'm not most men"—and how the simple statement had contained no bravado, just quiet certainty that proved true in ways I was still struggling to understand.

Alex was saying something about his firm, his hand now venturing a light stroke against my hip. I nodded at appropriate intervals, my body performing the role it knew while my mind drifted elsewhere—to coffee cups in morning light, to the weight of a key in my palm, to the press of lips against my forehead with unexpected tenderness.

"Would you like to dance?" Alex asked, mistaking my distraction for interest in the crowded floor.

I nodded, grateful for the excuse to move, to do something other than maintain conversation that felt increasingly like speaking a language I'd forgotten. His hand found mine as he led me into the press of bodies, his grip lacking the steady assurance, the deliberate pressure that had guided me through Ryker's apartment.

The music shifted to something with a deeper bass, bodies pressing closer in the limited space. Alex's hands settled at my waist, his movements competent but cautious. I tried to lose myself in the rhythm as I had so many times before, to let physical sensation drown out thought, to recapture the predatory focus that had defined my nights since George.

But my body betrayed me—steps faltering where they should have been fluid, muscles tensing where they should have yielded. When Alex pulled me closer, his breath hot against my ear as he spoke, all I could register was the sharp bite of whiskey overlaid with stale beer, so different from the clean mint and coffee that had accompanied Ryker's morning words.

The DJ caught my eye again as he moved from behind his equipment, apparently on break. He made his way toward us, his confidence evident in the direct line he cut through the crowd. Up close, his features were striking—sharp cheekbones, full lips, eyes slightly unfocused from whatever substance fueled his energy.

"You're too beautiful to look so bored," he said, leaning close enough that his breath brushed my cheek. The scent of beer and cigarettes enveloped me, and I fought the urge to step back.

Alex's hand tightened on my waist, a subtle claim of territory that might have amused me another night. Now it just felt constrictive, a reminder of performances I was struggling to maintain.

"I need another drink," I said to neither of them specifically, extracting myself from Alex's grip with practiced ease.

At the bar, I ordered another whiskey, more out of habit than desire. The glass was cool against my palm, the amber liquid catching light like a promise of warmth that never quite reached my core. My eyes drifted to a couple near the wall— her back pressed against the surface, his hands tangled in her hair as they kissed with the desperate hunger of strangers discovering temporary connection.

Only days ago, that had been me—pressed against bathroom walls, car seats, hotel mattresses, seeking oblivion in the temporary surrender of physical pleasure. Now, watching their performance, I felt nothing but a strange emptiness, as if viewing actors in a play whose plot I'd forgotten.

When Alex appeared at my elbow, his expression hopeful, I knew what came next in our particular script. "My place is just a few blocks away," he said, voice pitched low with practiced intimacy. "If you wanted to continue this somewhere more private."

The words hung between us, an invitation I'd accepted dozens of times from dozens of men whose names I'd forgotten by morning. But tonight, for the first time in six months, I felt no desire to say yes, no urge to use his body as temporary escape from the hollow space inside me.

"I think I'm going to call it a night," I said, the words feeling foreign on my tongue. "Alone."

His surprise was evident, confusion quickly masked by a practiced smile. "Another time, perhaps."

I nodded noncommittally, already turning away, leaving my half-finished whiskey on the bar—another departure from habit, another small rebellion against patterns that suddenly felt constricting rather than liberating.

Sam caught my eye from across the room, her eyebrows raised in question as she noticed me moving toward the exit alone. I gestured vaguely at my phone, mouthing "work emergency" with a shrug that she accepted without question. Another lie, another performance, another moment of distance between who I pretended to be and whoever was emerging from beneath that carefully constructed facade.

My heels struck the pavement in lonely percussion, each

click echoing through empty streets that had grown colder in the hours since sunset. No warm body pressed against mine as I walked, no whispered promises of pleasure to come, no hand at the small of my back guiding me toward temporary oblivion. For the first time in six months, I was heading home alone, the night spread before me like an empty canvas I no longer knew how to fill.

The air bit at my exposed skin with unusual sharpness, as if punishing me for the absence of shared body heat that had become my nightly ritual. I crossed my arms over my chest, the thin leather of my jacket offering minimal protection against the chill that seemed to seep past fabric, past skin, settling somewhere deeper inside me. Without the anticipation of someone else's hands warming my flesh, the night felt hostile in ways I hadn't noticed before.

My apartment building loomed ahead, windows dark except for scattered squares of yellow light marking other insomniacs, other lonely souls, other people whose stories I'd never bothered to wonder about. Six months of viewing my home as merely a starting point and occasional ending point— never the destination itself—had rendered it almost unfamiliar, a way station rather than sanctuary.

The lock clicked open under my key, the sound unnaturally loud in the silent hallway. Inside, darkness greeted me, no lights left on because I hadn't expected to return alone, hadn't planned for solitude when nightclubs were still pulsing with potential connections. I flipped a switch, wincing as harsh light flooded the space, revealing the stillness of unopened wine bottles, an undisturbed bed, a night that had ended before it truly began.

I kicked off my stilettos with unnecessary force, sending them skidding across the hardwood floor in separate directions. The relief of flat feet was immediate but insufficient, doing nothing to ease the hollow ache that had expanded beneath my ribs throughout the evening. With mechanical movements, I peeled off my jacket, dropping it over the back of a chair rather than hanging it properly—another small rebellion against patterns that suddenly felt suffocating rather than comforting.

The bed called to me despite its rumpled state, sheets still tangled from this morning's restless awakening. I collapsed onto the mattress fully clothed, the black dress riding up my thighs as I sprawled across the surface that had witnessed countless temporary connections but few genuine moments of vulnerability. The ceiling above me bore no answers, just the blank whiteness I'd stared at so many times before while waiting for strangers' breathing to deepen into sleep before making my escape.

My phone lay heavy in my hand, screen dark and silent. No messages. No missed calls. No digital evidence of Ryker's existence beyond the contact entry I'd created that morning. I pressed the power button, watching the screen illuminate with notifications—two texts from Sam asking if I was okay, an email from work, a news alert about market fluctuations that would have mattered to me yesterday. Nothing from him.

Why would there be? I hadn't reached out either, hadn't given any indication that I wanted more than what we'd shared. One night, coffee in the morning, a key returned to a mailbox with no note attached. Clean. Simple. Exactly what I'd trained myself to want.

So why did the absence of his name among my notifications feel like loss?

I set the phone aside, my fingers drifting to the inside of my wrist where his lips had pressed the night before—not in passion but in that quiet moment between rounds, a gesture of unexpected tenderness that had no place in the carefully choreographed encounters I'd perfected. I traced the spot, remembering the warm pressure, the slight scratch of evening stubble, the way he'd looked up at me afterward with eyes that sought connection beyond the physical.

The memory was more vivid, more present than anything I'd experienced at the club tonight—more real than Alex's tentative touch or the DJ's alcohol-heavy breath. Those men had been physically present but somehow less substantial than the ghost of Ryker that seemed to haunt my apartment, lingering in coffee mugs and rumpled sheets and the phantom sensation of his hands on my skin.

I stared at the ceiling, watching shadows shift as cars passed on the street below, their headlights momentarily illuminating my space before plunging it back into partial darkness. The emptiness inside me had a weight now, a presence I could no longer ignore or fill with temporary pleasure. It demanded acknowledgment, demanded naming, demanded reconciliation with the woman I'd become since George and the woman who had spent a night in Ryker's arms without fleeing before dawn.

My phone beckoned, offering the illusion of connection. I

reached for it again, opening my messages to Sam's concerned texts. My fingers hovered over the keyboard as I considered what to say, what could possibly explain the strange hollowness that had replaced my carefully cultivated confidence.

"I think I'm broken," I typed, the words appearing stark and vulnerable on the screen.

I stared at them for a long moment before deleting each letter, replacing the raw truth with a more acceptable fiction: "Just tired. Talk tomorrow."

The lie felt bitter even in digital form, another performance for an audience that included myself. But what was the alternative? To admit that one night with a stranger had somehow shifted something fundamental inside me? That after six months of emotional armor, I was suddenly vulnerable to the absence of a man I barely knew?

I set the phone aside again, rolling onto my side and curling inward as if physical compression might contain the expanding awareness in my chest. But as I closed my eyes, memories assaulted me with merciless clarity—Ryker's mouth exploring the sensitive hollow between my neck and shoulder, his hands pinning my wrists above my head with gentle firmness, his voice rough against my ear as he commanded me to stay present, to feel everything.

The ghost of his touch seemed more solid than the actual hands that had reached for me tonight, the echo of his voice clearer than the music that had pulsed through The Velvet Room. I remembered the weight of him above me, the perfect pressure of his body against mine, the way he'd somehow demanded emotional presence alongside physical surrender.

No one had asked that of me in six months. No one had seen past the carefully constructed facade to the hollow spaces beneath. No one had made me feel simultaneously exposed and protected, vulnerable and safe.

My carefully constructed walls—the defenses I'd built after George's rejection, the emotional distance I'd maintained through dozens of meaningless encounters—trembled under the weight of memory, of absence, of unnamed longing.

"Fuck," I whispered into the darkness, the single syllable containing frustration and confusion and something dangerously close to fear. Not fear of Ryker, but fear of what he represented—the possibility that the emptiness inside me couldn't be filled with physical pleasure alone, that the woman I'd become was less complete, less satisfied, less whole than the one I'd been before.

As silence settled around me like a shroud, the truth I'd been avoiding all day crystallized with painful clarity: for the first time in six months, I wanted more than forgetting. I wanted to remember, to feel, to connect—and the realization terrified me more than any rejection ever could.

CHAPTER THIRTEEN
Sam's Departure

I pushed open our apartment door, my mind still caught in the undertow of last night's revelation. The emptiness that had followed me home from The Velvet Room clung to my shoulders like a damp coat, heavy and uncomfortable, impossible to shrug off. I'd spent the entire workday distracted, my thoughts circling back to Ryker and the unsettling realization that for the first time in six months, casual encounters had lost their anesthetic effect. But as I stepped inside, the sight before me yanked me firmly back into the present: Same crouched amid a chaos of open suitcases, her usual meticulous organization replaced by frantic sorting and the unmistakable tension of emergency.

"SAM?" My voice came out smaller than intended, barely audible over the rustle of clothing being hastily folded and tucked.

SHE LOOKED UP, platinum hair falling across her face in unwashed strands, the pink tips faded to a soft peach, a detail she'd never allow on her Instagram grid. Her expensive ring light stood unplugged in the corner, her camera equipment carefully set aside on the coffee table, protected even in chaos.

"HEY." She pushed her hair back, revealing eyes rimmed with subtle redness. No elaborate makeup, no carefully crafted expression for her followers. Just Sam, stripped of the SamThompStyle persona she'd cultivated with such precision. "I was hoping you'd be home soon."

I SET MY BAG DOWN, moving cautiously through the obstacle course of half-packed belongings. "What's happening? Are you...leaving?" The question felt absurd given the evidence surrounding us, but my brain struggled to process the scene.

SAM'S HANDS stilled on the sweater she'd been folding. The confidence that typically radiated from her like heat from pavement seemed dimmed, her shoulders curving inward in a posture I'd never associated with her.

"MY MOM CALLED THIS MORNING. My sister's in the hospital—gallbladder surgery gone complicated. She needs help with the kids while my sister recovers." She tucked the sweater into a suitcase with unusual gentleness. "I need to go home for about a month."

"A month?" The words escaped before I could temper them with understanding or concern. My shoulders stiffened involuntarily, my throat constricting around a surge of panic I hadn't anticipated.

Home for Sam meant Minnesota—a world away from our carefully constructed life in the city, from the clubs and bars where she'd first encouraged me to spread my post-George wings. A month without her meant a month without my safety net, my cheerleader, my witness to the new Elara I was still learning to become.

"I know the timing sucks," she continued, avoiding my eyes as she sorted through a pile of jeans. "But they really need me. My mom can't handle the twins alone, and my brother-in-law has to work."

I nodded mechanically, trying to push down the selfish anxiety rising in my chest. "Of course you have to go. Is your sister going to be okay?"

"They think so." Sam reached for her phone, the case adorned with her brand colors and logo. "Here, look."

She handed me the device, open to a text thread with her mother. The messages were nothing like the carefully crafted captions Sam posted online—no clever phrases, no strategic emojis, just raw concern and family logistics. Photos of her sister in a hospital bed, looking pale and tired. Pictures of twin four-year-olds with Sam's eyes and none of her camera awareness.

"They're beautiful," I said, handing the phone back, my fingers trembling slightly.

"Yeah." Sam's expression softened in a way I rarely saw—genuine rather than posed for maximum engagement. "I haven't seen them in almost a year. Some aunt I am, right?" She laughed, but the sound held none of her usual vibrance.

I perched on the edge of our sofa, watching as she continued packing with movements that lacked her usual efficiency. "Have you posted about this?"

Sam's fingers paused on the zipper of her toiletry bag. "No," she admitted, the single syllable heavy with uncharacteristic hesitation. "I haven't figured out how to... package it, I guess."

"Package it?"

She sighed, abandoning the bag to sit beside me, her knee bouncing with nervous energy. "Family emergency content doesn't perform well unless it's really dramatic or has a clear redemption arc. A sick sister and babysitting duties don't exactly scream 'aspirational lifestyle.'" Her fingers reached for her nose ring, fidgeting with it in a nervous gesture I'd rarely seen. "Plus, my followers expect daily outfit posts, club recommendations, partnership content. Not me changing diapers in suburban Minnesota."

The bitterness in her voice caught me off guard. Sam had always spoken of her influencer career with pride, with the certainty that she was building something meaningful despite her parents' initial disapproval.

"It's just a month," I offered, unsure if I was reassuring her or myself. "Your followers will understand."

"Will they?" She pulled out her phone again, this time opening her analytics page. "I've been losing engagement for weeks. The algorithm already hates me because I haven't been posting as consistently." She scrolled through numbers I didn't fully understand but recognized as important from the tightness around her mouth. "If I disappear for a month, I might as well be starting from scratch when I get back."

I watched her face as she stared at the screen, seeing for the first time the weight she carried behind her curated captions and perfect poses. How had I missed this? I'd been so consumed with my own transformation, my own quest to fill the hollow space George had left, that I'd failed to notice the cracks in Sam's carefully constructed image.

"You could be honest," I suggested. "Tell them what's happening."

"That I'm a mess? That I've been running on four hours of sleep trying to keep up with content demands?" She laughed, the sound sharp-edged and unfamiliar. "That I've been pre-filming for weeks because some days I can't even get out of bed?" She gestured to her current appearance—joggers instead of stylish jeans, hair unwashed, face bare. "This isn't what they follow me for, Elara. They want the fantasy, not... this."

Her voice cracked on the last word, and I saw with startling clarity how much of herself Sam had sacrificed to maintain the illusion of effortless success. How she'd hidden her exhaustion behind filters and strategic angles, buried her family concerns beneath sponsored posts and carefully staged photos.

"What if they forget me?" she whispered, the vulnerability in her voice making her seem suddenly younger, smaller. "What if I go back to being nobody?"

I reached for her hand, surprised by the coolness of her skin against mine. In that moment, our roles reversed—me offering strength, her accepting comfort. For six months, she had been my guide through the world of reinvention, my cheerleader as I shed the "good girl" identity that had defined me before George. I'd never considered that her own identity might be just as fragile, just as carefully maintained.

"You're not nobody," I said firmly. "You're Sam. With or without the followers."

She squeezed my hand, her grip stronger than her expression suggested. "I haven't been just Sam in a long time," she admitted. "Sometimes I don't even know where SamThomp-Style ends and I begin."

I recognized the sentiment with uncomfortable clarity—the blurring of performance and authentic self, the masks we wore becoming so familiar we forgot they weren't our actual faces. Wasn't that exactly what had happened to me last night at The Velvet Room, when the seductress persona I'd cultivated suddenly felt like borrowed clothing that no longer fit?

"Maybe this month will be good for you," I said, surprised by the certainty in my voice. "A break from being on display."

Sam nodded slowly, though uncertainty lingered in her eyes. "Maybe." She looked around at the half-packed suitcases, the carefully separated camera equipment. "I'm pre-filming some content tonight to schedule while I'm gone. Trying to minimize the damage."

As she returned to her packing, I remained on the sofa, watching her with new awareness. My anxiety about being left alone still pulsed beneath my ribs, but it was joined now by genuine concern for my friend—concern that transcended my own needs. For the first time since that day at the Bluebird Café, I felt something crack in the shell of self-protection I'd built around myself. Something that felt dangerously close to regret.

Three hours later, our living room had transformed into a makeshift content studio. Sam stood before the ring light, now replanted by the window to catch the last of the natural daylight, her appearance miraculously restored to the SamThompStyle her followers knew. Perfect makeup, freshly styled hair, outfit changed three times already to create the illusion of different filming days. I sat cross-legged on the floor behind the camera, checking lighting and framing while she recorded another "casual" outfit recommendation that had required forty-five minutes of preparation and would eventually become a fifteen-second clip.

"And don't forget to swipe up to shop this look! Link in bio, besties!" Sam's voice shifted into her higher, more energetic "content voice" as she finished the segment with a practiced hair flip and smile. The moment the camera stopped recording, her shoulders dropped, the bright expression fading like a light switched off. "How was that one?"

"Perfect," I assured her, though I'd said the same about the previous seven takes. "No one would guess you're filming all these at once."

She nodded, already moving to change outfits again. Our apartment looked like it was being both assembled and dismantled simultaneously—half-packed suitcases competed for floor space with carefully arranged product displays. The bathroom counter was a battlefield of makeup tubes and skin-care products, some packed for travel, others positioned for upcoming beauty content.

I followed her into her bedroom, where the closet doors stood open, revealing shelves half-emptied of their contents. The carefully color-coordinated system she normally maintained had collapsed into piles sorted by necessity rather than aesthetic.

"Can you grab those jeans? The light wash ones?" Sam pointed toward a stack while struggling to zip a garment bag filled with outfits labeled by day. "I need them for the 'casual coffee run' reel I'm filming next."

I handed her the jeans, my fingers lingering on the expensive denim. "How many more do you need to film tonight?"

"At least ten more." She consulted a detailed spreadsheet on her tablet. "I've got the vacation content excuse for the first week—I've preloaded those sunset photos from Mexico last year. Then I need enough new content to cover three more weeks, plus the sponsored posts for BeautyBlend and FitFuel." She rubbed her temples, smearing her perfect eyeliner slightly. "I'll need to film those workout videos before I leave too."

"When will you sleep?" I asked, only half-joking as I glanced at the clock—already past nine, with seemingly endless content still to create.

"Sleep is for people with less than fifty thousand followers," she replied with a hollow laugh. "I'll catch up in Minnesota. Between diaper changes and bedtime stories."

I watched her methodically apply another layer of setting spray to her makeup, the practiced movements betraying years of repetition. The exhaustion behind her eyes contradicted the vibrant persona she projected online—the carefree, spontaneous influencer whose life was one endless adventure.

"I'll make some tea," I offered, retreating to the kitchen to give her space to change again.

Our kettle felt unusually heavy as I filled it, or perhaps it was just my arms that felt weaker tonight. The water sloshed dangerously close to the rim, my hands less steady than I liked to admit. I set the kettle on the stove with exaggerated care, focusing on the simple task to avoid the anxiety building in my chest.

The kitchen, at least, remained mostly unchanged—Sam's domain was living room, bathroom, closet. Places where lighting was good and backgrounds could be controlled. Here, surrounded by familiar mugs and the faint scent of this morning's coffee, I could almost pretend nothing was changing.

Almost, but not quite.

Steam whistled from the kettle, startling me from my

thoughts. I poured water over tea bags, watching the color bleed outward in murky clouds. By the time I returned to Sam's room, she had changed again—white linen shirt, different jeans, hair pulled into an artfully messy bun.

"Three outfits from one filming session," she explained, accepting the tea with grateful hands. "I'll edit them to look like different days." She scrolled through her content calendar, frowning at whatever calculations she was making. "If I post once a day instead of twice, I might be able to stretch what I've filmed."

I sat on the edge of her bed, careful not to disturb the clothes laid out in precise arrangements. "Can you film anything while you're there?"

"Maybe." She shrugged, the movement disrupting her carefully positioned shirt. "Depends on how bad things are with my sister, and if I can find any backgrounds that don't scream 'suburban family home.'" Her fingers traced the rim of the mug, leaving smudges of foundation. "My engagement drops thirty percent whenever I post anything that doesn't fit the aspirational city-girl aesthetic."

The brutal mathematics of her existence struck me anew—how she quantified her worth in likes and views, how each deviation from her established persona came with a measurable cost. I'd been doing something similar these past six months, I realized, measuring my healing from George in conquests and temporary pleasures rather than genuine connection.

. . .

HOURS LATER AND FILMING DONE, we sat with warm cups of tea, and we were just us again, Sam and Elara.

"What about you?" Sam asked, her tone shifting to something gentler. "Will you be okay while I'm gone? With... everything?" The vague gesture of her hand encompassed our shared history—my transformation after George, our nights out, the carefully reconstructed identity I'd built with her encouragement.

I sipped my tea to hide my expression. "Of course. Why wouldn't I be?"

She gave me a look that saw through the false confidence. "Because you've never done this alone before. The clubs, the men, the whole lifestyle—I've always been your backup."

The truth of it settled heavily between us. Sam had been my safety net, my guide, my witness. She'd held my hair back after tequila shots gave me the courage to approach my first post-George conquest. She'd helped me select outfits that transformed me from the "good girl" George had rejected to the woman who rejected attachment altogether. She'd waited up for my texts confirming I was safe, had listened to my stories of nameless men with encouraging whoops and high-fives.

Without her, what was I? Who was I?

"What if I can't do this without you?" The question slipped out before I could contain it, vulnerability cracking through the confident façade I'd worked so hard to perfect.

Sam paused her packing, looking at me directly for what felt like the first time all night. The influencer mask dropped completely, leaving just my friend, tired and worried and real.

"You don't need me anymore, Elara." Her voice was soft but certain. "You've become exactly who you wanted to be."

The statement hung between us, neither fully believing it. I'd become someone, certainly—a woman who took what she wanted without apology, who used men as they had used women for centuries, who refused to let emotional vulnerability threaten her carefully constructed independence. But was that really who I wanted to be? After last night at The Velvet Room, after Ryker, I wasn't sure anymore.

Before I could formulate a response, Sam's phone buzzed loudly against the dresser. She grabbed it, her shoulders tensing as she read the screen.

"My ride's three minutes away," she said, suddenly all efficient movement again. "Can you grab that last suitcase by the door? I need to finish in the bathroom."

And just like that, our moment of honesty was packed away like another outfit deemed unsuitable for public viewing. I nodded, gathering my empty mug and heading toward the living room where the final suitcase waited. Behind me, I heard Sam resume her influencer voice, recording one last sign-off for her followers.

"Love you, besties! Don't miss me too much while I'm on this amazing brand retreat! Can't wait to show you all the exclusive content coming your way!"

The contrast between her manufactured enthusiasm and the reality of where she was actually going—a hospital, worried family members, exhausted children—made my chest ache with a peculiar mixture of sadness and affection. Perhaps we were more alike than I'd realized, both of us hiding behind carefully constructed personas, both afraid of what might happen if the masks slipped completely.

The rideshare app showed the car circling our block, the little icon moving with ominous purpose. Sam stood by the door, transformed from the glossy influencer of an hour ago into someone almost unrecognizable—hair pulled back in a practical ponytail, face scrubbed clean of most makeup save for lingering mascara smudges, loose gray sweatpants and an oversized NYU hoodie replacing her camera-ready outfits. This was Sam stripped of SamThompStyle, a version her followers never saw, a version I rarely witnessed myself.

"They're here," she announced unnecessarily, her eyes fixed on the phone screen as if it might offer some reprieve, some last-minute excuse to stay. But the icon continued its approach, relentless as time itself.

I grabbed the handle of her last suitcase, the smallest of the three, though it still carried more belongings than I'd taken on my longest vacation. My fingers wrapped around the leather grip, holding tighter than necessary, as if through this connection I might somehow delay her departure.

"Did you remember your chargers?" I asked, falling back on practical concerns to mask the tightness in my throat.

"Triple-checked." Sam patted her crossbody bag, its practical nylon a stark contrast to the designer purses she showcased online. "And I've got all the content scheduled through next week, with notes for the weeks after. The engagement spreadsheet is shared with you, just in case..." She trailed off, leaving the possibility unnamed.

Just in case she needed to stay longer. Just in case her sister's condition worsened. Just in case the reality of family emergency refused to conform to her content calendar.

We stood in awkward silence, the weight of imminent separation pressing against us both. Through the door, I could hear the elevator ding down the hallway—someone arriving or departing, lives in motion while ours seemed momentarily suspended in this liminal space between together and apart.

"I've never done this alone," I admitted quietly, the words slipping out with unusual honesty. "Any of it."

It wasn't just the clubs, the men, the carefully constructed new Elara I'd become. It was existing without a witness to my transformation, without someone to validate that I was succeeding at my reinvention. Before Sam, it had been George whose attention had anchored me, whose approval had shaped my choices. I'd simply transferred that need from him to her, exchanging one form of dependency for another.

Sam's eyes softened, her hand reaching to squeeze my shoulder. "You're stronger than you think, Elara." Her voice carried a certainty I wished I could borrow, could wrap around myself like a protective cloak against the doubts already gathering at the edges of my thoughts. "You don't need me holding your hand anymore."

I nodded, not trusting my voice with a response. The suitcase between us seemed suddenly like a barricade, a physical manifestation of the distance about to separate us. I released the handle with reluctance, stepping back to allow her access to the door.

Sam reached for the knob but paused, her usual confident movements stilling. When she turned back to me, her expression held a vulnerability I rarely saw—the careful construction of SamThompStyle completely absent, leaving only Samantha Thompson, a woman with fears as ordinary and profound as anyone else's.

"Don't forget about me while I'm gone, okay?" she asked, her voice smaller than I'd ever heard it. Her fingers fidgeted with her nose ring, twisting it in a nervous gesture that betrayed how deeply the question mattered. "A month is a lifetime in social media. People move on so quickly."

The request revealed the core of her insecurity—the fear that her worth existed only in being seen, that without constant visibility she might simply disappear. I recognized the fear with uncomfortable clarity, having experienced my own version of it after George. Hadn't my entire transformation been driven by the terror of invisibility, of returning to the forgettable "good girl" he had so easily discarded?

"I'll call you every day," I promised, forcing my lips into a smile that felt too tight across my face. "Twice on weekends."

She laughed, the sound fragile but genuine. "You better. I want all the dirty details of whatever club adventures you get up to."

Neither of us acknowledged the unspoken question of whether there would be any adventures to report. Whether, without her encouragement, I would retreat back into safer patterns, abandon the boldness we'd cultivated together.

Her phone chimed again—the driver, waiting downstairs. The sound broke our momentary connection, pulling us back to the practical reality of departure. Sam straightened her shoulders, a shadow of her influencer posture returning as she gathered her composure.

"Okay, for real this time. I have to go." She pulled me into a hug, her arms wrapping around me with surprising strength. Against my ear, she whispered, "Be kind to yourself, Elara. Even when I'm not here to remind you."

Before I could respond, she released me, gathering her carry-on and pulling the suitcase over the threshold. I stood frozen in the doorway, watching as she moved down the hallway with determined steps, her usual runway strut replaced by the efficient pace of someone with a plane to catch.

At the elevator, she turned back one last time, raising her hand in a small wave that contained more emotion than any elaborate goodbye could have conveyed. Then the doors opened, she stepped inside, and she was gone.

I closed our apartment door with a definitive click that echoed in the sudden stillness. For a moment, I remained there, my palm flat against the cool surface, listening to the fading whir of the elevator carrying my friend away. Only when silence had completely settled did I step back, turning to face the apartment that suddenly seemed vast and emptier than its physical dimensions should allow.

Sam's presence lingered in the spaces she'd vacated—a forgotten scarf draped over a chair, the faint scent of her perfume hanging in the air, the wall of photos we'd accumulated over three years of friendship. But the vibrant energy she carried, the constant motion and chatter and plans that filled our shared space, had departed with her, leaving a stillness that felt almost oppressive in its completeness.

I moved through the rooms like a visitor in an unfamiliar house, noting the subtle but significant changes her packing had created. The bathroom counter, usually crowded with her extensive beauty collection, now held only my modest assortment of products, looking strangely inadequate in the expanded space. The living room, rearranged to accommodate her final content filming, seemed off-balance, furniture at odd angles, shadows falling in unfamiliar patterns.

In the kitchen, I found her favorite mug—the oversized ceramic one with "Main Character Energy" emblazoned across it in gold lettering—sitting upside down in the dish rack. Something about this ordinary object, this evidence of her last normal morning here, sent a surge of emotion through me that I hadn't been prepared for.

I sank onto the sofa, the leather cool against my bare legs. Without Sam's constant commentary, without her music playing or her phone chiming with notifications, I could hear the subtle sounds of the apartment itself—the hum of the refrigerator, the occasional creak of the heating system, the distant traffic filtering through closed windows. Sounds that had always existed but had been masked by the constant soundtrack of our shared life.

As I sat in this unfamiliar silence, a realization settled over me with uncomfortable clarity. I had escaped George's rejection by reinventing myself, but I'd done so with Sam as my constant validator, my witness, my safety net. I'd replaced dependency on his approval with dependency on hers, exchanging one form of external validation for another while convincing myself I'd become independent.

The hollow space inside me—the void that no amount of nameless encounters had filled, that even Ryker had only temporarily quieted—pulsed with renewed awareness. It wasn't just George-shaped anymore. It wasn't even Ryker-shaped. It was a space created by my own inability to exist without someone else's gaze defining me, anchoring me to myself.

As night settled around the apartment, wrapping the unfamiliar silence in deeper layers of solitude, I faced a truth I'd been avoiding since that day at the Bluebird Café: I had changed everything about myself except the one thing that mattered most—my need for someone else to make me real.

CHAPTER FOURTEEN
The Failed Night Out

I pushed through Obsidian's heavy door with deliberate force, as if physical momentum could propel me back into the woman I'd been before Ryker. The familiar wave of bass hit my chest, vibrating through my ribcage with a rhythm that should have felt comforting in its predictability. Three nights had passed since Sam's departure, three nights of empty rooms and conversations with myself, before I'd gathered the courage to venture out alone. My dress, black, tight, cut low enough to draw eyes but not desperate enough to seem eager, clung to my body like armor rather than invitation. Tonight would prove I needed neither Sam's validation nor Ryker's unsettling presence to be who I'd remade myself to be.

THE CLUB'S interior hadn't changed, same pulsing neon cutting through artificial fog, same overpriced drinks in crystal glasses, same beautiful people performing the same rituals of attraction. Only I seemed different, moving through the space with a hesitancy that felt foreign in my own skin. I scanned the VIP section reflexively, relief and disappointment tangling in my chest when I confirmed Ryker wasn't there. Of course, he wasn't. This coincidental meeting place wasn't his regular haunt any more than it was mine. I'd chosen Obsidian deliberately, a test of my immunity to the ghost of his presence, at least, that's what I told myself. If I were to be honest with myself, I had hoped to see him again.

I CLAIMED a spot at the bar with practiced ease, sliding onto a stool with a posture I'd perfected, back straight but not rigid, legs crossed at an angle that elongated them, one elbow resting lightly on the polished surface. The bartender approached, his eyes performing the quick assessment I'd grown accustomed to.

"WHISKEY, NEAT," I ordered, the familiar words feeling strangely hollow in my mouth. "Macallan 18."

HE NODDED WITH PROFESSIONAL EFFICIENCY, turning away to prepare my drink. I used the moment to survey the room through the mirror behind the bar, cataloging potential conquests with the detached calculation that had become second nature. A tall man in a tailored jacket caught my eye, his confident stance and carefully styled hair marking him as the type I'd usually target, successful enough to be interesting, attractive enough to be satisfying, self-absorbed enough to expect nothing beyond physical connection.

WHEN MY WHISKEY ARRIVED, I took a measured sip, letting the amber liquid burn a familiar path down my throat. The man in the jacket noticed my movement, his gaze lingering on the curve of my neck as I swallowed. I met his eyes in the mirror, offering the slight smile that had successfully baited dozens of men before him. He took the invitation as expected, detaching himself from his group to approach.

"THAT'S a serious drink for someone who looks like you," he said, sliding onto the stool beside me, his opening line as predictable as the tide.

I TILTED my head at the practiced angle that displayed my neck to advantage, lips curving into the smile that showed just enough teeth to suggest appetite without desperation. "I've never been particularly interested in meeting expectations."

THE WORDS EMERGED AUTOMATICALLY, the same script I'd performed countless times, but something in the delivery felt off, a pianist hitting all the right notes but missing the emotion behind the piece. The man responded as expected, leaning closer, his cologne, something expensive and forgettable, enveloping me in a cloud that felt suffocating rather than enticing.

OUR CONVERSATION PROCEEDED along familiar channels, his jokes slightly too loud, my laughter slightly too appreciative, his hand eventually finding its way to the small of my back in a touch that should have sent pleasant anticipation through me. Instead, I felt myself tensing beneath his fingers, the contact registering as an intrusion rather than a connection.

. . .

After fifteen minutes of increasingly strained interaction, I excused myself with a vague promise to find him later. His disappointment was evident but not concerning; dozens of other women in the club would respond to his attention exactly as expected. I was the variable that had changed, not him.

I moved toward the dance floor, determined to recalibrate. Perhaps conversation was the issue—too many opportunities to compare stilted exchanges with the unexpected depth I'd found with Ryker. Dancing required no words, just bodies responding to rhythm and proximity. I positioned myself near the edge of the writhing crowd, allowing the music to guide my movements in the patterns that had never failed to draw attention.

Sure enough, within minutes a new man materialized before me—younger than my usual targets, with the lean build of someone who spent serious time at the gym and knew exactly how good he looked in his fitted shirt. He moved with confidence, his body aligning with mine in a way that was technically perfect yet curiously empty of the charge I'd come to expect from such encounters.

I placed my hands on his shoulders, attempting to lose myself in the mechanical pleasure of attractive bodies in motion. My hips swayed, my back arched, my eyes locked with his in silent promise of possibilities beyond the dance floor. All the right movements, all the right signals—yet inside, a hollow space expanded with each passing minute, a sense of performing for an audience that included myself.

My jaw clenched with growing frustration, the muscles aching from maintaining a smile that didn't reach my eyes. When his hands slid lower than casual dancing warranted, I didn't feel the usual flicker of triumph at his predictable desire. Instead, I felt nothing but the increasing tempo of my own heartbeat, pounding with something closer to anxiety than anticipation.

After two songs, I stepped away, gesturing vaguely toward the bar to indicate my exit. The dancer shrugged, already turning toward other prospects as I retreated from the floor, my movements increasingly stiff, my confidence crumbling with each step.

At the opposite end of the bar, I ordered another whiskey, downing half of it in one swallow that burned more from desperation than appreciation. A third man approached— older, more polished, with the quiet confidence of serious money and the slightly loosened tie of someone unwinding from significant responsibilities.

"You look like someone with a story," he said, his opener more original than most, his eyes assessing me with genuine interest rather than mere appreciation.

This should have been perfect—exactly the type of man I would have selected before Ryker. Attractive without being obvious about it, successful without needing to announce it, interested without being desperate. Yet as I turned toward him with my practiced smile, my foot tapped an irregular rhythm against the barstool, betraying the disconnect between my external performance and internal discomfort.

"Everyone has a story," I replied, the words emerging flatter than intended. "Most aren't worth telling."

He raised an eyebrow, accepting the challenge in my tone. "I'd be willing to bet yours is."

Our conversation progressed in fits and starts, his questions thoughtful, my answers increasingly evasive. My fingers drummed against my glass, creating tiny ripples in the remaining whiskey. The noise of the club—the clink of ice in glasses, the hum of dozens of overlapping conversations, the thudding bass that vibrated through the floor—seemed to intensify with each passing minute, pressing against my skin like an unwelcome touch.

Perfume mingled with sweat, alcohol with expensive cologne, creating an olfactory assault that had once been the familiar backdrop to my hunting grounds but now felt overwhelming. Bodies pressed against each other on the dance floor, seeking connection through proximity, through rhythm, through the temporary surrender to shared movement. I watched them with growing alienation, as if observing a ritual from a culture I no longer belonged to.

The businessman continued speaking, unaware of my internal fracturing. I nodded at appropriate intervals, smiled when expected, performed all the external signs of interest while inside, a voice grew louder with each passing second: This isn't working. I'm not working. Something fundamental had shifted inside me, rendering my carefully crafted persona as ill-fitting as clothes borrowed from a stranger.

By the time I finished my second whiskey, the weight of my failure sat heavy in my stomach. Three attempts, three men who would have been perfect conquests a week ago, and not a flicker of the satisfaction I'd once found in these exchanges. My shoulders, once thrown back in deliberate display, now curved inward slightly. My eyes, once scanning the room with predatory focus, now darted toward the exit with increasing frequency.

The realization I'd been avoiding since walking through Obsidian's door settled with undeniable weight: I couldn't go back to being the woman I'd been before Ryker. Whatever had shifted during our night together—whatever walls had crumbled, whatever hollow spaces had been momentarily filled—had changed me in ways I couldn't simply reverse through force of will or practiced seduction.

I was failing at being the very person I'd worked so hard to become, and the worst part was that I couldn't tell if this was regression or growth.

I retreated to the darkest corner of the bar, claiming a high-top table partially hidden by a structural column. The shadows felt appropriate—a physical manifestation of my fading presence in a space where I'd once commanded attention. I signaled for another whiskey, my third of the night, no longer caring about maintaining the precise level of intoxication that enhanced confidence without compromising control. My practiced calculations had failed me tonight; perhaps surrendering to the burn of good scotch would succeed where strategy had not.

From my secluded vantage point, I watched the rituals of attraction play out across the club with the detached fascination of an anthropologist studying a foreign culture. Women who could have been mirror images of my pre-Ryker self moved through the space with effortless confidence— laughing at precisely the right moments, touching arms with calculated casualness, leaning forward to create the perfect angle of invitation. And men responded exactly as programmed, their desire as predictable as gravity.

Across the bar, a woman with copper hair twisted into an elaborate knot tilted her head back in practiced delight at something her companion said, exposing the elegant line of her throat. His eyes followed the movement as expected, his body leaning imperceptibly closer, pulled by the silent promise of her posture. I could read the entire exchange from fifty feet away—the subtle shifts in proximity, the mirrored body language, the gradual elimination of space between them that would ultimately lead to his apartment or hers, to the temporary connection of bodies without the complication of genuine intimacy.

It was a dance I'd perfected, steps I'd executed flawlessly night after night. Until now. Until Ryker had somehow corrupted the program, introduced a variable that rendered the equation unsolvable.

I took another sip of whiskey, the expensive liquid wasted on taste buds numbed by repetition. What had changed? The men were the same—attracted to confidence, responsive to suggestion, eager for uncomplicated pleasure. The club was the same—bass pulsing through bodies like a second heartbeat, lighting designed to flatter and conceal in equal measure, alcohol loosening inhibitions and judgment. Even my appearance was unchanged—the dress that had led to countless successful conquests, the makeup applied with surgical precision, the hair styled to invite fingers to test its softness.

Only I was different. Something inside me had shifted during that night with Ryker, some fundamental calibration altered by his insistence that I remain present, that I feel rather than simply perform. The hollow space I'd been trying to fill with nameless encounters seemed to have expanded rather than contracted, grown more demanding rather than satiated.

My shoulders hunched slightly inward, a physical manifestation of the contraction happening inside me. The confident mask I'd worn for six months felt like it was slipping, revealing glimpses of the vulnerable woman beneath—the one I'd buried after George, the one who still flinched at the memory of rejection, the one who craved genuine connection despite all evidence of its dangers.

Around me, the club continued its choreographed chaos—beautiful people finding beautiful distractions, everyone playing parts they'd rehearsed to perfection. Once, I had found comfort in this predictability, in knowing exactly how each interaction would unfold, in controlling every aspect of physical connection while maintaining emotional distance. Now, the performance felt hollow, a substitute for something I hadn't known I was missing until Ryker had offered a glimpse of its possibility.

My eyes darted toward the exit with increasing frequency, measuring the distance to escape, calculating the steps required to remove myself from this failed experiment in reclaiming my pre-Ryker confidence. My fingers tapped an irregular rhythm against the sticky surface of the table, betraying the anxiety I was failing to contain. The weight of my inadequacy pressed against my chest, making each breath shallower than the last.

This wasn't working. I wasn't working. Whatever version of myself I'd been building these past six months seemed to have collapsed under the weight of one night with a man who had somehow seen through all my carefully constructed layers.

I drained the last of my whiskey, the burn insufficient to cauterize the raw edges exposed by tonight's failure. Enough. Time to retreat, to regroup, to figure out what version of Elara emerged from the wreckage of my carefully constructed identity. I gathered my clutch, fingers clumsy with the unfamiliar weight of defeat.

As I prepared to leave a shift in the air behind me registered before any conscious recognition occurred, a subtle change in temperature, in pressure, in the very molecules surrounding my body. My pulse accelerated with primitive recognition, skin prickling with awareness before my mind could process the cause. A scent cut through the club's chaotic mixture of perfume and sweat and alcohol, sandalwood and something darker, earthier, achingly familiar.

WARM BREATH TICKLED the sensitive skin below my ear, raising goosebumps that raced down my neck and across my shoulders. The bass seemed to recede, the crowd noise fading to background static as my senses narrowed to the heat of the body behind me, close enough to feel but not quite touching.

"I was hoping I would find you here," Ryker's voice, lower than I remembered, rougher at the edges, vibrated through the minuscule space between us. "Let me take you to my car, bend you over the bonnet until you scream yourself hoarse."

The explicit promise in his words, so different from the measured conversation of our first meeting, yet delivered with the same quiet confidence, sent liquid heat pooling low in my abdomen. My breath caught, lungs suddenly forgetting their automatic function, as my body responded to his presence with embarrassing eagerness. "Breathe, Elara," he whispered closer, lips brushing my skin. Every nerve ending seemed to awaken at once, skin hypersensitive to the touch of him behind me.

For endless seconds, I remained frozen, caught between the primal urge to lean back into his heat and the defensive instinct to maintain the independence I'd fought so hard to establish. The club's chaos receded completely, my awareness contracting to this single moment, this proximity that somehow felt more intimate than the countless bodies that had been inside mine these past six months.

When I finally turned to face him, the movement felt like passing through water, slow, deliberate, requiring more effort than physics should demand. Ryker stood closer than I'd expected, his presence filling my visual field with disorienting immediacy. He looked exactly as memory had preserved him, the strong line of his jaw softened by evening stubble, the subtle grey at his temples, the green eyes that watched me with that unsettling mixture of desire and assessment.

But something was different too—a tension in his shoulders that hadn't been there at Obsidian or in his apartment, a tightness around his mouth that suggested my absence had affected him in ways I hadn't anticipated. The realization sent a confusing mixture of triumph and vulnerability coursing through me.

"Ryker," I managed, his name emerging with more breath than voice, betraying the effect his sudden appearance had on my carefully maintained composure.

His eyes traveled over my face with deliberate slowness, cataloging changes I wasn't aware of making. "Elara." My name in his mouth sounded like both question and answer, challenge and surrender.

We stood suspended in that moment, the air between us charged with possibilities—his explicit offer hanging between us, my body's eager response warring with my mind's determination to protect the fragile independence I'd constructed. Around us, the club continued its rhythmic pulse, bodies moving in practiced patterns of seduction and surrender, oblivious to the more complex negotiation happening in our small corner of shadow.

I had come to Obsidian to prove I didn't need him, that I could reclaim the confident seductress who required nothing beyond physical satisfaction. Instead, I found myself trembling at the mere proximity of the one man who had somehow slipped past all my carefully constructed defenses, torn between relief at his presence and resentment at my body's betrayal of all my hard-won independence.

CHAPTER FIFTEEN
The Animal Unleashed

H is words hung between us, explicit and demanding, sending a rush of heat through my body. I should have walked away, should have proven to myself that I didn't need him, that I could maintain the careful distance I'd established with all men since George. I knew it wasn't really true. So instead, I heard myself whisper, "Yes," the single syllable containing surrender I hadn't intended to offer when I first met him, but found myself wanting to offer now.

RYKER'S EYES darkened at my response, pupils expanding until only a thin ring of green remained. Without another word, his fingers circled my wrist, not gripping, just resting there with quiet possession that somehow felt more commanding than force would have. He turned and moved toward the exit, and I followed as if tethered, my legs obeying a directive my mind was still questioning.

THE NIGHT AIR struck my heated skin with shocking coolness as we emerged from Obsidian's throbbing interior. Stars punctured the darkness overhead, distant and indifferent to the turmoil inside me, Ryker guided me toward a concrete structure across the street, his pace unhurried yet purposeful, as if my compliance were a foregone conclusion.

"Second level," he said, his voice pitched low enough that I had to lean closer to hear him, the proximity sending another wave of awareness through my already sensitized nerves.

The parking garage loomed before us, its entrance gaping dark and hungry. Inside, fluorescent lights buzzed at irregular intervals, casting sickly pools of illumination that failed to reach the deepest corners. Our footsteps echoed against concrete, creating a percussion that matched my accelerating heartbeat. Each step carried me further from the carefully constructed identity I'd cultivated for six months, from the woman who took but never gave, who controlled every encounter with mechanical precision.

I stole glances at Ryker's profile as we ascended the ramp, the strong line of his jaw, the subtle tension at the corner of his mouth, the focused intent in his gaze. Nothing about him resembled the eager, easily manipulated men I'd selected since George. Nothing about this encounter followed the script I'd perfected.

"Having second thoughts?" he asked without looking at me, somehow sensing my internal struggle.

. . .

"No," I replied too quickly, the denial feeling hollow even to my own ears.

His lips curved into a smile that held knowledge rather than amusement. "Liar."

The second level was darker than the first; half the lights either burned out or were never installed. Shadows pooled in concrete corners like spilled ink, making the space feel both vast and confining. Ryker led me toward a sleek vehicle at the far end, German engineering in matte black, its lines cutting through the darkness with quiet aggression.

Before I could register which model it was, he turned suddenly, backing me against the hood with unexpected speed. His mouth claimed mine with none of the careful exploration of our previous kisses. This was possession, pure and uncompromising, his tongue demanding entrance, I was helpless to deny. I tasted whiskey and barely leashed hunger, my hands rising to grasp his shoulders for balance as much as desire.

The cold metal of the hood pressed against the backs of my thighs, a shocking contrast to the heat of Ryker's body against my front. His hands moved from my waist to my hips, fingers digging into flesh with calculated pressure that would leave marks.

. . .

He broke the kiss abruptly, his breathing ragged against my neck. "Turn around," he commanded, the words vibrating against my skin.

I hesitated for a fraction of a second, some last vestige of my carefully cultivated independence resisting the directive. His eyes met mine, holding a question beneath the desire, offering choice even in his demand. That paradox, control offered rather than taken, crumbled my final resistance. I turned, bracing my palms against the cool metal of the hood, my spine curving in unconscious invitation.

Ryker's hands skimmed down my sides, gathering the hem of my dress and drawing it upward with deliberate slowness until the fabric bunched around my waist. The garage air caressed newly exposed skin, raising goosebumps that had nothing to do with temperature. I heard him sink to his knees behind me, felt his breath against the sensitive skin of my inner thighs moments before his teeth grazed the same spot.

I gasped, the sharp edge of almost-pain sending sparks of pleasure radiating outward. His mouth moved higher, alternating between gentle kisses and sudden nips that made my legs tremble. Each point of contact seemed precise and designed to maximize response, to build tension without release.

When his fingers hooked the edges of my underwear, drawing the delicate fabric down my legs with torturous patience, I bit my lip to keep from begging him to hurry. The concrete floor would have bruised his knees, but he seemed unaware of any discomfort as he continued his careful attention to my thighs, his tongue tracing patterns that approached but never quite reached where I most wanted him.

Just as I was about to break and plead for more, he rose in one fluid movement, his body pressed against my back, one hand sliding around to grip my throat. The pressure was precise, firm enough to assert control without restricting breathing, his thumb resting against my pulse point where he could feel each accelerated beat.

"Head back," he murmured, exerting gentle pressure until I complied, my neck arching, exposing my vulnerable point to his hold.

His free hand slid around my hip, fingers tracing the curve of my stomach before dipping lower with unerring accuracy. I was already embarrassingly wet, my body betraying how completely his presence affected me despite all my attempts at emotional distance.

"You're so fucking wet," he growled against my ear, the explicit observation somehow more intimate than the touch itself. "Is this what you've been thinking about since that night? My fingers inside you, my cock filling you?"

· · ·

I WANTED TO DENY IT, to maintain some illusion that he was just another conquest, another temporary distraction from the hollow space inside me. But my body's response made lies impossible, my hips pushing against his hand in a silent plea for more pressure, more friction, more of him.

HE WITHDREW SUDDENLY, and I nearly whimpered at the loss until I heard the metallic slide of his belt buckle, the quiet rasp of his zipper. His hand returned to my throat, tilting my head back further until it rested against his shoulder, his lips brushing my ear.

"TELL ME YOU WANT THIS," he demanded, his voice rough with restraint.

"I WANT THIS," I whispered, the admission costing more than just pride. "I want you."

THE BLUNT PRESSURE of him against my entrance was my only warning before he thrust forward, filling me completely in one powerful stroke that forced a cry from my throat. My fingers scrambled against the hood's slick surface, seeking purchase as he established a rhythm that left no room for pretense or performance.

EACH THRUST DROVE me against the unyielding metal, the impact traveling through my body to collide with the next incoming wave. The angle was perfect, maddening, each stroke

277

hitting places inside me that sent white-hot pleasure spiraling outward. His grip on my throat tightened fractionally, the edge of danger adding another layer to the building tension.

My carefully constructed walls crumbled under the assault of physical sensation too intense to process. I heard myself making sounds I'd never made with other men, raw and honest and vulnerable in ways I'd never even known were possible.

Ryker's rhythm faltered slightly, his breathing harsh against my ear. "Come for me," he commanded, his free hand circling to find the exact spot that would push me over the edge. "Now, Elara."

My body obeyed before my mind could process the instruction, pleasure crashing through me with such force that my vision narrowed to pinpricks of light against darkness. I heard myself cry out his name, the sound echoing against concrete walls as my inner muscles clenched around him in rhythmic pulses. He followed moments later, his release coinciding with a final, deep thrust that pinned me against the car, his groan vibrating through both our bodies.

For several heartbeats, we remained locked together, the only sound our uneven breathing and the distant hum of garage ventilation. His hand released my throat, moving to brush damp hair from my neck with unexpected tenderness that contrasted sharply with the fierce claiming of moments before.

. . .

WHEN HE FINALLY WITHDREW, I felt suddenly unmoored, adrift without his solid presence anchoring me. Before I could gather myself, his hands were straightening my dress, his movements efficient but not rushed.

"GET IN," he said, opening the passenger door with the casual authority that had drawn me to him that first night. "We're going to my place."

IT WASN'T a question or an invitation, just a statement of fact that assumed my compliance. Previously, I would have bristled at such presumption. Tonight, with my body still trembling from the most intense climax I'd experienced, I slid into the leather seat without protest, my usual need for control temporarily silenced by the promise of more to come.

THE RIDE to Ryker's apartment passed in charged silence, my body still humming with aftershocks, my mind struggling to reconcile the woman who'd just surrendered against a car hood with the carefully constructed identity I'd maintained since George. I pressed my thighs together, the slight pressure sending renewed pulses of pleasure through my sensitized nerves. Beside me, Ryker drove with one hand on the wheel, the other resting possessively on my knee, his thumb tracing small circles against my skin, a gesture too intimate for the casual encounters I'd cultivated, too deliberate to dismiss as meaningless.

. . .

WHEN WE ARRIVED at his building, the doorman's carefully neutral expression suggested he'd seen this scenario before. The thought of being just another in a potential line of conquests sent an unexpected surge of jealousy through me, followed immediately by irritation at my own reaction. Wasn't that exactly what I'd been doing for months? Taking men for a night and discarding them by morning?

THE ELEVATOR ASCENDED with the same silent efficiency I remembered from our first night together, but the energy between us had shifted, raw and urgent where before there had been measured exploration. Ryker stood slightly behind me. I felt the heat from his body; it was like our bodies were sending small electric pulses between us. The anticipation was its own form of foreplay, my skin prickling with awareness of what was to come.

WHEN THE DOORS opened to his penthouse floor, he guided me forward with a hand at the small of my back, the pressure firmer than before, more directive than suggestive. Inside his apartment, the familiar scent of sandalwood greeted me, his cologne, his essence, the smell that had lingered on my skin for days after our first encounter. It mingled now with the jasmine notes of my own perfume, creating something new and complicated between us.

"BEDROOM," he said, the single word carrying more command than request.

. . .

I SHOULD HAVE BRISTLED at the tone, should have reasserted the control I'd fought so hard to maintain with every other man. Instead, I felt a treacherous heat curl through my abdomen, my body responding to his authority with an eagerness my mind still resisted.

THE BEDROOM WAS EXACTLY as I remembered: minimalist luxury with a massive bed as its focal point, the sheets still in midnight blue, the city lights creating patterns through partially opened blinds. Before I could take another step, Ryker moved with unexpected speed, turning me and backing me against the nearest wall, his hands capturing my wrists and pinning them above my head in one fluid motion.

HIS MOUTH FOUND mine with none of the gentle exploration of our first night. This was claiming, pure and uncompromising, his tongue demanding entrance, I was helpless to deny. I tasted whiskey and something darker, more primal, the essence of him beneath the civilized exterior. My body arched toward his despite my mind's protest, seeking contact, friction, the pressure I'd been craving since walking away from his apartment days ago.

"YOU DISAPPEARED," he growled against my mouth, the accusation unexpected in its vulnerability. "No message, no call."

"I DON'T DO FOLLOW-UPS," I gasped as his teeth scraped against my lower lip, the slight pain sending sparks of pleasure radiating outward. "You knew what this was."

His laugh held no humor, just acknowledgment of the challenge. "Did I?" One hand maintained its grip on my wrists while the other descended to the neckline of my dress, fingers hooking into the fabric with deliberate intent. "Did you?"

Before I could formulate a response, he pulled sharply, the expensive material giving way with a sound that echoed my fragmenting control. Cool air rushed against newly exposed skin, raising goosebumps that had nothing to do with the temperature and everything to do with the hunger in his eyes as they raked over me.

Not to be outdone, I freed one hand from his grip and reached for his shirt, buttons scattering across the hardwood as I tore the fabric open with matching urgency. The solid planes of his chest came into view, the defined muscles I remembered tracing with fingers and tongue during our first night. My palm pressed against his heart, feeling its accelerated rhythm that belied his outward control.

His response was immediate and uncompromising. Fingers tangled in my hair, gripping at the roots with calculated pressure that walked the exquisite line between pleasure and pain. He used this hold to tilt my head back, exposing my throat to the assault of his mouth, teeth, and tongue, marking territory with a possessiveness that should have triggered resistance but sent liquid heat pooling between my thighs.

"You're fighting this," he murmured against my collarbone, his free hand working the clasp of my strapless bodysuit. "Fighting me, fighting yourself."

The garment gave way, joining my ruined dress on the floor. I stood before him in nothing but thigh-high stockings and heels, the physical exposure a mirror to the emotional vulnerability I was desperately trying to contain. His eyes moved over me with deliberate appreciation, taking inventory of what he'd claimed once before and clearly intended to claim again.

"On the bed," he directed, releasing my hair but maintaining contact with a hand at the nape of my neck, guiding rather than forcing.

The Old Elara stirred within me, bristling at the command. "Make me." I challenged, chin lifting in defiance that felt simultaneously genuine and performative.

His smile held no malice, just recognition of the gauntlet thrown. "With pleasure."

The hand at my neck tightened, fingers twisting in my hair with renewed purpose as he guided me—not quite dragging but close—toward the massive bed. My heels caught on the rug, nearly sending me stumbling, but his grip was sure, his control absolute. When my legs hit the edge of the mattress, he pushed me forward with firm pressure, my hands breaking my fall against midnight blue sheets that still carried his scent.

Before I could push myself up, his weight settled behind me, one knee parting my thighs with insistent pressure. As he rolled me onto my back, I heard the whisper of fabric, felt something cool and smooth against my wrist—silk, I realized, as he bound first one hand and then the other to the posts of his headboard. The restraints were secure but not painful, snug enough to limit movement while allowing enough slack to prevent discomfort.

"What are you doing?" I asked, my voice betraying more breathlessness than alarm.

His hands skimmed down my sides, coming to rest at my hips. "Taking away your excuses," he replied, the simple explanation cutting through my practiced defenses. "Making it impossible for you to pretend this is just another conquest."

The truth of it silenced whatever protest I might have made. With other men, I maintained control even in supposed surrender, dictating the pace and depth of pleasure while keeping emotional distance. Ryker understood this strategy too well, recognized it perhaps from his own experience. By binding my hands, he forced me to accept pleasure rather than orchestrate it—to feel rather than perform.

His weight shifted as he moved down my body, his mouth tracing a path along my breast bone and stomach, that made me shiver with anticipation. When he reached between my legs, his hands gripped my hips, adjusting my position until I was displayed before him in a way that left no room for modesty or pretense.

The first touch of his mouth against my inner thigh made me jerk against the restraints, the sensation both expected and shocking in its intensity. His technique alternated between gentleness and sudden, sharp bites that pulled gasps from my throat. Each nip was immediately soothed by the warm stroke of his tongue, the contrast building a tension that had me straining against the silk ties.

"Is this what you came back for?" he asked, his breath hot against sensitive skin. "This physical release you could get from anyone?"

"Yes," I lied, the denial feeling hollow even to my own ears.

His laugh held no humor, just recognition of the falsehood. "Then why are you here, Elara? Why not one of your usual conquests? Why me?"

The questions struck too close to truths I wasn't ready to acknowledge, vulnerabilities I'd been hiding even from myself. Instead of answering, I raised my hips against him, seeking contact that might distract us both from dangerous emotional territory.

"Beg for it," he commanded, his hands stilling my movements with firm pressure at my hips. "Tell me what you want —what you really want."

The demand stripped away pretense, forced honesty I'd avoided in all my encounters since George. My throat tightened around words I couldn't bring myself to say, pride warring with desperate need for completion.

"Make me," I challenged again, the defiance in my tone undermined by the trembling of my thighs, the obvious evidence of arousal I couldn't conceal in this position.

I felt him shift, the blunt pressure of him against my entrance the only warning before he thrust forward, filling me completely in one powerful stroke that forced a cry from my throat. My hands clenched into fists above the restraints, nails digging into palms as pleasure so intense it bordered on pain radiated outward from where our bodies joined.

"Is this what you needed?" he growled, establishing a rhythm that left no room for performance or calculation. "To be taken? To surrender control just for tonight?"

Each thrust drove me upward, the headboard creaking in protest against the force of our movements. I heard myself making sounds I'd never made with other men—raw, honest, stripped of artifice. My practiced seductress persona crumbled under the assault of sensation too intense to process, leaving only the vulnerable woman beneath, the one I'd been hiding since that day at the Bluebird Café.

"Say my name," Ryker demanded, his voice rough with exertion and something darker, more possessive. "Say it."

"Ryker," I gasped, the syllables broken by the impact of his body against mine. "Ryker, please..."

The plea slipped out unbidden, genuine in a way I hadn't allowed myself to be in six months of calculated encounters. His rhythm faltered briefly at the naked honesty in my voice, then resumed with renewed intensity, as if determined to break through any remaining barriers between us.

My release built with frightening speed, muscles tensing in anticipation of pleasure I knew would be both salvation and destruction. With Ryker, orgasm wasn't just physical relief but emotional exposure—a moment of complete vulnerability I both craved and feared.

The world narrowed to sensation—the silk restraints against my wrists, the pressure of Ryker's body driving into mine, the approaching wave of pleasure threatening to sweep away the carefully constructed walls I'd built since George. I fought it even as I craved it, straining against the bindings not to escape but to ground myself against the overwhelming intensity. Just as the first tremors of release began to ripple through me, Ryker's movements stilled abruptly. His hands released my hips, moving instead to the ties at my wrists, freeing me with deft efficiency that suggested this wasn't improvised.

Before I could protest the interruption, he flipped me onto my stomach with surprising strength, my newly freed arms barely breaking my fall against the mattress. His weight settled over me, one hand tangling in my hair to turn my face sideways against the pillow, the other gripping my hip to lift me slightly. When he entered me again, the angle was deeper, more consuming, forcing a sound from my throat that I barely recognized as my own.

"I want to feel you come apart," he growled against my ear, his chest pressed against my back, surrounding me completely. "No more holding back, Elara."

His thrusts increased in both pace and force, driving me against the headboard with each forward movement. The wood struck the wall with rhythmic insistence, creating a percussion that punctuated my increasingly desperate sounds. I buried my face in the pillow, trying to muffle the evidence of how completely he was undoing me, how thoroughly he was dismantling the control I'd maintained through dozens of emotionless encounters.

The pillow absorbed my cries as pleasure built beyond anything I'd experienced with my careful conquests. Those men had been instruments I'd played for my own satisfaction, their bodies merely tools to temporarily fill the hollow space inside me. Ryker was something else entirely—a force I couldn't direct or control, a connection that threatened the very foundations of the identity I'd constructed since George.

My hands gripped the sheets with desperate strength, searching for anchor against the tide of sensation threatening to sweep me away. Just as I approached the edge of release, Ryker's hand tightened in my hair, pulling my head back from the pillow with calculated pressure that walked the exquisite line between pleasure and pain.

"No," he commanded, his voice rough with exertion and

something darker, more possessive. "I want to hear you. Every sound, every breath."

With my face no longer buried against the pillow, the sounds I'd been trying to contain escaped freely—raw, honest vocalizations that echoed against the walls of his bedroom. Each thrust seemed deliberately calculated to draw another cry from my throat, to force another surrender from a body that remembered him even as my mind tried to maintain distance.

"Look," he demanded, using his grip on my hair to turn my head toward the wall of windows where our reflection was visible in the darkened glass. "Look at what you do to me."

The image reflected back at us was primal and unrecognizable—my hair wild around my face, lips swollen from his kisses, eyes wide and vulnerable in a way I never allowed with other men. Behind me, Ryker moved with relentless purpose, his usual composure fractured by desire that seemed equal parts physical and possessive. The sight of us together—not just bodies aligned but somehow connected beyond the purely physical—sent a fresh wave of heat through me.

"You feel it too," he said, the words more statement than question. "This isn't like the others. Not for you, not for me."

The truth of it pushed me over the edge I'd been desperately clinging to. Release crashed through me with devastating force, muscles clenching around him in rhythmic pulses that drew a groan from deep in his chest. He followed moments later, his body tensing against mine, his arms tightening around my waist as if afraid I might somehow slip away at the moment of greatest connection.

For several heartbeats afterward, we remained locked together, breathing synchronized in the aftermath of shared pleasure. His weight should have felt oppressive, but instead provided a strange comfort—an anchor in the storm of sensation and emotion that had swept away my carefully maintained facades.

When he finally rolled to the side, taking me with him so that we lay facing each other, I felt exposed in ways that transcended physical nakedness. His eyes studied my face with the same intensity I remembered from our first night together, searching for something beyond the practiced expressions I'd perfected with other men.

"You're thinking too much," he murmured, one hand rising to brush hair from my face with unexpected tenderness.

I looked away, unable to maintain eye contact that felt more intimate than the joining of our bodies had been. My gaze fell instead to the marks his mouth had left across my collarbone, my breasts, my inner thighs—evidence I couldn't deny of passion that had transcended the controlled encounters I'd cultivated since George.

"I should go," I said, the words automatic, a defense mechanism against the vulnerability expanding beneath my ribs.

Ryker's hand stilled against my cheek, his expression shifting from post-coital satisfaction to something more guarded. "Running again?"

The quiet accusation struck deeper than it should have, piercing through the emotional armor I'd been crafting for six months. "I don't stay over," I reminded him, echoing words I'd said during our first night together. "It's one of my rules."

"Your rules," he repeated, the phrase carrying a weight of judgment I hadn't expected. "The ones that keep you safe? Or the ones that keep you lonely?"

I pulled away from his touch, rolling to the edge of the bed and scanning the floor for my ruined clothes. My dress hung in tatters from where he'd torn it earlier, my bodysuit similarly destroyed in our mutual urgency. Panic fluttered beneath my ribs at the thought of having nothing to wear, of being literally as well as figuratively exposed.

As if reading my thoughts, Ryker rose from the bed with fluid grace, moving to his closet and returning with a simple black t-shirt. "Here," he said, offering it without commentary on the state of my own clothing.

I took it with reluctant gratitude, pulling the soft cotton over my head. It fell to mid-thigh, the fabric carrying his scent —sandalwood and clean sweat and something uniquely him that I'd been trying to forget since our first encounter. The intimacy of wearing his clothes felt more dangerous than the sex we'd just shared, more revealing than physical nakedness.

"I still need to go," I insisted, gathering the tattered remains of my dress and underwear, shoving them into my small clutch with movements that betrayed more agitation than I wanted to reveal.

Ryker watched from the bed, making no move to stop me physically, but his eyes held a challenge I found difficult to meet. "Stay," he said simply, the word containing neither plea nor command, just quiet certainty that I was making a mistake.

I busied myself with locating my shoes, using the search as excuse to avoid his gaze. The heels I'd worn with such confidence into Obsidian now seemed like props from a performance I could no longer maintain. I slipped them on anyway, needing their familiar height to reestablish some sense of the woman I'd been before Ryker had once again dismantled my carefully constructed persona.

"Elara," he said, my name in his mouth carrying a weight that made me pause at the bedroom doorway. "What are you so afraid of?"

The question hung between us, penetrating deeper than it had any right to. What was I afraid of? Rejection, certainly— the crushing blow George had delivered that had catalyzed my transformation. But something else too, something more terrifying: the possibility that with Ryker, I might want more than physical satisfaction, might crave connection I'd convinced myself I no longer needed.

"Goodbye, Ryker," I said instead of answering, the words feeling inadequate even as they left my mouth.

I moved through his apartment with quickening steps, past the living room where we'd shared coffee that first morning, past the kitchen where he'd prepared it with thoughtful attention to my preferences. Each space held memories of moments where he'd seen past my carefully constructed facade, where he'd demanded presence rather than performance.

At the front door, I paused despite myself, catching my reflection in the decorative mirror hung nearby. The woman who stared back was barely recognizable—hair tangled from Ryker's grip, lips swollen from his kisses, makeup smudged beyond repair. But it was the eyes that stopped me—wide and vulnerable in a way I hadn't allowed myself to be since that day at the Bluebird Café.

I looked like a woman who'd been thoroughly claimed, not just physically but somehow deeper. The realization sent a fresh wave of panic through me, propelling me through the door and into the hallway before I could reconsider.

The elevator arrived with painful slowness, each second stretching as I imagined Ryker following, imagined having to face those perceptive eyes that saw too much, that demanded honesty I wasn't prepared to give. When the doors finally opened, I stepped inside with relief that turned quickly to a strange hollowness as they closed behind me, sealing me away from the man who had once again disturbed the careful equilibrium of my existence.

As the elevator descended, I pressed my thighs together, the slight pressure sending renewed pulses of pleasure through sensitized nerves. My body still hummed with awareness, with the aftershocks of release that had been as emotional as physical. Beneath Ryker's t-shirt, my skin bore evidence of his possession—marks I would see in the mirror tomorrow, reminders I couldn't simply dismiss as I had with other men.

The hollow space inside me—the void I'd been trying to fill with nameless encounters since George's rejection—felt different now. Not filled, exactly, but somehow altered, its edges less jagged, its emptiness less absolute. The realization was both comforting and terrifying, suggesting a healing I hadn't sought and wasn't sure I wanted—not if it meant vulnerability, not if it meant risking the devastation I'd experienced once before.

As the elevator reached the ground floor, I straightened my shoulders, attempting to reclaim some semblance of the confident woman who had walked into Obsidian hours earlier. But the mask felt ill-fitting now, the performance unconvincing even to myself. Ryker had seen through it, had demanded the authentic woman beneath, had touched places inside me I'd thought safely buried.

And despite the panic driving me from his apartment, despite the fear propelling me toward the building's exit, a treacherous part of me wondered when—not if—I would find myself drawn back to the man who made me feel too much, who made me remember what it was to be fully present in my own life, my own pleasure, my own pain.

CHAPTER SIXTEEN
The Gentle Queen

I stood frozen in the lobby of Ryker's building, my hand on the glass door that would return me to the night, to my carefully constructed life of emotional distance and physical satisfaction without complication. My body ached pleasantly beneath his borrowed t-shirt, my skin marked with evidence of his possession, my mind still spinning from the connection. I'd felt upstairs, a connection I'd been running from since our first night together. The doorman kept his eyes carefully averted, practiced in the art of not seeing the obvious: a woman fleeing a man's apartment in his clothes, disheveled and unsteady, caught between escape and return.

THE COOL GLASS beneath my palm offered no answers, no direction. Outside, the city continued its nighttime pulse, headlights tracing patterns across the darkened street, late-night pedestrians hurrying past with collars turned up against the chill, the distant wail of a siren marking someone else's emergency. Inside me, a similar chaos reigned, the practiced detachment I'd cultivated since George warring with the undeniable pull I felt toward the man I'd just left.

MY THIGHS PRESSED TOGETHER, the slight movement sending renewed awareness through nerve endings still sensitized from his touch. The marks he'd left throbbed gently beneath his shirt, badges of possession I should have resented but instead found myself touching through the thin cotton, physical reminders that what had happened between us transcended the carefully controlled encounters I usually orchestrated.

"IS EVERYTHING ALRIGHT MISS?" The doorman's voice startled me from my reverie, his tone professional but tinged with genuine concern.

"FINE," I managed, the single syllable emerging breathier than intended. "Just...deciding."

HE NODDED ONCE, returning to his studied neutrality, but his question lingered in the air between us. Was everything alright? Nothing had been "alright" since that first night with Ryker, since coffee in morning light, since the weight of a key in my palm, since a forehead kiss that had somehow felt more intimate than the joining of our bodies.

MY HAND REMAINED frozen on the door, unable to push it open, unable to commit to the exit I'd been so determined to make minutes earlier. What was I doing? This wasn't me, the woman who never looks back, who leaves before sunrise, who maintains control through careful distance. Yet here I stood, hesitating like the pre-George Elara who had sought connection rather than conquest.

THE SOFT DING of the elevator behind me registered a moment before the subtle shift in air pressure, the scent reaching me before I fully processed the sound of footsteps crossing marble.

I TURNED, knowing before my eyes confirmed it who would be standing there.

RYKER MOVED toward me with that same deliberate grace I'd found so unsettling from the beginning, a man who never rushed yet never hesitated, who moved through the world with quiet certainty that others would adjust to accomodate him. He wore only the sweatpants he'd pulled on after our encounter, chest bare and hair disheveled from where my fingers had gripped it minutes earlier. The elevator doors closed behind him with a quiet whisper, sealing us in the moment of confrontation neither of us had planned.

"ELARA." My name in his mouth carried the same weight it always did, both question and answer, both recognition and claim.

I SAID NOTHING, caught between the instinct to flee and the treacherous desire to stay. The borrowed t-shirt suddenly felt inadequate protection against his gaze, which traveled over me with deliberate thoroughness, taking inventory of what he'd claimed and what I was attempting to reclaim through escape.

He closed the distance between us with three measured steps, stopping close enough that I could feel the heat radiating from his skin. The restraint in his posture spoke of careful calculation, giving me space to retreat if I chose, but making it clear he wanted me to stay.

"I couldn't let you just leave again," he said, the words simple but weighted with implications neither of us had acknowledged aloud.

Before I could formulate a response, his hand rose to cup my cheek, the touch both gentle and assertive. I should have pulled away, should have maintained the emotional distance I'd cultivated so carefully, but I wanted him and I knew it, I leaned into his palm, the simple contact sending warmth cascading through me no matter how much I keep denying this connection between us, this warmth from his touch shows me I am wrong.

His mouth found mine with none of the raw hunger from earlier. This kiss was different, deliberate, thorough, questioning, it felt like love and emotion of words unsaid. My body responded before my mind could intercept, lips parting on a sigh that carried surrender I hadn't intended to offer.

. . .

WHEN HE FINALLY PULLED BACK, his eyes searched mine with that unsettling perception that had drawn me to him from the beginning. "Come back upstairs," he said, his voice low enough that only I could hear the slight roughness at its edges. "Stay the night. Just stay."

THE REQUEST WAS simple but represented everything I'd avoided since George—vulnerability, connection, the possibility of rejection come morning. Yet as his fingers twined with mine, I found myself nodding, the movement slight but unmistakable.

He led me back to the elevator, his grip firm but not constraining, offering guidance rather than demanding compliance. The doorman's gaze remained carefully averted, though I caught the slight upturn at the corner of his mouth— amusement or approval, I couldn't tell which.

The elevator ascended with the same silent efficiency it had descended minutes earlier, but the energy within its confines had shifted completely. Ryker stood beside me rather than behind me, his thumb tracing small circles against my palm in a gesture too intimate for casual connection, too deliberate to dismiss as meaningless.

His apartment welcomed us back with familiar scents and shadows, the spaces we'd moved through in urgent passion now quieter, more contemplative. He guided me toward the bedroom without words, his hand at the small of my back providing gentle pressure like he was trying to ensure I didn't turn and run.

The sheets still bore evidence of our earlier encounter,

tangled and bearing the imprint of our bodies, but when he drew me down beside him, the urgency had transformed into something I found more frightening than raw desire. His hands moved over me with soft tenderness, exploring rather than possessing, his mouth tracing paths that sought connection rather than submission.

I EXPECTED to fight this gentleness, to demand the physical intensity that allowed me to separate body from emotion, but I couldn't; I yielded to it, my own touches turning exploratory rather than demanding. We moved together with a synchronicity that felt both new and familiar, as if our bodies had always known this particular dance but had been performing only segments of it until now.

THIS TIME WE CAME TOGETHER, it was quieter than before but somehow deeper, waves of pleasure that radiated outward from where our bodies joined to suffuse my entire being. I heard myself whisper his name, not in desperate abandon but in recognition, in acknowledgement of what was happening between us despite all my attempts to prevent it.

AFTERWARD, he gathered me against him, one arm curved protectively around my waist, his chest warm against my back. I tensed momentarily, the position too intimate, too vulnerable for the woman I'd become. But when his lips pressed against my shoulder, not in renewed desire but simple affection, I felt something inside me uncoil, a tightness I'd been carrying for six months, relaxing incrementally.

· · ·

As HIS BREATHING deepened toward sleep, his arm remained firm around me, anchoring me to him, to this moment, to the connection I'd been fleeing. The hollow space inside me, the void I'd been trying to fill with nameless encounters, felt different somehow, its edges less jagged, its emptiness less absolute.

SLEEP PULLED at me despite my determination to remain alert, to maintain some semblance of the control I'd cultivated so carefully. The last thought before darkness claimed me was both comforting and terrifying: for the first time since George, I was falling asleep in a man's arms, not because I was too exhausted to leave, but because some part of me—some treacherous, vulnerable part—wanted to stay. "Fuck, this one is going to hurt," I thought to myself.

I WOKE TO UNFAMILIAR SOFTNESS, morning light filtering through partially open blinds. For a moment, just a moment, I felt nothing but contentment; I was sated and happy. Then the disorientation gripped me. I was still here, surrounded by tactile reminders of boundaries crossed, walls breached— evidence of last night's surrender. I promised myself not to let anyone in again. I was such an idiot, and I knew this time I was going to get hurt bad.

THE DIGITAL CLOCK on the nightstand read 7:26, early enough that I could still make a dignified exit, but late enough to confirm I'd truly spent the entire night in his arms. I sat up slowly, wincing at the pleasant soreness radiating from muscles that had been used thoroughly and repeatedly. Morning light revealed what darkness had concealed: faint marks across my collarbone, my inner thighs, and my wrists. Evidence of possession I couldn't dismiss as easily as I had with other men.

I LOOKED DOWN AT MYSELF, realizing I still wore only his t-shirt from the night before. In darkness, the borrowed garment had felt like enough protection. In sunlight, it felt like a confession, the fabric hanging loosely from my shoulders and brushing my mid-thigh, silently showing that I belonged, even if only for a moment, to this man. The vulnerability of it sent a new wave of panic through me, an urgent need to reclaim the carefully built identity I'd surrendered somewhere between his kiss in the lobby and falling asleep in his arms.

MOVEMENT from beyond the bedroom caught my attention— the gentle clink of ceramic, the subtle hiss of what sounded like an espresso machine, the quiet domesticity of morning rituals I rarely witnessed from my conquests. I slid from the bed, hesitating at the bedroom threshold. The hallway stretched before me like a gauntlet I wasn't prepared to run, the journey from sexual partner to something more compli- cated, from midnight shadow to morning light.

THE FLOORBOARDS FELT cool beneath my bare feet as I headed toward the kitchen, each step feeling like moving closer to something I'd been carefully avoiding for six months. Ryker stood with his back to me, dressed in loose sweatpants and a fitted T-shirt that showed off the width of his shoulders. He moved with the same quiet precision I remembered from that first morning—efficient yet graceful, each action purposeful rather than rushed.

HE TURNED AT MY APPROACH, his eyes locking onto mine with an intensity that made me fight the urge to cross my arms over my chest. I felt exposed in a way that had nothing to do with the inadequate coverage of his shirt and everything to do with the careful assessment in his gaze—how he seemed to catalog not just my physical appearance but also the tension in my shoulders and the vulnerability I was struggling to conceal.

"MORNING," he said, the single word devoid of the awkwardness I'd come to expect from morning-after encounters. "I was just about to bring this to you." He gestured toward the counter where two mugs sat ready, steam rising in delicate spirals from their surfaces.

"I DON'T USUALLY SLEEP that deeply," I said, the admission feeling more revealing than I meant. "Especially not in... unfamiliar places."

SOMETHING FLICKERED IN HIS EYES: recognition, perhaps, of what I wasn't saying—that I usually didn't sleep in men's beds at all. That last night marked a departure from my carefully established routines. That I was exploring territory without maps or weapons.

· · ·

He extended a robe toward me, plush navy fabric that looked soft enough to sink into. The gesture carried no expectation, just quiet consideration for my comfort. I took it with fingers that weren't entirely steady, slipping it on with gratitude I couldn't quite voice. The added layer felt like permission to breathe, to exist in this space without the sharp awareness of skin exposed to morning scrutiny.

"Black, no sugar," he said, lifting one of the mugs.

I nodded, feeling surprised and unsettled that he still remembered this detail. The mug he gave me was different from last time—heavier, made of ceramic in a deep forest green, instead of the sleek white porcelain we used the first morning. It felt solid in my hands, adding a sense of grounding with its weight and warmth.

"Thank you," I said, the words emerging more formally than intended, as if I were a guest rather than a woman who had spent the night screaming out his name.

He moved around the kitchen with the same quiet efficiency I remembered, getting cream for his coffee and adjusting the blinds to let in more light without causing direct glare. I stayed frozen near the island, unsure of my place in this morning routine.

. . .

"Sᴉᴛ," he suggested, gesturing toward the barstools at the counter. "Unless you need to rush off?"

Tʜᴇ ǫᴜᴇsᴛɪᴏɴ ʜᴀᴅ no expectation either way, no pressure to stay nor suggestion to leave. Its neutrality somehow made honesty easier.

"I ᴅᴏɴ'ᴛ ʜᴀᴠᴇ any meetings until noon," I admitted, sliding onto the nearest stool.

Rʏᴋᴇʀ ɴᴏᴅᴅᴇᴅ, moving to stand across from me, his own coffee cradled between hands that had mapped every inch of my body hours earlier. The memory sent warmth spreading through me that had nothing to do with the beverage I held.

"Tʜᴇ ᴄʜᴀɪʀ's ᴛᴏᴏ ʜɪɢʜ," he observed after a moment, setting down his mug and coming around the island. Before I could protest, he was adjusting the hydraulic lift, his movements matter-of-fact rather than invasive. The casual domesticity of it, his attention to my physical comfort in ways beyond the sexual, left me momentarily speechless.

Hᴇ ʀᴇᴛᴜʀɴᴇᴅ to his seat across from me, raising his mug in a small gesture that hinted at continuity, a thread linking this morning to the last, acknowledging a pattern forming between us despite my attempts to stop it.

· · ·

We drank in silence that should have been awkward, but somehow wasn't. The coffee was perfect, rich and complex rather than merely strong. Like the man who'd prepared it, it demanded attention rather than passive consumption.

When my mug was nearly empty, Ryker reached for the carafe behind him and refilled my cup without asking if I wanted more. The gesture carried an assumption that would have irritated me coming from other men, but from him, it felt like attentiveness rather than presumptuousness.

As he poured, his fingers brushed against mine on the mug's handle, the brief contact electric, sending awareness racing up my arm and across my chest. I flinched involuntarily, a reaction more revealing than words could be. The touch was accidental, incidental, yet my body responded as if it had been a deliberate caress.

If Ryker noticed my reaction—and I knew he had, those eyes missed nothing—he showed no sign. Instead, he kept pouring with the same steady hand, his expression revealing nothing about what he might be thinking regarding my skittishness or the contrast between last night's passion and this morning's caution.

"There's a good bakery a few blocks from here," he said, returning the carafe to its place. "Their croissants are worth the trip."

· · ·

THE CAUSAL SUGGESTION lingered between us, an invitation to prolong this morning, to step beyond the privacy of his apartment into public spaces where we would be seen together, recognized as a couple rather than just two people who had shared physical intimacy.

I TOOK another sip of coffee to delay my response, using the moment to gauge my own reaction to the situation. The old Elara, the one who had come out after George's rejection, would have already been planning her exit, making up an excuse to avoid more intimacy. But something had changed overnight, some wall had come down if not completely fallen.

"THAT SOUNDS NICE," I heard myself say, the simple acceptance feeling like surrender of a kind I hadn't offered in six months.

RYKER'S SMILE in response was slight but genuine, reaching his eyes in a way that transformed his entire face from merely handsome to something that tugged painfully at places inside me I'd thought safely numb. He didn't comment on my acceptance or draw attention to this departure from the woman who had tried to leave his apartment twice now. His restraint felt like another form of consideration—allowing me the dignity of evolution without forcing acknowledgment of what it might mean.

AS MORNING LIGHT strengthened around us, warming the kitchen with golden clarity, I wondered how many more of my carefully built rules would crumble under the gentle persistence of this man who somehow saw past all my defenses, offered coffee and croissants instead of demands, and adjusted chairs and refreshed cups with the same care he'd given to my pleasure the night before.

I slid into the passenger seat of Ryker's car—a matte-black BMW that managed to convey wealth without ostentation, much like the man himself. The leather was butter-soft beneath my thighs, still bare under his borrowed t-shirt and robe since my dress remained in tatters from the night before. Our first stop was planned for my apartment so I could grab some clothes—wearing his clothes in daylight carried different implications than the urgent borrowing of a t-shirt for a midnight escape. The car interior smelled of him—sandalwood and leather and something I couldn't name but recognized instantly as uniquely Ryker—and sitting beside him in this enclosed space felt more revealing than being naked in his bed had been.

He settled into the driver's seat with the same fluid economy of movement I'd noticed in his apartment, his hands resting on the steering wheel with casual confidence. The engine purred to life at his touch, responsive in a way that reminded me of my own body beneath his fingers hours earlier. I pushed the thought away, focusing instead on the technical precision with which he navigated from the parking garage into morning traffic.

WE ARRIVED AT MY APARTMENT. The thought crossed my mind to just say goodbye, but I didn't want to; I wanted to spend more time with him. I managed to push down the confusion of my feelings and just be in the moment. "I will be just a second," I said, slipping out of the car. I rushed inside, quickly shedding his borrowed clothes, and grabbed an appropriate dress for a breakfast outing—a mid-thigh skirt with a button-up shirt. However, unlike how I used to wear them, I didn't button it all the way to the throat.

I FELT something I hadn't truly felt in a long time...excitement. I was excited to go on this breakfast date, I thought. Then I paused, I just referred to it as a date, and for once the prospect didn't fill me with fear. I closed the door behind me and headed back out to Rykers waiting car. He smiled when he saw me approach and gave me a flirty wink as I slipped into the car and closed the door.

"Still okay with breakfast?" he asked, his eyes briefly meeting mine before returning to the road.

"Yes," I replied, though uncertainty still fluttered beneath my ribs in small doses. Breakfast meant sitting across from each other in daylight, meant being seen together, meant extending what should have been a single night into something with duration, with potential meaning.

Ryker drove with the same quiet authority that characterized everything he did—confident without aggression, aware of other vehicles without being intimidated by them. At a red light, his fingers tapped a gentle rhythm against the wheel, the only indication of energy contained within the calm exterior. I found myself studying his profile with unwanted fascination—the strong line of his jaw softened by morning stubble, the subtle gray at his temples catching sunlight, the curve of his mouth that had been pressed against my skin hours earlier.

"You're staring," he observed without turning his head, the slight upturn at the corner of his lips indicating he'd felt my gaze.

"Just thinking," I deflected, turning to look out the window at pedestrians hurrying toward coffee shops and office buildings, their routines untouched by the seismic shifts occurring in my carefully constructed world.

"Dangerous activity," he responded, the light humor in his tone a contrast to the intensity that had characterized our night together.

I didn't answer, unsure how to navigate this new territory of morning-after banter, of daylight conversation with a man I'd meant to leave at midnight. The ease with which he shifted between the commanding lover of last night and this relaxed morning companion was unsettling, suggesting a complexity I hadn't encountered—or perhaps hadn't allowed myself to notice—in my previous conquests.

The sky darkened suddenly, and clouds that had been gathering unnoticed now released their burden in a sudden downpour, transforming the street into a blur of reflected headlights and hunched shoulders as pedestrians scurried for cover. Ryker pulled smoothly to the curb beneath an architectural overhang that provided temporary shelter.

"Perfect timing," he commented, nodding toward the café just visible through the curtain of rain. "It's right there, but we might want to wait a few minutes for this to let up."

I nodded, grateful for the reprieve. The rain created a strange intimacy, isolating us in this quiet bubble while the world rushed past in watery distortion. Ryker reached behind my seat, retrieving something from a compartment I hadn't noticed.

"Here," he said, extending a sleek black umbrella toward me. "In case it doesn't let up."

I took it, our fingers brushing in the exchange. This time, I managed not to flinch, though the brief contact still sent awareness skittering across my skin.

"And this," he continued, leaning closer to tuck something into the pocket of my shirt. His proximity brought with it his scent— morning-clean with traces of coffee and that underlying note that was purely him. "So you'll be able to return later."

I put my hand in my pocket and pulled out a card. It had a key taped to it and a phone number in big, bold numbers. I looked up at him, shocked. He was giving me a key? "Is this?" I couldn't finish the sentence. "A key to my apartment," he finished. "So you can come anytime and not feel locked in," he whispers and brushes a loose strand of hair behind my ear. His hand lingers on my cheek, and his eyes hold mine. "Ryker, I…" My words are cut off when his mouth finds mine—soft, gentle, tender—and I lean into him. I want more. The kiss starts off so gently, but I find the heat of it consuming me. My hand rises up to the back of his hair. "We should go inside, or I am going to pull you onto my lap right here," he says against my lips with a smile.

The rain slackened slightly, shifting from downpour to steady shower. Ryker's hand settled at the small of my back as we exited the car, the contact light but grounding as I navigated the curb in borrowed loafers that were slightly too large. I opened the umbrella, holding it above us both as we crossed the short distance to the café entrance.

Inside, warmth surrounded us—the heat of ovens, the rich aroma of baking pastry, and the soft hum of morning chats over steaming mugs. The space was smaller than I expected, with tables arranged carefully to maximize both capacity and a sense of privacy. A server approached right away, her features lighting up with recognition as she saw Ryker.

"Mr. Davis," she greeted, her tone professional but warmed with genuine pleasure. "Your usual table?"

"Please," he replied, his hand remaining at the small of my back as we followed her toward a corner spot partially shielded by an indoor planter, offering views of both the rain-washed street and the café interior.

He pulled out my chair with a gesture so smooth it felt choreographed, the old-fashioned courtesy somehow lacking the performative quality I'd encountered in other men. This wasn't chivalry for show but a natural extension of his movements, as automatic as holding a door or offering an umbrella.

"The almond croissants are worth the trip," he said as we settled, "but their egg dishes are excellent too."

When the server returned, he ordered for both of us with quiet confidence that should have irritated me—I'd spent six months regaining control over every part of my life, including what I ate and when—yet I instead saw it as a continuation of his earlier thoughtfulness. He didn't assume my preferences but suggested options, his choices reflecting the attention he'd paid to my tastes at breakfast in his apartment.

"So," he said after the server departed, his eyes finding mine across the small table, "tell me about this noon meeting you have. Client or internal?"

The question—specific, interested, remembering a detail I'd mentioned casually earlier—caught me off guard. My usual conquests rarely asked about my work, and when they did, their questions were generalized, performative rather than genuinely curious.

"Client," I answered, adding with deliberate lightness, "A tech startup with more funding than direction. They're hoping I can help them look like they know what they're doing."

"And do you?" he asked, his expression serious, but his eyes held a warmth that invited continuation rather than defense.

"Know what I'm doing?" I laughed, my voice coming more easily than I expected. "More than they do, at least. Digital transformation is my specialty, but half the battle is convincing executives to actually transform rather than just digitize their existing problems."

He nodded, his attention unwavering in a way that made me increasingly aware of how rarely I was truly listened to. "That's the challenge with most change initiatives," he said. "People want different results without different behaviors."

The conversation flowed with surprising ease; his questions revealed actual engagement with my responses, rather than mere politeness while waiting for his turn to speak. I found myself sharing details about projects I rarely discussed outside work, drawn out by his genuine interest and insightful comments.

As our food arrived—almond croissants flaking golden layers beside perfectly poached eggs—I caught myself relaxing into the exchange, momentarily forgetting the reminders I'd been silently repeating since waking in his bed: This is just physical. Don't get attached. Remember George.

I watched Ryker interact with the server—thanking her by name, asking about her graduate studies with specific questions that indicated this wasn't their first conversation—and found myself cataloging the differences between the man across from me and the men I'd selected for temporary pleasure since George. Ryker commanded attention without demanding it, earned respect without intimidation, and existed in the world with a groundedness I found increasingly compelling.

The realization sent a fresh wave of panic through me. I had spent six months carefully avoiding this—this noticing, this appreciating, this dangerous territory of seeing a man as fully human rather than just useful. I took a bite of my croissant, using the moment of chewing to rebuild the walls that seemed to crumble in his presence.

"Just physical," I reminded myself as he poured more coffee into my cup without being asked, a gesture that felt domestic in a way that tugged at places inside me I thought were safely numbed. But as his fingers brushed mine in passing the sugar I hadn't asked for but he'd remembered I occasionally added to my second cup, I wondered how much longer I could keep up this fiction—not just with him, but with myself.

My phone rang. "Sorry, I need to take this," I say. Ryker nods in understanding. "Elara? It's Hannah. The noon meeting has been moved to next week—something about travel conflicts with the client. Given how hopeless they are at organizing anything, they most likely double-booked, so no need for you to come in today. Take a break, girl—you deserve it," she said. "Okay, can you email the details of the new time, Hannah?" I ask. "Sure thing, see you tomorrow," she says, ending the call. I look at Ryker, who is looking at me inquisitively. "Everything okay?" he asks. "Yes, my noon meeting has been moved, so I guess I don't have anywhere to be today," I reply, immediately feeling like I've shared too much but also filled with warmth at his returning smile at the prospect of more time.

Rain kept falling as afternoon settled over the city, turning Ryker's living room into a cozy space of warm light against the gloom reflected in the glass. Floor-to-ceiling windows revealed the storm's drama—clouds heavy between skyscrapers, droplets racing down the large panes in uneven patterns, the world outside appearing as watercolor smudges of gray and muted colors. Inside, lamps cast pools of amber that defined our space without sharp edges, the gentle light creating an intimate atmosphere that matched the strange comfort I'd been feeling in Ryker's presence since breakfast. I sat at one end of his sectional sofa, legs tucked beneath me.

After returning from the café, we'd moved through his apartment with surprising ease—he'd made more coffee, I'd helped clear mugs to the kitchen, our movements finding unexpected synchronicity in these simple domestic tasks. The rain had intensified, eliminating any practical reason to venture out again, creating a natural cocoon around this unplanned day together.

Now Ryker sat at the opposite end of the sofa, one arm stretched along its back, not quite touching me but close enough that I remained aware of the potential for contact. A book rested in his other hand—something leather-bound and well-worn, its pages slightly yellowed at the edges. He'd selected it from a shelf lined with similar volumes, his fingers running along spines with the familiarity of frequent touch before selecting this particular one.

"I found this during a trip to London," he said, noticing my interest in the book. "Small shop in Bloomsbury that probably isn't there anymore." His voice held the quiet reverence of someone who understood the value of things beyond their price tag.

I nodded, studying his profile as he opened to a page marked with a thin leather bookmark. The rain-filtered light caught the angles of his face differently than the club's artificial illumination or his bedroom's intimate glow—revealing complexities I hadn't allowed myself to notice in our previous encounters. Fine lines at the corners of his eyes suggested laughter rather than just age; a small scar near his temple hinted at stories I suddenly wanted to hear.

"Listen to this," he said, settling more comfortably into the cushions. Then he began to read, his voice dropping to a lower register that seemed to vibrate through the space between us:

"'What are we but our histories and how they have shaped us? We carry our past not as burden nor badge, but as the sculptor's chisel that reveals what we might become from the formless stone of possibility.'"

The words themselves were beautiful, but it was his voice that captured me—a low rumble that seemed to touch my skin directly, raising goosebumps along my arms and the back of my neck. I'd heard that voice command and seduce, had felt it against my ear in moments of intimate instruction, but this was different—Ryker sharing something he found meaningful, inviting me into an appreciation that transcended the physical connection we'd established.

He continued reading, passages about time and perception, about the space between what we show and what we feel, about connections formed and broken, and sometimes, rarely, rebuilt. I found myself leaning slightly toward him, drawn not just by the words but by the resonance they created between us—ideas that seemed to speak directly to the strange liminal space we now occupied, neither strangers nor established lovers, neither casual nor committed.

When he paused, closing the book with careful precision, the silence felt weighted with potential. He extended the volume toward me, the gesture casual yet somehow deeply personal.

"Take it," he said. "I think you'd enjoy the rest."

My fingers brushed against his as I accepted the book, the contact brief but electric. The leather was warm from his hands, the weight of it in my palms somehow significant beyond its physical presence. This wasn't like borrowing his clothes out of necessity or using his umbrella against the rain —this was deliberate sharing of something he valued, an invitation to understand him through what he found meaningful.

"Thank you," I said, my voice sounding strangely formal even to my own ears. "I'll return it when I've finished."

His smile shifted subtly, eyes crinkling at the corners in a way that suggested he heard the unspoken acknowledgment in my words—that there would be a "when," not an "if," that our connection would extend beyond this rain-enclosed day.

"No rush," he replied. "We can discuss it over dinner next week. I have reservations at Lumière on Thursday, if you're free."

The casual certainty of his words—the assumption of continuation, of future plans beyond our current encounter— sent a sharp spike of panic through me, accelerating my heart-beat to a rhythm I couldn't control. Six months of carefully managed encounters had never included a "next week," never extended into planning, into potential patterns that might lead to expectations, to vulnerability, to the possibility of rejection.

"Thursday," I echoed, striving for lightness I didn't feel. "That's thinking ahead. I usually don't plan my hook-ups with quite so much advance notice."

The attempt at humor fell flat, the words revealing more

than I'd intended about my usual patterns, about the careful distance I maintained through deliberate casualness. Ryker's expression didn't change, but something in his eyes—a slight sharpening of focus, an increased attentiveness—told me he'd caught both my deflection and the fear beneath it.

"I know what you're doing, Elara," he said, his voice gentle but direct, containing neither judgment nor retreat. "You're afraid I'll hurt you."

The simple statement—accurate in its assessment, devastating in its perception—struck with the precision of a surgeon's blade, exposing what I'd been hiding beneath layers of practiced indifference. I looked away, unable to bear the clarity of his gaze, fixing my attention instead on the rain still tracing patterns down the massive windows, on the city below continuing its rhythms despite the weather, despite my internal turmoil.

"You don't know me," I said finally, the protest weak even to my own ears.

"I'm beginning to," he countered, making no move to close the physical distance between us, respecting the space my body language had created while refusing to retreat from the emotional territory we'd entered. "And regardless of you trying not to, I think you are learning who I am too."

A slight shiver passed through me—from his words or the room's temperature, I couldn't be sure. Before I could respond, he rose with that fluid grace I'd come to expect, moving to a chest near the window and returning with something draped across his arms—a throw in soft heather gray, the cashmere catching amber light as he settled it around my shoulders with careful hands.

The gesture—attentive without being invasive, caring without demanding acknowledgment—undid me more thoroughly than any passionate embrace could have. I clutched the edges of the impossibly soft fabric, drawing it closer around me, a physical barrier against the emotional exposure I felt in his presence.

"Thank you," I managed, the words encompassing more than just the blanket, though I couldn't bring myself to articulate precisely what else I was acknowledging.

Ryker nodded, returning to his place on the sofa but making no attempt to push past the boundaries I'd re-established with my reaction to his invitation. Instead, he shifted the conversation to safer topics—a documentary he thought I might enjoy, a new restaurant that had opened downtown, observations about the changing skyline visible from his windows. I responded with growing ease, grateful for the reprieve from emotional intensity while still aware of the undercurrents flowing beneath our seemingly casual exchange.

Shadows lengthened across the floor as afternoon surrendered to early evening, the rain finally subsiding to leave the city washed clean, buildings gleaming in the break of sunlight through dispersing clouds. The natural conclusion of our unexpected day together approached with the changing light, creating a decision point I'd been avoiding since waking in his bed.

"I should probably go," I said finally, the familiar words feeling strange in this context—not the hasty exit line I'd delivered to countless men, but a reluctant acknowledgment of responsibilities beyond this rain-cocoon we'd created. "I need to prepare for another meeting tomorrow."

Ryker nodded, making no attempt to convince me to stay longer, respecting the boundary I'd established even as his eyes suggested he saw through my excuse to the fear driving it. He rose as I did, accepting the folded throw I returned to him with the same quiet attentiveness that had characterized his actions all day.

At his door, I hesitated, suddenly unsure of the appropriate goodbye for whatever this had become—not quite lovers in the casual sense I'd cultivated for six months, not quite something more defined. Before I could decide, he leaned forward, his lips pressing gently against my forehead in a gesture of such unexpected tenderness that I felt my breath catch.

The kiss—chaste yet somehow more intimate than the passionate exchanges we'd shared in his bed—lingered like a physical presence as he drew back, his eyes holding mine with that same penetrating perception that had unsettled me from our first meeting at Obsidian.

"I'll call you about Thursday," he said, neither demanding confirmation nor accepting my earlier deflection.

I nodded, unable to form words that wouldn't either commit me to something I feared or reject something I increasingly wanted. As the door closed behind me, I remained standing in the hallway, my fingers lingering on the doorknob, caught in the liminal space between his world and mine, between running from him and running from myself.

For six months, I had perfected the art of leaving, of maintaining control through careful distance, of taking physical pleasure without risking emotional vulnerability. Now, as I finally forced myself to move toward the elevator, I realized with uncomfortable clarity that the real danger Ryker presented wasn't that he might hurt me as George had—it was that he might heal me in ways I wasn't sure I was ready to accept.

CHAPTER SEVENTEEN
The Walls

The wine tasted rich and dark on my tongue, a cabernet that probably cost more than my entire liquor cabinet at home. I swirled it in the crystal glass, watching how the deep burgundy caught the warm lamplight in Ryker's living room. Three days had passed since I'd walked out of his apartment, since I'd felt the struggle between staying and leaving. Yet here I was again, drawn back to him like a moth to a dangerous flame, sitting on his plush velvet couch with bare feet tucked beneath me and his borrowed shirt grazing my thighs.

RYKER SAT at the opposite end, one arm stretched along the back of the sofa, his fingers close enough that I could feel their phantom touch against my shoulder. The space between us hummed with unspoken questions, the text message I had finally responded to after two days of silence, and the way he had opened his door two hours ago and simply pulled me inside without asking for explanations.

· · ·

"Tell me about him," Ryker said, his voice low and measured, the words dropping into our comfortable silence like stones into still water.

My glass paused halfway to my lips. "About who?"

His eyes, those perceptive green eyes that seemed to strip away my carefully constructed layers, held mine with gentle insistence. "The one who hurt you. The reason you run."

I forced a laugh that sounded brittle even to my own ears. "What makes you think there's a him?"

"Experience," he replied. "Recognition."

The wine suddenly tasted sour. I set the glass down and shrugged with deliberate casualness. "There's nothing to tell. Ancient history. Nothing worth rehashing."

He leaned forward, closing some of the distance between us, his expression serious without being intimidating. "I disagree. Whatever happened changed you fundamentally. I can see it in how you protect yourself, in how you use your body to maintain distance rather than create connection."

· · ·

MY FINGERS CLENCHED around the stem of my wineglass, the delicate crystal suddenly feeling fragile under my grip. The room seemed to close in on us, the warm, amber-lit space becoming suffocating and tight. I hadn't come here for this, for excavation, for exposure, for the gentle persistence that threatened to crack these foundations I have spent months reinforcing.

"GEORGE," I said finally, the name tasting like ash on my tongue. "His name was George."

RYKER WAITED, his silence an invitation rather than a demand.

I TOOK another sip of wine, buying myself time. "Like I said, ancient history. We dated for two years. It ended. I moved on." Each sentence emerged clipped and final, doors slammed shut against further inquiry.

"AND THAT'S why you've spent six months having meaningless encounters? he asked, his tone free of judgment but laden with that damnable perception that seemed to see through every defense. "That's why you never stay until morning, why you flinch when I touch you outside of sex, why you're sitting there right now calculating your escape route?"

HEAT FLOODED MY FACE, not the warm flush of desire but the burning acknowledgment of being seen too clearly, of being known in ways I hadn't granted permission for. My jaw tightened as I set my glass down with a deliberate click against the coffee table.

"WHAT ARE YOU AFRAID OF, ELARA?" he asked, his voice softening further, the gentleness more devastating than any accusation could have been.

THE QUESTION HOVERED BETWEEN US, dangerous in its simplicity, in its accuracy. What was I afraid of? Rejection. Inadequacy. The overwhelming realization that I could give everything of myself and still be found wanting. The knowledge that the good girl I was with George hadn't been enough, that he shattered my heart and praised me for taking it well. That the seductress I'd become since might be nothing more than elaborate armor around the same insufficient woman.

I SWALLOWED HARD, my throat suddenly dry despite the wine. Fight or flight instinct surged through me, and in this moment, fight meant using the one weapon I knew would distract him, would shift the power back to me, would transform this dangerous emotional territory into the physical landscape I controlled with practiced expertise.

"I'D RATHER DO something more interesting than talk," I said, my voice dropping to the husky register I'd perfected in recent months.

．　．　．

BEFORE HE COULD PRESS FURTHER, I moved toward him with deliberate grace, every motion calculated for maximum impact. I rose to my knees and swung one leg over his thighs, settling my weight against him with precision that made his breath catch. My hands found his shoulders, fingers digging slightly into the firm muscle beneath his shirt.

"ELARA," he began, but I silenced him by rolling my hips against his, feeling him respond despite his obvious desire to continue our conversation.

"SHHH," I whispered against his ear, my lips brushing the sensitive skin just below. "Isn't this better than talking about the past?"

MY TEETH GRAZED HIS EARLOBE, applying just enough pressure to send shivers down his spine. I felt his hands settle at my waist, uncertain whether to push me away or pull me closer. I took advantage of his hesitation, threading my fingers through his dark hair and tugging just hard enough to expose his throat to my mouth.

"THIS IS DEFLECTION," he managed, though his voice had roughened with evident desire.

"MMM," I agreed, nipping at the sensitive spot where his neck met his shoulder. "Expert-level deflection. The kind you'll thank me for."

I SHIFTED AGAINST HIM, the thin fabric of my underwear providing a minimal barrier between us. His hands tightened on my waist, his body betraying his mind's reservations. I felt the growing hardness beneath me and smiled against his skin, victorious in this small battle of wills.

MY FINGERS MOVED to his belt, working the leather free with practiced efficiency. The metallic sound of his zipper seemed unnaturally loud in the quiet room, punctuated only by our increasingly uneven breathing.

"WE DON'T HAVE to do this," he said, though his hips shifted upward slightly when my hand slipped beneath the waistband of his boxers.

"I WANT TO," I insisted, the words not untrue. My body did want this, wanted the physical connection, the temporary oblivion, the familiar territory of pleasure without vulnerability.

IT WAS my mind that recognized the desperation in my actions, the fear driving my fingers as they wrapped around him, stroking with deliberate skill that made his head fall back against the couch.

. . .

I USED every trick I'd learned in the months of casual conquests, the precise pressure of my palm, the twist of my wrist that made his breath stutter, the rhythm that built sensation without pushing too quickly toward release. His hands moved restlessly at my waist, torn between surrendering to my expertise and maintaining the emotional ground he'd been trying to claim.

"LOOK AT ME," I commanded, my free hand gripping his jaw.

WHEN HIS EYES MET MINE, I saw the conflict there, desire warring with something deeper, something that threatened the careful distance I was trying to maintain through physical connection. I crushed my mouth to his before that look could undo me, kissing him with an intensity that was both distraction and desperation.

OUR TONGUES MET in a familiar dance, the taste of expensive wine mingling between us. I pressed against him with increasing urgency, my body serving as the best distraction from the questions still hanging between us. His hands finally moved from my waist to my thighs, slipping beneath the borrowed shirt to grip my hips with bruising intensity.

IN THIS, at least, I knew precisely what I was doing—how to use my body to silence questions, how to turn emotional vulnerability into physical surrender, and how to maintain control even while seeming to let it go. As Ryker's breathing grew faster and his restraint visibly weakened, I celebrated this small victory over intimacy with the desperation of someone clutching to the only safety they've ever known.

RYKER'S HANDS moved to take control, attempting to flip our positions, but I caught his wrists in a firm grip. I recognized the shift in his eyes—the dominant lover from our previous encounters emerging—but tonight I couldn't risk surrendering even that form of control. "No," I said, my voice firm as I pressed his wrists into the velvet cushions on either side of his head. "My way tonight." I needed to dictate every moment, every touch, every sensation. Allowing him to lead would risk the very vulnerability I was using sex to avoid.

A flash of surprise crossed his features before settling into something more complex—arousal mixed with assessment, as if he recognized exactly what I was doing but was willing to let me play it out. The slight upturn at the corner of his mouth suggested he understood more than I wanted him to, but his body relaxed beneath mine, surrendering this round of our unspoken battle.

I released his wrists slowly, testing his compliance. When his hands remained where I'd placed them, I sat back, straddling his thighs. With deliberate movements, I grasped the hem of his borrowed shirt and pulled it over my head in one fluid motion, discarding it onto the floor beside the couch.

I held his gaze as I revealed myself to him, a reverse strip-tease designed to command rather than entice. The lamplight cast my skin in warm gold, highlighting the fading marks from our previous encounter—slight bruises on my inner thighs, a faint redness around my wrists, the shadow of his teeth at the curve where my neck met my shoulder. Evidence of possession I now reclaimed as my own.

His eyes darkened as they traveled over me, pupils expanding until only a thin ring of green remained. I watched his throat work as he swallowed, his chest rising with a deep breath he couldn't quite control. His muscles tensed beneath me, the restraint visible in the cording of his forearms, in the slight tremor of his hands still pressed against the cushions where I'd placed them.

"You can look," I said, trailing my own fingers down my body with performative slowness, "but don't touch. Not until I say."

Power thrummed through me—the familiar, hollow power of physical control that had become my armor since George. I leaned forward, bringing my mouth to his chest, where I traced my tongue along the defined muscles visible through his thin t-shirt. The cotton dampened beneath my lips as I moved lower, pushing the fabric up to access bare skin.

His breath hitched when I reached the waistband of his already-unfastened pants. I glanced up through my lashes, meeting his heated gaze with cool assessment. Then I slid backward off his lap, kneeling between his thighs on the plush carpet. With efficient movements, I tugged his pants and boxers down his legs, leaving him exposed to my calculated attention.

"Elara," he began, his voice roughened with desire but still carrying that damnable hint of perception—as if even now, he saw through my performance to the fear driving it.

"Shh," I commanded, placing one finger against his lips. "No talking. Just feeling."

Before he could respond, I lowered my head, taking him into my mouth with practiced skill. I'd perfected this art over six months of meaningless encounters—learned exactly how to use lips and tongue and the careful scrape of teeth to drive a man beyond coherent thought. I applied this expertise now with methodical precision, watching Ryker's reactions through hooded eyes.

His hands finally moved from where I'd placed them, one fisting in the velvet cushion beside him, the other hovering uncertainly before settling in my hair. I allowed this small liberty, the weight of his palm against my scalp a grounding presence as I worked him with deliberate intensity.

I could read his responses like a familiar text—the tightening of his abdomen when I hollowed my cheeks, the slight upward thrust of his hips when I used my tongue just so, the sudden catch in his breathing that signaled approaching release. When his fingers tightened in my hair, I pulled back, denying him completion with the same calculated control with which I'd offered pleasure.

His frustrated groan carried notes of both protest and admiration for my skill. I smiled up at him, a predator's smile that contained challenge rather than affection. "Not yet," I said, rising to straddle him again. "I'm not finished with you."

I positioned myself above him, my body hovering just out of reach. When his hands moved to my hips, seeking to guide me down onto him, I captured his wrists again, pressing them firmly against the back of the couch.

"I said no touching," I reminded him, my voice honey-smooth but unyielding. "This is about my pleasure now."

Without releasing his wrists, I lowered myself onto him with excruciating slowness, watching his face contort with the effort of remaining still. When he was fully seated inside me, I paused, savoring the fullness, the stretch, the physical connection that demanded nothing more than bodily response.

Only then did I release his hands, placing them deliberately on the couch beside his thighs. "Keep them there," I instructed, "or I stop."

I began to move, setting a rhythm designed for my pleasure rather than his—rolling my hips in the precise motion that created friction exactly where I needed it. My hands splayed across his chest for balance, nails digging slightly into the fabric of his shirt. I hadn't bothered to remove it completely, another small act of control, of keeping him partially clothed while I was naked—vulnerable physically but armored emotionally.

Sweat beaded along my collarbone as I increased my pace, chasing the physical release that would temporarily quiet the anxiety still churning beneath my performance. I threw my head back, eyes closed to avoid the intensity of Ryker's gaze. I knew what I'd see there—not just desire but understanding, not just heat but connection—and I couldn't risk it, not when I was using this act specifically to avoid such intimacy.

My focus narrowed to physical sensation—the delicious friction where our bodies joined, the tightening coil of pleasure building at my core, the slight burn in my thighs as I lifted and lowered myself with increasing urgency. I was vaguely aware of Ryker's hands still pressed against the couch where I'd commanded them to stay, of his ragged breathing matching my own, of the occasional sounds that escaped his throat when I clenched deliberately around him.

But I maintained my distance even in this closest of connections—keeping my eyes closed, focusing on my own body's responses rather than our shared experience, using him as the instrument of my pleasure rather than a partner in creating it. This was sex as I'd perfected it since George—physical without being emotional, intimate without being vulnerable, intense without requiring trust.

I felt my release approaching and chased it with single-minded determination, adjusting my angle slightly to increase pressure against my most sensitive point. My hands moved from his chest to his shoulders, nails digging crescents into his skin as my movements became less controlled, more urgent.

"Look at me," Ryker commanded suddenly, his voice cutting through the haze of approaching orgasm.

I kept my eyes firmly closed, shaking my head slightly as I continued to move. His hands finally disobeyed my earlier instruction, rising to grip my hips—not guiding my movements but simply establishing contact, connection, the very thing I was trying to avoid.

334

"Elara," he said again, my name both request and demand. "Look at me when you come."

I bit my lip hard, focusing on that small pain to center myself as pleasure built to nearly unbearable levels. I wouldn't give him this—this final surrender, this moment of unguarded vulnerability. I turned my face away, pressing my forehead against my own raised arm, creating yet another barrier between us as my body tensed on the edge of release.

When it finally crashed through me, I muffled my cry against my shoulder, body shuddering with waves of pleasure that radiated outward from where we joined. I felt Ryker follow moments later, his hands tightening on my hips as he pulsed inside me, his groan carrying notes of both satisfaction and something that sounded dangerously like surrender of a different kind.

I rode out the aftershocks with my eyes still closed, my breathing gradually slowing, my body humming with a temporary sense of peace even as my mind registered the hollow victory. I had avoided his questions, prevented the emotional exposure he'd been seeking, and maintained control through physical distraction. Yet, the emptiness that followed felt deeper than before, and the strategy that had served me for six months suddenly offered diminishing returns.

We collapsed against each other, my body still trembling with aftershocks, our skin sticky with sweat and satisfaction. I felt suddenly, acutely aware of my nakedness while Ryker remained partially clothed—my strategy for maintaining control now feeling like exposure of a different kind. The velvet of the couch caught against my overheated skin as I shifted, creating the slightest distance between our bodies without fully breaking contact. My breathing gradually slowed, matching the gentle rise and fall of his chest beneath my palm. This was typically when I'd make my exit—task accomplished, physical release achieved, no lingering required—but exhaustion held me in place, my limbs temporarily boneless from exertion.

Ryker's fingers found the curve of my spine, tracing each vertebra with maddening gentleness. The touch wasn't sexual —that would have been easier to categorize, to respond to— but something worse: tender, exploratory, the kind of touch that sought connection rather than arousal. I fought the instinct to arch into it like a cat, to surrender to the simple pleasure of being touched without agenda.

"We should clean up," I murmured, the words sounding hollow even to my own ears—another deflection, another retreat.

His fingers continued their gentle exploration of my back, undeterred. "In a minute," he said, his voice a low rumble I could feel vibrating through his chest. "I like you like this."

"Like what?" The question slipped out before I could stop it.

"Unguarded," he replied simply. "Even if it's just for a moment."

I stiffened against him, muscle memory preparing for escape, for the reconstruction of walls his words threatened to breach. His hand flattened against my lower back, not restraining but present, aware.

"Why won't you let me in, Elara?" he asked, the question hanging between us like smoke—intangible yet impossible to ignore.

I pushed up from his chest, reaching for the discarded t-shirt on the floor—armor I suddenly needed desperately. Before I could grab it, Ryker's arm tightened around my waist, not forcefully but with enough intention to pause my retreat.

"I'm not asking for your life story," he said, his voice softening further. "Just something real. Anything."

I stared at the shirt, just inches beyond my fingertips, my throat working as I swallowed against the pressure building there. The space between us filled with all I couldn't say— about George, about the woman I'd been before him, about the hollow freedom I'd constructed from the wreckage of rejection.

"I don't do real," I finally replied, the words emerging rougher than intended. I gestured vaguely between our naked bodies, still joined at the hips, though the passion had subsided. "This—this is all I have to offer."

Ryker shifted beneath me, propping himself up on one elbow, his free hand still gently resting on my waist. The movement brought his face closer to mine, those perceptive eyes studying me with an intensity that made me want to look away but somehow I couldn't.

"I don't believe that," he said, the simple statement striking deeper than any accusation could have.

My hand twitched at my side, almost reaching for his face before I caught myself, fingers curling into a fist instead. I needed to leave—needed to escape this couch, this apartment, this man who somehow saw through every defense I'd spent six months perfecting. My eyes darted toward the door, calculating the steps required: retrieve shirt, find underwear, gather purse, exit before vulnerability could take root.

"You're doing it again," Ryker observed, his thumb tracing small circles against my hip bone. "Planning your escape route."

"I should go," I said, the words automatic, a script I'd performed dozens of times with other men. "It's getting late."

"It's barely nine o'clock," he countered, the faint smile playing at his lips containing no mockery, only gentle understanding that somehow hurt worse than ridicule would have.

My hands trembled slightly—a betrayal of my body I couldn't control. I tucked them under my thighs, out of sight, but Ryker had already noticed, his eyes missing nothing. I felt exposed in ways that had nothing to do with my physical nakedness and everything to do with the emotional layers he kept stripping away with such careful precision.

"What do you want from me?" I asked, frustration bleeding into my tone, making it sharper than intended.

"Just you," he replied. "Not the seductress, not the ice

queen, not the woman who uses her body as both weapon and shield. Just Elara."

"That woman doesn't exist anymore," I said, the words emerging with a finality that surprised even me. "George made sure of that."

The admission hung between us—the first piece of truth I'd offered voluntarily, the first acknowledgment of the man whose rejection had catalyzed my transformation. Ryker's expression remained carefully neutral, neither pushing for more nor dismissing what I'd shared.

"I think she does," he said after a moment. "I catch glimpses of her sometimes—when you forget to perform, when something genuinely amuses you, when you're half-asleep and your guard slips."

My throat tightened further, making breathing a conscious effort. He was describing moments I'd barely registered— vulnerabilities I hadn't realized I'd shown, cracks in an armor I'd thought impenetrable. The realization sent fresh panic spiraling through me, my heart rate accelerating despite my attempts to maintain composure.

"You don't know what you're talking about," I insisted, my voice sounding brittle even to my own ears. "You don't know me."

"I'm learning," he countered, echoing words he'd spoken days earlier in his apartment, when I'd tried to leave after our rain-soaked day together. "And I think you're learning me too, despite your best efforts not to."

. . .

THE ECHO of that previous conversation—the recognition that we were circling the same truth, approaching the same vulnerability from different angles—sent an unexpected warmth through my chest. I looked away, unable to bear the gentle persistence in his gaze, the patient certainty that I was more than the carefully constructed facade I presented.

Ryker shifted again, his hand moving from my waist to my face, tucking a strand of hair behind my ear with a tenderness that made my breath catch. The gesture was achingly simple yet devastating in its care—the kind of touch that acknowledged me as a person rather than merely a body, that saw value beyond physical pleasure.

"When you're ready to talk, I'll be here," he said softly, his fingers lingering against my cheek. "About George, about what happened, about whatever you're so afraid of. No rush, no pressure. Just... here."

The promise in his words—the offered patience, the lack of demand, the simple assurance of presence—threatened to undo me completely. I felt something crack inside my chest, a hairline fracture in foundations I'd thought solid. My hand moved of its own accord, covering his where it rested against my face, our fingers intertwining in a connection that felt more intimate than the sex we'd just shared.

For a breathless moment, I allowed it—this simple touch, this wordless acknowledgment of something growing between us that transcended physical chemistry. Then fear resurged, the specter of George and rejection and inadequacy rising like a tide to drown the momentary courage.

I pulled away first, my fingers reluctantly releasing his, my body shifting to create distance without completely breaking contact. Caught between contradictory impulses—the growing desire to stay versus the ingrained instinct to flee, the longing to be known versus the terror of being rejected once known—I remained suspended in indecision, torn between the safety of emotional isolation and the dangerous allure of whatever Ryker was offering.

As silence settled around us, broken only by the soft sounds of our breathing and the distant hum of the city beyond his windows, I realized with uncomfortable clarity that for the first time in six months, I didn't know what came next in my carefully constructed script of emotional avoidance. The hollow space inside me—the void I'd been trying to fill with meaningless encounters—ached with new awareness, with the possibility that perhaps it couldn't be filled with physical connection alone.

And that terrified me more than any rejection ever could.

CHAPTER EIGHTEEN
The Return of George

The martini glass sat between my fingers like a crystal shield, olive-speared and gin-cold against my palm. I'd chosen this upscale hotel bar for its anonymity—dark corners, discreet service, the kind of place where no one knew your name unless you wanted them to. Three days had passed since I'd left Ryker's apartment, since I'd fled the dangerous vulnerability he kept coaxing from me. I checked my phone, the screen's glow illuminating my face in the dim light, wondering if he'd try again tonight. That's when I caught it—a familiar scent cutting through the ambient notes of leather and liquor. Fresh linen cologne. My body recognized it before my mind did, muscles tensing, pulse quickening, the primitive response of prey sensing a predator's return.

I didn't need to look up. I knew it was George.

The bar's amber lighting caught the rim of my glass as I raised it, taking a deliberate sip while keeping my eyes fixed on the wall of bottles behind the bartender. Jazz notes floated through the air—a mournful saxophone weaving between quiet conversations, ice clinking against crystal, the soft creak of leather as patrons shifted in their seats. I'd chosen this place specifically because it wasn't connected to my past, wasn't part of the geography of my heartbreak. Yet here he was, his presence transforming my sanctuary into another scene of potential ambush.

"Elara?"

His voice hadn't changed. Still that perfect blend of authority and warmth, the slight rasp at the edges that had once made my name sound like a caress in his mouth. My fingers tightened around the stem of my glass, knuckles whitening beneath the strain of appearing unaffected.

I turned, arranging my features into what I hoped was polite disinterest rather than the storm of contradictory emotions battering my ribs. George stood beside me, his tailored suit impeccable as always—navy wool that probably cost more than my monthly rent—but something was off. His hair, usually styled with meticulous precision, looked slightly mussed, as though he'd been running his fingers through it. His smile, that practiced curve that had once melted my defenses, didn't quite reach his eyes.

"George." I managed to make his name sound like a period rather than a question. "What a surprise."

He slid onto the stool beside me with the fluid grace that came from a lifetime of being welcomed into spaces—boardrooms, exclusive clubs, women's lives—without having to justify his presence. His cologne enveloped me entirely now, that clean scent I'd once buried my face in his shirts to capture after he left for work.

"I'll have what she's having," he told the bartender, then seemed to reconsider. "No, make it a Macallan. Neat."

Of course, he'd order that. Of course, he'd remember it was my preferred drink, the one I'd started ordering after we split. I wondered if he'd been watching me longer than I realized.

"You look amazing," he said, turning those assessing eyes on me fully. "I almost didn't recognize you."

My mouth went dry, a physical betrayal that had nothing to do with the alcohol. "That was rather the point."

His laugh held genuine amusement, the sound triggering a cascade of memories I'd thought safely buried—Sunday mornings in his kitchen, holiday parties where he'd kept his hand possessively at the small of my back, the way his eyes had crinkled at the corners when he was genuinely pleased. Before everything changed. Before the Bluebird Café.

"The hair, the dress..." His gaze traveled over me with the practiced assessment of someone cataloging improvements to property they still considered partly theirs. "You've changed your style completely. It suits you."

My hand trembled slightly as I reached for my drink, the barest ripple disturbing the clear surface of the gin. I took another sip, using the moment to rebuild walls that had begun to crack at the mere sound of his voice.

"People change," I said, the banality of the response frustrating me even as the words left my mouth.

"Some things don't," he countered, his voice dropping lower as the bartender placed his scotch before him. He lifted the glass in a small toast before taking a sip, his eyes never leaving mine. "I've heard things, you know. About your... new lifestyle."

My spine stiffened, years of conditioning making me want to defend myself before I remembered I owed him nothing— no explanations, no justifications, no glimpse into the woman I'd become in his absence.

"Have you?" I kept my tone light, bored even, though my heart hammered against my ribs with increasing urgency. "How fascinating for you."

He smiled—that particular smile I'd seen him use in negotiations, the one that suggested he knew more than he was saying. "The clubs, the men... quite the transformation from the girl I knew." His fingers brushed against mine as he reached for the small dish of bar nuts between us. "Though I suppose we all have our ways of coping."

The casual touch sent an electric current up my arm, anger and awareness tangled together in a response I couldn't control. I pulled my hand back slightly, hating the flush I could feel warming my cheeks.

"Is there something you want, George?" I asked, finally looking directly at him. "Some reason you've sought me out after all this time?"

Something flickered across his face—a momentary crack in

the polished veneer, a glimpse of something raw beneath the practiced charm. He took another drink, longer this time, before setting the glass down with precise control.

"Madison left," he said, the admission delivered with calculated vulnerability, his eyes watching for my reaction. "Two months ago. Said I was 'emotionally unavailable.'" He gave a short laugh that contained no humor. "Apparently, I talk about you too much."

My breath caught in my throat, a complicated tangle of vindication and suspicion warring in my chest. This was precisely what the old Elara would have dreamed of—George realizing his mistake, coming back, admitting he'd been wrong. The fantasy I'd clung to in those first devastating weeks after he'd ended things.

"I'm sorry to hear that," I managed, the polite response a shield against the dangerous hope trying to take root. "Breakups are difficult."

"I made a mistake, Elara." His voice softened to that intimate register that had once made me feel like the only woman in any room. His hand moved across the bar, fingers brushing against my wrist with deliberate gentleness. "I've missed you."

I pulled back instinctively, a physical recoil that happened before conscious thought could intervene. But even as I created distance, some treacherous part of me—the part still damaged from his rejection, the part that had spent six months proving I was desirable, valuable, worth wanting—hesitated, then allowed his fingertips to maintain contact with my skin.

The touch burned like ice, both familiar and foreign at once. My eyes darted toward the exit, calculating the steps required to escape, to return to the safety of emotional distance I'd so carefully constructed. I swallowed hard, my throat clicking audibly in the small space between us.

"You don't miss me," I said, the words emerging with a steadiness that surprised me. "You miss how I made you feel. There's a difference."

His fingers tightened slightly around my wrist, not enough to hurt, just enough to assert presence, to demand attention. "I miss everything about you," he insisted, leaning closer. "The way you used to look at me, the way you'd curl against me in the morning, the way you always knew exactly what I needed before I did." His thumb traced small circles against my pulse point, a gesture he knew had once melted my resistance. "We were good together, Elara. We could be again."

The words I'd once longed to hear now rang hollow, practiced, the script of a man who always got what he wanted through careful application of pressure to precisely the right points. I looked at him—really looked—and saw not the man who had destroyed me, but a carefully constructed facade with cracks beginning to show. Behind his practiced smile lurked something desperate, something needy.

And for the first time since that day at the Bluebird Café, I wondered if perhaps it wasn't that I hadn't been enough for George, but that George hadn't been enough for himself.

. . .

I stared at George's hand on my wrist, at the manicured nails and the faint dusting of hair along his knuckles. This hand had once mapped every inch of my body, had held mine through movies and dinners and family gatherings, had gestured emphatically as he'd explained why we needed to end things at the Bluebird Café. Now it rested against my pulse point like a claim being reinstated, and I couldn't decide whether to pull away or lean in. The decision was made for me when a different scent cut through George's fresh linen cologne—sandalwood and something darker, earthier. My body recognized it instantly, every nerve ending suddenly alert. I didn't need to turn around to know Ryker had entered the bar.

The air in the room seemed to shift, molecules rearranging themselves around this new presence. I felt the weight of his gaze before I saw him, a physical pressure between my shoulder blades that sent heat spiraling through my chest. George was still talking, something about reconnecting, about second chances, but his words had become background noise to the approaching footsteps I could somehow distinguish from all other sounds in the crowded bar.

When I finally looked up, Ryker was moving toward our table with that measured grace that had unnerved me from our first meeting—not hurried yet utterly purposeful, a man who moved through the world with quiet certainty. He wore a simple black button-down, sleeves rolled to expose forearms corded with subtle strength, dark jeans that emphasized his height. But it was his expression that caught in my throat—the tightness around his mouth, the careful assessment in those green eyes as they moved from George's hand on my wrist to my face.

"Elara," he said, my name in his mouth carrying the same weight it always did—both question and acknowledgment. The single word somehow conveyed everything he wasn't asking aloud: Are you okay? Do you want me to leave? Do you need help?

George sensed the shift in my attention, his fingers tightening slightly on my wrist before releasing it to turn in his seat. I watched his face rearrange itself, the intimate expression he'd worn for me transforming into the polished social mask he presented to potential rivals. His eyes performed a quick assessment—taking in Ryker's height, his build, the quiet authority in his stance—before his lips curved into that perfect smile that had charmed boardrooms and cocktail parties with equal success.

"Everything okay here?" Ryker asked, his voice measured but with an undercurrent of tension I'd come to recognize— the careful control that masked stronger emotions beneath.

George stood, extending his hand with a politician's smile. "You must be the new guy," he said, the casual phrasing deliberate in its dismissiveness. "I'm George, Elara's ex." The emphasis he placed on "ex" somehow managed to imply both past and potential future simultaneously.

I watched the two men shake hands, the contrast between them suddenly stark under the bar's amber lighting. George all fluid motion and practiced charm, every gesture calculated for maximum effect; Ryker contained energy and genuine presence, his movements economical yet graceful. They were approximately the same height, but Ryker seemed somehow larger, more solid—a man comfortable in his own skin rather than one performing his identity for an audience.

My fingers moved unconsciously to the small pendant resting at my collarbone—a delicate silver key on a fine chain that Ryker had given me two days ago. It had arrived at my apartment in a simple box with a note: "For when you're ready to stop running." I'd put it on without fully understanding why, the metal warming against my skin like a promise I wasn't sure I could keep.

George's eyes tracked the movement, narrowing slightly as he noticed the jewelry he hadn't seen before. "That's new," he observed, his tone casual but his gaze sharp. "Not your usual style."

"People change," I repeated my earlier words, fingers still touching the pendant like a talisman.

Ryker remained standing, not quite at my side but positioned in a way that established presence without claiming possession. "I was just meeting Elara for a drink," he said, the statement neutral yet somehow making it clear he had every right to be there.

"What a coincidence," George replied with a laugh that contained no actual humor. "So was I. After all, we have so much to catch up on." He gestured to the empty chair at our small table. "Please, join us. I'd love to hear how you two met."

The invitation was perfectly polite, utterly reasonable, and completely insincere. I caught the subtle tightening of Ryker's jaw—the only outward sign of his recognition of the underlying challenge.

"That's up to Elara," Ryker said, his gaze finding mine with a question I could read clearly: Do you want me to stay?

Before I could respond, George leaned slightly toward Ryker, his posture deceptively casual. "It's fascinating, really," he said, swirling the amber liquid in his glass. "Meeting someone who knows the current version of Elara. I'm curious —has she told you about who she was before? The real Elara?"

The implication hung in the air between us—that the woman I'd become was somehow inauthentic, a creation rather than an evolution. That George alone knew the "real" me, as if identity were fixed rather than fluid, as if I were a fossil rather than a living being.

"George," I warned, but he continued as if I hadn't spoken.

"We were together for two years," he told Ryker, his tone conversational but his eyes calculating. "Long enough to know someone's truths, their patterns, what they need even when they don't know it themselves."

Ryker's expression remained neutral, but I caught the slight shift in his stance—feet planted more firmly, shoulders squared, the posture of a man preparing for impact rather than retreat. "People are more than their past," he said.

George's smile tightened at the edges. "Are they? Or do they just put on new costumes to hide old wounds?" He turned back to me, his gaze softening in that practiced way that had once made me feel seen but now struck me as performative. "Elara always needed security, certainty. Needed to know exactly where she stood." His eyes flicked back to Ryker. "Does she know where she stands with you?"

The question struck closer to the truth than I was comfortable with—the ambiguity of whatever was growing between Ryker and me, the undefined nature of our connection that both terrified and compelled me. I felt caught between past and potential future, between the man who had shaped my transformation and the one who challenged its foundations.

"I think Elara can speak for herself," Ryker said quietly, the respect in his tone a stark contrast to George's assumption of knowledge.

George's laugh held genuine amusement this time. "That's new, too. The Elara I knew preferred to let others lead the conversation." He leaned toward me, close enough that I could smell the scotch on his breath mingling with his cologne. "Is that who you are now? Someone who speaks for herself? Someone who takes what she wants without apology?" His eyes held a knowledge that made my skin burn with sudden shame. "I've heard interesting things about your... adventures these past few months."

My throat tightened, the implications clear—he knew about the clubs, the men, the calculated seductions I'd used to rebuild myself after his rejection. The hollow victory of becoming someone he might want but could no longer have.

"Do you still love me?" George asked suddenly, the direct

question cutting through the careful dance of insinuation and defense. He ignored Ryker's presence entirely, his eyes fixed on mine with an intensity that once would have melted my resolve. "Who is he, really, to you? A distraction? A replacement? Something serious?"

The questions hung in the air between us, weighted with history and implication. The bar seemed to recede around us, ambient noise fading beneath the roaring in my ears. Ice clinked in glasses, muffled conversations continued at nearby tables, the saxophone wailed a lonely note that seemed to echo the confusion twisting in my chest.

I looked between them—George with his expectant expression, the familiar face that had once been the center of my world, and Ryker with his patient gaze, offering presence without demand, connection without condition. Two versions of myself reflected back at me through their eyes: the woman I had been and the woman I was becoming.

And I suddenly wasn't sure which one was more real, more authentic, more truly me.

The weight of their expectations pressed against my chest, constricting my lungs until each breath felt shallow and insufficient. George's question hung between us, demanding an answer I wasn't prepared to give. Did I still love him? The man who had dismantled my world with careful words over cooling coffee? And Ryker—what was he to me? The man who saw through every defense I'd constructed from the wreckage

George had left behind? Their gazes pinned me like a butterfly to velvet, waiting for me to declare a truth I hadn't yet discovered for myself. Something cracked inside me, a fault line splitting open after months of careful containment. I stood abruptly, my chair scraping against the floor with a sound like bone against stone.

"Elara—" George began, his hand reaching toward me with practiced concern.

I stepped back just beyond his reach. My spine straightened, shoulders squared into the rigid posture I'd honed after our breakup—a physical armor of perfect posture and deliberate distance. What had been uncertainty moments before hardened into something colder, a defensive shell forming around the sudden flood of vulnerability.

"Don't," I said, the single syllable emerging sharper than I'd intended.

Memories surged like a tide breaking through weakened barriers—George across from me at the Bluebird Café, his expression carefully composed as he explained why we needed to "take a break," how he "needed space to evaluate what he really wanted." The precise way he'd placed his napkin beside his half-finished muffin, how he'd insisted on paying despite having just shattered my world, the practiced sympathy in his eyes that hadn't quite masked the relief beneath. The humiliation of realizing I'd been blindsided by an exit he'd been planning for weeks.

My gaze moved between them—George with his expectant expression, the slight upturn at the corner of his mouth suggesting confidence in his ability to reclaim what he'd discarded; and Ryker, his eyes holding concern rather than expectation, patience rather than demand. Two men who represented such different versions of myself: the woman who had built her identity around being wanted, and the woman who was learning, painfully, to exist without external validation.

"I can't do this," I said, my voice tight as a wire pulled to breaking. "Not with either of you."

George's expression shifted to one of practiced understanding. "You're overwhelmed. That's natural. We can talk tomorrow when you've had time to process—"

"No." The word came out with surprising force. "There's nothing to process, George. You don't get to walk back into my life and act like you have any claim to it. Not after—" I stopped, reluctant to put into words the extent of the devastation he'd caused, unwilling to reveal that wound in Ryker's presence.

My hands trembled as I reached for my purse, fingers clumsy with adrenaline as I gathered my jacket from the back of the chair. The leather felt cool against my overheated skin, a slight shock of sensation that helped anchor me in the moment.

"Elara," Ryker said, my name in his mouth so different from how George pronounced it—not a possession being reclaimed but a person being acknowledged. "You don't have to decide anything now."

The gentleness in his voice threatened to undo me

completely, to crack the rigid shell I'd constructed in the face of George's unexpected appearance. His understanding was somehow more dangerous than George's manipulation—offering space rather than demanding resolution, respecting boundaries rather than attempting to breach them.

George stepped closer, his cologne enveloping me in unwanted familiarity. "We have history, Elara," he said, voice dropping to that intimate register that had once made me feel chosen, special. "Two years isn't something you just erase. What we had—what we could have again—"

I shook my head sharply, cutting him off. "What we had was a relationship where I molded myself into exactly what you wanted, and you still walked away." My voice held a steadiness that surprised me, though I could feel the slight tremor beneath the words. "I won't do that again. Not for you, not for anyone."

My eyes flicked to Ryker, catching the flash of something like pride in his expression before I looked away. I took another step backward, maintaining equal distance from both men, my posture tight as a coiled spring. The bar suddenly felt claustrophobic, the air too thick with expectation and history and possibility.

"I need space," I told them, my voice cracking slightly despite my attempt at firmness. "From both of you."

George's expression hardened slightly, the practiced charm slipping to reveal the frustration beneath. "You're overreacting. If you'd just—"

"She said she needs space," Ryker interrupted quietly, his tone even but with an edge of steel beneath the calm surface. The contrast between their responses—George's dismissal versus Ryker's respect—only reinforced the certainty growing inside me.

I needed distance not just from George but from Ryker too —from the vulnerability he coaxed from me, from the walls he kept dissolving with such gentle persistence. I needed to find solid ground within myself before I could navigate whatever lay between us.

"Goodbye," I said, the word directed at both of them and neither specifically. I turned and pushed through the bar's heavy door, the sudden weight of it requiring more strength than I expected, as if the universe itself were testing my resolve.

Behind me, I heard both men call my name, their voices overlapping in a dissonant chord that followed me into the night air. The cool breeze against my flushed skin provided momentary relief, the city sounds—passing cars, distant sirens, the muffled bass from a nearby club—creating a buffer between me and the emotional turbulence I'd just escaped.

I walked quickly down the street, my heels striking concrete with purposeful rhythm. My arms wrapped around my torso, holding myself together when it felt like I might fly apart with each step. Streetlights cast my shadow long and solitary on the pavement, stretching and contracting with each light I passed, a visual echo of the expansion and contraction happening inside me.

For six months, I'd been building a fortress around the wound George had left—using men's bodies, using Ryker's body, to prove I was desirable even as I kept my heart carefully guarded. But something had changed in these past weeks with Ryker; some fortress wall had crumbled under his patient siege. And now, with George's unexpected reappearance, I found myself caught between past and potential future, between the woman I'd been and the woman I might become.

I walked alone through the night-quiet streets, retreating into the emotional fortress I'd constructed—not to hide forever, but to gather myself, to find the center that had been shaken by both men in different ways. The key pendant Ryker had given me rested against my collarbone, its weight both comfort and question as I put distance between myself and the choices I wasn't ready to make.

CHAPTER NINETEEN

War of Words

L ast night, after walking away from both George and Ryker at the hotel bar, I found myself standing at Ryker's door, my finger hovering over his doorbell. His text had been simple: "We need to talk." No pressure, no ultimatum, just four words that had gnawed at me until I'd finally relented. The key pendant he'd given me felt unnaturally heavy against my collarbone as I pressed the bell, the soft chime echoing my racing heartbeat. I'd told them both I needed space, yet here I was, voluntarily stepping back into the very situation I'd fled.

When Ryker opened the door, the familiar scent of sandal-wood washed over me. He wore simple black sweatpants and a fitted gray t-shirt, his feet bare against the hardwood floor. No words of greeting, just a slight step aside—an invitation rather than an insistence. I moved past him into the dimly lit apart-ment, my shoulders tight with tension I couldn't disguise.

City lights winked through his floor-to-ceiling windows, a constellation of artificial stars against the night sky. The space felt both familiar and foreign—I'd been here often enough to know the layout intimately, yet tonight the shadows seemed deeper, the air charged with something I couldn't quite put my finger on.

"Drink?" he asked, his voice carrying that same measured control I'd come to expect, though a subtle roughness at its edges suggested emotion held carefully in check.

"No," I replied, standing my ground even as he gestured to the couch. "I'm not staying long; I just wanted to see what your text was about."

Ryker nodded once, moving toward the kitchen island that gleamed like obsidian in the low light. He rested his palms against its cool surface, the posture placing him directly across from me, the granite slab a physical barrier between us that somehow mirrored all the others I'd erected since our first meeting.

"I'm tired of only getting half of you," he said finally, the words dropping between us like stones into still water.

I crossed my arms, the familiar defensive gesture automatic as my chin lifted slightly. "I never promised you more than that."

"Didn't you?" His eyes—so perceptively green even in this dim light—held mine with uncomfortable intensity. "Every time you come back, every time you stay a little longer, every text you answer... those are promises, Elara. Small ones, maybe, but they add up."

My laugh sounded brittle even to my own ears. "That's quite the interpretation. I come here for sex, Ryker. Good sex, admittedly, but let's not pretend it's something more significant."

His expression didn't change, but something flickered in his eyes—a hurt quickly masked, a patience wearing thin. "Last week," he said, his voice deliberately even, "you fell asleep in my arms watching that documentary. When you woke up, you looked at me with such openness, such vulnerability. Then the moment you realized what was happening, you manufactured an excuse about an early meeting and left."

Heat crawled up my neck, embarrassment mingling with anger at having my patterns so accurately named. "Analyzing my sleep habits now? That's not obsessive at all."

"Tuesday night," he continued as if I hadn't spoken, "you were telling me about your childhood pet, that ridiculous one-eared rabbit. You were laughing, really laughing, and then suddenly stopped mid-sentence. Made a joke about boring me and changed the subject to something sexual."

My fingers curled tighter around my biceps, nails digging crescent moons into my own skin. "Sorry for trying to keep things interesting. Next time I'll be sure to bore you with my complete childhood pet catalog."

"And yesterday morning," he pressed on, his voice dropping lower, "when I kissed you goodbye, you kissed me back—really kissed me. Not the calculated seduction you've perfected, not the performance you've been giving for six months. Something real. Then you practically ran out the door."

"Are you keeping a diary of my perceived emotional failures?" I snapped, heat rising in my cheeks. "Making a list of all the ways I don't meet your expectations?"

Ryker's hands tightened on the countertop, knuckles whitening with pressure. "They're not failures, Elara. They're glimpses of you—the real you, not the carefully constructed facade you've been hiding behind."

My fingers found the key pendant at my collarbone, twisting it nervously between thumb and forefinger. The metal had warmed against my skin, a constant reminder of his silent invitation: For when you're ready to stop running. I wasn't ready. I wasn't.

"You don't know the first thing about the 'real me,'" I said, the words emerging sharper than intended. "You've constructed this fantasy woman from bits and pieces you think you've seen. Congratulations on your imagination, but I'm not some puzzle for you to solve."

"You're right," he agreed, the unexpected concession momentarily throwing me off balance. "I don't know the whole you. You've made damn sure of that. But I know more than you think, and definitely more than you're comfortable with."

"This is ridiculous." I took a step backward, closer to the door, my escape route already mapping itself in my mind. "I didn't come here to be psychoanalyzed."

"Why did you come, then?" He pushed away from the island, walking around it with deliberate steps. "Because I asked? Because despite all your careful distance, you can't quite stay away? Because whatever's happening between us scares you exactly because it matters?"

Each question felt like a precision strike against walls I'd spent six months reinforcing. I continued backing up until my shoulders met the cool surface of his living room wall. "Nothing's happening between us," I insisted, the lie bitter on my tongue. "We fuck. We occasionally share a meal. We're two adults enjoying each other's bodies without complications."

"Bullshit." The rare profanity from his usually measured mouth startled me. "You're here wearing my necklace. You kept my borrowed shirt. You've left a toothbrush in my bathroom. Those aren't the actions of someone maintaining casual distance."

"Don't make this into something it's not," I warned, my voice tight with the effort of maintaining control. My fingers worked the pendant faster, a nervous tell I couldn't seem to stop. "You knew what this was from the beginning."

Rykcr took another step closer, the space between us narrowing to dangerous proximity. "No, I knew what you wanted it to be. I knew what you were trying to convince yourself it was. But we both know it's become something else."

"Stay back," I warned, pressing myself harder against the wall as if I could somehow melt through it.

He paused, studying my face with that damnable perception that seemed to see straight through every defense. "What are you so afraid of, Elara? That I'll hurt you like George did? Or that I won't, and then you'll have no excuse to keep running?"

The mention of George's name sent a shock of fresh pain through me, memories of the hotel bar still raw and unprocessed. Ryker was too close now, his presence overwhelming my senses—the sandalwood scent of him, the heat radiating from his body, the intensity of his gaze that demanded truth I wasn't ready to give.

"You don't get to use him against me," I hissed, anger finally overtaking anxiety. "You don't get to pretend you understand what happened."

"Then tell me," he said, closing the final distance between us. "Help me understand."

Something inside me snapped—the tenuous thread of control I'd been clinging to finally breaking under the weight of his gentle persistence, his refusal to accept the barriers I'd erected. My hands shot out without conscious direction, connecting solidly with his chest in a hard shove that sent him stumbling backward.

"I said, stay back!" The words came out as a half-shout, my voice cracking with emotion I couldn't control, tears starting to leak uncontrollably from my eyes.

Ryker regained his balance quickly, his expression shifting from surprise to something more complicated—concern mingled with determination. We stared at each other across the small space I'd forcibly created, both breathing heavily, the air between us charged with potential energy—a storm building pressure without release.

"I'm not him," Ryker said finally, his voice quiet but firm. "I'm not going anywhere, Elara. No matter how hard you push."

The silence between us stretched taut as a wire, vibrating with the aftermath of my physical outburst. My palms tingled where they'd connected with his chest, the solid warmth of him lingering against my skin. Ryker's words—"I'm not going anywhere"—hung in the air between us, a declaration that felt like both threat and promise. I couldn't bear the gentleness in his eyes, the patience that eroded my defenses more effectively than any anger could have. Something wild and desperate clawed at my insides, demanding release, demanding escape. I lunged forward again, hands aimed at his chest, but this time he was ready.

His fingers closed around my wrists with precise strength, halting my advance mid-motion. The sudden restraint sent electricity racing along my nerves, a confusing mixture of panic and something darker, more primal. He backed me against the wall again, my shoulder blades pressing into the cool surface as he pinned my hands at either side of my head. Our bodies aligned—chest to chest, hip to hip, thigh to thigh—his heat radiating through the thin fabric separating us.

"Let go," I hissed, the demand undercut by the breathless quality of my voice.

"No," he replied, his face inches from mine. "I'm done letting you run."

I struggled against his grip, testing the boundaries of his restraint. His hold remained firm but careful, containing without hurting. The controlled strength in his hands sent heat pooling low in my abdomen, my body responding to him with embarrassing eagerness despite—or perhaps because of—the charged confrontation.

"I hate you," I whispered, the lie tasting bitter on my tongue even as it left my mouth.

"No, you don't," he countered, his eyes searching mine with that penetrating gaze that always saw too much. "You hate that I make you feel. You hate that I see past the walls you've built. You hate that I want all of you, not just the parts you've decided are safe to show."

The truth in his words burned like acid, dissolving the last threads of my restraint. With a sudden twist, I freed one hand and tangled my fingers in his hair, yanking sharply at the roots. His sharp intake of breath was my only warning before his mouth crashed against mine, the kiss nothing like the measured explorations of our previous encounters. This was claiming, consuming, teeth clashing, and lips bruising as we poured months of frustrated longing into the contact.

I bit his lower lip hard enough to draw the metallic tang of blood, my free hand clawing at his shoulder, nails digging through the thin cotton of his t-shirt. His response was imme-diate—one hand releasing my captive wrist to grasp my hip with bruising intensity, pulling me harder against him until I felt the rigid evidence of his arousal pressing into my stomach.

My newly freed hand reached between us, fingers curling into the fabric of his shirt. With one violent tug, the material gave way, buttons scattering across the hardwood floor like tiny missiles. The sound of tearing fabric mingled with our ragged breathing as Ryker retaliated, ripping my blouse open with equal ferocity, exposing the black lace beneath to his hungry gaze.

"Is this what you want?" he growled against my mouth, the question containing both challenge and consent-seeking despite the aggression in his tone. "To tear each other apart instead of talking?"

"Yes," I gasped, arching into him as his teeth found the sensitive juncture where my neck met my shoulder. "No more talking. No more analyzing. Just this."

His hands moved to the backs of my thighs, lifting me in one fluid motion. My legs wrapped around his waist instinctively, ankles crossing at the small of his back as he carried me from the living room. My mouth found his again, our kiss devouring rather than savoring, tongues battling for dominance that neither would concede.

The journey to his bedroom was punctuated by collisions with walls, my back pressing against various surfaces as Ryker paused to adjust his grip, each stop another opportunity for our mouths to wage war, for hands to claw at remaining clothing. By the time we reached his room, my blouse hung in tatters from my shoulders, his shirt completely gone, our skin marked with crescent indentations from grasping fingers.

He pressed me against the wall beside his bed, one hand supporting my weight while the other worked at the fastening of my pants. I retaliated by dragging my nails down his back, leaving red trails I knew would linger for days—physical evidence of this moment neither of us could deny later. The pain seemed to spur him on, his movements becoming more urgent, less controlled.

"Mark me," I demanded, tilting my head to expose my neck further to his mouth. "Make me feel it."

His teeth scraped against my collarbone, then bit down with careful force—hard enough to leave an impression, controlled enough to balance pleasure with pain. The sensation sent shockwaves through my nervous system, a moan escaping my throat that contained no performance, no calculated seduction, just raw response.

With fumbling urgency, we managed to rid ourselves of remaining barriers—my pants shoved down and discarded, his sweatpants pushed just low enough for access. When he entered me with one powerful thrust, the force of it drove the air from my lungs in a gasping cry. My head fell back against the wall, eyes squeezing shut against the overwhelming intensity.

"Look at me," he commanded, one hand moving to grasp my jaw, forcing my gaze to his. "Stay with me. Right here."

The demand pierced through the haze of physical sensation, requiring a presence I typically avoided in these moments. I forced my eyes open, meeting his with reluctant vulnerability as he established a rhythm that left no room for performance or calculation—hard, deep thrusts that sent me pushing back against the wall with each forward motion.

My fingers dug into his shoulders, seeking an anchor against the rising tide of sensation threatening to overwhelm me. "Harder," I gasped, the challenge both deflection and genuine desire. "I won't break."

Something flashed in his eyes—recognition of my strategy, perhaps, but acceptance of the challenge nonetheless. He adjusted his grip, hands sliding beneath my thighs to spread me wider, changing the angle to one that sent sparks of almost unbearable pleasure radiating outward from where our bodies joined.

We tumbled onto his bed moments later, a tangle of limbs and grasping hands against midnight-blue sheets. Ryker used our momentum to pin me beneath him, capturing both my wrists in one strong hand and pressing them above my head against the mattress. The position left me exposed, vulnerable in a way that should have triggered panic but instead sent fresh heat coursing through my veins.

"Is this what you need?" he asked, his voice rough with exertion and emotion. "To be taken? To surrender control just for tonight?"

The echo of our previous confrontation—these same questions asked in a different context—sent a tremor through me. Instead of answering, I arched upward, using the leverage of my legs around his waist to flip our positions. The move caught him by surprise, allowing me to straddle him, hands pressing his shoulders into the mattress as I established a new rhythm—riding him with an intensity that bordered on punishment, for him or for myself, I couldn't be sure.

His hands found my hips, fingers digging into flesh with calculated pressure that would leave marks—evidence I couldn't deny of passion that had transcended the controlled encounters I'd cultivated since George. I leaned forward, my hair creating a curtain around our faces as I pressed my forehead against his, our breath mingling in the small space between us.

"Tell me to stop," I challenged, my voice barely recognizable to my own ears. "Tell me this is too much."

Instead of words, his response was to thrust upward with renewed force, matching my intensity with his own. One hand tangled in my hair, pulling sharply to expose my throat to his mouth. The slight pain merged with pleasure, boundaries blurring until I couldn't distinguish where one ended and the other began.

Our bodies moved together with none of the practiced coordination of our previous encounters—this was raw, primal, a physical manifestation of emotional wounds we'd both been circling for weeks. Every touch contained anger and tenderness in equal measure, every kiss both punishment and reward. We marked each other with deliberate intent—his teeth against the sensitive skin of my breast, my nails carving temporary ownership into the muscles of his back.

When release finally claimed me, it crashed through with devastating force, muscles clenching around him in rhythmic pulses that drew a guttural groan from deep in his chest. He followed moments later, his body tensing beneath mine, his arms tightening around my waist as if afraid I might somehow slip away at the moment of greatest connection.

The intensity of our shared release left me boneless, my limbs heavy with exhaustion as I collapsed beside Ryker on the tangled sheets. The frantic energy that had driven our encounter dissipated like smoke, leaving behind a strange stillness I didn't know how to navigate. This was typically when I'd begin planning my exit—task accomplished, physical release achieved, no lingering required—but my body refused to cooperate, muscles still trembling with aftershocks that felt deeper than merely physical. Ryker's breathing gradually slowed beside me, his chest rising and falling in a rhythm that somehow anchored me to the present moment, preventing the usual mental escape that preceded my physical one.

City lights filtered through the uncovered windows, casting blue-tinged shadows across our bodies—illuminating the evidence of what had just transpired between us. In the gentle glow, I could see the marks we'd left on each other—red welts from grasping fingers, the faint impression of teeth against his shoulder, the darkening bruise where my collarbone met my neck. Physical manifestations of something I couldn't bring myself to name.

My gaze fixed on a particular scratch that curved from

Ryker's shoulder toward his chest—slightly deeper than the others, the raised line angry against his skin. Had I done that? The realization sent an uncomfortable wave of something like shame through me. My hand moved of its own accord, fingers reaching out to trace the mark with feather-light pressure. I felt the slight tremor in my touch, an uncharacteristic unsteadiness that betrayed my usual post-sex confidence.

Ryker remained perfectly still beneath my exploring fingers, his only movement the continued rise and fall of his chest. When I finally gathered the courage to meet his eyes, I found him watching me with that penetrating gaze that always seemed to see straight through my carefully constructed facades. He didn't speak, didn't pressure me with questions or demands, just maintained that steady eye contact I typically avoided after sex—the kind that threatened the emotional distance I fought so hard to maintain.

This wasn't like me—this lingering touch, this silent acknowledgment of what had passed between us. My usual pattern was well-established: passionate encounter followed by practiced nonchalance, perhaps a shower if the exertion warranted it, then a perfectly reasonable excuse to leave. The script had served me well for six months, keeping men at precisely the distance I required—close enough for physical satisfaction, far enough to prevent emotional entanglement.

Yet here I was, my fingertips still resting against the mark I'd left on Ryker's skin, my eyes locked with his in a connection that felt more intimate than the joining of our bodies had been. Something had shifted during our violent coming together; some wall had cracked that I couldn't seem to repair in the quiet aftermath.

"I didn't mean to hurt you," I whispered, the words emerging unbidden, surprising me with their honesty.

The corner of Ryker's mouth lifted slightly—not quite a smile, more an acknowledgment. "Yes, you did," he replied, his voice gentle despite the blunt assessment. "We both meant everything we did tonight."

The truth in his words sent a tremor through me, a hairline fracture spreading through foundations I'd thought solid. My eyes burned suddenly, a pressure building behind them that I recognized with dawning horror as unshed tears. I blinked rapidly, turning my face slightly to hide this unprecedented betrayal of my body.

Ryker's hand moved to cup my cheek, turning my face back toward his with gentle insistence. "Don't," he said softly. "Don't hide from me. Not now."

I swallowed hard, the movement visible and audible in the quiet room. Something was happening inside me—walls crumbling faster than I could rebuild them, emotions surging through cracks I couldn't seem to seal. Six months of careful distance, of using my body to maintain control rather than create connection, and now this: trembling in the aftermath of passion that had been as emotional as physical, unable to deploy my usual defenses against the tenderness in Ryker's eyes.

A single tear escaped despite my efforts, tracking a warm path down my temple and into my hair. Ryker brushed his thumb across the damp trail, the gentle touch undoing me further. More tears followed, silent but unstoppable, like a dam giving way after months of increasing pressure.

"It's okay," he murmured, fingers threading through my hair, brushing it back from my face with a tenderness that contrasted sharply with the aggression of our earlier encounter. For the first time, I didn't pull away from this gentleness, didn't deflect with practiced seduction or manufactured distance.

My lower lip quivered slightly, a physical tell I couldn't control. My fingers curled into the midnight-blue sheets, grasping at the fabric as if seeking an anchor against the emotional tide threatening to sweep me away. The hollow space inside me—the void I'd been trying to fill with meaningless encounters since George—ached with new awareness, with the possibility that perhaps it couldn't be filled with physical connection alone.

"I don't know how to do this," I admitted, my voice barely audible even in the quiet room.

"Do what?" Ryker asked, his hand continuing its gentle movement through my hair.

The question hung between us, deceptively simple yet impossibly complex. What was "this," exactly? Vulnerability? Intimacy beyond the physical? The possibility of connection I'd convinced myself I no longer needed or wanted?

"Be here," I managed finally. "Without performing. Without calculating my exit. Without keeping parts of myself hidden."

His expression softened further, something like under-standing mixed with relief crossing his features. "You don't have to know how," he said. "You just have to be willing to try."

The simplicity of his response cracked something funda-mental inside me—the belief that I needed to be perfect, to have everything figured out, to protect myself from ever being hurt again. A sound escaped my throat—not quite a sob, but close—as the full weight of what I'd been doing for six months crashed down on me. The men, the clubs, the calculated seduc-tions... none of it had healed the wound George had left. It had merely numbed me to the possibility of genuine connection.

Ryker's arms encircled me, drawing me against the solid warmth of his chest. Unlike every other time he'd held me, I didn't stiffen or immediately begin planning my escape. Instead, I let myself be held, my ear pressed against his heart, its steady rhythm somehow both comforting and terrifying in what it represented—consistency, presence, the opposite of the temporary connections I'd cultivated since George.

"I'm scared," I whispered against his skin, the words so quiet they were barely sound at all—just breath shaped into my deepest truth.

His arms tightened around me, one hand cradling the back of my head while the other traced soothing patterns along my spine. "I know," he replied, his lips pressing gently against my forehead. "I know you are."

We lay like that—my body curled against his, his arms forming a shelter I hadn't realized I was seeking—as city lights continued to cast blue shadows across his bedroom. For the first time in six months, I let myself be fully present in this moment of connection, without planning my escape, maintaining no careful distance, and without using my body as both weapon and shield.

The key pendant he'd given me rested between us, warmed by our shared body heat. For when you're ready to stop running. I wasn't sure if I was ready—wasn't sure I would ever be completely ready—but as Ryker's heartbeat echoed beneath my ear, steady and unwavering, I found myself taking the first tentative step away from flight and toward something I'd been too afraid to name.

CHAPTER TWENTY
The Revelation

Morning light pierced through a gap in Ryker's curtains, casting warm stripes across my face that pulled me from sleep. I blinked into awareness, my body registering several sensations at once: the luxurious weight of his high-thread-count sheets against my bare skin, the pleasant ache in muscles that spoke of the previous night's exertions, and most alarmingly, the empty space beside me where Ryker's warmth should have been. I sat up, clutching the sheet to my chest, my heartbeat quickening as I realized I'd done the one thing I vowed never to do again: to let someone in—if they can get in, they can hurt me.

THE REALIZATION SENT a jolt of panic through me. Six months of careful patterns broken, six months of maintaining control shattered in a single night of vulnerability. My fingers traced a tender spot at the junction of my neck and shoulder, the slight sting confirming what I already knew—Ryker had marked me in ways that would linger for days, maybe longer. I examined my wrists, finding faint bruises from where he'd pinned me against the wall, from where I'd asked him to hold me tighter.

. . .

MY GAZE SWEPT THE ROOM, searching for my scattered clothes. The previous night replayed in flashes— the confrontation in his living room, the desperate clash of our bodies, the tears I'd let fall as we lay tangled together afterward. I'd been more exposed than naked with him, more vulnerable than I'd been with anyone since George. Who was I kidding? I was never even that vulnerable in front of George. The memory ignited fresh panic, triggering the familiar escape route in my mind.

I SAW my underwear near the foot of the bed, and my torn blouse was draped over his dresser. I really needed to start bringing extra clothes with me, I thought to myself. I began calculating how quickly I could get dressed and leave; I would need to borrow another top and think about how to explain my quick departure in a text later—something about an early meeting, a friend in crisis, or any excuse that would help me regain the distance I'd let dissolve.

THE SHEET WRAPPED around me like a toga. I slid from the bed, my bare feet connecting with cool hardwood. The movement awakened new twinges of pleasant soreness, physical reminders of passion that had been as emotional as it was physical. I reached for my underwear, fingers closing around the black lace when I heard the unmistakable sound of foot-steps approaching.

MY BODY FROZE, caught in the act of escape. The bedroom door swung open, and there was Ryker, two steaming mugs in his hands, his expression shifting from neutral to something more complex when he spotted me standing there, sheet clutched to my chest, underwear dangling from my fingertips like evidence at a crime scene.

"MORNING," he said, his voice carrying that same measured control I'd come to expect, though a slight roughness at its edges suggested emotion held carefully in check.

MY EYES TRAVELED OVER HIM, cataloging details with involuntary precision. He wore only low-hanging sweatpants, his chest bare and marked with evidence of our encounter. Thin red lines tracked across his shoulders where my nails had dug in, a darkening bruise visible just above his collarbone where my teeth had been less than gentle. The sight of those marks sent heat rushing to my face, an unfamiliar embarrassment washing over me.

"I MADE COFFEE," he continued, crossing to the nightstand to set one mug down before offering the other to me. The familiar scent of fresh coffee mingled with his cologne; it was a smell I'd come to associate exclusively with him, affecting me in ways I wasn't prepared for.

I DROPPED MY UNDERWEAR, accepting the mug with fingers that weren't entirely steady, the warm ceramic providing a welcome anchor for my hands. Ryker settled on the edge of the bed rather than beside me, maintaining a careful distance that somehow felt more intimate than closeness would have been

—a deliberate choice to give me space rather than an instinctive withdrawal.

"Thank you," I managed, my voice coming out huskier than I intended. I took a sip, the bitter warmth spreading across my tongue, a familiar taste from mornings in the kitchen. The warmth made me feel sated. I closed my eyes and took a deep breath.

The silence between us stretched, electric with unspoken words. I remained standing, the sheet clutched to my chest with my free hand, suddenly aware of my nakedness. This wasn't calculated nudity I'd wielded like a weapon; this was something raw, unadorned, a vulnerability I wasn't entirely sure how to navigate.

Ryker watched me over the rim of his mug, those perceptive green eyes missing nothing, not the way my gaze kept darting to my discarded clothing, not the slight tremor in my fingers around the mug, not the tension evident in my shoulders as I stood poised between staying and fleeing.

"Why do you always run?" he asked finally, the question soft but demanding.

My spine stiffened, muscles tensing as if preparing for physical impact rather than the emotional blow his words delivered.

The instinct to deflect, to erect walls between his perception and my truth, surged through me.

"I have things to do," I replied, the excuse sounding hollow even to my own ears. "Work, responsibilities. The usual."

His expression didn't change, but something in his eyes; a slight sharpening of focus, an increased attentiveness, told me he'd caught the lie beneath my words. "It's Saturday, Elara."

I took another sip of coffee, using the moment to rebuild walls that seemed to crumble in his presence. "I still have things to do."

"Like what?" he pressed, his tone gentle but persistent. "What's so urgent that you need to run away from this? From me?"

"I'm not running," I insisted, even as my eyes darted toward the door, calculating the steps required to escape this conversation, this room, this moment of dangerous honesty.

After taking a sip, Ryker set his mug down on the nightstand, the deliberate movement drawing my attention back to him. The morning light caught the angles of his face differently than the club's artificial illumination or his bedroom's intimate glow, revealing complexities I'd allowed myself to notice in unguarded moments but had never fully acknowledged. The slight crease between his brows as he studied me, the patient set of his mouth, the careful way he held himself still, as if afraid any sudden movement might spook me into flight.

"You're still holding your clothes," he observed quietly, nodding toward my free hand that had somehow reclaimed my underwear without conscious decision.

I glanced down, surprised to find the black lace tangled around my fingers again. My throat tightened, making speech suddenly difficult. The sheet slipped slightly as I adjusted my grip on the coffee mug, revealing the curve of one shoulder marked with evidence of his mouth from the night before.

"I think we need to talk about last night," Ryker said, the words a gentle invitation rather than a demand.

My defenses rose immediately, a reflexive shield against the vulnerability his words threatened to expose again. "It was just sex," I said, the familiar deflection automatic, "Intense, yes, but nothing we need to analyze over coffee."

His eyes held mine with uncomfortable intensity. "You know it wasn't just sex, Elara."

. . .

THE TRUTH in his simple statement sent a tremor through me, nearly spilling coffee over the rim of my mug. In all these months of carefully managed encounters, I had never felt like this, exposed, uncertain, caught between conflicting desires to flee and to fall.

I TIGHTENED my grip on the sheet, as if the thin fabric could somehow shield me from the truth in Ryker's words. "Look, last night was..." I trailed off, searching for a word that would minimize what happened between us. "Intense. Different. But that doesn't mean..." The words died in my throat as Ryker stood, closing the distance between us with measured steps. My body tensed, preparing for either confrontation or escape, but he took the coffee mug from my unsteady hands and placed it beside his on the nightstand.

"SIT WITH ME," he said, the words somewhere between invitation and gentle command. When I didn't move, frozen in indecision, he added, "Please."

SOMETHING IN HIS TONE—a hint of vulnerability beneath the usual confidence—made refusal impossible. I perched on the edge of the mattress, the sheet still wrapped tightly around me. Ryker settled beside me, close enough that our shoulders touched, his skin warm against mine through the thin fabric. The contact sent awareness skittering across my nerves, my body responding to his proximity with embarrassing eagerness despite my mental reservations.

. . .

"THIS DOESN'T HAVE to be complicated," I said, forcing lightness into my tone. My hand dropped to his thigh, fingers tracing a deliberate path upward. We could skip the morning-after analysis and just..." I leaned closer, my lips brushing the sensitive spot below his ear that I'd discovered made his breath catch.

HIS HAND CAUGHT my wrist before I could continue my advance, his grip firm but gentle. "Elara," he said, my name half-sigh, half-warning. "You can't seduce your way out of this conversation."

HEAT FLOODED MY CHEEKS, not the warm flush of desire but the burning acknowledgment of being seen too clearly, of having my strategy named so accurately. I tugged my hand away, frustration rising at having my usual method of deflection neutralized so easily.

"THEN WHAT DO you want from me?" The question emerged sharper than intended, edged with the fear I was trying desperately to disguise as irritation.

INSTEAD OF ANSWERING, Ryker reached toward his nightstand, pulling open the drawer and withdrawing something I couldn't immediately identify. When he settled back beside me, I saw it was a photograph—well-handled, its edges softened from frequent touch. He held it between us, allowing me to see without forcing it upon me.

. . .

The image showed a younger Ryker, perhaps five years or so ago, his face more open, less guarded, with his arm around a woman whose smile didn't quite reach her eyes. They stood on what looked like a beach at sunset, the colors faded slightly with age or exposure.

"Her name was Vanessa," he said, his voice dropping to a register I hadn't heard before, lower, rougher, scraped raw by old pain. "We were together for almost five years. I thought we'd get married."

I stared at the photograph, taking in the details, the way his body curved protectively around hers, the slight distance in her expression despite their physical closeness. Something about that disconnection felt unnervingly familiar, as if I were looking at a mirror reflecting my own careful maintenance of emotional barriers.

"What happened?" The question slipped out before I could stop it, genuine curiosity overriding my usual disinterest in others' histories.

Ryker's thumb brushed over the image, a gesture so gentle it made my chest ache with unexpected recognition. "She was building her career in finance. I was expanding my business. We were both ambitious, driven." His shoulders rose and fell in a small shrug that didn't quite disguise the lingering hurt. "I thought we were partners in it all. Turns out, I was just a stepping stone."

My fingers trembled against the sheet still clutched to my chest. I recognized the careful neutrality in his tone, the same voice I used when discussing George, when pretending the wound had scarred over completely.

"She was offered a position in London—the kind of opportunity that comes once in a lifetime. I was ready to make it work, to build a life there together and manage long-distance until I could join her." His jaw tightened momentarily before he continued. "I told her about a new model that I was designing and how it would have set us up for life once it was completed. That was why I couldn't join her immediately; I paid for the new apartment two years' rent in advance so it was secured for us. Since she was there and I wasn't, it made sense for it all to be in her name. Then, two weeks after she moved, I discovered she had taken my idea to her boss, with whom she had been sleeping with for at least the past twelve months. They copyrighted it together, and they made a fortune. The job offer was just the public reason for her departure; her boss had moved the week prior."

The familiar pattern of betrayal, different circumstances but the same core of rejection, sent an unexpected wave of empathy through me. I resisted the urge to reach for his hand, to offer comfort I wasn't sure how to provide.

"I'm sorry," I said, the words inadequate but sincere.

. . .

He tucked the photograph away and turned slightly to face me more directly. "I don't keep this to remind me of her, but to remind myself of how easily someone fooled me. For a year afterward, I did exactly what you've been doing—used people, kept them at a distance, and made sure I never stayed long enough to risk getting hurt again."

The recognition in his words, the accurate naming of my strategy, made my breath catch. "Sounds efficient," I managed, attempting to maintain some semblance of emotional distance even as his story struck uncomfortably close to home.

"It was," he agreed, surprising me. "Very efficient. Very empty. And then I met you that night." His eyes found mine, their green depths holding both understanding and challenge. "I know what it's like to build walls, Elara. To use your body as both shield and weapon. To convince yourself that control means safety."

I swallowed hard, my throat suddenly dry. "Maybe it does."

But I also know those walls keep out the good along with the bad," he continued, his voice softening further. "They keep out possibility. Connection. The chance to feel something real again."

My coffee mug sat abandoned on the nightstand, cooling as rapidly as my defenses were weakening under his careful siege.

I clutched the sheet tighter, as if the thin fabric could somehow protect me from the truth in his words, from the dangerous parallels between his experience and mine.

"WHAT IF REAL ISN'T WORTH the risk?" I asked, the question containing more honesty than I'd intended to reveal.

HIS HAND MOVED to cover mine, where it gripped the sheet, his touch careful, questioning. "What if it is?"

THE SIMPLE COUNTER-QUESTION hung between us, weighted with implications I wasn't sure I was ready to consider. My fingers trembled beneath his, the physical betrayal of emotion I couldn't quite contain. The key pendant he'd given me felt suddenly heavy against my collarbone, its weight both comfort and question as I sat suspended between flight and possibility.

"YOU'RE afraid I'll hurt you," he said, the statement containing neither accusation nor demand, just quiet certainty. "The way George did. The way Vanessa hurt me."

I NODDED SLIGHTLY, the admission more than I'd granted anyone since my transformation. "Fear is a pretty reliable compass," I said, attempting to inject lightness into my voice and failing completely. "It's kept me safe for six months."

. . .

"Safe," he repeated, the word carrying a weight of assessment. "But are you happy, Elara?"

The question hit home, exposing the hairline fracture in my carefully built facade. Happy wasn't a metric I'd been tracking. Satisfied, yes. In control, definitely. But happy? The empty space inside me, the void I'd been trying to fill with pointless encounters, suddenly ached with awareness.

"I don't know if happy is the point," I deflected, my voice barely above a whisper.

Ryker's hand remained steady on mine, his thumb tracing small circles against my knuckles. "Then what is?"

"Not getting hurt again," I answered immediately, the truth emerging before I could dress it in something more sophisticated, more calculated.

His expression softened further, understanding rather than pity filling his eyes. "I can't promise I won't hurt you," he said, the honesty in his words more compelling than any easy reassurance could have been. "No one can make that promise. But I can promise to never deliberately cause you pain. To be careful with what you trust me with."

My breath caught, the simple declaration penetrating defenses more effectively than any grand romantic gesture could have. The morning light filtering through his curtains caught the marks on his body—evidence of passion that had transcended the controlled encounters I'd cultivated since George. My own skin bore similar marks, a physical record of connection I couldn't deny.

For the first time in six months, I allowed myself to consider that perhaps vulnerability wasn't weakness but another kind of strength—one I'd been too afraid to reclaim since George's rejection had shattered my world.

A slight movement caught my eye, drawing my attention to the mirror mounted on Ryker's dresser across the room. The woman reflected there startled me—wrapped in navy sheets that highlighted my paleness, hair tousled from sleep and the previous night's passion, eyes wider and more vulnerable than I had allowed them to be in months. For six months, I had carefully crafted my reflection—calculated makeup, deliberately chosen clothing, practiced expressions—but this woman looked stripped of artifice, simultaneously stronger and more fragile than the image I'd cultivated since George.

The recognition sent a strange stillness through me, a quieting of the constant internal voice that had been urging escape since I'd awakened. I studied my reflection with new awareness—the visible marks on my neck and shoulders not badges of conquest but evidence of connection I couldn't deny, the slight tremor in my hands not weakness but acknowledgment of something that mattered enough to fear its loss.

With deliberate care, I reached for my abandoned coffee mug, took a sip, and then set it beside Ryker's on the nightstand. The gesture felt symbolic somehow—a conscious choice to stay rather than flee, to engage rather than deflect. The ceramic made a soft sound against the wood, punctuating the decision forming inside me.

My fingers brushed the key pendant resting by my collarbone, its weight familiar after days of keeping it close to my skin. For when you're ready to stop running. When Ryker handed it to me, I slipped it on without fully understanding why, the metal warming against my skin like a promise I wasn't sure I could keep. Now, as morning light reflected off its silver surface, the meaning felt less threatening, more like an invitation than a demand.

"George and I were together for two years," I said quietly, the words emerging with surprising steadiness. "I thought we were building something real, something lasting."

Ryker remained still beside me, his breathing the only movement, giving me space to continue at my own pace. His silence felt different from other men's, not disinterest or impatience, but an attentive presence, offering the gift of being heard without interruption.

"We met at a charity event. He was charming, successful, seemed genuinely interested in my thoughts, my ambitions." My throat tightened around memories I'd spent months burying beneath meaningless encounters. "I molded myself to fit what I thought he wanted, the supportive girlfriend, the perfect hostess for his business dinners, always put-together, never demanding too much."

. . .

My FINGERS CLENCHED around the pendant, drawing strength from its solid presence. "Six months ago, he asked to meet at the café we frequented, the Bluebird, it was my birthday. I thought..." A bitter laugh escaped me. "God, I actually thought he might be proposing. We'd talked about the future, about building a life together."

RYKER'S HAND moved to cover mine, where it clutched the sheet, offering silent support without interrupting my flow of words. The warmth of his palm against my knuckles anchored me to the present as I navigated the painful past.

INSTEAD, he explained—so reasonably, so compassionately— that he needed space to evaluate what he truly wanted. That I was wonderful, but perhaps not the right fit for his long-term goals. I was predictable, and he was seeing a girl from work; he needed spontaneity in his life." My voice hardened around the remembered phrases that had dismantled my world. "Two hours later, I saw pictures of him with Madison at a gallery opening. She was everything I wasn't—bold where I was reserved, demanding where I was accommodating, confident in ways I'd never allowed myself to be."

THE SHEET SHIFTED SLIGHTLY as I moved, but I no longer felt the desperate need to clutch it like armor. "That night, Sam did my hair, makeup, and lent me clothes I'd never have worn when we were together, and I went to a club. I picked up a man whose name I didn't bother to remember. And it felt...power-ful. Like reclaiming something George had taken from me."

. . .

RYKER'S EXPRESSION remained carefully neutral, though his eyes betrayed understanding rather than judgment. "And that became your pattern."

I NODDED, the admission easier than I'd expected. "I thought power meant never letting anyone close enough to hurt me. Using men the way I felt used, being the one to walk away before they could." My voice dropped to barely above a whisper. "But beneath it all, I've been terrified of being hurt again, of being found insufficient again."

"YOU WERE NEVER INSUFFICIENT, ELARA," Ryker said, the quiet certainty in his voice making my chest tighten with emotion I couldn't quite name. "George's inability to recognize your worth reflects his limitations, not yours."

THE SIMPLE TRUTH in his words, the perspective I'd been unable to find in six months of carefully constructed indifference, sent an unexpected warmth through me, melting something frozen at my core.

"I THOUGHT I WAS SO CLEVER," I continued, a sad smile tugging at my lips. "Building this new identity, this woman who took what she wanted and needed no one. But I was just running, from pain, from rejection, from the possibility of caring enough about someone to give them the power to hurt me again."

· · ·

RYKER'S FINGERS tightened around mine, his thumb tracing small circles against my skin. "Real power isn't never getting hurt," he said, his voice low and certain. "Real power is knowing someone could hurt you, and letting them close anyway."

OUR EYES MET, the connection between us suddenly as tangible as the sheet wrapped around my body, as real as the marks we'd left on each other's skin. The key pendant felt warm against my collarbone, its message no longer a challenge but a possibility I was finally ready to consider.

"I'M STILL AFRAID," I admitted, the confession both terrifying and liberating.

"I know," he replied, the simple acknowledgment more comforting than any reassurance could have been. "So am I."

Our bodies gravitated toward each other with a naturalness that surprised me, closing the small distance between us on the edge of the bed. When his free hand rose to cup my cheek, I didn't flinch away as I might have days ago, instead leaning slightly into his touch, allowing the connection rather than retreating from it.

HIS LIPS MET mine without the urgent hunger of our past encounters. This kiss was different—gentle, questioning, an invitation instead of a demand. I responded with gentle tenderness, the exchange lacking the calculated passion I had perfected over six months of meaningless encounters. This wasn't seduction, distraction, or power play—this was presence, acknowledgment, the start of something I had been too afraid to name.

When we finally separated, my hands had somehow found their way to his shoulders, the sheet pooled around my waist, my body no longer seeking to hide behind fabric barriers. The physical exposure felt like metaphor for the emotional walls I was consciously choosing to lower—not all at once, not completely, but enough to allow possibility in.

"I can't promise I won't run again," I said honestly, holding his gaze despite the vulnerability the admission created. "Six months of patterns won't disappear overnight."

Ryker's smile held understanding rather than disappointment. "I'm not asking for overnight," he replied. "Just for you to run a little less far, a little less often. Maybe eventually, to stay."

The woman in the mirror caught my attention again—still wrapped in Ryker's sheets, still bearing the marks of our passion, but something had shifted in her expression. The tension that had tightened her features upon waking had softened into something more open, more present. This wasn't surrender or weakness, I realized with startling clarity. This was transformation—my strength not diminished by vulnerability but deepened by it, made more authentic by the willingness to risk rather than retreat.

My fingers traced the key pendant at my throat, its meaning shifting from challenge to choice. For when you're ready to stop running. I wasn't entirely ready—might never be completely free of the fear George's rejection had sown—but for the first time in six months, I found myself willing to pause, breathe, and consider the possibility that what lay beyond my carefully built walls might be worth the risk of pain.

"I think I'd like to try," I said finally, the words emerging soft but certain. "Not running, I mean. At least for today."

Ryker's answering smile—genuine, reaching his eyes in a way that transformed his entire face—held neither triumph nor demand, just quiet pleasure in the small victory we'd both won over fear.

"Today is a good place to start," he agreed, his fingers intertwining with mine in a connection that felt more intimate than the joining of our bodies had been. The morning light strengthened around us, warming the room with golden clarity that seemed to promise not endings but beginnings—not certainty, perhaps, but possibility.

CHAPTER TWENTY-ONE
The Reunion

The coffee had gone cold in my mug, forgotten in the wake of confessions I hadn't planned to make. Morning light filtered through Ryker's bedroom curtains, casting gentle patterns across the rumpled sheets that still held the memory of our bodies. I sat perched on the edge of his bed, one foot tucked beneath me, the other grazing the hardwood floor— positioned for flight even as I'd just promised to stay. The weight of that promise pressed against my chest, heavier than the key pendant resting against my collarbone.

I stared into the dark liquid, watching how the faint light caught its surface, turning it into a tiny mirror that reflected nothing clearly—much like the uncertain future stretching before me. The mug felt unreasonably heavy in my hands, as if the ceramic contained not just cooling coffee but the accumulation of six months of carefully maintained distance, of walls built brick by emotional brick after George had left me in ruins.

My fingers found the silver key at my throat, its edges smooth from days of nervous touching. For when you're ready to stop running. Was I ready? The thought sent a tremor through me, subtle but impossible to hide from myself. Stopping meant staying, and staying meant risking, and risking meant potential pain—a circular logic that had kept me safely moving, safely disconnected, for half a year.

The bedroom door opened with a soft click, and Ryker appeared, holding a fresh mug of coffee. He'd pulled on sweatpants but remained shirtless, the marks I'd left on his skin during our passionate night still visible in the morning light—evidence of connection I couldn't deny, couldn't dismiss as meaningless. He approached with careful steps, like someone approaching a wild animal they didn't want to startle. The bed dipped slightly as he sat beside me, close enough that I could feel the warmth radiating from his skin, far enough that our bodies didn't touch.

"Thought you might want a fresh cup," he said, offering the steaming mug. "That one's probably cold by now."

I nodded, exchanging mugs with him, our fingers brushing in a brief contact that sent awareness skittering across my skin. The fresh coffee smelled rich and inviting, but I merely held it, letting its heat seep into my palms.

Silence settled between us, not the comfortable quiet of longtime intimates nor the awkward pause of strangers, but something in-between—a space filled with things unsaid, with possibilities neither of us had dared name. I could feel his presence beside me, solid and patient, making no demands but offering no retreat either.

The words rose in my throat, pressing against my lips until I couldn't contain them anymore. "I've spent so long building these walls," I confessed, my voice emerging softer than intended, a slight tremor undermining my attempt at steadiness. My fingers traced the rim of the mug, giving me something to focus on besides the vulnerability of my admission. "I'm terrified of what happens if I let them down."

I didn't look at him as I spoke, couldn't bear to see whatever expression might cross his face—pity, triumph, disappointment, any of them would have sent me retreating back behind my carefully constructed barriers. But I felt his attention like a physical touch, his gaze a weight against my skin.

"I know," he said after a moment, his voice carrying that same measured control I'd come to expect, though a subtle roughness at its edges suggested emotion carefully contained. "I'm scared too."

The simple acknowledgment—his admission of fear that echoed my own—made me finally turn to look at him. His expression held none of the responses I'd feared, just open honesty that made my chest tighten with an emotion I couldn't quite name.

"You? Scared?" The question emerged with genuine surprise. In all our encounters, Ryker had seemed the embodiment of certainty, of confidence without arrogance.

A slight smile touched his lips, not reaching his eyes. "Terrified," he confirmed. "Every time you walk out my door, I wonder if it's the last time I'll see you. Every time you build another wall between us, I wonder if it's the one I won't be able to get past."

His hand moved toward mine, where it rested on the mattress between us, not grasping but offering—palm up, an invitation rather than a demand. "I'm afraid of rejection, too, Elara. Of caring for someone who doesn't want to be cared for. Of opening myself to someone who might decide I'm not worth the risk."

Something shifted inside me at his words—at the recognition that vulnerability wasn't one-sided, that in my careful protection of myself, I'd been causing the very pain I so feared experiencing. My hand moved of its own accord, fingers sliding against his palm until they intertwined with his—a simple connection that somehow felt more intimate than the passionate joining of our bodies had been.

"I want to be worth the risk," I whispered, the admission costing me more than I'd expected, each word pulled from somewhere deep and tender that I'd kept carefully guarded since George.

Ryker's fingers tightened around mine, the pressure gentle but grounding. "You already are," he said, the quiet certainty in his voice making my eyes burn with unexpected tears. "The question is whether you believe I am."

I didn't have an answer—not one I could voice aloud, not yet. But my body seemed to know what my mind still wrestled with. I found myself leaning toward him, the space between us narrowing until my shoulder pressed against his arm, the contact sending warmth cascading through me that had nothing to do with the coffee cooling in my hands.

Ryker's arm moved slowly, deliberately, lifting to wrap

around my shoulders—not pulling or demanding, just offering shelter that I could accept or reject. For the first time in six months, I allowed myself to lean into someone else's strength, to accept support without calculating the cost or planning my escape.

My head rested in the hollow of his shoulder, fitting perfectly as if made for that curve. The coffee mug wobbled in my hands, and Ryker reached to take it, placing it beside his on the nightstand. Freed from that small barrier, my body leaned further into his, craving a connection I had been denying myself for longer than I could remember.

When his free hand lifted to tilt my chin upward, I didn't resist. Our eyes met, his searching mine with a question I could understand without words. I gave a small nod, both permission and invitation. His forehead pressed against mine, our breath mixing in the small space between us.

In that moment of connection—simpler and more profound than any passionate embrace—I felt something inside me shift and settle. Not all my walls had fallen, not every fear had been vanquished, but a door had opened, a possibility had been acknowledged, a first step taken away from the isolation I'd mistaken for strength.

The space between us seemed charged with possibility, our foreheads still touching, breath mingling in shared air. His eyes —those perceptive green depths that had seen through my defenses from our first meeting—held a question I finally felt ready to answer. My hand rose of its own accord, fingers tracing the line of his jaw with a gentleness I'd rarely allowed myself to show. The coffee sat forgotten on the nightstand as I tilted my face upward, offering my lips to his in silent invitation.

Ryker hesitated, his gaze searching mine for certainty. When he finally closed the distance between us, his kiss was nothing like the demanding pressure I'd come to expect from our previous encounters. This was tentative, questioning—a brush of lips so gentle it sent an unexpected shiver down my spine. His hands moved to frame my face, palms warm against my cheeks, fingers threading into my hair with a reverence that made my chest tighten with emotion I couldn't name.

In our past collisions, kissing had been a means to an end —passionate but calculated, a step on the path to physical release. This felt like its own destination, a connection sought for its own sake rather than what might follow. I leaned into his touch, my eyes drifting closed as I allowed myself to simply experience the moment without planning its progression or calculating my escape.

His thumb brushed across my cheekbone with feather-light pressure, the small gesture somehow more intimate than the most explicit touches we'd shared in the darkness of his bedroom. I felt myself softening beneath his careful attention, walls lowering brick by emotional brick as the kiss gradually deepened. His tongue traced the seam of my lips, requesting rather than demanding entry. I opened to him with a small sound of surrender that surprised us both.

The heat between us built slowly, banked embers catching rather than erupting into an explosive flame. My hands grew restless against his shoulders, fingers tracing the contours of muscle beneath warm skin. With deliberate intent, I slid my palms beneath the hem of his shirt, exploring the terrain I'd previously mapped in urgent haste but now discovered anew with careful attention. The ridges of his abdomen contracted beneath my touch, his skin surprisingly soft over hard muscle.

"Elara," he murmured against my mouth, my name transformed into both question and plea.

I answered by tugging at his shirt, suddenly needing to eliminate barriers between us. He leaned back just enough to pull it over his head, the morning light catching the planes of his chest, highlighting the marks I'd left during our night together—evidence of passion now reframed by this new tenderness. When his hands returned to me, they carried the same careful deliberation, as if touching something precious rather than merely desirable.

With gentle pressure, he guided me backward until I lay against his pillows, his body following mine down to the mattress. The weight of him above me felt different than before—not the thrilling restriction of dominance but the comforting pressure of shared vulnerability. His lips found the pulse point at my throat, lingering there as if memorizing my heartbeat.

The scent of him enveloped me—sandalwood and clean sweat and something darker that was uniquely Ryker. I breathed him in, letting the familiar notes anchor me as we ventured into unfamiliar emotional territory. My fingers traced the muscles of his back, not clawing in desperate passion but exploring with appreciative touch.

The silk of his sheets whispered against my skin as I shifted beneath him, cool fabric a counterpoint to his radiating heat.

Piece by piece, our remaining clothes fell away—my borrowed t-shirt lifted over my head with reverent hands, his sweatpants pushed down and discarded, my underwear sliding down my legs with deliberate slowness. Each removal felt like more than just shedding fabric—layers of defense stripped away, leaving us naked in ways beyond the physical.

He paused above me, elbows braced on either side of my head, creating a private space that contained just the two of us. The morning light filtered through the curtains, painting patterns across his face, illuminating flecks of gold in his green eyes that I'd never noticed before. His expression held a vulnerability I'd never allowed myself to see—uncertainty, wonder, and something deeper that made my breath catch.

"I need to know this is different," he said, voice rough with restrained desire. "That this isn't just—"

"It's not," I interrupted, knowing exactly what he meant. Not just sex. Not just physical release. Not just another performance of passion without meaning. My hand rose to cup his cheek, thumb brushing across his lower lip. "I trust you," I whispered, the words emerging with surprising ease, truth I hadn't planned to offer but couldn't withhold.

Something shifted in his expression—relief mingled with determination, desire tempered by care. I reached for him, pulling him down until our bodies aligned, skin against skin with nothing between us—no barriers, no performance, no calculated seduction. Just Ryker and Elara, seeing and being seen.

When he entered me, the physical connection felt like an extension of the emotional bond we'd been building since I'd stopped running that morning. My breath escaped in a gasp that contained no artifice, no practiced sound designed to boost his pleasure, just a genuine response to sensation that went beyond the merely physical.

His movements were measured, deliberate—the commanding presence I'd come to expect now balanced with attentive care, responding to my every reaction. I found myself unusually vocal, not with the performative moans I'd perfected over six months of meaningless encounters, but with words I couldn't seem to contain.

"Yes," I breathed against his shoulder, "like that, please," and "stay with me," phrases I'd never allowed myself to utter, admissions of need and pleasure that felt dangerously vulnerable yet impossible to withhold.

His rhythm faltered at my unexpected openness, green eyes finding mine with an intensity that might have made me look away before. But I held his gaze, allowing him to see me— really see me—as we moved together toward shared release. His hand found mine, fingers intertwining against the sheets in a connection that mirrored our bodies.

"Tell me what you need," he urged, his voice rough with emotion and restraint.

"Just you," I answered truthfully, the simple words

containing depths I was only beginning to understand. "Just this."

He seemed to comprehend what I couldn't fully articulate —that "this" meant not just the physical act but the vulnerability we were sharing, the walls we were dismantling together, the trust being built with each unguarded moment. His forehead pressed against mine, maintaining that connection even as our bodies found an increasingly urgent rhythm.

When release finally claimed me, it felt different from every climax we'd shared before—not just physical pleasure cresting and breaking but something deeper, more complete. I called his name without calculation or artifice, the sound torn from somewhere deep and true within me. He followed moments later, my name on his lips like a prayer, his body tensing above mine before collapsing into my waiting arms.

We remained connected, neither rushing to separate, my hands tracing lazy patterns along the sweat-dampened skin of his back as our breathing gradually slowed. The vulnerability I'd feared for so long felt less like weakness and more like unexpected strength—the courage to be seen completely and still valued, still wanted, still held.

We lay tangled in sheets damp with sweat, our breathing gradually slowing to match the peaceful rhythm of the morning. Ryker's arm curved around my waist, his palm flat against the small of my back, holding me against him with gentle pressure that felt like an anchor rather than a restraint. Unlike every other time we'd shared his bed, I felt no immediate urge to calculate my exit, no mental inventory of excuses to disengage from this intimacy. Instead, I found myself memorizing details I'd never allowed myself to notice before—the exact cadence of his heartbeat beneath my ear, the specific pattern of freckles across his shoulder, the way his breathing changed slightly when my fingers traced absent patterns along his ribs.

A slight shiver passed through me—from cooling sweat or newfound vulnerability, I couldn't be sure. Ryker noticed immediately, his body shifting beside mine as he reached toward the foot of the bed, retrieving a thick blanket I hadn't seen him use before. With careful movements, he draped it over us both, tucking it around my shoulders with a tenderness that made my throat tighten.

"Better?" he asked, his voice carrying that same gentle concern that had characterized our lovemaking—attentive without demanding, caring without smothering.

I nodded against his chest, unable to find words for how this simple act of care affected me. In all our previous encounters, the aftermath had been carefully orchestrated performance—quick kisses, casual banter, calculated indifference masking my impatience to escape. This genuine attention to my comfort felt more intimate than the passion we'd just shared.

The morning light had strengthened, no longer the soft filter of dawn but the clear illumination of day. Golden patterns stretched across our bodies, highlighting the places where we connected—his arm around my waist, my leg thrown over his, our fingers loosely intertwined against his chest. The light revealed us completely to each other, not just physically but emotionally—no shadows to hide in, no darkness to mask vulnerability.

Ryker's free hand moved to my face, brushing a strand of hair that had fallen across my eyes. His fingertips lingered on my cheek, tracing the curve with a reverence that made me want to both pull away and lean closer. I'd grown accustomed to his touch in passion, in desire, in commanding moments that set my body aflame. This gentleness was newer territory, more frightening in its quiet intimacy than any dominant display had ever been.

"Stay," he said simply, the word hanging between us like both gift and question.

In the past, this request would have triggered immediate panic, activating well-worn escape routes in my mind. Today, I felt the flutter of anxiety but didn't surrender to it, didn't allow it to dictate my response. I turned slightly to face him more fully, studying the vulnerability in his eyes that matched my own.

"I'm not running anymore," I replied, my hand finding the key pendant at my throat—his gift from weeks before, the one I'd put on without fully understanding why, the symbol I'd been carrying against my skin even as I'd continued to flee emotionally. My fingers curved around its silver edges, feeling its weight as something chosen rather than imposed.

Something shifted in Ryker's expression—relief mingled with cautious joy, as if he'd been offered something precious but was afraid to grasp it too tightly. His thumb brushed across my lower lip with gentle pressure.

"I should make us some fresh coffee," he said after a moment, the ordinary suggestion somehow containing extraordinary meaning—an invitation to domestic intimacy I'd carefully avoided, an extension of our time together beyond the boundaries of physical connection.

I nodded, releasing him from our tangle of limbs. "I'd like that."

He pressed a kiss to my forehead before sliding from the bed, his movements carrying the same fluid grace that had first caught my attention at Obsidian so many weeks ago. I watched him retrieve his boxers from the floor and pull them on, making no attempt to hide my appreciation of his body in the clear morning light.

What struck me wasn't just his physical beauty—the broad shoulders tapering to narrow waist, the defined muscles moving smoothly beneath skin marked with evidence of our passion—but the ease with which he occupied his space, the comfortable confidence of a man who knew exactly who he was. As he padded toward the kitchen, I found myself captivated by this ordinary moment, this glimpse of Ryker beyond the bedroom, beyond the carefully controlled encounters I'd permitted until now.

The bed felt suddenly too large without him. I slid from beneath the blanket, scanning the floor for my borrowed t-shirt from the night before. Instead, I found his button-down draped over a chair—the one he'd worn yesterday before our emotional confrontation had turned physical. I pulled it on, the fabric still carrying his scent—sandalwood and something uniquely him, a combination that had once made me want to flee but now felt strangely like comfort.

I rolled the too-long sleeves to my elbows and followed the sounds of domestic activity to his kitchen. Ryker moved with practiced efficiency, measuring coffee grounds into a filter, filling the reservoir with water, his back to me as I leaned against the doorframe. The muscles of his shoulders flexed with each movement, his boxers riding low on his hips, and I found myself appreciating this unguarded version of him as much as the commanding lover I'd previously allowed myself to know.

He turned, seeming unsurprised to find me watching him. His eyes traveled over me—taking in his shirt hanging to mid-thigh on my frame, my bare legs, my uncombed hair—with an appreciation that felt different from mere desire. This was recognition, acknowledgment of something significant in finding me still here, wearing his clothes, making no move toward the door.

"You look good in my shirt," he said, a small smile playing at the corners of his mouth.

"It smells like you," I replied, honesty replacing the calculated response I might have given before.

The coffee maker gurgled behind him, filling the kitchen with a rich aroma that mingled with the scent of morning and lingering traces of our lovemaking. Ryker leaned against the counter, making no move to close the distance between us, allowing me this space to choose proximity rather than having it imposed.

I crossed to him, my body moving of its own accord, drawn to his warmth without the urgent need that had characterized our previous encounters. He handed me a steaming mug, our fingers brushing in an exchange that felt significant in its ordinariness. We stood side by side at his kitchen counter, bodies close but not touching, comfortable in the new silence between us.

This was unfamiliar territory—not the heated passion we'd perfected nor the careful distance I'd maintained, but something in between. Domestic intimacy, ordinary connection, the quiet comfort of shared space without agenda. I sipped my coffee, finding it prepared exactly as I preferred—strong with just enough sugar to cut the bitterness without overwhelming it.

"You remembered how I take it," I observed, surprise coloring my tone.

Ryker's shoulder brushed against mine as he shifted slightly closer. "I remember everything about you, Elara."

The simple statement should have triggered my defenses, should have activated the fear of being known too well, seen too clearly. Instead, I found myself leaning into him, my head coming to rest against his shoulder as we stood in comfortable silence, watching morning light stream through his kitchen windows.

Between us stretched something new—not the charged tension of unacknowledged desire nor the careful distance of emotional withdrawal, but a quiet understanding that required no words, no physical distraction, no performance to maintain. For the first time in six months, I wasn't running, wasn't hiding, wasn't calculating my escape. I was simply present, the key pendant warm against my skin, no longer a question but an answer I was finally ready to give.

I step toward him, taking the cup from his hand and placing it on the counter. I lean in, my lips barely brushing his, and whisper, "This scares the shit out of me, I have felt more connection with you in the past weeks while trying not to feel it than I have ever felt, and I realize something," I pause for a moment, "I want this. I want you." A smoldering smile spreads across his face, reaching his eyes. "I want you too, from the moment you sat beside me at the Obsidian, there was something about you, and each day you take up more space in my heart." His hands find my waist, lifting me into his arms, turning and setting me on the table. He pulls a chair closer, his face level with my stomach, and begins unbuttoning his shirt, letting it fall open. "You are so fucking sexy, Elara," he growls, rising to lick and gently nibble my nipples. This feels different, more intimate, more intense. He runs his fingers down my sides, lowering my back onto the table. He lowers himself, pushing my legs open, lapping at my opening, twisting his tongue around all my most sensitive areas. I arch my back, letting myself feel, really feel. "I want it all," I manage to say. He lifts his head, inserting two fingers inside me, curling them in that way that sends electricity through me. "What is it you want?" he growls, gently biting my inner thigh. "I want you to take control, push me to the edge," I say. He smiles with that wickedly sexy grin. "Don't move," he commands.

. . .

RYKER DISAPPEARS FOR A MOMENT, returning with two silk scarves. He ties my left wrist to my left ankle and repeats it on my right. I am trussed up, exposed, sitting on his kitchen table, and it's as sexy as hell. He stands between my bound ankles, pulling my ass down the table closer to him, beginning his relentless assault on my senses. He uses his fingers, his mouth, then pulls a toy from his pocket that buzzes like a jar of trapped bees, pushing it against my clit as he fucks me with his mouth. My body convulses, the sensation too much, too little, too extreme. I don't know if I want to cum or cry. Finally, he undoes the binds, spreads me as far as my legs will allow, and pushes into me hard. I scream out in pleasure. I sit up, wrapping my legs around his waist. One hand pulls me closer on my lower back as he thrusts with force and grinds into me. He lifts me from the table and fucks me hard against the wall. I cum again. He pauses, stopping himself from finding release, and takes me to the bedroom while still inside me, my body pulsing around his hard cock. He stands me up at the edge of the bed, kisses me hard, then turns me around. "Put your knees on the bed," he orders. I am on all fours on the edge of the bed. I feel the sting of his hand as he slaps my ass, then enters me again in a sudden, hard thrust that pushes away all my worries. He fucks me like it's a matter of life and death, punishing my pussy with thrusts so hard they will leave marks, and I love every second. I love that he can be loving and then fuck me like an animal.

AFTERWARD, we fall into bed, tangled in each other's arms, a silent acknowledgment that everything has changed.

413

CHAPTER TWENTY-TWO
The Integration

Morning light crept through a gap in Ryker's curtains, warming my face as I blinked awake. The first thing I noticed was his gaze—steady, attentive—his head propped on one hand as he watched me with an expression I'd rarely allowed myself to see before yesterday. The second thing I noticed was the rich aroma of freshly brewed coffee wafting from the mug he held in his other hand, steam curling into the space between us like an offering.

"How long have you been watching me sleep?" I asked, my voice still rough with rest, a vulnerability I would have hidden before.

His lips curved into that half-smile that had first caught my attention at Obsidian all those weeks ago. "Long enough to memorize the way your eyelashes flutter just before you wake up."

Instead of the discomfort such scrutiny would have triggered days ago, I felt a strange warmth spreading through my chest. I propped myself up against his headboard, accepting the coffee he offered. Our fingers brushed during the exchange, a small contact that sent awareness skittering across my skin.

"Perfect," I murmured after the first sip—strong with just enough sugar, exactly how I liked it. The fact that he remembered such a detail made something twist pleasantly in my stomach.

Ryker leaned forward, pressing his lips against my forehead before sliding from the bed. "I need to get ready for work. Make yourself at home."

I watched him move around the bedroom, gathering clothes from drawers with practiced efficiency. He disappeared into the bathroom briefly, emerging with damp hair and a towel wrapped around his waist. The domesticity of the moment struck me—me in his bed, him preparing for his day, the easy comfort between us feeling both foreign and strangely right.

When he dropped the towel to dress, I made no pretense of looking away. His body was familiar territory now, yet somehow different in the morning light—not just an instrument of pleasure but the physical manifestation of the man who had somehow slipped past my defenses. I noticed details I'd previously overlooked—the small scar on his left hip, the way his shoulders tensed slightly as he buttoned his shirt, the careful precision with which he selected a tie from his closet.

I slid from the bed, pulling on his discarded t-shirt before padding toward his sound system. My fingers trailed across his album collection—vinyl records organized alphabetically, another glimpse into the man beyond the bedroom. I selected something with a soft jazz rhythm, letting the music fill the space between us.

Ryker emerged from the bathroom fully dressed save for his unbuttoned shirt sleeves. He moved to a basket of clean laundry, folding each item with methodical care. The sight of this powerful man performing such an ordinary task made something loosen inside me—walls I hadn't even realized were still standing began to crumble.

I moved past him toward the kitchen, drawn by hunger and the need to do something with my hands. As I passed, his palm brushed against my lower back—not grabbing or demanding, just acknowledging my presence with a touch so casual it felt more intimate than our most passionate embraces had been.

In his kitchen, I found bread and slipped two pieces into the toaster. While waiting, I leaned back against the counter, watching as Ryker appeared in the doorway, now folding a dark blue shirt with careful precision. My eyes traced the movement of his hands, remembering how they had felt against my skin just hours before.

He set the folded laundry aside and crossed to where I stood. Without speaking, I shifted to lean back against his chest, his arms encircling my waist as we waited for the toast to pop. His chin rested atop my head, our bodies fitting together with a comfort that should have terrified me but somehow didn't.

My fingers found the key pendant at my throat, twisting it absently as I savored this moment of simple connection, for when you're ready to stop running. The inscription echoed in my mind, no longer a challenge but a choice I was actively making with each passing minute I remained in his space.

"I have meetings until six," Ryker said, his voice vibrating against my back. "But I could pick up dinner after. Come back here?"

The invitation hung between us—another step toward something I'd spent six months avoiding. My fingers tightened around the pendant, tension coiling in my chest even as I pressed more firmly against his warmth.

"I should probably go home tonight," I said, testing the words even as they left my mouth. "I have laundry and—"

The toast popped up, interrupting my half-formed excuse. Ryker reached around me to retrieve it, his body still pressed against mine. He didn't push, didn't express disappointment, just handed me a piece with a nod.

"Whatever you need," he said, the absence of pressure somehow more compelling than any persuasion could have been.

I turned in his arms, studying his face—the quiet patience in his eyes, the slight tension in his jaw betraying that my answer mattered more than he wanted to show. Something shifted inside me, a recognition that his patience wasn't manipulation but genuine respect for my process.

"Maybe you could bring dinner to my place instead," I offered, the invitation emerging before I'd fully decided to extend it. "I have a perfectly good kitchen that rarely sees any action."

The smile that spread across his face reached his eyes, crinkling the corners in a way that made my chest tighten with an emotion I wasn't ready to name. "I'd like that," he said, fingers brushing a strand of hair from my face.

I glanced at the clock on his microwave, calculating how much time I had before needing to leave for work. "I should get going soon."

"Not yet," Ryker murmured, his hand sliding to the back of my neck, drawing me toward him with gentle pressure.

When our lips met, what began as a goodbye kiss quickly transformed into something more urgent. His hands slid beneath the t-shirt I wore, palms warm against my bare skin as he backed me against the counter. I responded without hesitation, my leg hooking around his waist, pulling him closer with a need that surprised me despite our history.

His mouth moved from my lips to my neck, teeth grazing the sensitive spot below my ear that he'd discovered made me shiver. "You're going to be late," I gasped, even as my hands fumbled with his carefully knotted tie.

"Worth it," he growled against my skin, his fingers tracing patterns along my inner thigh that made coherent thought increasingly difficult.

With reluctance that felt genuine on both sides, we finally separated, both breathing heavily. Ryker pressed his forehead against mine, eyes closed as if memorizing the moment. "Tonight," he promised, the word containing layers of meaning beyond the obvious.

"Tonight," I echoed, the commitment feeling both terrifying and right.

As I gathered my things to leave, I caught sight of my reflection in his hallway mirror—cheeks flushed, lips slightly swollen, wearing his clothes with a comfort that would have been unthinkable weeks ago. The woman looking back at me seemed simultaneously familiar and strange—still Elara, but somehow more open and present than the carefully constructed façade I'd maintained since George.

For the first time in six months, the thought of returning to someone, of continuing something beyond a single encounter, didn't trigger my flight response. Instead, I felt a cautious anticipation building as I stepped out of Ryker's apartment, the key pendant warm against my skin—no longer a question but an answer I was finally allowing myself to give.

I strode through the glass doors of Meridian Marketing with a confidence that felt both foreign and natural. My heels clicked decisively against the marble floor of the lobby, each step punctuating the subtle but significant shift in how I carried myself. The fitted crimson pencil skirt and ivory silk blouse I'd chosen that morning were a deliberate departure from the muted grays and navy blues that had dominated my professional wardrobe before George—professional still, but with an assertion of presence I'd previously avoided.

"Morning, Ms. James," called the security guard, his customary greeting warmer than usual as he noticed my outfit. "Looking sharp today."

I smiled in response—not the polite, tight-lipped acknowledgment I would have offered weeks ago, but something genuine that reached my eyes. "Thanks, Joe. Beautiful day, isn't it?"

The conference room was already half-full when I arrived for our 9:30 strategy meeting. I selected a seat near the middle of the table rather than my usual position at the far end. David Chen, our creative director, raised an eyebrow slightly at my choice but made room for my portfolio as I settled beside him.

"The Henderson campaign needs a complete overhaul," Melissa, our account manager, was saying as she flipped through a presentation on the large screen. "Their target demographic has shifted, and the current approach isn't generating the engagement metrics they want."

I felt the familiar tightening in my chest that usually preceded my contributions in these meetings—the remnant of old insecurities that had kept me deferential and cautious. But today, something different happened. I straightened my spine, set my shoulders back, and raised my hand without hesitation.

"I think we're approaching this from the wrong angle," I said when Melissa acknowledged me, my voice clear and steady. I maintained eye contact rather than glancing down at my notes as I would have before. "The data suggests it's not just their demographic that's changed, but the way that demographic consumes media. I've drafted an alternative strategy that pivots to a multi-platform approach with emphasis on interactive content."

I passed copies of my proposal around the table, noticing with satisfaction how David's eyes widened slightly as he reviewed my work. For the next ten minutes, I walked the team through my concepts, fielding questions with confidence I'd always possessed professionally but had somehow muted in my presentation. When our CEO asked about implementation timelines, I answered directly, meeting his gaze without the nervous smile that had once been my reflex.

"This is excellent work, Elara," he said, using my first name in a departure from his usual formality. "Let's develop this further. Can you lead a small team on a comprehensive proposal?"

"Absolutely," I replied, the word containing none of the surprise I might have felt before.

After the meeting broke up, I gathered my materials, feeling a new energy humming through me. My boss, Christine, approached as I organized my portfolio. "You've been doing excellent work lately," she said, leaning against the conference table. "Not that you weren't always good, but there's something different in your presentations now. More conviction."

I thanked her, accepting the compliment without deflection or self-deprecation. As I turned to leave, Christine studied me with the perceptive gaze that had made her one of the youngest female executives in the industry.

"Whatever's happening in your life," she added with a knowing smile, "it clearly agrees with you."

At my desk, I immersed myself in drafting the implementation plan for my Henderson proposal, the creative energy flowing more freely than it had in months. I was so absorbed that I barely noticed Amber from the design team approaching until she perched on the edge of my desk.

"Okay, what gives?" she asked, her voice lowered conspiratorially. "You're practically radiating this new energy, your outfit is fire, and you just dominated that meeting like a boss. Spill."

I laughed, surprised by how easily the sound emerged. "Just feeling good lately," I replied, offering a mysterious smile that revealed nothing yet somehow everything.

"Hmm," Amber narrowed her eyes playfully. "This wouldn't have anything to do with that incredibly hot guy who sent flowers the other week, would it? The ones you pretended weren't a big deal?"

The memory of Ryker's first gesture—white peonies with a simple card that read "For when you're ready to pause"—sent warmth spreading through my chest. Before I could respond, my phone vibrated against my desk with an incoming message.

"The blush on your cheeks says it all," Amber teased,

pushing away from my desk. "Just know I expect details at happy hour sometime. You can't glow like that and not share your secrets."

After she left, I turned my phone over, Ryker's name illuminating the screen alongside a photo notification. My breath caught as I opened the message—a close-up image of a deep blue tie with subtle silver threading, draped across what I recognized as his desk. The accompanying text read: "Thinking of using this later. Not necessarily around my neck."

Heat pooled instantly between my legs, memories of our previous encounters where he'd bound my wrists with his ties flashing vividly in my mind. I crossed my legs, then uncrossed them, the sudden pressure both relief and torment. My fingers hovered over the keyboard, several responses forming and dissolving before I settled on one.

"I was thinking of wearing that blue lace set you like. But I could be persuaded to wear nothing but your tie instead."

I hit send before I could second-guess myself, a delicious anticipation building as I watched the message status change to "read." Six months ago, such an exchange would have been calculated seduction, a power play designed to maintain emotional distance through physical connection. Today, it felt like a playful promise between equals, desire deepened rather than diminished by the emotional intimacy we'd begun to build.

Three dots appeared, indicating Ryker was typing a response. They disappeared, then reappeared, suggesting he was crafting and recrafting his reply—a rare indication of impact from a man who typically maintained such careful control. Finally, his message appeared: "You've just made every meeting on my calendar an exercise in restraint. 7 pm can't come soon enough."

I smiled, satisfaction spreading through me that had nothing to do with power games and everything to do with genuine connection. I placed my phone face down on my desk, forcing myself to return to the Henderson proposal despite the pleasant distraction of anticipation humming beneath my skin.

As LUNCHTIME APPROACHED, my excitement grew. Sam's mother had rented an apartment nearby where Sam was going to move in with her. The short time Sam helped her with her sisters' children showed Sam that her mother needs more help with everyday things, so Sam was able to convince her to come back with her. We had decided to meet for lunch. I missed her so much; I knew she would want to hear all about Ryker.

THE OUTDOOR PATIO at Café Lucie hummed with lunchtime conversation, sunlight dappling through the green canvas umbrellas as I spotted Sam already seated at our usual corner table. She waved enthusiastically, rising to embrace me as I approached. The familiar scent of her signature perfume—something floral and expensive—enveloped me as we hugged, her platinum blonde hair with pink tips tickling my cheek. When we separated, her shrewd eyes performed a quick assessment, taking in my crimson skirt and confident posture with the practiced evaluation of someone who made her living noticing details.

"Well, well, well," she said, settling back into her chair with a knowing smile. "Someone's looking like she stepped off a 'confidence queens' Pinterest board today."

I laughed, arranging my napkin across my lap as the waiter appeared with Sam's already-ordered iced tea and took my request for sparkling water. "Good to see you too, Sam."

"Don't 'good to see you too' me," she countered, leaning forward conspiratorially. "I want details. Is this Ryker guy responsible for that sex goddess energy you're radiating? Because honey, you are glowing in a way that face masks and green juice definitely did not create."

Heat crept up my neck at her directness, though I'd long ago grown accustomed to Sam's unfiltered observations. In the six months since George, she'd been my constant companion through club nights and casual hookups, cheering each conquest as a victory over heartbreak.

"Maybe," I admitted, taking a sip of water as the waiter delivered it. "Things have... evolved, I actually am meeting him tonight."

Sam's perfectly shaped eyebrows arched higher. "Evolved? Last time we talked, you were insisting he was just another notch on your bedpost, albeit a particularly skilled one." She studied me, something flickering behind her playful expression. "This looks like more than good sex face. This looks dangerously close to feelings face."

I fingered the key pendant at my throat, a gesture that had

become almost unconscious. Sam's eyes tracked the movement, her gaze sharpening as she recognized jewelry she hadn't seen before.

"Did he give you that?" she asked, pointing to the pendant.

"A few weeks ago," I replied, surprised by how easily the admission came. "It's... significant."

Sam's expression shifted, something vulnerable breaking through her carefully curated exterior. She took a long sip of her tea, ice cubes clinking against glass as she set it down with deliberate care.

"So this is serious," she said, the statement somewhere between question and conclusion. "Like, actual relationship serious."

The waiter's return with menus provided a brief reprieve from the sudden intensity. We ordered our usual—Niçoise salad for me, avocado toast with poached eggs for Sam—before the conversation resumed.

"I'm not sure what to call it," I said honestly. "But it's not like the others. Not like what we've been doing these past months."

Sam adjusted the napkin in her lap, her movements containing a nervous energy I rarely saw in her. "So what does this mean for Thursdays at Velvet? Or Saturdays at Obsidian?" She attempted a lighthearted tone that didn't quite mask the genuine concern beneath. "Is the legendary Elara James retiring from the scene already?"

The question contained layers—concern about our friendship rituals, anxiety about change, perhaps even fear of abandonment, wrapped in casual inquiry. Six months of club nights and shared conquests had formed the foundation of our post-George bond. Sam had been my guide through transformation, my cheerleader in reclaiming power through calculated seduction.

"I think my club days might be winding down," I admitted, reaching across the table to touch her hand. "But that doesn't mean you and I are."

Sam nodded, withdrawing her hand to fidget with her silverware. "Of course not. I just... I've seen this before, you know? Friend meets guy, friend disappears into a relationship vortex. Six months later, you're lucky to get a text back."

The hurt beneath her bravado was real, and I felt a pang of guilt for not considering how my evolution might affect her. Sam's influencer lifestyle depended on constant content creation, on being seen at the right places with the right people. Our club nights weren't just friendship for her—they were part of her brand, her livelihood.

"You're still my person, Sam," I said firmly. "That hasn't changed just because I have someone warming my bed regularly now." I smiled, injecting lightness into my tone while maintaining sincerity. "I might not be prowling Obsidian every weekend, but I'm not disappearing. Promise."

Our food arrived, beautifully plated as always. Sam drizzled hot sauce over her avocado toast, a habit that had initially horrified me but now registered as one of her endearing quirks.

"So tell me about him," she said, cutting into a poached egg with deliberate precision. "And not just the bedroom high-lights, though obviously I require those too. What makes this guy different?"

I considered the question, searching for words that wouldn't sound trite. "He sees me," I said finally. "Not just the after-George version I created, not just the before version I lost. Something more complete than either."

Sam chewed thoughtfully, studying me over her toast. "That's either really beautiful or really terrifying."

"Both," I admitted, surprised by my own candor. "Definitely both."

"And the sex is still mind-blowing?" she pressed, a hint of her usual playfulness returning.

I laughed, grateful for the shift back to familiar territory. "Let's just say I'll never look at kitchen tables the same way again."

"That's my girl," Sam grinned, raising her glass in a mock toast. After a moment, her expression softened into something more genuine. "I'm happy for you, Elara. Really. Even if I'm a little jealous someone else is getting all your attention now."

"Not all of it," I corrected, seizing the opening. "In fact, what are you doing next Thursday? Not for clubs—just us.

Wine, takeout, those ridiculous face masks you're always trying to get me to use. Your place or mine."

The relief that washed over Sam's face made me realize how much this conversation had mattered—not just for her but for me too. For six months, she'd been my constant, my cheerleader through reinvention. The fact that I was evolving again didn't diminish her importance in my journey.

"My place," she decided, perking up visibly. "I just got this Korean skincare set that will change your life. And I want to hear every dirty detail about kitchen table guy that you're comfortable sharing."

"Deal," I agreed, feeling a warmth that had nothing to do with the sunshine filtering through the café umbrellas. "Though I reserve the right to maintain some mystery."

Sam laughed, the sound lighter now, more genuine. "Mystery is just details I haven't extracted yet."

As we finished our lunch, the conversation drifted to Sam's latest brand deal and an influencer event she was planning. I listened attentively, aware that while one part of my life was transforming, this friendship remained a constant I valued—different perhaps from what it had been during my six-month reinvention, but no less important.

When we parted with another hug, Sam held on a moment longer than usual. "I'm really happy you found someone good," she whispered against my ear. "You deserve that. Just don't forget about the friend who helped you through the bad stuff, okay?"

"Never," I promised, the word containing all the sincerity I could muster.

Walking back toward my office, I realized that opening myself to vulnerability with Ryker hadn't weakened me as I'd feared. Instead, it had somehow expanded my capacity for genuine connection in all areas of my life, including the friendship that had sustained me through my darkest days after George.

THE REST of the afternoon passed in productive focus, my professional confidence somehow enhanced rather than diminished by the personal vulnerability I'd begun to embrace. As I refined marketing strategies and budget projections, I realized something fundamental had shifted—the compartmentalization I'd maintained for six months between my professional persona and my personal life was dissolving, not into chaos as I'd feared, but into a more integrated sense of self.

When I finally powered down my computer at 5:30, I gathered my things with purposeful movements, my mind already shifting toward the evening ahead. For the first time since George, work wasn't merely escape or distraction but part of a life I was actively choosing to build—one that included professional ambition, personal agency, and the frightening, exhilarating possibility of genuine connection.

. . .

Steam rose from the simmering pot of risotto as I stirred, my hips swaying slightly to the soft jazz playing from my rarely-used sound system. The rich aroma of sautéed mushrooms and white wine filled my kitchen—a space that had seen more takeout containers than actual cooking in the months since George. Tonight felt different. I'd left work early to shop for ingredients, uncorked a bottle of cabernet to breathe, and even arranged fresh flowers on my dining table. The domesticity of these actions would have terrified me weeks ago, would have felt like dangerous backsliding into the woman I'd been before. Now, they felt like reclamation—cooking not to please someone else but because I wanted to, creating comfort in my space on my own terms.

I was so absorbed in my stirring that I didn't hear the knock at first. When it came again, louder, I lowered the heat and wiped my hands on a dish towel. My heartbeat quickened as I moved toward the door—not with anxiety but with an anticipation I was still getting used to feeling.

Ryker stood in my doorway, the deep blue tie from his earlier text now loosened at his neck. His eyes traveled over me —taking in my bare feet, simple black dress, hair loosely pulled back—with an appreciation that felt both physical and something more.

"Hi," I said, suddenly shy despite our history.

Instead of answering, he stepped inside, closing the door behind him. His gaze moved past me to the apartment—taking in the lit candles, the open wine bottle, the evidence of effort

I'd rarely bothered with for anyone, including myself, in the past six months.

"You cooked," he observed, his voice carrying that same measured control I'd come to expect, though a slight roughness at its edges betrayed his pleasure at the discovery.

"Don't sound so surprised," I replied, turning back toward the kitchen. "I do possess skills beyond the bedroom."

I felt him follow rather than heard him, his presence registering like a physical touch across my skin. When I reached for the wooden spoon to resume stirring, his arms encircled my waist from behind, his chest pressing against my back as his lips found the sensitive spot where my neck met my shoulder.

"I've never doubted your skills," he murmured against my skin, the words sending a shiver down my spine.

I leaned back into his embrace, allowing myself to savor the solid warmth of him, the sandalwood scent of his cologne mingling with the aromas of cooking food. His hands splayed across my stomach, holding me against him without demanding, offering a connection that I could accept or reject.

"The risotto will burn," I warned halfheartedly as his lips continued their exploration of my neck.

In one fluid motion, he reached past me to turn off the burner, then spun me to face him. His hands found my waist, lifting me effortlessly onto the counter. The granite felt cool against my thighs, where my dress had ridden up, a sharp contrast to the heat of his palms as they slid beneath the fabric.

"I'm suddenly less interested in dinner," he said, his voice dropping to the register that never failed to make my pulse quicken.

When his mouth found mine, the kiss contained both the urgency of desire and something slower, more deliberate— exploration rather than conquest. I tasted wine on his lips, suggesting he'd stopped for a glass on his way to me, the rich flavor complementing the natural taste of him that I'd come to crave.

My legs wrapped around his waist, drawing him closer to the edge of the counter where I sat. His hands moved with practiced confidence, one tangling in my hair to tilt my head back for deeper access, the other tracing patterns along my inner thigh that made coherent thought increasingly difficult.

"Here?" he asked against my mouth, the single word somehow containing proper respect for my space while making his preference clear.

"Yes," I breathed, already reaching for his tie, the silk sliding through my fingers as I loosened it completely. "Right here."

What followed was both familiar and entirely new—our bodies connecting with the same physical chemistry that had drawn us together initially, but now enhanced by the emotional intimacy we'd begun to build. When he entered me, I kept my eyes open, maintaining contact with his gaze in a way I'd always avoided before. The vulnerability of being seen so completely during our most physical connection sent tremors through me that had nothing to do with approaching climax and everything to do with walls continuing to crumble.

His hands guided my hips with firm but gentle pressure, setting a rhythm that built slowly rather than rushed toward completion. Unlike our kitchen encounter at his apartment days before, this wasn't about proving something or avoiding emotional exposure through physical distraction. This was presence, connection, the joining of bodies mirroring the tentative joining of something deeper.

"Stay with me," he urged when I began to close my eyes as sensation threatened to overwhelm me. "I want to see you."

The request would have sent me running weeks ago—too intimate, too exposing, too demanding of vulnerability I wasn't willing to give. Now, I found myself nodding, holding his gaze as pleasure built and crested, my release washing through me in waves that felt deeper for being witnessed so completely.

Later, after we'd managed to salvage the risotto and eat at my rarely-used dining table, we settled on my couch with refilled wine glasses. My legs stretched across his lap, his fingers absently stroking through my hair as we talked about nothing in particular—work anecdotes, a documentary he thought I might enjoy, small details of our days that would have seemed mundane with anyone else but somehow mattered in the sharing.

"What were you like as a kid?" he asked during a comfortable lull in conversation, the question casual but holding genuine curiosity.

I took a sip of wine, considering. "Serious," I replied finally. "The responsible one. Always trying to meet expectations—my parents', teachers', my own."

"That tracks," he said with a gentle smile. "I can see little Elara with perfectly done homework, raising her hand with all the right answers."

"What about you?" I deflected, uncomfortable with how accurately he'd imagined my childhood self.

His expression shifted, something vulnerable flickering across his features. "The opposite, probably. Always testing boundaries, seeing what I could get away with." His fingers continued their gentle movement through my hair. "My dad left when I was eight. I think I was trying to make sure my mom had enough to worry about that she wouldn't leave too."

The casual admission of childhood pain made something twist in my chest. Before I could consider the implications, I found myself speaking. "My parents stayed together, but sometimes I think it might have been better if they hadn't. They barely spoke to each other except to argue about my academic performance or my father's long hours."

The words emerged with surprising ease, memories I rarely examined spilling into the space between us. "I learned early that perfection was the price of peace. If my grades were high enough, if the house was clean enough, if I was quiet and helpful and never caused problems... maybe they wouldn't fight that night."

Ryker's hand stilled in my hair, his eyes holding mine with that perceptive gaze that always saw too much. "You're still doing it, aren't you? Being perfect to keep others from leaving."

The insight struck with uncomfortable precision, naming patterns I'd never fully articulated even to myself. George had rejected me despite my attempts at perfection, sending me spiraling into the opposite extreme—the deliberately imperfect woman who needed no one, who left before she could be left. Yet both versions had been reactions to the same core fear, different sides of the same wounded coin.

"I'm trying not to," I admitted, the confession containing more vulnerability than any physical nakedness had.

His fingers resumed their gentle exploration of my hair, neither pushing for more nor dismissing what I'd shared. "That's all any of us can do. Try to recognize our patterns and maybe choose differently sometimes."

The simple wisdom in his words, the absence of judgment or pity, made something loosen inside me. I found myself sharing more fragments of my childhood—the piano lessons I'd excelled at but never enjoyed, the summer I'd broken my arm falling from a tree and been more worried about disappointing my father than about the pain, the stray cat I'd secretly fed despite my mother's allergies. Small pieces of myself I'd kept carefully guarded, deemed too mundane or too revealing to share with the men who had briefly passed through my life.

As the evening deepened into night, my head found its way to Ryker's chest, his arm curving around me with protective warmth. The steady rhythm of his heartbeat beneath my ear created a lullaby more soothing than the jazz still playing softly in the background. My eyes grew heavy, the combination of wine, emotional openness, and physical satisfaction creating a peaceful exhaustion I couldn't fight.

The last thing I remembered before sleep claimed me was the gentle pressure of Ryker's lips against my forehead, the slight tightening of his arm around me as if ensuring I remained safely anchored against him through the night. We were both still fully clothed, no deliberate seduction or calculated passion between us—just the profound intimacy of trust beginning to take root where fear had previously dominated.

For the first time since George, I fell asleep in someone's arms without planning my morning escape, without maintaining careful emotional distance, without using physical connection to avoid something deeper. The key pendant rested against my collarbone, warm between our bodies—no longer a challenge but a choice I was making with increasing certainty with each passing day.

CHAPTER TWENTY-THREE
The Full Circle

Morning light streamed through my kitchen windows, casting golden patterns across the marble countertop as I measured coffee grounds with practiced precision. The silk of my robe whispered against my skin with each movement, cool and sensuous in the quiet of early day. I inhaled the rich aroma of fresh coffee, savoring this moment of solitude that no longer felt like loneliness but like peaceful anticipation—a subtle yet profound shift I was still getting used to.

The coffee maker gurgled to life, its familiar rhythm a counterpoint to the unusual comfort I felt in my own skin. Six months ago, mornings had been exercises in avoidance—quick showers, hurried makeup application, carefully selected armor of conservative clothes, anything to escape the emptiness of my apartment and the thoughts that threatened to consume me when I was alone. Now, I found myself lingering in these quiet moments, present in a way I hadn't been even before George.

I heard Ryker before I felt him—the almost imperceptible

sound of bare feet on hardwood, the slight change in the air that always preceded his presence. Then his arms encircled my waist, strong and certain, and his lips found the sensitive curve where my neck met my shoulder. I leaned back into his solid warmth, my body responding with a familiar heat that showed no signs of diminishing despite our increasing familiarity.

"Good morning," he murmured against my skin, his voice carrying that same measured control I'd come to expect, though sleep had roughened its edges in a way that sent pleasant shivers down my spine.

His hands splayed across the silk covering my stomach, the heat of his palms seeping through the thin fabric. I covered his hands with mine, our fingers intertwining in a gesture that felt both possessive and protective. The simple contact—this moment of connection that required nothing more—would have terrified me months ago. Now, I found myself sinking deeper into it, seeking rather than fleeing the intimacy it represented.

My fingers brushed the key pendant around my neck, a habit that had become almost subconscious since Ryker gave it to me. The metal was warm against my skin, having soaked up my body heat through the night. For when you're ready to stop running. The inscription had felt like both a challenge and a promise when he'd first placed it around my neck. Now, it was a tangible reminder of how far I'd come—not just in our relationship, but in my relationship with myself.

I traced the pendant's outline, thinking about the woman I'd been when George had sat across from me at the Bluebird

Café, his expression carefully composed as he explained why we needed to "take a break." How I'd hunched my shoulders then, making myself physically smaller as if I could somehow diminish the target of his rejection. How I'd clutched my mug with both hands to hide their trembling, my voice pitched higher as I fought to maintain composure.

The woman I'd been before that day had spent years molding herself into what she thought others wanted—soft-spoken, accommodating, careful not to take up too much space. I'd disguised my curves in boxy blazers and loose slacks, spoke only when directly addressed in meetings, apologized for opinions before I even expressed them. I'd been so eager to prove my worth through perfect compliance that I'd nearly erased myself in the process.

Now, I stood with my shoulders back, spine straight, chin lifted. The robe I wore didn't hide my body but celebrated it—the silk clinging to curves I'd once considered flaws but now recognized as assets. My voice had dropped to its natural register, no longer artificially raised to sound more pleasing. I took up space unapologetically, both physically and metaphorically.

I remembered George's face on my birthday, the practiced sympathy in his eyes as he'd delivered the lines he'd clearly rehearsed. "You're wonderful, Elara, but I need someone more...spontaneous. More confident. Someone who challenges me." The irony wasn't lost on me—that in rejecting me for being too predictable, too accommodating, he'd catalyzed my transformation into exactly the woman he claimed to want.

But that transformation hadn't been for him. The woman who emerged from the wreckage of his rejection—the woman who now stood wrapped in Ryker's arms—hadn't been created to prove George wrong or to lure him back. She'd been forged in the fire of necessary reinvention, in the slow, painful process of recognizing my own worth independent of external validation.

"You're thinking awfully hard for someone making coffee," Ryker observed, his breath warm against my ear. His hands tightened slightly around my waist, grounding me in the present moment rather than the memories that had temporarily claimed me.

I turned within the circle of his arms, the silk of my robe catching slightly on the cotton of his t-shirt. He'd pulled on boxers and the shirt he'd discarded on my bedroom floor the night before, his hair still mussed from sleep in a way that made my fingers itch to run through it. The stubble along his jaw caught the morning light, highlighting the strong line of his face that had first drawn my eye across the dimly lit expanse of Obsidian.

My hands found their way to his chest, feeling his heart-beat steady and strong beneath my palm. I rose on tiptoes, pressing my lips to his in a kiss that began with gentle intention but quickly deepened into something more urgent. His hands slid down to my hips, pulling me closer as mine tangled in his hair, neither of us particularly concerned with the coffee growing cold behind us.

When we finally separated, both slightly breathless, Ryker's eyes searched mine with that perceptive gaze that had always seen through my carefully constructed facades.

"What were you thinking about so intensely?" he asked, one hand rising to tuck a strand of hair behind my ear, the gesture so tender it made my chest ache.

I smiled, the expression reaching my eyes in a way that still felt new and slightly foreign. "Just how much has changed," I replied, my fingers finding the key pendant once more. "How much I've changed."

His answering smile contained equal parts pride and understanding, as if he recognized both the distance I'd traveled and the journey still ahead. "For the better," he said, not a question but a statement of fact.

"For the better," I agreed, turning back to the coffeemaker, his arms still looped loosely around my waist. Through the window, morning light continued to strengthen, illuminating not just my kitchen but the woman I was becoming—neither the perfect, accommodating ghost I'd been with George nor the deliberately detached seductress I'd crafted in the aftermath of his rejection, but someone more authentic, more complex, more fully myself than either version had been.

∾

The boutique's door chimed softly as I stepped onto the sunlit sidewalk, the weight of shopping bags a pleasant reminder of purchases made without the guilt or second-guessing that once shadowed such indulgences. My reflection caught in a storefront window—a woman in a burgundy dress that followed the lines of my body with appreciative attention, neither hiding nor flaunting but simply acknowledging what was there. Six months ago, I would have tugged at the hemline, worried about drawing attention. Today, I adjusted my sunglasses with a small smile, recognition rather than surprise registering at the confident stranger looking back at me.

I'd spent the morning browsing boutiques in the upscale shopping district that I'd once walked past with wistful glances, convincing myself I didn't belong among their carefully curated displays and attentive staff. Now, I moved through these spaces with the easy assurance of someone who knew her worth wasn't determined by others' assessments. The dress I wore had been my first purchase of the day—its deep burgundy fabric draping in a way that accentuated my curves without apology, the neckline revealing just enough collarbone to display the key pendant that had become my talisman.

Shopping had transformed from an exercise in self-denial to an act of self-appreciation. Before George, I'd approached each purchase with anxious calculation—was it modest enough, professional enough, unobtrusive enough? I'd stood in fitting rooms mentally cataloging potential criticisms, selecting clothes that helped me disappear rather than be seen. After George, shopping had briefly become a rebellion— choosing pieces designed to provoke reaction, to announce my sexuality as a weapon rather than vulnerability. Now, I selected items simply because they pleased me, because they felt right against my skin, because they expressed rather than disguised who I was becoming.

I was contemplating which café might offer the best spot for a late lunch when my gaze drifted across the street and locked with a pair of eyes I'd once known better than my own. George sat at a table outside Café Lucien, a half-empty espresso cup before him, his expression shifting from distraction to surprise to something more complicated as recognition dawned.

My body registered his presence before my mind fully processed it—a sudden tightening in my chest, a momentary acceleration of my pulse, my fingers instinctively finding the key pendant at my throat. But the panic I might have expected, the urge to duck into the nearest store or hurry in the opposite direction, never materialized. Instead, I felt a strange calm descend, a clarity that surprised me with its steadiness.

Six months of avoidance, of carefully selecting restaurants and shops unlikely to intersect with his routine, and now here he was—sitting alone at a café I'd almost chosen myself. The coincidence felt significant, a test I hadn't known was coming but suddenly realized I was prepared to face.

I waited for the pedestrian signal, then crossed the street with measured steps. Each click of my heels against the pavement felt deliberate, percussive punctuation to the decision I'd made. I watched George's posture change as he realized my approach was intentional—the straightening of his spine, the quick adjustment of his tie, the practiced smile that didn't quite reach his eyes.

"Elara," he said as I neared his table, rising from his seat with the polished manners that had once seemed so sophisticated but now struck me as performative. His coffee cup rattled slightly against its saucer as he set it down, a small betrayal of nervousness in his otherwise composed demeanor. "This is... unexpected."

"George," I replied, my voice emerging with a steadiness that matched my posture—shoulders back, chin level, weight distributed evenly between feet planted firmly on the ground. I made no move to hug him or offer my cheek for the air-kiss he might have expected, maintaining a distance that felt like reclamation of boundaries I'd once surrendered too easily.

His eyes traveled over me with an assessment that attempted subtlety but achieved none, lingering on the curves his hands had once known, the neckline that revealed more skin than I'd have dared display when we were together, the confident posture that made me appear taller than he remembered.

"You look... different," he said finally, gesturing vaguely toward an empty chair across from him, the invitation awkward in its presumption.

I remained standing, not out of rudeness but simple preference. "I am different," I replied, the simplicity of the statement containing layers he couldn't possibly understand.

Silence stretched between us, George shifting his weight from one foot to the other, clearly uncertain how to navigate this unexpected version of the woman he'd left behind. I felt no obligation to ease his discomfort, no reflexive urge to fill the space with nervous chatter or self-deprecating jokes as I once would have.

"Are you still at Meridian?" he asked finally, retreating to the safety of professional inquiry, the same tactic he'd employed at dinner parties when conversation veered toward emotional territory that made him uncomfortable.

"I am. Recently promoted, actually." I offered the information without elaboration, without the eager details I would once have provided in hopes of holding his interest.

"That's great," he nodded, his smile tightening at the edges. "You always were talented." The words emerged with the slight condescension that had once been subtle enough to escape my notice but now rang clear as bells. "I'm sure they recognize that now."

"They always did," I corrected gently. "I just needed to recognize it myself."

His eyes narrowed slightly, registering the implied criticism. Another silence fell, this one more charged than the last. I watched him recalibrate, shifting strategies with the same calculation he'd likely used in boardrooms and breakups alike.

"You're seeing someone?" he asked, nodding toward the key pendant at my throat, the question casual but his eyes sharp with assessment.

I touched the pendant briefly, the metal warm against my fingertips. "Yes."

"Anyone I know?" His attempt at lightness fell flat, the question revealing more interest than he'd intended to show.

"No," I replied simply, offering no details about Ryker, no opening for George to insert himself into this new chapter of my life, even peripherally.

He nodded, taking a long sip of his espresso before setting the cup down with exaggerated care. When he looked up again, his expression had softened into something that might have appeared genuine to anyone who hadn't spent two years studying its nuances.

"Listen, Elara, seeing you like this..." He gestured toward me, his hand encompassing the dress, the posture, the confidence he'd never witnessed during our time together. "Sometimes I wonder if I made a mistake. If I didn't fully appreciate what I had."

The words hung between us—words that six months ago might have unraveled me completely, might have sent me spiraling into hope or vindication or renewed pain. Now, they registered as simply what they were: a man's belated recognition of value only after it had been withdrawn from his reach.

A genuine smile curved my lips, surprising both of us with its warmth. "It was the best thing you could have done for me," I said, the truth in the statement coursing through me like a cleansing current. Not because he was unworthy, not because the relationship had been meaningless, but because its ending had forced me to confront the emptiness I'd created within myself in my desperate attempt to be wanted.

Something shifted in George's expression—confusion giving way to understanding, then a flash of something that might have been regret. Before he could respond, I adjusted my shopping bags, prepared to continue on my way.

"It was good to see you, George," I said, meaning it in ways I couldn't have imagined when he'd walked away from our relationship six months earlier. "Take care of yourself."

I turned and walked away, my steps neither hurried nor hesitant. No backward glance, no wondering if he watched me leave, no calculating my movements for maximum effect. For the first time since I'd known him, George's opinion of me—his desire or lack thereof—held no power over my sense of self. The realization settled over me like sunshine, warming places within that had been cold for longer than I cared to admit.

The scent of lemongrass and ginger greeted me before I'd fully opened my apartment door—the distinctive aroma of Thai Palace, my favorite restaurant that required a forty-minute round trip to reach. Ryker stood in my kitchen, trans-ferring food from paper cartons to the ceramic plates I rarely used, his back to me as he arranged everything with the same attention to detail he brought to all aspects of his life. The sight struck me with unexpected force—this man who had seen through my carefully constructed facades from the beginning, now moving through my space with the easy familiarity of someone who belonged there.

He glanced up as I set my shopping bags beside the door, his eyes warming with something that made my chest tighten pleasantly. "I thought you might be hungry after your shopping expedition," he said, his voice carrying that same measured control I'd come to expect, though an undercurrent of affection softened its edges.

"Starving," I admitted, slipping off my heels with a sigh of relief. I crossed to where he stood, pressing a kiss to his shoulder before peering at the spread he'd arranged. "You got the crispy duck too?"

"And extra spring rolls," he confirmed, his hand finding the small of my back with casual intimacy. "Wine's breathing on the counter."

The domesticity of the moment struck me—how easily we'd fallen into these rhythms over the past weeks, how natural it felt to return to someone rather than an empty apartment. Six months ago, such comfort would have terrified me, would have sent me searching for the nearest exit. Now, I leaned into it, savoring rather than fleeing the connection it represented.

We settled at my dining table—the one I'd purchased during my post-George transformation but had rarely used for actual meals until Ryker began spending evenings here. He poured wine into glasses that had been gathering dust in my cabinet, the rich burgundy liquid catching the afternoon light filtering through my windows.

"So," he said, passing me a plate heaped with pad thai and crispy duck, "how was your day? Find anything worth buying?"

I took a sip of wine, considering how to transition from shopping to my unexpected encounter. "I did, actually. A dress I'll wear to Christine's gallery opening next week." I twirled noodles around my fork, then set it down, meeting his eyes. "And I saw George."

Ryker's expression remained neutral, though I caught the slight tightening of his jaw, the momentary stillness of his hand around his wine glass. "That must have been... interesting," he offered, his tone carefully even.

"It was," I agreed, appreciating his restraint, the space he created for me to process the experience in my own way. "I saw him sitting at Café Lucien as I was leaving that boutique on Hawthorn Street."

"Did you speak with him?" Ryker asked, resuming his meal with deliberate casualness that didn't quite mask his interest.

I nodded, recounting the interaction—George's awkward invitation to sit, his carefully casual questions about my professional life, the moment his eyes had lingered on my pendant. Ryker listened attentively, his eyes rarely leaving my face, his hand occasionally brushing mine across the table when I paused between bites.

"He told me he sometimes wonders if he made a mistake," I said, watching Ryker's reaction closely. "If he didn't fully appreciate what he had."

Something flickered in Ryker's eyes—not jealousy, exactly, but a protective alertness. "And how did that make you feel?" he asked, the question genuine rather than leading.

I considered this, surprised by the clarity of my answer. "Validated, in a way, but not in the way I would have expected six months ago. Not because I needed his approval, but because it confirmed how far I've come." My fingers found the key pendant at my throat, a gesture that had become almost unconscious. "I told him it was the best thing he could have done for me."

The smile that spread across Ryker's face reached his eyes, crinkling the corners in a way that made my chest tighten with an emotion I was becoming increasingly comfortable naming, even if only to myself. "I'm proud of you," he said simply, the words containing no condescension, only genuine recognition of the journey they represented.

After dinner, we moved to the couch, the casual migration feeling as natural as breathing. Ryker settled into the corner, arm extended in silent invitation. I curled against him, my head finding that perfect hollow between his shoulder and chest, my legs tucked beneath me. He reached for the remote, dimming the overhead lights through the smart-home system he'd helped me set up weeks before. The apartment transformed—shadows softening, ambient light creating a gentle cocoon around us.

My fingers found their way beneath the sleeve of his t-shirt, tracing the lines of the tattoo that curved around his bicep—an abstract design of flowing lines that reminded me of water currents. His skin felt warm beneath my touch, slightly rough with the fine hair that caught the light when he moved. I breathed in the scent of him—sandalwood cologne mingling with the natural musk that was uniquely Ryker, a combination that had once made me want to flee but now felt like coming home.

His heart beat steady beneath my ear, the rhythm somehow both calming and exhilarating. His fingers threaded through my hair, gentle strokes that contained no demand, no expectation, just appreciation of connection that could exist without needing to progress toward something more physical.

I marveled at how different this felt from every relationship I'd known—not just from the calculated seductions of my post-George phase, but even from what George and I had shared. With George, vulnerability had been something I'd offered as proof of devotion, carefully measured doses designed to bind him closer without revealing too much. With the men who followed, I'd avoided vulnerability entirely, using physical intimacy as both shield and distraction.

With Ryker, vulnerability wasn't transaction or weakness but shared strength—the courage to be seen completely and valued for that authenticity rather than despite it. His fingers continued their gentle exploration of my hair, occasionally brushing against my neck in touches that sent pleasant shivers across my skin.

"I used to think power meant not feeling anything," I said softly, the realization crystallizing as I spoke it aloud. "After George, I convinced myself that the way to avoid being hurt again was to turn everything off—to use my body to maintain control without risking my heart."

Ryker's hand stilled momentarily, then resumed its gentle movement, encouraging me to continue without words. I shifted slightly to look up at him, needing to see his eyes as I articulated this truth.

"But there's more strength in this—in feeling everything and still standing tall," I continued, my voice steady despite the vulnerability of the admission. "In acknowledging that connections matter, that pain is part of the journey, that opening yourself to possibility means accepting both joy and hurt."

His eyes held mine with that perceptive gaze that had seen through my defenses from our first meeting. "That's what I've always seen in you," he said, his voice low and certain. "Not the walls you built or the distance you maintained, but the courage underneath—the woman strong enough to feel everything, even when it terrified her."

The truth in his words—the recognition of strength I'd always possessed but had mistaken for weakness—sent warmth spreading through my chest. I reached up, tracing the line of his jaw with fingertips that carried none of the calculated seduction I'd once deployed but instead simple appreciation of the man who had waited patiently for me to stop running.

My other hand found the key pendant, the metal warm against my skin after a day of wear. For when you're ready to stop running. What I understood now, what the encounter with George had crystallized, was that true empowerment came not from absence of emotion but from its complete embrace—not from shutting out vulnerability but from finding the strength within it.

I settled back against Ryker's chest, listening to the steady rhythm of his heartbeat beneath my ear. His arms tightened around me, not possessive but protective, offering shelter that demanded nothing in return. The pendant rested against my collarbone, no longer a question but an answer I had finally discovered for myself—that the key to freedom wasn't in flight but in the courage to remain present, to feel deeply, to risk everything for connections that mattered.

"Thank you," I whispered against his chest, the words containing multitudes he somehow understood without explanation.

His lips pressed against the top of my head, lingering there in a kiss that held more intimacy than the most passionate embrace we'd shared. "For what?" he asked, though his tone suggested he already knew.

"For seeing me," I replied simply. "Even when I was hiding from myself."

HE TOOK a finger and lifted my chin; our eyes met, and there was more in that look than I had ever felt before. I felt my breath hitch. "I see you, and I love you," he whispered. "I love you too." I smiled.

His answering smile contained no triumph, no self-satisfaction, just quiet joy in the journey we'd undertaken together —his patient siege against my carefully constructed walls, my gradual surrender to vulnerability that felt like victory rather than defeat. As evening deepened around us, I realized that the woman I'd become wasn't defined by either George's rejection or Ryker's acceptance, but by my own willingness to embrace every aspect of myself—strength and vulnerability, confidence and fear, independence and connection—not as contradictions but as essential elements of a whole, authentic self I was still discovering.

The Future
Unwritten

The balcony wrapped the northwest corner of our building, thirty stories above the city, catching the last dregs of sunset as they bled lavender and gold into the hazy blue. The air was just cool enough to raise goosebumps on my forearms, but I refused to shiver, not tonight. I braced my palms against the brushed steel railing and took in the grid of lights below, neon and halogen flickering to life, windows brightening in the office towers as janitorial crews began their invisible night shift. The city had a rhythm I'd never noticed when I was living on the ground. Up here, it felt almost orchestrated—like a living thing holding its breath for the next measure.

I wore a cream silk blouse, French cuffs undone and rolled back, tucked into midnight blue slacks that hugged my hips with tailored precision. My hair—no longer forced into corporate submission—fell in soft waves just past my shoulders, catching the wind and flickering with static. The silver key pendant Ryker had given me gleamed at my throat, cold against my skin until my body warmed it. It felt right, the weight of it a talisman rather than a burden now.

Inside, the glow from our open-concept loft spilled onto the balcony, painting slanted rectangles of light around my feet. I could hear faint sounds of music and the clink of glassware from someone's rooftop party across the street, but mostly I heard the city's layered soundtrack: distant sirens, a solitary honk, the steady whoosh of wind up the sheer face of our building.

The sliding door whispered open. I didn't turn. I didn't have to. Ryker's presence was as specific as a fingerprint; I felt it in the shift of air, in the gentle vibration of the floorboards, in the way my pulse always adjusted to sync with his when he entered a room. He stopped a step behind me, waited for the length of one breath, and then his hands found my waist with that paradoxical tenderness I'd come to crave—strong enough to make me feel small, gentle enough to make me feel safe.

"You're going to freeze out here," he murmured, voice low and familiar, lips brushing the shell of my ear.

"I don't mind the cold," I said, leaning back into his touch, my spine aligning with the heat of his chest. "You know that."

His arms encircled me, crossing just above my navel, and his chin came to rest lightly atop my head. The scent of his cologne—sandalwood and something peppery, warm—mingled with the clean, ozone-tinged wind, making it hard to distinguish where he ended and the city began.

"Habit," he said, squeezing me once. "Can't help myself."

We stood like that for a while, watching the city's nervous

system light up for the night. The sky had gone from pastel to steel, clouds layering and layering until it felt like we were floating in a bubble above the world. I let myself relax against him, my hands covering his where they lay, not needing to speak. Sometimes I could communicate with Ryker better without words at all, like we'd developed a tactile language that said everything words never could.

He broke the silence first. "Did you get Christine's email?"

I nodded, feeling the movement echo through both our bodies. "Yeah. She wants me to take point on the brand relaunch. Said she'd announce it at the next all-hands." I paused, rolling the words over in my mind. "It's a step up. Not just a title thing, either."

"Congratulations," he said, and I heard pride in his voice— subtle but unmistakable. He squeezed me again, this time with a note of celebration, as if hugging the accomplishment into reality. "Told you they'd see it eventually."

"They always did," I said, echoing what I'd told George weeks ago, but it felt different now, truer. "I just needed to let myself be seen."

He ran a thumb along the exposed skin between my blouse and my hairline. "You're beautiful when you're smug."

"I'm not smug," I countered, twisting in his embrace until I was facing him, my back pressed against the railing. The city stretched out behind his head like a private galaxy. I looped my arms around his neck, let my fingers toy with the hair just above his collar. "I'm right. That's different."

He laughed, a low rumble that vibrated through his chest into mine. "Keep telling yourself that."

I pulled him closer, until only the thickness of our clothes separated us, and tilted my face up to meet his mouth. The kiss was deliberate—no urgency, just heat slow-burning beneath the surface, the kind of connection that didn't have to prove itself anymore. His lips parted mine, tongue sweeping in with the same confidence he used in boardrooms and bedrooms alike. I matched him, not yielding, but meeting him in the middle, our breath mingling, bodies angled into each other as if designed that way.

When we finally broke apart, the city lights below had multiplied, each window or streetlamp adding to the sense of momentum. I traced a finger along the line of his jaw, rough with evening stubble.

"I like you in soft light," he said, tucking a stray strand of hair behind my ear. "Makes you look dangerous."

I snorted, resting my forehead against his shoulder. "You're so full of shit."

He slid his hands down to cup my hips, making it clear who was in control of this gravity. "Says the woman who closed her first six-figure campaign this quarter, outperformed every other account manager, and still finds time to humiliate me at chess three nights a week."

"You love being humiliated," I said, voice dropping half an octave.

"Only by you," he agreed.

I grinned, feeling a satisfaction that went deeper than lust, deeper even than love. I felt seen. The woman I was now—the one who wore silk and power and confidence like they were all the same fabric—wasn't afraid of her own hunger anymore.

"So," I said, "what time is your board meeting tomorrow?"

"Seven. Which means I'll be up at five, running that pitch for the billionth time." He kissed the top of my head, just a brush of lips and warmth. "You still want to come with, or did you decide to have your own breakfast with the girls?"

"Depends," I said, shifting so the pendant at my throat caught the last sliver of sunlight and threw a sharp glint against his collarbone. "If I go with you, will you make time for that little Italian bakery down the block?"

He considered, squinting theatrically into the distance. "I think I could be persuaded."

"I'll be the one in the corner booth with a brioche and the Financial Times. You'll recognize me by my smugness."

He laughed again, letting it linger. The sound always surprised me—the first time I'd met Ryker, I'd thought him incapable of genuine laughter, a man who lived entirely in control. But with me, he laughed often, and always as if he was sharing an inside joke with the universe.

The wind picked up, tugging at the hem of my blouse, and I

shivered for real this time. Ryker immediately peeled off his blazer and draped it over my shoulders, sleeves swallowing my arms whole. The fabric was still warm from his body and faintly smelled of his cologne; I burrowed into it, not bothering to play coy.

He settled beside me, propping an elbow on the railing, and we both stared at the city. There was a lull in our conversation, but it didn't feel empty. We'd reached the kind of intimacy where silence wasn't a void to be filled but a shared resource, something to be savored.

"Remember when you told me I was the best thing that ever happened to you?" he said after a moment, voice so quiet I almost missed it over the wind.

"Mm," I replied, arching a brow. "Are you about to ask for a favor?"

"No," he said, smiling. "Just thinking how I should have said the same about you."

I tilted my head, considering. "Too late now," I deadpanned.

He made a wounded face. "Brutal."

I elbowed him gently in the ribs. "You love it."

His hand slid around my waist, fingers splaying possessively across my hip, and he pulled me into his side. "God, I really do."

We stayed on the balcony as the last color drained from the sky, the city below shifting into a full-throttle pulse of movement and light. Inside, our loft glowed with soft lamps and the promise of comfort, but I wasn't ready to move yet. Not while the night still hummed around us, not while his touch still lingered on my skin.

Finally, Ryker straightened and held out his hand, palm up, as if inviting me to step onto a dance floor only we could see.

"Come on," he said, voice gentle but laced with intent. "Let's go inside before you turn into an icicle."

I hesitated, savoring the wind one last time. Then I took his hand, letting him lead me in—knowing that, this time, it was a choice I made for myself. I belonged here, in this city, in this moment, in this life we'd stitched together from the threads of every version of ourselves. The view from thirty stories up wasn't just scenery anymore. It was home.

The moving box squatted in the center of our bedroom like an accusation, black marker bleeding "Elara's Things" across its cardboard chest. Everything else had found its place— Ryker's books alphabetized and slotted into his custom shelves, his shirts hung with military precision in the walk-in closet, kitchenware nested like Russian dolls in the deep drawers of our new chef's kitchen. My art prints were already framed and hung, my plants breathing green into the corners of the loft, my shoes lined up in a row along the low windowsill. But this box remained, as if waiting for me to decide which version of myself deserved unpacking.

Ryker hovered in the doorway, arms folded, shoulder propped against the jamb. He wore a soft black henley and those faded jeans that never failed to make my pulse flicker. I could feel his eyes on me as I knelt by the box and sliced the packing tape with the key pendant at my neck, using it as an impromptu letter opener. The sound of tearing adhesive was loud in the hush of the room, underscored by the muffled thud of city life filtering up through double-paned glass.

I peeled back the cardboard flaps. A faint, sweet scent drifted out—a blend of old perfume, dust, and something floral from the tissue paper I'd used to wrap the more delicate things. The first layer was a stack of pale blue blouses, high-collared and starched, buttons shining like tiny pearls. I lifted one, smoothing the sleeve with a thumb, and laid it over the edge of the box.

Ryker said nothing, but the air seemed to tighten around his silence.

Next came a tangle of silk and lace: a crimson slip, a velvet choker, the micro-mini skirt Sam had dared me to wear out to Velvet one night, the tags still attached because we'd never quite made it to the club. I didn't bother to sort them—just set them aside, soft piles bleeding color onto the pale carpet. Beneath those, I found my old Moleskine planners, each thick with the detritus of a year: coffee-stained sticky notes, receipts, pressed flowers, and the looping, anxious handwriting of a woman who measured her worth in checklists.

Ryker moved closer, his steps quiet but sure, and crouched beside me. He took the blue blouse from where I'd draped it and ran his fingers over the fabric, then—surprisingly—folded it neatly and set it aside.

"You hated these," he said. It wasn't a question.

"I did." I thumbed through the planners, then let them fall shut with a small, final-sounding thwack. "But I wore them anyway. Felt like armor."

He nodded, eyes on the blouse. "I remember you in them, at that first dinner. You looked like you wanted to sink into the floor."

"I did," I admitted. "But I also wanted to be noticed. It was... complicated."

He picked up the velvet choker, held it against his wrist as if measuring its length. "And this?"

I laughed, a real one, unfiltered. "That was for you."

"Only for me?" His voice was gentle, teasing.

"Mostly for me, now," I said, and the words didn't feel false.

We worked through the box in tandem: conservative sheath dresses and barely-there club wear, a pair of battered ballet flats next to spiked heels that had never survived a full night out. There were photos, too—my parents, Sam, and me in various stages of drunken bravado, even one of George and me at some mutual friend's wedding, our smiles a study in polite discomfort.

I stared at that one longer than I meant to. Ryker's hand closed over mine, his thumb tracing a slow circuit along the edge of the photograph.

"You don't have to keep it," he said, and I realized he was permitting me to let go.

I slipped the photo into a small trash pile, not because I needed his permission but because, for once, it felt like a choice rather than a compulsion. "I don't want to erase my history," I said, mostly to myself. "But I don't want to live in it, either."

He nodded, picking up one of my old work notebooks and flipping through the first few pages. "You always use pen," he said. "No room for edits."

"Permanent record," I said, shrugging. "Even the mistakes."

He smiled, soft at the corners. "I like that about you."

There was a rhythm to our unpacking—a give-and-take, a negotiation of what belonged to the past and what fit into the present. For every buttoned-up dress, there was a bralette or a plunging neckline; for every meticulous planner, a handful of nightclub wristbands, each still sticky with the memory of spilled drinks and sweat and bad decisions. We didn't separate them into old life/new life, good girl/slut. I let the silk and the starch hang side by side in the closet, a palette of contradictions that felt more like me than any single hue ever had.

At the bottom of the box, cradled in bubble wrap, was the perfume I'd worn in college—Chanel, sharp and powdery, a little too much for my taste now. I uncapped it, sprayed a fine mist into the air, and watched as Ryker's expression shifted from bemused to genuinely surprised.

"God, that must bring back memories," he said, voice thickening. "What was that, four years ago? Five?"

"Six," I said, "but who's counting?"

He took the bottle from me, sniffed the sprayer, and then— without warning—dabbed a little behind my ear. The touch was almost reverent, like he was blessing me with some lost sacrament.

"There," he said, satisfied. "Now you smell like memory."

I turned, giving him a look. "You're such a sap."

He grinned, but didn't deny it.

I looked around at the piles we'd made: nothing sorted, everything blended, fragments of the woman I'd been and the woman I was now existing in the same physical space. There was no plan for where it all would go, but I realized I didn't need one. It would find its own order.

I picked up the key pendant, untangling it from my neck,

and rolled it between my fingers. It still bore the faint etching on the back, the one I'd never shown him: my initials, scrawled in Ryker's own blocky hand.

Without warning, I pressed the pendant into his palm and closed his fingers around it.

"For you," I said.

He opened his hand, studying the key as if seeing it for the first time. His thumb traced the initials, then he looked up at me, confusion and wonder warring in his eyes.

"What do you want me to do with it?" he asked.

"Hold it," I said, "for a minute."

He obeyed, closing his fist around the silver. The room felt electric, as if the action had reset the current between us.

I filled the silence. "I spent so much time thinking I had to pick a side, you know? Either be the good girl or the bad girl, the career woman or the party slut, the planner or the risk-taker. But it's all just me." I gestured to the piles at our feet. "All of this. I don't want to hide any of it anymore."

Ryker's gaze was steady, warm. "I never wanted you to."

I knelt in front of him, knees pressed into the carpet, and took his hand in both of mine. Gently, I pried his fingers open, reclaiming the key. This time, when I looped the chain around my neck, I felt nothing but lightness.

"I choose you," I said, not as a declaration but as a simple fact. "But I also choose me. Both."

He leaned in, pressing his forehead to mine. "That's all I ever wanted."

We sat there for a long time, cross-legged and surrounded by the evidence of our intertwined lives. He touched my thigh absently, fingers tracing circles on bare skin beneath the hem of my shorts, as if reminding us both that bodies could contain history and desire and possibility all at once.

When the last item was put away, when the box was finally empty, I looked at our closet—a riot of colors and textures, heels next to loafers, silk brushing up against cotton. It was imperfect and messy and alive. It was home.

Ryker watched me from the bed, eyes tracking my movements as I hung the final dress and shut the closet door. There was something in his gaze—pride, yes, but also relief. Like he'd been holding his breath for months and could finally exhale.

I crawled onto the bed beside him, burrowing under his arm and pulling his hand to rest over my stomach. He squeezed me, grounding us both.

We lay in silence, staring at the ceiling, listening to the city's distant heartbeat. I felt him turn, felt the heat of his gaze before I looked over and met it.

"You did it," he said quietly.

"So did you," I replied.

He smiled, then pressed a kiss to my temple, soft and sure.

The box was gone. There was only us, and everything we'd chosen to keep.

We'd always done our best talking in the kitchen. Maybe it was the acoustics—hard surfaces, high ceilings, the way sound bounced off glass and marble. Maybe it was the fact that neither of us could quite cook, so the only heat came from us, from the conversations that simmered and boiled over late into the night. Tonight, the counters were cleared of moving-day debris and scrubbed to a shine; candles flickered along the island in fat glass cylinders, and a bottle of champagne— Veuve Clicquot, Ryker's splurge—rested in an ice bucket next to a plate of strawberries.

The only thing out of place was the manila folder on the counter, thick with legal documents, each page bristling with colored flags marking where our signatures were required.

Ryker stood across from me, his sleeves rolled back, forearms braced on the stone as he flipped through the paperwork, his expression intent and almost boyishly eager. The kitchen light caught in his hair and turned it to dark gold, the color deepening as he bent over the papers and squinted at some detail.

"Second page in," he said, tapping the document and sliding it toward me. "Initial there, and at the bottom."

I leaned across the counter, pen at the ready, and signed my name with a flourish that was almost theatrical. "You really trust me to manage your money?" I asked, lifting a brow.

He grinned. "I trust you with more than that."

I signed the page, then the next, then the next, the stack of papers shrinking between us as the future we'd mapped out over weeks and months took physical form. The joint investment account. The LLC for our speculative side hustle—a little marketing consultancy, our skills merged and leveraged for clients who didn't know they needed us yet. The travel fund, which was mostly my idea: a quarterly escape, even if just for a long weekend, so neither of us would get swallowed by work.

I reached for the champagne and twisted off the wire cage with expert speed. The cork popped, echoing in the tall room, a rush of bubbles threatening to escape. I caught the spill with my tongue and poured two glasses, the liquid fizzing and gold and indecently expensive.

"To the most ridiculous business plan ever conceived by two overachievers with control issues," I said, raising my flute.

"To new beginnings," Ryker countered, tapping his glass to mine. The sound was delicate, crystalline, like a secret note only we could hear.

We sipped. The champagne was icy, tart, bracing. I watched him over the rim of my glass, studied the way his throat worked as he swallowed, the softening of his eyes as the alcohol took the edge off his perpetual readiness.

He set down his flute, picked up the pen, and scrawled his name on a dotted line. When he finished, he slid the pen across the counter, but I was already moving; our fingers met halfway, skin on skin, the contact electric in a way that had nothing to do with nerves and everything to do with recognition.

"You realize what this means," I said, voice low, letting my hand linger in his.

"That we're stuck together?" he deadpanned.

"That you're never getting rid of me," I corrected, and it felt good to say it, to make the threat and the promise in equal measure.

He gripped my hand, tugged me around the end of the island until I was within arm's reach. "I never wanted to."

We finished the documents, signatures layering like brush-strokes, each one a commitment, a promise, a dare to the universe. Ryker sorted the papers into piles, the neatness of it almost ceremonial. I watched, amused, as he double-checked every page.

"You're such a freak," I said, fondness coloring the insult.

He shrugged, not at all bothered. "You're the one who likes me this way."

"God help me, I do."

He gathered the signed stack and set it aside, then pulled me in close, so our hips were flush and my hands found their natural place—curled at the small of his back, fingers tracing the waistband of his jeans. The candles painted his face in moving golds and shadows, sharpening his jaw, setting his eyes aglow.

"We did it," I said, half-dazed.

He kissed my forehead, then the tip of my nose, then my mouth—each touch a period at the end of a sentence. "We did."

"Did you ever think we'd make it here?" I asked, surprising both of us with the tremor in my voice.

Ryker hesitated, eyes searching mine. "I hoped. But your walls were pretty solid."

I nodded, feeling the weight of everything that had come before. Eighteen months ago, I couldn't have imagined this: me, happy in my own skin, in my own home, building a life with a man who saw and cherished every version of me. The champagne was a celebration, but it was also a boundary marker—a reminder that the life before, the woman before, were part of me but not the whole.

I leaned into him, my head tucked beneath his jaw, and let myself feel the solidity of his arms, the heat of his chest, the way our bodies synced up without thinking. I heard the city outside, muffled and restless, and knew that whatever happened—success or failure, ease or struggle—I'd chosen this. Not out of desperation or fear, but because I wanted it. Wanted him.

Ryker stroked my hair, fingers lingering at the nape of my neck, thumb tracing lazy circles over my collarbone. "You remember the first night we met?" he asked, voice a vibration in my hair.

"At Obsidian?" I laughed, the memory sharp and sweet. "You were so sure of yourself. Suave. Knew exactly what to say to get my attention."

"Lies," he murmured. "I was terrified. You looked like you'd eat me alive."

I grinned, pulling back to meet his eyes. "You loved it."

He shrugged, the movement disarmingly self-effacing. "I still do."

I took another sip of champagne and let the bubbles settle in my bloodstream. The next signature would be on a different kind of document—a travel itinerary, a client contract, a lease on a space for our fledgling consultancy. Or maybe, eventually, something more permanent. But I wasn't rushing. I liked the uncertainty. I liked the not-knowing, as long as it was with him.

We left the paperwork on the counter, candles burning low, and drifted out onto the balcony, glasses in hand. The city was a sequined blanket beneath us, every window a promise, every headlight a wish in motion. The wind had shifted; it was cooler, carrying the first hints of rain from the river.

Ryker wrapped an arm around my waist, drawing me in so

the line of my body fit perfectly against his. We stood in silence, not needing to speak, just watching the world spin on.

"You know," I said after a while, "this doesn't feel real yet."

He sipped his champagne, thoughtful. "Want me to pinch you?"

I laughed, teeth on glass. "Not unless you want me to pinch you back."

He grinned, and I saw the man beneath the confidence, the boy who'd learned to mask vulnerability with jokes and bravado. I loved that man. I loved that boy, too.

I set down my glass and turned in his arms, threading my fingers behind his neck. "Here's to new ventures," I said, and kissed him, slow and deep, until the city faded and there was only us.

He lifted me—effortlessly, like I weighed nothing—and spun me once, just to make me laugh, before settling me back on my feet. My heart felt huge, so swollen with possibility it was almost painful.

He rested his forehead against mine. "Here's to us," he whispered.

We stood at the edge of our world, the city blazing below, our silhouettes merging in the flicker of candlelight and neon. I didn't know what came next. I didn't care.

I squeezed his hand and stepped forward, the threshold of the future wide open before us.

We stepped into it together, neither leading nor following, but moving as one.

Also by Laci Mae Wyld

Buried With You

A decade since the night they buried a dark secret in the shadows of the woods, Harper Lane is thrust back into the chilling embrace of Ash Pines, her reluctant return shrouded in impending doom. With her father's life waning and her past haunting her every step, she must face not only the memories she fled but also the man she once abandoned.

Eric Ransom harbours a festering wound from that fateful night—a wound reopened when Harper arrives at his garage, her presence reigniting a dangerous flame long thought extinguished. Amidst whispered threats in the dead of night and ominous messages left at the desolate grave site, they find themselves ensnared in a sinister game of retribution.

As they unravel a sinister web of deceit and betrayal, they realise their victim was no ordinary stranger. With allegiances crumbling and shadows closing in, Harper and Eric must unite to unmask their relentless stalker before they become mere pawns in a deadly chess match.

In a town where alliances shift like whispers in the wind and buried secrets claw their way to the surface, Harper and Eric are faced with an impossible choice—embrace the flames of passion reigniting between them as a beacon of hope or succumb to the darkness that threatens to consume them whole.

Amidst looming threats and betrayals lurking within familiar faces, Harper and Eric must navigate treacherous waters to uncover the truth behind their shared past. Will they emerge unscathed from the shadows of their sins, or will they be swallowed whole by the echoes of the grave that refuse to stay silent?

Vex Me: The Widow Queen

First Book in Vex Me Series: In a world teeming with danger and deceit, Kiera Moore's life takes a treacherous turn when her husband's death leaves her drowning in both grief and debt. Enter the enigmatic figure of Hudson Vex, a man shrouded in mystery and power, who offers Kiera a chilling deal she can't refuse - one night of boundless pleasure in exchange for erasing her late husband's debts and safeguarding her daughter.

As Kiera navigates the treacherous underworld of crime and betrayal, she embraces her transformation into the formidable "Widow Queen," unearthing her own strength and resilience. With Vex by her side, their twisted bond blurs the lines between love and manipulation as they build an empire fuelled by fear and respect.

But when her daughter falls prey to a ruthless cartel, Kiera must unleash her newfound ferocity to save her child, even if it means embracing the darkness within herself. As alliances shift and tensions rise, Kiera and Hudson find themselves entangled in a dangerous dance of passion and manipulation where love and vengeance blur into one.

Can Kiera navigate this treacherous path to reclaim her life, or will she succumb to the seductive allure of power and corruption? Prepare for a gripping tale of obsession, danger, and moral ambiguity in "The Widow Queen," where the line between hero and villain blurs beneath the intoxicating allure of the underworld's most dangerous game.

Fiery Fate (Vex Me: Book 2)

What began as a desperate bid for survival twists into a mesmerising metamorphosis. Immersed in Vex's clandestine world, Kiera unearths a seductive allure in the very violence that shattered her existence. Each brutal lesson and fiery encounter propels the grieving widow towards an unsettling evolution—a queen reborn amidst the chaos.

As an old nemesis resurfaces from Vex's past, Evelyn is forced to confront her escalating duality. With empires crumbling and blood staining her path, she teeters on the precipice between saviour and savage. Her daughter's fate hangs by a thread, and the boundaries between prey and predator blur into oblivion.

In this intoxicating thriller of power and fixation, Kiera will learn that certain debts demand payment in blood—and some reigns can only be forged in flames.

The Heir Will Not Turn (Vex Me: Book 3)

When Sophie is abducted by Falcom, the shadowy puppet masters steering global crime, Kiera and Hudson unleash their full power to rescue her. Their bond—fierce, primal, and unshakeable—drives a perilous chase across continents as they rally allies from the depths of their clandestine Shadow organisation. Clues lead through a web of brutal confrontations, where every victory costs blood and all threats point back to Sophie's fate.

As Falcom tightens its grip, the lovers push past fear toward a final, fortified base where extraction erupts into a desperate war. A heart-stopping gamble ends in a brutal revelation: Sophie's fate hinges on a line between loyalty and danger that could cost them everything. Love for Sophie becomes resolve as Kiera and Hudson vow to crush Falcom, harnessing every ally, every skill, every daring instinct to save the girl who has always been their guiding light—and to claim their own, hard-won happiness in the process.

Awakenings: Legacy of Shadow and Light

From the ashes of tragedy, her fate began to unfold...

Unveiled to a destiny she never fathomed, Suri Taylor emerges from the ruins of her shattered life. Taken captive by the malevolent Lyle Shawcross, she unearths a startling revelation: she is an immortal being bearing dormant powers, safeguarded to shield her from an age-old conflict.

Rescued by enigmatic saviours emanating celestial light, Suri is propelled into a clandestine realm where immortal entities coexist with mortals. As she hones her supernatural gifts under the tutelage of the guardian Drake Tudor, a rare bond sparks between them—a glimmering aura branding them as uniquely united.

Yet Lyle refuses to relinquish his coveted prize without a fight. Embracing her regal lineage and electing her allegiance in the immortal strife, adversaries encroach from every angle. With treachery lurking in the recesses and her extraordinary abilities still unfolding, Suri must discern whom to confide in while navigating her emotions for Drake and bearing the burden of her newfound legacy.

In a realm where luminescent gazes unveil true motives and everlasting existence exacts a dire toll, Suri's emergence may either reconcile ancient rifts or cast both worlds into eternal obscurity.

Content warning: Book contains scenes of sexual abuse and violence

Texting Fate

In the glittering world of Hollywood, he's the enigmatic heartthrob whose every move makes headlines. She's a refreshingly unfiltered woman who just wants to survive an epic Tinder disaster. But when a chance encounter lures them into a whirlwind of mistaken identities and electric chemistry, their lives are about to collide in the most unexpected way.

When a sassy text message meant for a Tinder date gone wrong lands in the hands of A-list actor Charlie Benton, it sparks a digital dance of wit and warmth with a mystery woman known only as Bee. Little do they know that amidst the virtual sparks lies the beginning of an uncharted romance that transcends fame and fortune.

As their playful banter deepens into a magnetic pull, Charlie and Bee find themselves entangled in a hot and steamy connection. But can they navigate the treacherous waters of stardom's spotlight without losing themselves in its glare? With paparazzi lurking and fans clamouring for every detail, their connection is put to the ultimate test.

Amidst the chaos of Hollywood whispers, Charlie and Bee search for authenticity in a world defined by illusions, and they must choose: embrace the unpredictable journey of love despite the odds or retreat to the safety of their separate worlds. Will their hearts find solace in each other's embrace, or will fame's cruel glare shatter their fairy tale dreams?

Haunted Memories of a Broken Girl

Haunted by visions of a violent crime, Kelly's melodic voice offers solace amidst the chaos of her past. Lawyer Michael Lawson is captivated by her singing, his own memories stirred by her haunting presence. When he rescues her from danger, a chilling realisation sets in - Kelly bears an uncanny resemblance to a long-lost childhood friend's deceased wife.

As their connection deepens, Kelly's fragmented past unravels. Each revelation brings them closer to a shocking reality: Kelly is Helayna Cook, the missing daughter of arms tycoon Richard Cook.

Navigating the treacherous waters of truth and deception, their unexpected romance blossoms. But sinister forces lurk in the shadows, determined to keep buried what should never see the light of day. Threats loom and loyalties are tested as Kelly and Michael find themselves ensnared in a dangerous game of obsession and vengeance.

To survive, they must confront the ghosts of their pasts and unearth the secrets shrouding Kelly's mother's untimely demise - before a malevolent force silences them forever.

You Will See Me

When the lifeless body of Louise Mansfield is found on the bustling Chicago River Walk, seasoned detective Samuel Barron is thrust into a macabre investigation that unravels a web of dark secrets and chilling connections. Louise, daughter of the influential Senator James Mansfield, had been striving to escape her turbulent past as an exotic dancer and reconcile with her powerful father before she became the target of a sadistic killer's wrath.

As Samuel delves deeper into the case, he uncovers a sinister pattern linking Louise to five other tormented women, all tied to the charismatic senator. The discovery hints at a twisted serial killer fixated on beautiful victims associated with the prominent politician. The tension escalates when the primary suspect meets a gruesome demise in a manner mirroring the previous murders, pushing Samuel to confront a ruthless and calculating murderer with a disturbing agenda.

The investigation takes an alarming turn when someone they least expected, is driven by a volatile obsession to protect the Senator's reputation, escalating their vendetta by targeting the Mansfield family. In a heart-pounding race against time, Samuel finds himself in a deadly showdown with the killer, unearthing the depths of their malevolent rage. Their harrowing clash culminates in an intense confrontation of wits and wills, revealing a tapestry of hidden truths, envy, and intricate familial bonds.

Haunted by the specter of this chilling case and facing a new wave of brutal crimes, Samuel realises that history has a way of resurfacing when least expected. To thwart the cycle of violence and deceit, he must confront his own demons and navigate through treacherous waters to prevent further tragedy. In this riveting tale of suspense and redemption, Samuel grapples with the enduring legacy of past sins in his relentless quest for justice amid shadows that refuse to fade.

Betrayal of Blood

In a whirlwind of betrayal, Sarsha Mitchell's once-promising future implodes when she catches her fiancé, James, entangled with her very own sister. Reeling from the heartbreak, Sarsha takes flight, leaving the shards of her shattered dreams behind. With her picture-perfect life in ruins, she seeks solace on an impromptu getaway to their abandoned honeymoon destination with her loyal confidante, Jess.

From the sun-kissed shores of Perth to the dazzling allure of the Gold Coast, Sarsha attempts to outrun her anguish amidst carefree escapades and electrifying nights out. Just as the shadows of her past threaten to engulf her present, a chance encounter at a club propels Sarsha into an unexpected charade with a mysterious stranger named Riley.

As sparks ignite between Sarsha and Riley during their fabricated romance, healing begins to seep into her wounded soul. However, upon their return to Melbourne, old wounds are ripped open anew as James refuses to relinquish his hold on her heart while envious desires stir chaos within her own family.

Supported by Riley's unwavering presence and unwavering gallantry, Sarsha finds the courage to confront the toxicity suffusing her familial bonds. Yet just as hope blossoms for a brighter tomorrow, a cruel act of revenge orchestrated by James and Megan threatens to shatter everything they hold dear.

In a race against time and treachery, Sarsha stands vigil by Riley's bedside, clinging to hope amidst the turmoil. Together, they uncover the depths of deceit woven by those she once trusted most. With Riley's love paving the way towards redemption and renewal, Sarsha severs the ties that bind her to darkness and steps boldly into a future brimming with promise

From Hatred to Heat

When fate entwines two souls marked by enmity, can they rewrite their story before the darkness consumes them both?

Within the walls of Hidden Chapters Bookstore, Jetta Kinsley revels in the sanctuary she's created with her partner-in-crime, Brandi. Embracing the solitary bliss of her life, Jetta's world is upended when Brandi's heart veers off course to Owen Cooper, leading Jetta down a path she never wished to tread again. Standing before her is Ethan Cole, the ghost of her past whose cruel grip once shattered her world and scattered the pieces.

Bound by loyalty to their friends, Jetta and Ethan forge a fragile alliance. Buried beneath their animosity smolders an undeniable attraction, stirring emotions neither thought possible. When danger lurks in the shadows of a nightclub, Ethan emerges as Jetta's fierce protector, unveiling a side she never dared to imagine.

From Broken Roads to Healing Hearts

When Natalie's car breaks down on a secluded Tasmanian road, little does she know it will lead her to a ruggedly handsome stranger named Kai and his highland cow farm. Far from the city bustle, Natalie and Kai find themselves tangled in a web of past heartbreaks and hidden scars.

Amidst the picturesque countryside, they form an unexpected bond, discovering solace and passion in each other's arms under the starlit sky. But as secrets unravel and old flames flicker back to life, they must confront their demons together or risk losing everything they've found.

A Dark Descent into Chaos

Caught in the sinister grip of Sydney's underworld, at just 23, she becomes Diego's pawn, a mere facade of a girlfriend to the heartless crime lord. Imprisoned in opulence at Diego's Rose Bay mansion with no way out, Mila endures a life of torment and manipulation. Joe Sullivan is no stranger to shadows and secrets. With a steely gaze that betrays his hidden motives, he infiltrates Diego's inner circle on a covert mission for the authorities. Witnessing Diego's brutal nature firsthand, Joe risks everything to shield Mila from the savagery that lurks within their glamorous facade.

Bound by a dangerous game of deception and desire, Mila and Joe must join forces to uncover the truth amidst a battlefield of power-hungry adversaries. As their partnership deepens, forbidden attraction ignites, threatening to consume them both. With danger closing in and lives hanging in the balance, Joe is determined to protect Mila at any cost, even if it means forsaking everything he holds dear.

In a whirlwind of perilous escapades, high-stakes confrontations, Mila and Joe must navigate a treacherous path towards freedom and justice. But in a world where loyalties shift like shadows and love teeters on the edge of ruin, will they emerge unscathed from the dark empire they're entwined in?

Friend or Foe weaves a tale of passion, loyalty, and sacrifice against the backdrop of Sydney's underworld glamour and danger. In a battle where survival could mean surrendering to love's embrace, will Mila and Joe triumph over the sinister forces that seek to tear them apart?

When We Close Our Eyes

After tragedy strands Casey and Kirk in separate worlds of longing, an unlikely encounter entwines them in a slow dance toward solace. Their love, a tender construction of two battered hearts, finds a tenuous rhythm until a specter from Kirk's past tears through the fragile façade. Obsessed and ruthless, Layla—his ex-wife—emerges from shadow with a plan to reclaim what she believes is hers. As threats mount, Casey and Kirk must fight not only for their love but for their lives, finding strength in their scars and shelter in each other.

Lucky in Love and Bullets

Kitty and Peter are madly in love. Kitty, a successful hair stylist, and Peter, a partner in a prestigious law firm, celebrate a lavish wedding in Hawaii. Their perfect day turns tragic when a gunman appears. Kitty is shot in the head. She regains consciousness in the hospital with no memory of Peter, though she recalls everything else. Kitty struggles to reconnect with Peter, who moves into a separate bedroom. Suspecting he is hiding something, she returns to work and meets Fynn, a handsome new client.

Kitty and Fynn find themselves in dangerous territory with criminals as they try to uncover the truth about why she was shot on her wedding day, with each discovery they see how involved Peter was with the wrong kind of people

Twisted Obsession In the shadows of a seemingly perfect life, Anya Willows discovers that the past she thought she'd escaped is about to collide with her present in the most terrifying way imaginable. After years of uncertainty, Anya finally finds stability with a loving boyfriend, a loyal best friend, and a newfound relationship with the father she never knew. But when tragedy strikes and her world begins to crumble, Anya finds herself at the centre of a twisted web of obsession, deceit, and murder. As the body count rises and the lines between friend and foe blur, Anya must confront a darkness that has been stalking her since childhood. With each shocking revelation, she's forced to question everything and everyone she thought she knew. Who can she trust when the very foundations of her life prove to be built on lies? In this heart-pounding psychological thriller, love becomes a weapon, trust becomes a liability, and the truth becomes the most dangerous thing of all.